A PALE HORSE

WENDY ALEC

Warboys Publishing

A PALE HORSE
THE CHRONICLES OF BROTHERS—BOOK 4

Published by Warboys Publishing (Ireland) Limited
77 Sir John Rogerson's Quay, Dublin 2, Ireland

A CIP record for this book is available from the British Library.

ISBN: 978-0-9571498-3-0

First paperback edition

Cover design by W. Alec, C. Bown and Studiogearbox.com
Typeset by CRB Associates, Potterhanworth, Lincolnshire, UK
Printed in the United States

Chronicles of Brothers: A Pale Horse
www.chroniclesofbrothers.com

And I looked, and behold a pale horse:

and his name that sat on him was Death,
and Hell followed with him.

And power was given unto them over the fourth
part of the earth, to kill with sword,
and with hunger, and with death,
and with the beasts of the earth.

(Book of Revelation 6:8 KJV)

CHRONICLES
BROTHERS

Dedicated to our beloved Lulu Auger
who so loved these books
You now see Him face to face . . .

ACKNOWLEDGMENT

With great love to all who have so *very* patiently and so *very* impatiently waited over three years for *A Pale Horse*!—finally it is in your hands!

To all who have understood the reasons for the tremendous opposition and the challenges encountered during the writing of this particular book. A million thanks.

That fantasy and truth at times intersect in the Chronicles Series, is inevitable.

As is the fact that truth will always generate confrontation in a parallel realm.

To all who will travel the chronicles road – until we all arrive with Michael and Lucifer at the White Gorge on the eastern shores of the Lake of Fire . . .

. . . when this story will finally be told.

W.A.

"WHEN IT IS DARKEST, MEN SEE THE STARS."

(*Ralph Waldo Emerson*)

CHRONICLES
BROTHERS

THE CHARACTERS

Jason De Vere, eldest brother, De Vere dynasty. Place of birth: New York, U.S.A. U.S. media tycoon. Chairman, owner, and CEO of multibillion-dollar media corporation VOX Entertainment. Owns a third of the Western world's television and newspaper empires. Married to Julia St. Cartier for twenty years. One daughter, Lily De Vere. Divorced. Current residence: penthouse, Central Park, New York.

Adrian De Vere, middle brother, De Vere dynasty. Place of (recorded) birth: London, England. Ex-prime minister of the United Kingdom (Labour, two terms), newly appointed president of the European Union (ten-year term). Nobel Peace Prize nominee. Currently negotiating the Ishtar Accord—the Third World War peace treaty. Married to Melissa Vane Templar for five years. Melissa deceased in childbirth. One son, Gabriel, deceased. Current residence: Winter Palace of the European president, Mont St. Michel, Normandy, France.

Nick De Vere, youngest brother, De Vere dynasty. Place of birth: Washington, D.C., U.S.A. Archaeologist, celebrity playboy. Dying of AIDS. No children. Currently in relationship with Jotapa, princess of the royal house of Jordan. Previous relationship: Klaus Von Hausen, senior curator of Department of the Middle East, British Museum. Current residences: penthouses, Los Angeles, New York, London.

James De Vere—Father of Jason, Adrian, and Nick De Vere. Deceased.

Lilian De Vere, chair of the De Vere Foundation. Mother of Jason, Adrian, and Nick De Vere. Current residences: penthouse, New York; mansions, Oxfordshire and London. Deceased.

Julius De Vere—grand master of the Brotherhood. Warlock. Chairman of De Vere Continuation Holdings AG. Father of James De Vere. Grandfather to Jason, Adrian, and Nick De Vere. Deceased.

Julia St. Cartier, former editor of Cosmpolitan. Present, founder/CEO of LOLA PR. Major clients: England Football Team and European Union Presidential Office. Married to Jason De Vere for twenty years. Mother to Lily De Vere. Divorced. Seeing Callum Vickers. Current residences: seafront town house, Brighton, England; Artists' Colony, New Chelsea, London.

Lily De Vere, Julia and Jason De Vere's daughter. Confined to a wheelchair following a car accident (Nick De Vere driving). Student at Roedean School for Girls, Brighton, England.

Melissa Vane Templar De Vere—Adrian's wife. Died in childbirth.

Rosemary De Vere—James De Vere's half-sister, Lilian's companion.

Maxim—James and Lilian De Vere's butler.

Pierre and Beatrice Didier—James and Lilian De Vere's chauffeur and housekeeper. Currently working for Adrian De Vere at Mont St. Michel, Normandy.

THE DE VERE DYNASTY
— EXTENDED CIRCLE —
FRIENDS, ASSOCIATES

Lawrence St. Cartier, Jesuit priest; retired CIA; antiquities dealer. Julia St. Cartier's uncle. Residence: Cairo, Alexandria, Egypt.

Alex Lane-Fox, son of Rachel Lane-Fox. Investigative journalist in training, working at the Guardian, London. Starting at New York Times, January 2022. Close family friend of Julia, Jason, and Lily De Vere.

Rachel Lane-Fox—supermodel. Julia's best pal. Killed aboard aircraft in 9/11 attack.

Rebekah and David Weiss—Rachel Lane-Fox's parents.

Polly Mitchell, Lily De Vere's best friend. Alex Lane-Fox's girlfriend.

Klaus Von Hausen—youngest senior curator of Department of the Middle East, British Museum. Former lover of Nick De Vere.

Charles Xavier Chessler, warlock. Former chairman of Chase Manhattan Bank. President of World Bank. Retired. Jason De Vere's godfather.

Callum Vickers, top London neurosurgeon. Seeing Julia de Vere.

Dylan Weaver—genius IT specialist holding high-level freelance positions with global banks, institutions, and various software companies. Nick De Vere's old school friend.

Jontil Purvis, long-term executive assistant to Jason De Vere—nineteen years.

Levine and Mitchell—Jason De Vere's aides.

Kurt Guber—first head of security at Downing Street, now director of EU Special Services Security Operations. Exotic-weapon specialist.

Neil Travis—Adrian's personal body guard.

Anton—Adrian De Vere's butler.

Father Alessandro—Dr Gabriele Alessandro—eminent glaciologist, Jesuit Priest and leader of the Vatican's Ice Man Three expedition.

Frau Vghtred Meeling—Austrian employee of De Vere household. Nanny to Jason, Adrian, and Nick. Also, Abbess Helewis Vghtred.

Brother Francis—monk, Alexandria, Egypt.

General Magruder—1st Special Forces Operational Detachment—Delta (1st SFOF-D) James De Vere's oldest and most trusted friend.

THE BROTHERHOOD
(ILLUMINATI)

His Excellency Lorcan De Molay—former superior general of the Jesuit order. Supreme high priest of the Brotherhood, Jesuit priest. Birthplace: indeterminate. Current age: indeterminate. Current places of residence: London, Washington, D.C., Rome.

Kester Von Slagel (Baron)—Lorcan De Molay's emissary.

Piers Aspinall—Head of MI6/British intelligence.

Charles Xavier Chessler—former chairman of Chase Manhattan Bank. President of World Bank. Retired.

Ethan St. Clair—grand master of the Scottish Brothers.

Dieter Von Hallstein—former German chancellor.

Naotake Yoshido—Chairman of Japan's Yoshido banking dynasty.

Raffaello Lombardi—patriarch of the black nobility family of Venice. Director of Vatican Bank.

Julius De Vere—grand master of the Brotherhood. Warlock. Chairman of De Vere Continuation Holdings AG. Father of James De Vere. Grandfather to Jason, Adrian, and Nick De Vere. Deceased.

Jaylin Alexander—former executive director of the Central Intelligence Agency.

Commander General Omar B. Maddox—NORAD commander.

Gonzalez—U.S. Secret Service Presidential Protective Detail.

Lewis—deputy secretary of defense.

Drew Janowski—special assistant to the president for Defense Policy and Strategy.

Werner Drechsler—president of the World Banks.

Vincent Carnegie

THE ROYAL HOUSE
OF JORDAN

King of Jordan—Jotapa, Faisal, and Jibril's father. Deceased (heart attack).

Jotapa, princess of Jordan. In relationship with Nick De Vere. Namesake of ancient Princess Jotapa, who lived over 2,000 years ago.

Jibril, Jordanian king's younger son. Appointed crown prince.

Faisal—Jordanian king's older son.

Safwat—head of security and Jotapa's personal bodyguard.

Crown Prince Mansoor of Arabia.

General Ahmed Kareem—Safwat's brother—Jordanian Special Security Forces.

General Hamid Assaf—Jordanian Royal Air Force

OTHER CHARACTERS

Professor Hamish MacKenzie—Scottish genetic scientist, world expert on animal and hybrid cloning.

Jul Mansoor—grandson of Abdul-Qawi, Bedouin archaeologist.

Abdul-Qawi Aka Jedd—Bedouin archaeologist.

Matt Barto—VOX's Teheran bureau chief.

Jordan Maxwell III—investment banker, Neal Black Securities.

Powell—Neal Black's vice president of IT.

Von Duysen—colleague of Jordan Maxwell.

Laurent Chastenay—assistant to Adrian.

General Kjellberg—Norwegian—Ice Man Three security forces.

Raffaele Ricci—special assistant to Chief Astronomer of the Vatican Observatory

Father d'Angelis—eminent glaciologist, Chief Astronomer of the Vatican.

FIRST HEAVEN

Jesus—Christos, the Nazarene.

Michael—chief prince of the royal household of Yehovah, commander in chief, First Heaven's armies, president of the Warring Councils.

Gabriel—chief prince of the royal house of Yehovah, lord chief justice of Angelic Revelators.

Jether—imperial warrior and ruler of the twenty-four ancient monarchs of the First Heaven and High Council. Chief steward of Yehovah's sacred mysteries.

Xacheriel—Ancient of Days curator of the sciences and universes, one of the twenty-four kings under Jether's governance.

Lamaliel—member of the Ruling Council of Angelic Elders.

Issachar—member of the Ruling Council of Angelic Elders.

Methuselah—member of the Ruling Council of Angelic Elders.

Maheel—member of the Ruling Council of Angelic Elders.

Joktan—ruler of Gabriel's Revelator Eagles.

Obadiah, Dimnah—*younglings*—an ancient angelic race with characteristics of eternal youth and a remarkable inquisitiveness, expressly designed as apprentices to assist the ancient ones in their custodianship of Yehovah's countless new galaxies.

Sandaldor—Gabriel's general.

Zadkiel—Gabriel's general.

Zalialiel—guard of the Portal of Shinar.

THE FALLEN

Lucifer—Satan, king of Perdition. Tempter; adversary; sovereign ruler of the Race of Men, Earth, and the nether regions.

Charsoc—dark apostle, chief high priest of the Fallen. Governor of the Grand Wizards of the Black Court and the dreaded Warlock Kings of the West.

Marduk—head of the Darkened Councils and Lucifer's chief of staff.

The Twin Wizards of Malfecium—the grand wizard of Phaegos and the grand wizard of Maelageor. The superscientists.

Mulabalah—ruler of the Black Murmurers.

Astaroth—commander in chief of the Black Horde. Michael's former general.

Moloch—satanic prince, Butcher of Perdition.

Sargon the Terrible of Babylonia—champion of Gehenna, great prince of Babylonia.

Balberith—Lucifer's chief attendant.

Nisroc the Necromancer—Keeper of Death and the Grave.

The Dark Cabal grand wizards—666 Black Murmurers.

Dracul—ruler of the Warlocks of the West, and ancient leader of the Time Lords.

Nephilim—A hybrid between the angelic and the Race of Men.

"SARAH, THERE'S A GOVERNMENT INSIDE THE
GOVERNMENT, AND I DON'T CONTROL IT."

(*Bill Clinton*, as quoted by senior White House reporter
Sarah McClendon in reply to why he wasn't doing
anything about UFO disclosure)

"WE ARE GRATEFUL TO THE *WASHINGTON POST*,
THE *NEW YORK TIMES*, *TIME* MAGAZINE AND OTHER GREAT
PUBLICATIONS WHERE DIRECTORS ATTEND OUR MEETINGS
AND RESPECTED THEIR PROMISE OF DISCRETION FOR
ALMOST 40 YEARS. IT WOULD BE IMPOSSIBLE FOR US TO
DEVELOP OUR PLAN IF WE HAD BEEN SUBJECTED TO THE
LIGHT OF PUBLICITY DURING THOSE YEARS. BUT THE
WORLD IS NOW MORE SOPHISTICATED AND PREPARED
TO MARCH TOWARDS A WORLD GOVERNMENT.
THE SUPRANATIONAL SOVEREIGNTY OF AN INTELLECTUAL
ELITE AND WORLD BANKERS IS SURELY PREFERABLE
TO THE NATIONAL AUTODETERMINATION PRACTICED
IN PAST CENTURIES."

(*David Rockefeller*, Founder of Trilateral Commission,
New World Order godfather, Baden, Germany, June 1991)

"WE HAVE, INDEED, BEEN CONTACTED—PERHAPS EVEN VISITED—BY EXTRATERRESTRIAL BEINGS, AND THE U.S. GOVERNMENT, IN COLLUSION WITH THE OTHER NATIONAL POWERS OF THE EARTH, IS DETERMINED TO KEEP THIS INFORMATION FROM THE GENERAL PUBLIC."

(*Victor Marchetti*, former Special Assistant to the Executive Director of the CIA)

"THE FEDERAL RESERVE IS ANSWERABLE TO NO ONE."

(*President Ronald Reagan*)

"ABANDONED" RUSSIAN RESEARCH STATION
LAKE VOSTOK
EAST ANTARCTIC ICE SHEET
SOUTHERN POLE OF COLD
OCTOBER 15, 2024

D R GABRIELE ALESSANDRO, eminent glaciologist, Jesuit priest, and leader of the Vatican intelligence's classified Iceman Three expedition, looked directly into the camera lens of the Vostok iris recognition system.

A moment later, huge steel doors slid open to reveal the most sophisticated underground communications center in the Southern Hemisphere.

The belly of the top secret intelligence base, which, to all intents and purposes, was invisible to the outside world.

Contrary to disinformation reports of its collapse and subsequent burial under millions of tons of ice, the abandoned Russian research station was, in reality, a living, heaving underground intelligence complex, under the control of the combined intelligence communities of the United States, the UK, the Russian Federation, and the Vatican. And gateway to the largest archeological dig in the world—an ancient subterranean city that had lain buried for centuries, two miles beneath the ice.

After decades of intense research, Gabriele Alessandro was almost persuaded that Admiral Byrd's secret diary of a subterranean city that lay beneath secret Antarctic doors, inhabited by Nordic-looking extraterrestrials and their flying craft, existed.

He was, however, thoroughly convinced that the fantastic tales that echoed through the deep underground levels of the Pentagon and the corridors of both the Kremlin and MI-6—reports of mummified giants frozen miles under the Antarctic ice—were based on fact.

Whispered tales of eighteen-foot Goliaths with monstrous heads, bright yellow hair, and staring lilac irises. Hybrid creatures that were alluded to in both the ancient books of Genesis and Enoch. The product of fallen angels' intercourse with the human race, buried for thousands of years in the floodwaters of Gilgamesh—Noah's flood.

Hitler's "*Übermenschen.*"

To locate the frozen monsters had become more than Alessandro's passion.

It had become his (and the Vatican covert intelligence service's—*Servizio Informazioni del Vaticano's*) sole obsession.

Forty-eight months ago, he had hit gold, quite literally, in the form of four unidentified flying machines, each emblazoned with a golden swastika and measuring over a hundred meters in height and width.

Then, six months later, far below the southeastern sector of the subterranean city, Alessandro had unearthed the first mummified Nephilim. The sector was now the site of the global intelligence community's highly restricted Red Ice zone.

The doctor walked inside and surveyed the members of the Iceman Three task force. Forty-five of the world's leading geophysicists, geologists, geomorphologists, anthropologists, and glaciologists, who had been secluded from all human contact. Training night and day for today's retrieval exercise.

A tall man with cropped pale blond hair, in uniform, strode into the communications center. The intelligence personnel immediately stood to attention and saluted.

General Kjellberg motioned them to stand down. He nodded to Dr. Alessandro, and together they walked to the far side of the chamber.

"Dr. Alessandro, time is not on our side." The general spoke with a soft Norwegian accent, but his tone was forceful. "Our security forces are waiting at the shaft entrance to accompany you. The destiny of the human race may rest on your success . . . "

The general looked at Gabriele Alessandro steadily.

" . . . or your failure."

"Understood, General. We shall work fast. And smart."

Dr. Alessandro turned to the task force. "Operation Iceman is in play, gentlemen."

General Kjellberg watched silently as, one by one, the red-jacketed expedition members of Iceman Three followed Alessandro through monstrous steel doors in the direction of the underground ice shaft.

Their mission: to destroy the hidden secrets of the Antarctic.

Maybe even the secrets of Hell itself.

TWO MILES UNDERGROUND
EIGHT WEEKS LATER

Although Gabriele Alessandro had been preparing for over two years to take possession of the "cargo," what they had discovered was nonetheless mind-blowing. Staggering.

Over two hundred frozen mummified bodies had lain two miles beneath the ice for centuries. Giants. Nephilim—the mythical hybrids of human and fallen angelic DNA—*actually existed.*

Their calculations had been exact.

Two decades of preparation had been successful. Beyond their wildest imagination.

"Hey, Doc!" Jesse Tate, the youngest member of Project Iceman, a brilliant MIT grad with a Mensa IQ, ran up to Gabriele Alessandro.

"Doc . . . ," he gasped. "I need you to come with me." He hesitated. "*Now*, please."

Alessandro frowned, then followed Tate swiftly over to the left of the cavern, where a colossal mummified figure rested on top of the ice.

The giant's head was at least three times the size of a man's, but the features were definitely human. Except for the staring eyes.

The irises were the strange pale lilac color that now seemed consistent with all Nephilim. The same chiseled mouth and nose, strong chin, coarse yellow hair.

Six fingers on each hand. Six toes. Wrists and ankles bound by wide copper bands.

The creature's jaw was open. Alessandro squatted down next to the giant.

"Two perfect rows of teeth," he murmured. "Note the incisors, Tate."

"Doc, it's the shoulders. Look at the *shoulders* . . . "

Alessandro's gaze dropped to the monster's shoulders. Jutting from the massive scapulae, half concealed by the icy matrix, was what looked like an outcrop of bone.

Impossible.

"Fused together," he muttered, tugging gently with his gloved hand at the bone jutting from the shoulder.

"Joint axes of the skeleton support the creature's wings," he murmured in wonder.

" . . . Set perpendicular to the longitudinal axis. Enables it to extend and flex. It's actually part of the hybrid's *skeleton.*"

He looked up at Tate, incredulous.

"You realize what this means, Tate?"

Jesse Tate stared at Alessandro in elation. "It means that this Nephilim had *wings*, Doc."

"It also means," Alessandro said softly, "that the angelic DNA in this hybrid had to have superseded the human DNA. Get the DNA sample, Tate. Then proceed with the extermination procedure."

Gabriele Alessandro tore his eyes away from the eighteen-foot mummy and pressed his transmit button.

"Bayliss, confirm the number of cargo still to be terminated."

"One hundred and ten, Doc." The words in a strong cockney accent reverberated in his earpiece.

Alessandro spoke softly again into his mouthpiece. "Keep me post—"

A barrage of machine-gun fire erupted through the

caverns. Seconds later, the entire battalion of special security forces lay dead or dying on the ground.

"*Congratulations,* Dr. Alessandro."

The blood drained from Gabriele Alessandro's face. Slowly he turned around.

Walking toward him was a tall, bony man with a gray complexion, humorless eyes, and badly dyed cropped jet black hair.

Kurt Guber, Director of E.U. Special Service Operations, and exotic-weapons specialist.

"You have some lost property belonging to us, I believe."

Alessandro stared back at Guber with unconcealed disgust.

"Oh, come, *come,* Dr. Alessandro, we are fully aware of your discovery of our flying machines. In fact, we are *most* indebted to you, Herr Doktor. You have single-handedly discovered the passage under ice to Agharta."

He held out a gloved hand grasping a map with the title "Deutsche Antarktis Expedition 1938–9."

"A map of the underground passages under Antarctica. Grand Admiral Doenitz gave it to my father."

Alessandro stiffened visibly at the mention of Guber's father. Ulrich Guber, "*the* Wolfman," had been in charge of one of the Nazis' most advanced covert superweapons programs until his disappearance in April 1945.

"What is the English saying? I think it goes, 'Don't exterminate your chickens'—in this case, your Nephilim—'before they are hatched.'"

"You're trapped, Guber," Alessandro snapped. "The communications base two miles above us will be tracking you and your thugs."

Guber reached over and ripped open Alessandro's Big

Red parka at the neck, revealing a clerical collar. He smiled contemptuously, then nodded to a swarthy mercenary who pushed the butt of his machine gun savagely between Alessandro's shoulder blades. Alessandro collapsed to his knees in pain.

"Yes, *pray*, Reverend Doctor—you will need your prayers. How do you think we got in? Let's just say that your associates from the intelligence base in Antarctica are no longer with . . . " Guber broke off in mid sentence. Gabriele Alessandro was staring, transfixed, at the Nephilim to his left.

Guber carefully followed his line of sight.

A shallow but definite pulse was beating under the pallid flesh.

"*Dio Abbi pietà*," Alessandro whispered, his face as pale as the form on the ice before him.

"God have mercy." He stared up at Guber "It's *alive!*"

"Of *course* it is alive, Herr Doktor Alessandro." Guber swigged a drink of brandy from the hip flask at his waist. "They are *all* alive." He smiled dispassionately at Alessandro.

"They have just been *sleeping*. For thousands of years."

He leaned over and pressed the transmit button on his comm system.

"Your assistance has been invaluable to us, Bayliss. Crate the cargo; then transfer the containers to the shafts. Our transport planes have entered Antarctic airspace. We airlift them out at 0200 hours. *And* the viruses. Leave him till last."

He nodded at the trembling Alessandro, then turned to the terrified scientists being herded into the cavern by Guber's mercenaries. Finally, all forty-five stood in silence before Guber.

"Execute them." There was so much loathing in Guber's voice that Gabriele Alessandro knew with certainty that he would slaughter them all. He bowed his head, grasping for his rosary with trembling fingers.

The South polar underworld had indeed released its grisly secret: the ancient race of flaxen-haired supermen that Ulrich Guber and the Nazis had combed Neuschwabenland for eight decades earlier.

Hitler's *Übermenschen*. Sons of the Fallen.

The Nephilim had been exhumed.

Operation Pale Horse was under way.

It was Resurrection Day.

VATICAN OBSERVATORY
CASTEL GANDOLFO, ITALY
2024

It was eight p.m., the first Sunday in December. And it was Raffaele Ricci's nineteenth birthday.

He had recently been transferred from the Osservatorio Astrofisico di Arcetri, in Florence, to serve as special assistant to the revered chief astronomer of the Vatican Observatory, Father d'Angelis. Raffaele knew instinctively that the sealed document he clutched in his right hand contained "*il più terribile segreto.*"

The terrible secret. The secret that Father d'Angelis had probed the cosmos and the glaciers of Antarctica for these past thirty years.

The terrible secret that could now set in motion the annihilation of the entire human race.

Il Catastrofico scenario—the Doomsday Scenario.

Raffaele wiped the perspiration from his upper lip, stared down once more at the document, then ran like lightning through the cloisters' ancient winding corridors, his long dark hair flying across his beatific features.

He ran through the vast observatory library housing the priceless antique works of Copernicus, Galileo, Newton, and Kepler. Past four Italian carabinieri holding their submachine guns, and out into the palace's inner courtyard. He caught his breath, then headed toward the newly renovated edifice on the east side of the Castel.

He pushed open the heavy eighteen-foot chestnut doors of the palace apartments.

Since the appointment of Pope Boniface Xl in 2022, Castel Gandolfo had ceased to function as the Pope's summer palace. It was now the international headquarters of the new state-of-the-art Vatican Observatory, and permanent residence of the current Pope's beloved old mentor and confidant: chief astronomer of the Vatican, and eminent glaciologist Father d'Angelis.

Unknown to the outer world—unknown even to the Pope—was the fact that Castel Gandalfo was also a top secret base for the most covert expedition ever planned by the Illumines: Project Iceman.

Raffaele stopped to catch his breath outside the exquisitely carved door of Father d'Angelis's private cloister. He knocked loudly.

He was greeted by silence.

He knocked again, then took a deep breath and pushed the door open.

"What *is* it, Raffaele?"

The 80-year-old Jesuit priest looked up from his papers

in mild irritation, but his pale blue eyes twinkled with affection.

"I thought I made it *abundantly* clear." Father d'Angelis elegantly removed his pince nez glasses and rubbed his eyes.

"There are to be *no* disturbances . . . " He broke off in mid sentence, catching sight of the distinctive copper seal of the Servizio Informazioni del Vaticano."

The Vatican's covert intelligence service, established to monitor secret information regarding extra- and intra-terrestrial intelligence activities.

The copper seal to be used only in one event: *il Catastrofico scenario*—the Doomsday Scenario.

Father d'Angelis's glasses slid out of his hand and onto the antique wooden desk.

Slowly he rose to his feet. Ashen.

"*Dio Abbi pietà*," Father d'Angelis murmured.

He held out trembling fingers to Raffaele, who handed him the sealed pages.

Father d'Angelis took the documents, broke the copper seal, then spread the papers out on his desk with meticulous care.

"*God have mercy.*"

Raffaelle watched his tutor in awe. He well knew that at this precise moment, the chief astronomer was deciphering the lines at lightning speed, using the thousands of proprietary algorithms and classified cryptography that he had meticulously accumulated over sixty years of intense analysis and study of both the cosmos and the Antarctic.

He put on his glasses, his eagle eyes scanning the pages of encoded data.

"The secret Antarctic doors of the South Pole," he

whispered. "They are open. *Essi sono qui . . .* " His voice quavered.

He read in silence, then rose slowly to his feet.

"Over a hundred frozen Nephilim bodies were secretly airlifted from below the Southern Polar entrance by Kurt Guber and his mercenaries over twelve hours ago."

He walked over to the window.

"To what end, we dare not contemplate."

He stared out at the calm waters of the volcanic Crater Lake that glistened in the falling Italian dusk.

"They are now housed in Mont St. Michel's secret bioterror containment levels, connected by a set of deep tunnels and railcars to the underground base at the Franco-Swiss border."

He turned back to the pale 19-year-old before him.

"To CERN."

"The expedition?" Raffaele whispered.

"Project Iceman was successful." The old man closed his eyes. "Successful beyond imagination. Over one hundred frozen Nephilim bodies. Giants. Hybrids of human and fallen angelic DNA. Our calculations were exact. Precise."

Ashen, he turned back to stare out over Lake Albano. He was silent a long time.

"As we knew they would be." He bowed his head.

"The expedition was tracked, Raffaele." His voice was very soft. "By Kurt Guber and his mercenaries. The Antarctic underground base. Blown to smithereens.

"The security forces—over a hundred killed. Our scientists, all forty–five, murdered in cold blood. Decapitated, their heads strewn on the ice."

Raffaele ran over to the small sink in the far corner of the cramped office and retched violently.

Father d'Angelis sighed deeply. His features began to glow with a strange luminosity. Raffaele turned from the sink just as the Jesuit priest transformed before his eyes into the form of Maheel, ancient angelic king of the High Council of the First Heaven.

Raffaele had seen the transformation only once before, but still he stared transfixed at Maheel's noble angelic features as the ancient king walked toward him, towering over him.

"We must alert Jether the Just."

Very gently Maheel placed his hand on Raffaele's back and smiled down in compassion at the trembling boy before him.

"We find ourselves in the most coveted place of all, my son," he said softly. *"La mani de Dio."*

He fingered his rosary with trembling fingers, then stared up at the beautifully carved statue of Christ in the alcove far above him.

"We find ourselves in the very hand of God."

CHAPTER ONE

DE VERE MANSION
LONDON
DECEMBER 2024
11 P.M.

J ASON STARED IN DISBELIEF at the figure standing outside the mansion's back garden security gate. He rubbed his eyes. He was seeing things. Hallucinating.

It was a ghost. But he was the CEO of the largest media conglomerate in the Western Hemisphere. A consummate pragmatist.

He didn't believe in ghosts.

Jason took a slug of his whisky.

The figure was a hallucination. A figment of his imagination. *What with Mother's sudden death tonight, the old professor's revelations about Adrian's birth . . . and the whisky . . .*

He stared down at the half-empty glass in his left hand. *God, the whisky.*

With his free hand, Jason fumbled in his pocket for the last cigarette in the now crumpled packet, shook it free, and lit it with trembling fingers.

31

He inhaled deeply on the cigarette; then very slowly, inch by inch, he raised his head toward the back gate.

The hallucination was still there.

In fact, not only was it still there. It must have keyed the private code into the security gate, because the steel gate was now open and the figure was walking.

Straight toward *him*.

The whisky glass slid out of Jason's hand and smashed onto the concrete floor of the garden terrace.

Jason stood rooted to the spot. Stunned.

"Nick?"

"Yeah, it's really me, Jas—Nicholas."

Jason's cigarette slipped out of his fingers and made a faint hiss as it hit the snow.

"You're *dead*," he whispered.

He was greeted by silence.

"You . . . you've been dead . . . "

He took two steps back, his mind reeling. Dear God, now he was conversing with a ghost.

" . . . for over three years."

Jason stared at Nick for a full minute, at a loss for words.

"I'm alive, Jas."

Nick took a step toward him. "Flesh and blood."

"How—I mean, where . . . ?"

"Look, Jas, I'll explain everything later," Nick said softly. He held out an envelope. "I can't stay."

"What the *hell* kind of game do you think you're playing?" Jason rasped. "Disappearing for three years. The whole family thinking you're *dead*."

Jason's grasp on Nick tightened so fiercely that Nick winced.

A PALE HORSE

"And you tell me you can't *stay*?"

"It's not a game, Jason," Nick replied. "I have no option."

"Don't." Jason brought his face a hairsbreadth from Nick's. "*Don't* you for one moment think you can just walk back into my life after three years of everyone thinking you were *dead . . .* " He took a deep breath, still shaking with fury. " . . . and *casually* tell me you'll explain everything *later.*"

He released Nick, then walked over to the rose beds. He spun around, his mind still reeling.

"Damn it, Nick, we had *a funeral* for you!" he yelled. He froze, then ran his hands through his cropped, silvering hair.

"Oh, God, Nick," he gasped. "It's been a rough night. Mother . . . she's . . . "

Nick nodded. "It's okay, Jas," he said softly. "I know. She's dead. A heart attack."

"*How?*" Jason rubbed his eyes wearily, then shook his head.

Nick looked back at him steadily. "You need to take the envelope, Jas."

"Nick . . . " Jason ran his palm over his face, feeling the old, familiar frustration rising. "You're not back on the *coke*."

Nick shook his head at his older brother, completely composed. "For *once* in your life, Jas, give me the benefit of the doubt."

"Okay, Nicky." Jason held up both hands. "The benefit of the doubt."

Nick held out the envelope again.

Jason frowned, took the envelope from him, and reluctantly tucked it in his pocket.

"An unmarked car will pick you up from here at four a.m. sharp. It'll be one of ours."

Jason stared at him in bemusement.

"Take out the sim card before you leave. No X-pads. No cabs. You're under surveillance. Your handheld, transaction data, GPS—Guber and his thugs are monitoring your every move."

"Guber? What's he got to do with this?"

"We'll explain everything once you arrive."

"Where, Nick? Arrive *where*?"

"Ireland. The northwest of Ireland. It's all in the envelope."

Jason took another step back, scrunching the empty cigarette pack in his fist.

Nick's eyes narrowed. "You stopped smoking years ago."

Jason shook his head. "Not mine," he grunted. "Dad's hidden stash. It's been *quite* an evening."

Jason scanned Nick up and down for the fourth time in as many minutes.

Faded Levi's. Brown leather jacket. Satchel. Same sun-bleached hair. Much longer, though, than the last time he'd seen Nick—now it skimmed the top of his shoulders. And he was tanned.

Nick De Vere still looked the pretty celebrity boy, except that the last time Jason had seen him he was gaunt, his body consumed by AIDS. He had filled out. In fact, he was looking like his old self.

"You're looking good, Nick," he said awkwardly.

Nick grinned. "More than I can say for *you*."

34

Jason gave a grudging half smile. He was fully aware that his 48 years looked more like 55. But vanity was not Jason De Vere's Achilles' heel. He was still ruggedly handsome but well worn, his tanned face creased and the cut of his cropped, silvering hair unbecomingly severe.

He paused, then frowned. "How did you get through the curfew?"

"Same as you." Nick held up a neon orange card. "Special pass. Except mine's a flawless forgery."

Nick handed Jason a silver and teal pen.

Jason frowned. It was a Conway Stewart Westminster —hellishly expensive.

"It's a fake," Nick said. "A very *good* fake. It's a secret camera. For Julia. We need her to do something for us, Jas. To go to the Redgrave Medical Registry on Wimpole Street."

"Wimpole Street," Jason muttered, his mind racing.

"We need her to photograph two sets of documents," Nick continued. He handed Jason a memory stick.

"Details of the files, for Julia."

Jason slowly took the memory stick from Nick's hand.

"Tell her you saw me. Whatever she photographs will be transmitted straight through to Ireland."

"What's in Ireland?" Jason held up the envelope. "The Ark of the Covenant?" He gave a wry smile.

Nick looked at him without a glimmer of humor.

The sound of voices echoed from the front hall. Nick looked around, uneasy.

"I can't stay, Jas. Adrian's on his way here from the hospital."

Jason stared at him, completely bewildered.

"Adrian," Nick said softly. "I know who he *is*, Jason."

Jason's mind raced back to Mackenzie's disclosures.

"You're not . . . " He looked at Nick incredulously. "You're not seriously trying to tell me you believe the old professor?" He shook his head in disbelief

Jason fell silent. Strangely troubled.

"We'll talk. In Ireland. I promise."

Jason nodded. "We'll talk. In Ireland."

He put his hand on Nick's shoulder, then clasped him fiercely to his chest.

They stood completely still, eldest and youngest brother embracing in the snow.

Finally, Jason released Nick. Nick walked toward the back gate. Jason noticed a slight limp in his left leg.

"Your leg . . . "

"From the accident. By the way, Jas, Maxim's fifth column. One of us," he said softly. He punched in the code to the gate. "Brothers," he whispered. "For eternity."

"Brothers," Jason echoed.

"I love you, Jason." Nick turned. "Always have."

Jason stared blankly after Nick as he disappeared out the back gate. He had never felt so good but, at the same time, so shaken in his entire life.

There was something different about Nick. Something indefinable—he couldn't put his finger on it. All he knew was that, against all his misgivings, he liked it.

"Love you, too, Nicky," he whispered. His eyes watered. "Always have."

But Nick had already vanished into the falling snow.

CHAPTER TWO

DUBLIN AIRPORT
FINGAL, IRELAND
DECEMBER 2024

IKE AND THE ALIENS: THE URBAN LEGEND

From July 13 to July 29, 1952, the world was stunned by newspaper headlines and photos of a series of unidentified flying objects appearing repeatedly over the United States Capitol in Washington, D.C.

Four months later, World War II hero Gen. Dwight Eisenhower was elected president.

Testimony by former from New Hampshire state representative Henry McElroy verifies that in May 2010, McElroy viewed a document, addressed to President Eisenhower and prepared by a governmental department, briefing him on the current situation and the history of UFOs on planet Earth.

The document advised Eisenhower that aliens existed on planet Earth and that a meeting with representatives of the aliens could be arranged. He was further advised that security would not be a problem, since the aliens had shown no hostility toward the human race.

On February 24, 1954, President Eisenhower reportedly made a secret trip to Muroc Airfield (now Edwards Air Force Base), in the California desert, accompanied by generals and four eminent leaders in the religious, economic, and media sectors.

Urban legend has it that while at Muroc Airfield, Eisenhower witnessed the landing of an extraterrestrial craft. Several extraterrestrial beings emerged to converse with the president and his generals. A researcher named Gabriel Green, on the base at the time, stated that he had earlier seen five UFOs fly in overhead and land. A retired Air Force test pilot stated that he had seen the UFOs under guard in the hangar. He described two as cigar shaped and three as disks.

The foundations were laid for a treaty between the United States and the extraterrestrial beings, which would be cemented less than a year later.

The treaty was known as the Greada Treaty.

An exchange was agreed. The aliens would furnish the United States with advanced technology and would assist in technological development that would allow the USA to maintain technological supremacy over the Soviet Union.

It was also agreed that the United States would allow the visitors to abduct a small number of humans, on a limited and periodic basis, for the purpose of medical examination and monitoring of human development only, with the stipulation that the humans would not be harmed, would be returned to their point of abduction, and would retain no memory of the event. Reporters were fed the cover story that the president needed to see a dentist.

On the night in question, events took a strange turn. The Associated Press reported: "President Eisenhower died tonight of a heart attack in Palm Springs."

Two minutes later, the report was retracted. The AP reported that Eisenhower was still alive.

Decades later according to urban legend, it became apparent that the aliens had deceived Eisenhower. The U.S. government received far less than the technology agreed on, and abductions increased a thousandfold.

The Greada Treaty had been broken.

Disclosure of the aliens' existence would mean the inevitable exposure of the U.S. government's covenant of death: the exchange of human software for extraterrestrial hardware.

Exposure of the U.S. government's complicity would result in revolution—a risk the government could never afford to take.

As of today, the existence of an extraterrestrial race continues to remain undisclosed.

—Alex Lane Fox
Staff writer, *New York Times*

Alex yawned, tapped his glass X-pad, then glanced down at the time. It was past midnight. He walked over to the window of the nondescript airport hotel and gazed out at Dublin Airport's recently completed new runway.

It was 12, 008 feet long. Postponed in December 2008—a result of the 2008–09 global financial crisis and falling consumer demand for air travel—it was recommissioned in 2020. Estimated cost: two billion euros. Actual cost: two billion eight hundred million euros.

He ran his fingers through his thick, dark shoulder-length hair in frustration. With an investigative journalist's ability to retain inane trivia, he had long ago discovered that the devil was indeed in the details.

Which brought him back to the present: the Greada Treaty.

Alex stared down for the tenth time that evening at the cutout of the now dog-eared article on Eisenhower's rumored meeting with ETs in the UK tabloid the *Daily Mail*, dated February 15, 2012.

Someone had shut the story right down twelve years ago—someone powerful. But Alex Lane Fox intended to get to the truth, whatever that may be.

He would finish his report first thing in the morning and file it before driving straight across to Easkey on the northwest coast, to meet Dylan Weaver.

And Nick.

Nick . . . Alex couldn't wipe the grin off his face.

If he hadn't seen Nick last night in Dublin, he wouldn't have believed it himself. Incredible as it seemed, it was an indisputable fact.

Nicholas De Vere was alive.

CHAPTER THREE

DE VERE MANSION
LONDON
DECEMBER 2024

"A HEM, SIR, your brother is waiting for you in the kitchen, Master Jason."

Jason turned. Maxim, Lilian's valet, who had raised him, stood at the back door.

Jason studied Maxim warily.

Maxim looked back at him, inscrutable. Jason walked inside.

Adrian De Vere, President of the European Union Superstate, stood at the kitchen table, looking the epitome of "presidential." Expensive tailored suit, fading Caribbean tan, chiseled movie-star features, not one raven hair out of place. His manicured fingers toyed idly with the blue card attached to the whisky bottle from Lilian.

Neil Travis, his personal bodyguard, and two ex-SAS men paced restlessly in the hall.

"You okay, Jas?" Adrian's piercing steel blue eyes surveyed Jason. "You look pretty rough. It's freezing out there, in case you hadn't noticed."

"Just having a cigarette," Jason muttered.

"You don't . . . "

"Still don't," Jason replied. "One from Dad's old stash. It's been quite a night."

"I thought I heard voices."

Jason held up his glass cell phone. "Purvis," he lied. "She'll liase with Rosemary about the funeral arrangements."

"It was peaceful, Jas." Adrian scanned Lilian's card. "Mother's passing."

Jason nodded. Adrian felt in his top pocket and took out his cell phone. He tapped the flexible willow glass display screen. "Copy of Mother's death certificate."

Jason stared down at his own phone screen as the certificate appeared. "Cause of death: acute myocardial infarction."

"She had a good life, Adrian," he said softly.

"She did, Jas." Adrian smiled. "She had a really good life." He looked down at his watch. Distracted. "Look, I'm sorry, but I have to get back. To Babylon. Tonight. Second session of the bailout talks starts at eight a.m. Then final session moves to Normandy Sunday night. I'll fly out to Mother's funeral from the abbey."

Jason nodded. "I'll stay a few days and wrap things up."

They clasped hands.

"Thanks, Jason. You're a brick." Adrian watched as Jason clipped the Conway pen into his shirt pocket, then laid his cell phone on the kitchen table, next to an unfashionable black accordion file.

Adrian's gaze fell down onto James De Vere's crest.

"Mother's papers," Jason mumbled. "Found them in the safe. I was going through them. You know she always preferred paper to the I- and X-pads."

He could feel his face turning red. He had always been a lousy liar, and he knew it. So did Adrian.

Adrian studied him, then lazily opened the black file. He picked up the grubby envelope containing the wad of blue paper from Professor Hamish Mackenzie.

His cell phone purred.

"Yes, I'm leaving now."

Adrian removed the letter, scanned the bank account numbers, then flipped through the grimy blue-lined pages.

"It's *garbage*, Adrian. Not worth the paper it's written on. Some senile old professor's ramblings."

"It was in the safe?"

"Addressed to Father."

Adrian studied the hurried, untidy cursive scrawl.

I have followed the genetic clone's rise intently since that day in 1998.

In December of that year, he graduated with five A-levels from Gordonstoun.

In 2002 he received his B.A. (Hons) in Philosophy, Politics, and Economics from Oxford.

In 2005, after two years at Princeton, he spent a year specializing in Arab studies in Georgetown.

From 2006 to 2010, he served as a director in the family business. Asset management.

He became chancellor of the exchequer in 2010.

In 2012 he became British prime minister.

Slowly Adrian turned the last page. Jason watched as Adrian read.

This is the secret I have held for over three decades.
His father was James, his mother Lilian.
The clone incubated in the Jesuit laboratory all those decades
ago is none other than the present prime minister of the United
Kingdom.
Adrian De Vere.

Adrian stared for a long moment at Hamish Mackenzie's scrawled signature, then finally looked back up at Jason. His gaze was inscrutable as ever. Finally, he spoke.

"You *were* going to show me this drivel?"

"Not worth the paper it's written on . . . " Jason found himself lying a second time.

"You don't mind if I take it with me?"

"I've got no use for it." Jason shrugged. "Do whatever you want, pal. It's that or the fireplace. Didn't think you'd give it a second thought. It was stashed with a pile of marriage certificates, death certificates. You know Mother; she kept *everything*. Even our kindergarten reports."

"James De Vere and his Illuminus friends," Adrian murmured. "Conspiracy theorists to the last." He smiled slightly. "Jason." He embraced his elder brother affectionately. "You're a good man."

He picked up the black file, strode down the hallway, opened the door, and walked out without a backward glance. The door shut behind him.

Jason watched Adrian walk through the gate and get into the black limousine purring outside. He walked back into the hallway—straight into Maxim.

"Your coat, Master Jason."

Maxim held out Jason's overcoat. Jason looked at him strangely but took the coat.

"And your gloves, Master Jason. Inclement weather is predicted."

A huge clap of thunder sounded overhead. Maxim raised his eyebrows.

"Forgive me, Master Jason, but I took the liberty of parking Madam Lilian's new Bentley outside." His brows knitted. "May I strongly suggest that you abandon your phone."

Jason looked at the valet even more strangely, then handed him the glass cell phone. Maxim gave a satisfied smile, then dismantled it and laid it on the hall console table.

"The Bentley is secure. I swept it."

Jason frowned. "You *swept* it?"

"For bugs, Master Jason," Maxim declared. "I have in my possession my own portable X-ray machine for checking the insides of objects and walls, a time-domain reflectometer, frequency scanner, nonlinear junction detector. I conduct regular magnetic anomaly inspections: thermal imaging, X-ray, radiographic, and fluoroscope inspections."

Sleet bucketed down as they walked toward the Bentley. Maxim opened the car door for Jason.

"By the way, Master Jason, I took the liberty of duplicating Master James De Vere's files before Master Adrian arrived. You will find them on the backseat, on a memory stick."

"Damn it, Maxim." Jason glared at his old servant, then settled back into the plush gray leather seat. The door closed automatically. He picked up the memory stick and tucked it in his wallet, then took the envelope from his pocket and tore it open.

He studied the contents. One passport in the name of Alexander Monaghan. A safe-deposit box key. A ticket for the 8:25 a.m. Aer Lingus flight from Heathrow to Dublin.

Jason slipped the passport and key into his pocket, and the ticket inside his wallet.

Maxim got into the front seat and attached a neon orange curfew pass, courtesy of Adrian De Vere, to the windshield.

"Maximus Basil Pinkerton, did you know Nick was alive?" Jason growled. Maxim stared straight ahead.

"On second thought, don't answer that," Jason sighed.

"May I inquire as to our destination, Master Jason?"

"I don't know what the hell's going on," Jason growled, "but I have the distinct feeling you already know *exactly* where I'm going."

Maxim twirled his mustache and smiled broadly. He placed both his enormous hands firmly on the steering wheel.

"Start," he commanded. The Bentley's voice-activated ignition system roared to life.

"One-o-four Cheyne Walk, Chelsea." The Bentley's auto-pilot program illuminated the dashboard. "To Madam Julia," Maxim said.

Adrian reclined in the backseat of the limousine. He looked up from the black file, then casually pressed the intercom.

"Mr. President, sir," Chastenay answered in his clipped English accent.

"Check if a call from Jontil Purvis was placed to my brother's handheld between eleven and eleven fifteen this evening."

"Yes, Your Excellency." Chastenay entered "Jason De Vere" into the holographic visual database built into the dashboard of the limousine.

Adrian returned to his reading. He looked up once more.

"My instructions. Concerning my mother's body."

Chastenay nodded. "The body goes directly to the Chapel of Rest. No autopsy. Our people are dealing with it."

Adrian nodded.

Chastenay looked up from the database. "Only one call registered to Jason De Vere's cellular phone the entire evening. From your handheld, Your Excellency. Your location. Chelsea Hospital. At precisely twenty-two fifteen this evening. No calls received on the house phone. Again, only your call."

Adrian frowned. "Surveillance on my brother."

"Already in hand, Your Excellency."

Adrian pressed a remote, and the glass divider slid up. He handed Chastenay the black file.

"The three law firms mentioned in these papers—each holds a duplicate of this file. Deal with them in the normal fashion. And *very discreetly*."

"Of course, Your Excellency.

Adrian stared out at the stylish interactive glass advertising panes of West London.

"One more thing: Aveline. Aveline Biological Institute."

"Ivanovich owes us a favor," Chastenay said.

Adrian nodded. "Very good. No loose ends."

"Of course, Your Excellency. Arson is his speciality. By the time we reach Babylon all instructions shall be executed."

Adrian leaned back in the plush seat, deep in thought.

The intercom buzzed.

"Kurt Guber on satellite phone for you, Mr. President."

Guber's precise German tones resonated through the limousine. "The transport arrived at Mont St. Michel at o-three-hundred hours. The cargo is now safely housed in biocontainment three. Level Subzero."

"Job well done, Guber."

Adrian settled back in his seat, a satisfied smile on his face. Everything was going precisely as planned. He glanced down at his watch. In less then twenty-one days, the entire human race would be under his total control.

He was about to commit the ultimate crime. He was about to execute genetic Armageddon on an unsuspecting world.

Operation Pale Horse was under way.

CHAPTER FOUR

CHEYNE WALK
NEW CHELSEA, LONDON
ONE A.M.

THE WEATHER had deteriorated into what was fast becoming a virtual blizzard.

Jason struggled against the gale-force winds and blinding snow, through Julia's gate, and up the icy path.

He looked up. Julia's bedroom light was still blazing.

Jason picked up the brass lion's head and knocked loudly on the freshly painted door of Julia's recently refurbished white flat-fronted Georgian house.

Julia's light clicked off.

Jason paced impatiently up and down the small paved path, then knocked again. Loudly.

Lights clicked on in a window of the adjoining house. A disheveled blonde glared out at him. Jason lifted his hand in apology, then bent his head to the mail slot.

"Julia!" he hissed. "I know you're in there. It's a blizzard out here."

He looked back up toward the blonde, who had now been

joined by a young man. They both stared suspiciously down at him through the driving snow.

"Open the door, damn it!"

A military van drew up outside, and a soldier with a sub-machine gun got out. Jason watched as Maxim displayed the special pass. The soldier nodded, saluted Jason, and headed back into the van, which roared off down the road.

Jason rolled his eyes. He had never thought he would see the day. Curfews and military patrols in *London*.

"Julia!" he shouted through the mail slot. "*Julia, do you want me arrested?*"

There was a long silence, then the sound of keys jangling and a lock turning. The front door slowly opened.

Julia stood barefoot, her duck-egg blue chenille dressing gown wrapped tightly around her. The blustery winds blew her blond hair and gown violently. She pushed her hair back from her face and stared up at Jason in sheer disbelief.

The wind blew Christmas cards from the hall side table onto the carpet.

"You're letting the cold air in," she snapped.

Jason, now drenched as well as frozen, pushed unceremoniously past Julia's petite frame and into the hallway and slammed the door. He pulled off his leather gloves and fiddled with his watch.

"Look, Julia, I know I haven't been in touch," he said, wiping the snow off his face.

"*Not been in touch,*" Julia muttered, rapidly regaining her composure. "*Three and a half years* and not a word, and now you have the audacity . . . " She stared at him in disbelief. "And God knows, Jason, only *you* would do it—you have the *audacity* to pitch up on *my* doorstep at one in the morning, during the worst snowstorm in living memory."

She frowned.

"How did you get past the curfew?" she added suspiciously.

She strode toward the kitchen and flicked on the touch-sensitive display glass. "*Don't* bother to answer that."

The lights switched on.

"Three and a half years, Jason." Her mouth was a thin line. "Not so much as a text message, let alone a phone call."

He followed her into the kitchen.

"You took the note from Nick I gave you the day after his funeral, and just *disappeared.*"

She tapped the kitchen display pane, and immediately the electric kettle started to heat up. She turned, seething.

"For three whole years. You and Lily are together one weekend out of four. But me? Not even a phone call."

"Look, Julia . . . " Jason threw his hands up in frustration. "I should have known. What *possessed* me to think you'd be rational?"

He strode back down the hall.

"Rational—*you* want *me* to be *rational!*" she hissed.

Jason turned. "Fine. I'll be rational," he snapped. "Mother's dead. A heart attack."

Julia stared at him. Stunned into silence.

"Earlier this evening." He glared at her.

Julia put her hand on his arm in shock. Jason stared down at the large diamond on her left ring finger and stiffened involuntarily.

Callum Vickers. Julia's British neurosurgeon fiancé. The wedding was six months away.

"I . . . I'm sorry, Jason . . . I didn't know," she said softly.

He looked up into Julia's bewildered hazel gaze. He still loved her. He always would.

Lily had been living in New York for the past two years. He took her out to dinner every Sunday night when he was home. They debated and chatted, were vocal about every subject under the sun. But Lily knew not to violate Jason's unspoken rule. Any mention of Julia was verboten. And Jason deliberately never asked.

He was out of his mind. He should never have come. He'd go to Wimpole Street himself.

He gingerly removed Julia's hand from his arm, retraced his steps, and opened the front door. He hesitated, then strode toward the Bentley in the driving rain.

Julia ran after him in her slippers, slipping on the snow that was now rapidly turning to sleet. She stood in front of the gate, the wind lashing her face, snow mingling with her tears. The wind died down to an icy breeze.

She waved feebly to Maxim, who extricated his huge feet from the Bentley, put up a large multicolored golfing umbrella, and handed it to her.

Julia took it and smiled weakly.

"Thank you, Maxim."

The lights went on next door. Jason glared up at the nosy blonde, then sighed.

"Look, Jason, I'm sorry. I didn't realize Lilian was . . . oh, hell, listen, I was a jerk."

Jason grudgingly looked down into her honey brown eyes.

"Truce?" She smiled up at him. "Still Earl Grey with Darjeeling?"

She ran over to Maxim's car window.

"Maxim?"

The Bentley window rolled down.

"Come in for tea?"

Maxim shook his head, pointing to a thermos flask on the passenger seat. He started unwrapping a bacon sandwich. "My emergency rations," he declared. "I shall have to decline your generous offer, Madam Julia."

Julia leaned over and kissed his blushing cheek. "Lovely to see you, Maxim."

Jason followed Julia up the path to the house and through the hallway to the kitchen. He sat down heavily in one of the white leather kitchen chairs.

"Where's Callum?"

"Hamburg," she replied. "Neuro conference. He comes back Sunday. On Tuesday I fly out to New York. Exclusive interview."

Jason grunted. "Staying at the Gramercy apartment?"

Julia nodded. She handed him the the cup of tea.

"I didn't come just because of Mother." Jason sipped the tea, then set it down. "I need to talk to you, Julia," he said quietly.

"About Lily?"

He shook his head. "About Nick."

Julia's expression softened. "You've got to forgive yourself, Jason," she said.

She gently laid her free hand on his arm.

"It's been over three years since he died. You've *got* to move on."

"Look . . . " Jason closed his eyes. "There's no easy way to say this, so I'll just spit it out." He hesitated. "Nick's *alive*."

Julia sighed. "Yes, of *course* he's alive, Jason. He'll always be alive in our hearts."

"No. I mean he's *alive*. I saw him tonight . . . at the house."

The bone china teacup slipped out of Julia's hand, smashing into smithereens on the kitchen floor.

"That's below the belt, Jason De Vere." Julia knelt down and began picking up the broken pieces with trembling hands. "Even for *you*." She looked up at him, seething.

"Nick's *dead*."

"Nick is *alive*, Julia." Jason looked at her, unwavering. "Did you actually *see* his body at the funeral?"

Julia rose from the floor, still staring straight at Jason. "What do you mean, *alive*?" she whispered.

"*Alive*. I saw him. Flesh and blood. Forty-five minutes ago."

"You . . . you actually *saw* him?"

Jason nodded. "Here in London, at the mansion."

"You actually *saw* him." Julia put the broken china in the dustbin and sat shakily at the table. "I don't *believe* it."

"Believe it." Jason shrugged. "It's true."

"I *can't* believe it." She pushed her hair off her forehead, bewildered.

"God, Jason, we had a *funeral* for him."

Jason raised his hands. "That's what *I* told *him*." He rolled his eyes in frustration.

"What did he *say*?"

"Not much." Jason shrugged. "Normal cryptic Nick. I fly to Dublin . . . " He glanced down at his watch. " . . . in a few hours to meet with him. He said he'd explain everything. You *have* to keep it secret, Julia."

She frowned. "Why? Why doesn't he want anyone to know he's alive?"

Jason looked at her intently, then sighed. "I don't know. He's going to tell me everything once I'm in Ireland." She opened her mouth. Jason placed his finger gently on her lips. He shook his head and sighed. "He must have good reason, Julia. We have to trust you."

"*We*," Julia snapped. "You didn't speak to him for over eight years when he was alive, and suddenly it's '*we*.'" She glared.

"Look, I don't expect you to understand," Jason said in exasperation. "I'm not sure *I* understand. Nick gave me this. And something else . . . for you."

He held out the silver and teal pen.

Julia stared down at the Gothic-style engraving on the cap and barrel, then reached out and took it from him. Her eyes softened.

"Oh, it's beautiful," she whispered. "Oh, Nicky."

Jason rolled his eyes in irritation. "It's a *camera*, Jules," he said. "Not a present. A very *sophisticated* camera."

"Oh," Julia muttered weakly.

"Nick said he needs you to photograph two documents. At the Redgrave Medical Library on Wimpole Street. Today. There are two sets of papers filed in its archive. Medical records."

He handed her the memory stick Nick had given him.

"Those are the codes for the records. You have to photograph them using the pen." He took the pen back from Julia and clicked the button. "Nick said whatever you film will be instantaneously transmitted back to Ireland."

"Ireland?" she repeated.

Jason shrugged. "Julia, I told you, Nick was cryptic. You just have to click the pen. I can't believe I'm actually doing this. Listen, as soon as you've photographed the documents, get out of there—your job's done."

He handed her a card.

"Nick said you'd need this. It's a security clearance. I'll see you at Mother's funeral."

Jason strode to the door and turned back to face her. He nodded at the ring.

"I'm glad you're happy, Jules," he said awkwardly. "With Callum, I mean."

And then he was gone, leaving Julia staring after him in the now softly falling snow.

CHAPTER FIVE

SOFITEL ELITE HOTEL
TERMINAL 6, HEATHROW AIRPORT
LONDON

J ASON LOOKED at his watch. It was four thirty a.m. He was exhausted. He stared around the Sofitel Hotel's deserted lobby.

He removed the safe-deposit tag from his wallet and walked up to the blonde, foreign duty clerk behind the reception desk. He pushed the tag over the counter, then his new forged passport.

He watched as the young woman scanned his photo, then pushed the passport under the reader.

It illuminated blue. She pushed the passport back over the counter. He ran his fingers through his hair. He couldn't *believe* he was doing this.

She smiled up at him.

"Good to have you back, Mr. Monaghan."

He breathed a sigh of relief.

The clerk nodded to the concierge, who beckoned Jason back to the newly manufactured state-of-the-art security center behind the reception area. He took Jason's security pass and held it up to a scanner. It reactivated. The number 787 appeared in flashing cobalt blue, and a steel door slid open. The concierge nodded and stayed outside the door.

Jason walked into the security center, past hundreds of silver boxes flashing yellow. He scanned the numbers, then walked over to 787 and slid the key into the lock.

The box slid open, and a slim steel drawer slid out. Jason stared down at the glass handheld phone. He picked it up and tapped the screen.

One Aer Lingus boarding pass. Flight 204. Heathrow to Dublin. Terminal 6.

He frowned. There was a second passport, also in the name of Alexander Monaghan.

He studied the screen and instantly recognized the blue top-security clearance insignia reserved for top-level diplomats from Babylon. He raised his eyebrows. Nick had his contacts, all right.

He picked up an old set of car keys, then slowly tucked the new phone in his inside pocket, unzipped his briefcase, put the car keys into the pocket, and walked out.

"Thank you, Mr. Monaghan, sir." The clerk pushed a digital passkey over the counter. "The key to your suite, sir. The usual."

Jason was about to pass when he realized how desperate he was for a shower and a shave. He also realized that under the regulations of the curfew, Heathrow's terminals did not open until six a.m. He took the suite keys and disappeared into the elevator.

An hour and forty-five minutes later, he arrived back down in the lobby. He held out his ticket to the concierge, who nodded in the direction of the white and silver personal rapid-transport courtesy podcars to the newly built Terminal 6, directly outside the hotel's glass and stainless steel revolving doors.

When was the last time he'd had to board a commercial jet? He scowled. It must be over fifteen years ago. His own plush personal Gulfstream 7 was at that very moment parked at the largest of the newly opened Thames Estuary airports in London. Nick's precautions had better be worth the inconvenience.

He tore the second envelope open as he walked toward the podcar. Two breakfast vouchers for Gordon Ramsay Plane Food, Terminal 6. He suddenly realized that he was ravenous.

Ten minutes later, he was standing at security in front of the iris scanner.

"Thank you, Mr. Monaghan."

Jason grinned. How had his little brother organized *that* one? Jason De Vere's irises were now the property of one Alexander Monaghan.

He walked through the body scanner, into the recently opened Terminal 6. He'd read that it was erected on an area bigger than London's Hyde Park. He stood staring up at the massive white steel "trees," then scanned the shopping arena: Tiffany's, Harrods—no wonder Julia had learned to love flying.

He caught sight of the restaurant, then checked his watch. The sign outside Gordon Ramsay's said it opened at six thirty a.m. *Damn.* Five minutes to go. He vaguely remembered the hotheaded London chef from *Hell's Kitchen*, back in 2012. When he was younger, much younger, and still caught some TV. He yawned.

A smartly dressed server escorted him to a cream-colored booth. He picked up the menu and stared idly through the glass panes, then back to the menu.

Classic Breakfast. Coffee.

He looked down. He couldn't wipe the smile off his face.

Nick De Vere was alive and *well*.

And living in Ireland.

୶

WELBECK STREET
LONDON WI

It was nine a.m. precisely. The rain and sleet had stopped. Julia parked her silver VW Beetle on Welbeck Street, pressed the remote locking mechanism, and walked around the corner to Wimpole Street.

She walked briskly toward number 64. She had pulled on a pair of faded jeans and sneakers. Her hair was pulled off her face in a simple ponytail, and she wore no makeup, only lip gloss and sunglasses. Passing the specialists' offices until she came to number 64 Wimpole Street, she walked up the steps of the red brick building and stopped outside a gold plaque that read "THE REDGRAVE MEDICAL LIBRARY." It started to snow lightly.

She pressed the buzzer.

Chapter Six

PERDITION
CYDONIA MENSAE REGION
PLANET MARS
2024

MICHAEL STOOD, his cloak wrapped tightly around his lean imperial form, his flaxen braids lashing his face, his cape flying wildly in the freezing arctic tempests.

He stared out beyond the southern polar cap of Mars, toward the great silver battlements of the Ice Citadel of Gehenna, glistening in the nine magenta ice suns that rose from the murky, cold skies above the brooding ice-capped crags of Vesper.

The Second Heaven.

Lucifer's forbidding realm.

The wild, barren ice plains of Gehenna stretched for miles, surrounding the great looming fortress. Freezing arctic blizzards and tempests from Mars circled the citadel continually, venting their fury on Lucifer's winter palace.

The skies grew dark as packs of monstrous scaled gray-winged leviathans flew through the Martian skies, their powerful translucent webbed seraphim wings beating the air frenziedly, seething ice smoke spewing from their nostrils. A ghoulish screeching filled the solar system as thousands of white devourer vultures circled overhead.

Michael turned. There, striding toward him over the barren landscape, was Lucifer.

The familiar magnificent figure stopped directly in front of him.

Michael studied his brother. Nine feet tall, lean, his waist-length raven hair lashing his face in the freezing wind.

Lucifer raised his scarred imperial features in ecstasy to the dark blizzards that blew in from the White Dwarf Pinnacles. Then he turned to face Michael. He smiled brilliantly.

"It has been many moons since we last fellowshipped, brother." He bowed.

Michael bowed in return.

Lucifer ascended, his black wings outstretched, and hovered above the planet.

Michael followed his elder brother into the bleak sky. Far below them rose a steep-flanked mass of rock eight hundred feet high.

The shadowy likeness of a sphinxlike face, nearly two miles from end to end, stared back at them.

"A memorial to the fallen cherub, the light bearer," Michael murmured.

A strange, evil smile flickered on Lucifer's lips.

"Quite a good likeness of me—I was gratified," he murmured. "The Gray Magus conceived the blueprints. My shaman kings built it—a memorial to my eternal presence in the solar system. However, let us dispense with trivialities. You summoned me."

Michael held out a missive with the royal seal of the House of Yehovah.

Lucifer snatched the missive and tore it open. He turned his back to Michael, pacing up and down as he read.

"He *dares*," Lucifer muttered. "He *dares* to give me an ultimatum."

He swung around to Michael, his eyes rabid with rage.

"He threatens me with *expulsion* from both the First *and* the Second Heavens . . . unless we, the Fallen, desist in our genetic experimentation."

"That *includes* your nefarious scheme involving the Nephilim bodies transported to Mont St. Michel from Antarctica."

Michael watched intently as Lucifer's expression changed to one of sheer hatred.

"The Second Heaven is legally *my* territory," he hissed. "*I possess* the title deeds. Eternal Law cannot be overruled."

"Unless you violate it by your *own* hand." Michael stared at him. Fierce. "You have gone too far this time, Lucifer," he warned. "You have contravened Eternal Law by your schemes to manipulate the Race of Men's DNA. Even as the Watchers of old. Your legal claim on the Second Heaven became invalid the *moment* you contravened Eternal Law."

"I am chief prince, seraphim, second only to His throne," Lucifer snarled. "I will enter the First Heaven just as and when *I please.*"

Michael grasped his arm. "Those days are long gone. It would behoove you to heed it. Yehovah well knows your ill-founded schemes to mutate the Race of Men's DNA. Your extraterrestrial creatures and your flying machines are known both to Yehovah *and* to the High Councils of the First Heaven."

Lucifer looked in revulsion at Michael, then removed himself from his grasp.

"And will shortly be disclosed to the Race of Men," he snarled. "The Race of Men—their television, movies, video games—all propagate my gospel, the gospel of extra-terrestrial beings. How *fervently* they believe in us, not as the Fallen but as *ascended masters*, as a benevolent race from an older planet.

"The revelation of an ancient civilization will prove that intelligent life other than man exists in the universe. Proof of artificially built structures on the moon and Cydonia, Mars, will eventually lead the Race of Men to the conclusion that the entities responsible designed and guided them throughout history—that our presence on Mars and in UFOs confirms that we are their *gods*.

"*Then* we shall wreak our final revenge. We shall instruct them that the Nazarene was one of our own. No more, no less.

"We shall persuade them that *we* are the gods they seek. They will worship us, their masters. The truth of the Nazarene and Golgotha will be *obliterated*."

The two brothers stared at each other, their hands on their broadswords, Lucifer with loathing, Michael with disgust.

"You are drunk with your own importance, brother," Michael snapped.

"Michael, the ever *sanctimonious*."

"Lucifer, the deluded."

"Why should we not war right this minute, *brother*?"

Lucifer grasped the hilt of his broadsword handle.

"But oh, no." He drew his sword and raised it to the skies. "Yehovah requires an *army*."

With a deft thrust, he struck the sword from Michael's grasp. It clattered to the icy ground.

"I was always faster than you, younger brother."

Lucifer returned his broadsword to its sheath at his side, his eyes hard as flint.

"The war is not between you and me," Michael said through gritted teeth.

"Whom is it between, Michael? *Pray* enlighten me. I earnestly seek to be enlightened by my pious younger brother. Should I fight Yehovah? Will He descend from His holy hill? Will He descend from His rubied sanctuary. From His place of safety? His asylum?

"Will He descend in the likeness of the angelic and have the nerve to fight me face to face?" he snarled.

"*Oh, no*, my naive younger brother. Yehovah will stay out of harm's way, in His anodyne habitation, His safe haven. Instead, He sends my brother to wage war against me."

"I *tire*, Lucifer," Michael sighed. "Your beguiling speeches that once found their mark leave no trace on me."

"You have received Yehovah's ultimatum, yet you dare continue with this folly. Hark back to the days of the fallen Watchers. They crossed the point of no return by committing intercourse with the daughters of men."

Lucifer grinned. "The Nephilim. What fun!"

"You well know that the mutation of the Race of Men's DNA carries the severest judgment. The Watchers lie chained these past millennia, reeking of sulphur in the lowest pits of hell beyond the abyss."

Lucifer's expression grew dark. "I do not need my earnest younger brother to remind me of their eternal damnation."

"I warn you, Lucifer," Michael continued. "If you reject Yehovah's ultimatum and persist in your schemes of genetic Armageddon, you shall not only be expelled from the gates of the First Heaven, but I shall personally drive you and your Fallen from your monstrous citadels on the planets and constellations of the Second Heaven. Earth *alone* shall be your habitation."

Michael stood, his hand on his broadsword.

"You have forty moons to comply. Yehovah's ultimatum runs out on the eve of the Great Tribulation of the Race of Men. At the rise of the two crimson moons.

"You have been *warned*, brother."

He vanished.

Lucifer stood trembling with rage, staring after him. The warlocks of the west materialized in front of him.

"Summon the Dread Councils of hell," Lucifer murmured. He raised his head to the warlocks of the west, whose hands were raised as they murmured their dark incantations.

Summon the royal princes of Grecia, of Babylonia, the black ice magus. Summon the warlocks of Ishtar, the wort seers of Diabolos. Summon the necromancer kings. The Cyclops of Diabolos. Summon the legions of the damned to gather on the ice plains of Gehenna."

He held up the missive high.

"We will conspire!"

CHAPTER SEVEN

GABRIEL'S PALACE BEDCHAMBER
PALACE OF ARCHANGELS

G ABRIEL TOSSED and turned on his bed. Sweat from his brow soaked his pillow.

"War," he muttered, his eyes glazed and unseeing. "War . . . Hell and death ride with the Dragon."

Michael stood at the balcony doors, staring out at the seven pale blue moons glimmering on the First Heaven's horizon.

"You have returned from Mars," Jether said. Michael turned. Jether stood in the bedchamber doorway.

"Lucifer would war." Michael sighed. "His self-importance has become insatiable these past eons."

Jether walked over to Michael. They stood together in silence.

Finally Jether spoke. "It is his final answer?"

Michael shook his head. "No," he said softly. "He summons the Dread Councils of hell. They hold court."

He gazed back toward Gabriel.

"Each night, it is the same, Jether. Gabriel falls into a deep and restless sleep; then the dreamings grip him like a vise. He is tormented by the visions he sees."

"He sees the Third Great War," Jether murmured. "The War of the Revelation of St. John—the war between Michael and the Dragon."

"He is the Revelator," Michael stated. "We knew it would be so. It would seem my elder brother has learned absolutely nothing from his defeat these past millennia."

"As eons pass, the wisdom of Yehovah recedes from him," said Jether. "In its place grows the unruliness of lawlessness and pride. He becomes defiant. Reckless with his own self-importance." Jether heaved a deep sigh. "Reckless because he knows that a millennium chained in the bottomless pit awaits him . . . and the Lake of Fire. We cannot act officially until the full forty moons of the ultimatum have passed. Yehovah's justice demands he be given the allotted time."

"He will not go quietly to his doom," Michael answered. "His intention remains. To set himself up as ultimate ruler, to set up the fallen angelic host in our place and rid the First Heaven of every trace of the Race of Men."

"Yes." Jether looked at Michael with compassion. "Because of the victorious sacrifice of the slain Lamb on Golgotha, judicially, victory is ours. But practically, Michael, we are still required to enforce his defeat in the heavenlies. It is written in the High Courts. You, Michael, must prepare our armies."

"War." Gabriel sat bolt upright in horror, his eyes glazed. "There was war in heaven," he muttered. "Michael and his angels fought against the Dragon, and the dragon fought, and his angels . . . "

Sweat dripped from his brow.

"At the rise of the two crimson moons, forty moons hence, the Great Portals shall open. I see Lucifer. He storms the gates of the First Heaven, his wrath unbridled."

Jether walked over to Gabriel, but Gabriel stared through him, unseeing, then placed his head in his hands, trembling violently.

"It is the Great War of the Apocalypse—war between Michael and the Dragon."

Jether bent over him, stroking his matted hair. "But the Dragon was defeated, Gabriel," he whispered. "And there was no longer any place for them in heaven. The great Dragon was hurled down—that ancient serpent called the devil, or Satan, who leads the whole world astray."

Gabriel's countenance changed. His eyes focused first on Jether and then on Michael.

"He was hurled to the earth, and his angels with him," Gabriel said softly. "It will result in the greatest conflagration that the Race of Men and planet Earth have ever seen. This last war—it precedes the great battle of Armageddon."

He rose and walked across the amethyst floors of his bedchamber.

Jether watched as Gabriel bathed his face in the hot springs.

"Let us ride," said Gabriel. "It will clear my head."

He led the way down white marbled balcony steps onto the sands of infinity below his palace apartments. He mounted a beautiful winged white stallion, as did Michael, while Jether climbed astride Vesper the giant eagle's saddled back.

Together they ascended the skies, flying past the pale blue moons beyond the enormous Pearled Gates of the First

Heaven. Out into the galaxies, far beyond them, was the faint silhouette of the Fourth Horse and its rider.

"Nisroc, keeper of hell and death, rides a pale horse. The fourth seal of Revelation is about to be broken. The fifth seal yet awaits. The Rapture of all who wear the Nazarene's seal will take place. Then the Great Tribulation of the Race of Men."

They stared out as one toward planet Earth and the galaxies surrounding it.

"The Harpazo—the great snatching away of the church —the Rapture," Jether murmured. "It draws near. Lucifer, in his obsessive envy of the Race of Men, will not share heaven with the Race of Men."

Michael moved his hand across the galaxies. Instantly, Moloch and his black horde became visible on Saturn. Their black braided hair hung well below their thighs. Their pale straw-colored eyes stared pitilessly out from their scarred, mangled faces. Alongside the fallen horde, a pack of snarling black jaguars paced, chained to their depraved masters, their poisonous black fangs visible, each with a tail of seven snakes.

"The Fallen hone their warring skills. Moloch and his bloodthirsty black horde battle each other on Venus and Saturn."

"There is worse," Jether murmured. "The Dread Councils of hell gather on the ice plains of Gehenna. The Twins of Malfecium create Lucifer's supersoldiers: hybrids, chimeras. Monsters."

"We await his response to Yehovah's ultimatum," said Michael.

"Lucifer's visits to the First Heaven have become strangely

rare these past moons," Gabriel said. "These past seventy moons, he has come to our High Council Chambers, to the Supreme Angelic Courts, with his legislative host only seven times."

"He schemes," said Michael.

"For eons, his fallen judges have brought case after case against the Race of Men. He is accuser of the brethren," Gabriel said softly. "He rails against the just. His envy of the Race of Men is unappeasable." He paused. "Jether, what if Lucifer chooses war?"

"He will enter officially through the Pearl Gates, as is still his legal right. Then, in his takeover bid, his armies will storm the gates."

The brothers followed Jether's gaze over to the glistening Rubied Door, so colossal in its beauty that it was still visible from the higher heavens. Their gaze fell to Eden, whose beauty was visible throughout the galaxies. They watched the glistening aurora borealis of Eden in silence.

"Lucifer himself will battle for Eden, the garden of Yehovah Himself," Jether continued. "This war will be the most gigantic, unprecedented event in the annals of angelic warfare.

"If it comes to battle, we, the holy angelic host, must defeat him, for once and for all time. And we must defeat him in our own backyard."

Michael nodded. "My task will be to drive him from the First Heaven and rid every planet in the Second Heaven—Venus, Saturn, Mars—of him and his evil cohorts."

"At the time of the Great Tribulation, directly after the Rapture occurs, the Great Portals will reopen. I will cast down Lucifer and his Fallen through the Portal onto planet

Earth. We rid the First and Second Heavenlies of the Fallen forever."

"And if we lose?" Gabriel whispered.

"We will not lose," stated Michael. "We must keep our heads. Yehovah will keep our souls. Justice will prevail."

Michael stood in the balcony doorway. He raised his palm. Earth came into view. "For the devil has come down to you enraged, in great fury, because he knows that his time is short."

Jether stared at planet Earth for a long time. His voice was very soft. "If we lose, the consequences for the Race of Men . . . " He raised his face to Michael and Gabriel. " . . . are untenable. Yet if we win, for a short time, Lucifer will vent his unbridled fury on the Race of Men. Planet Earth will be ravaged by Lucifer and the Fallen.

"However, for now we wait."

CHAPTER EIGHT

DUBLIN INTERNATIONAL AIRPORT
IRELAND

JASON WALKED OUT into the Dublin Airport parking lot. He surveyed the unappealing concrete horizon, then made for a smaller rental car lot directly across the road. It was midwinter, but unlike London's currently clear blue skies, Dublin's skies were gray and overcast, and the wind was mind-numbingly cold.

Jason pulled his coat collar close around him and stared out at the sea of parked cars: Budget, Avis, Europcar, Hertz. Finally, he spotted it, beyond the rental signs: the long-term parking lot.

He walked up and down the rows of VW Eoses and Mazdas. Nothing. *Damn.* More Volvos, BMWs, and Land-Rovers. Nothing. *Damn.* Finally, his eyes fell on a small, battered red 2008 Ford Escort.

It started to rain.

He fumbled for the car keys in his pocket as a car accelerated past, splashing him with mud. Exasperated, Jason brushed at his suit jacket.

He looked up, coming eye to eye with an elderly couple in the car opposite him, eating sandwiches wrapped in newspaper. They glared at him suspiciously. He glared back and then, with some difficulty, opened the Escort's door, crammed his lanky frame into the front seat, and slammed the door.

He stared down at the gearshift. It must have been at least twenty-five years since he last drove a manual vehicle.

"Damn it, Nick," he muttered, then stopped himself. His little brother must have had good reason.

Shivering with cold, Jason opened the glove compartment to find a brand-new map of Ireland still in its plastic wrapping, with a yellow sticky note attached. "Post Office, EASKEY—County Sligo West" was scrawled on it with a thick red felt-tipped pen. He tore off the wrapper, unfolded the map over the steering wheel, and studied the coast until he found the M4 out of Dublin, heading west.

He placed the map on the seat next to him, buckled his seat belt, and started the engine, then stowed his phone minus the sim card in the cubby hole. Were all these precautions *necessary*?

The woman in the car opposite him was still glaring at him.

He scowled back at her. Where were the heat controls? He turned on the old-fashioned heating system, and a blast of freezing air came through the vents. He scowled again, put the Escort into gear, and sped out of Dublin airport, following the large–format, moving-display glass signs to the M4.

⌒

REDGRAVE MEDICAL LIBRARY
WIMPOLE STREET
LONDON

Julia walked into the huge medical library, signed her name in the registry book, then walked over to the medical registry reception. She stared around the vast room. Six people sat at the long oak tables, engrossed in their research. Not a pin dropped.

She handed the security clearance to the nondescript clerk behind the large oak desk. He studied her clearance and her request form, then disappeared.

⌇

EASKEY
NORTHWEST IRELAND

Three hours later, Jason turned into the coastal village of Easkey. The main street consisted of one carry-out eatery, a local pub, a butcher shop, a hair salon—hardly Nick's usual sprawling metropolis. He grinned.

There was the post office. And Nick, hanging out of a sky blue Jeep.

"Follow me!" Nick yelled.

Jason lowered the window and gave a thumbs-up. He pulled out after Nick, roaring up the R297 toward Sligo. Five minutes later, Nick made a sharp left down a rambling dirt track half covered in melting snow.

Jason followed Nick for a full mile and a half until a low-lying thatch-roofed cottage came into view.

He parked behind Nick, directly outside the front door, then grabbed his phone from the cubby hole, and his briefcase from the backseat and extricated himself, with some difficulty, from the front seat of the Escort. Jason stared out at the spectacular view of the Atlantic, a hundred yards below the cottage.

Nick stood watching him from the doorway. "Hey, Jas," he said, grinning.

The sight of his youngest brother standing there, very much alive, still had the most profound effect on Jason.

"Nicky . . . " He embraced Nick, who then steered him into the hallway.

"Welcome to our humble abode."

The entire far side was built on an open plan and crammed with what appeared to be extremely sophisticated sur-veillance equipment. Above it was a colossal holographic display screen.

Dylan Weaver sat hunched over a server. To his left were five supercomputers, all transmitting information in real time. To his right, three Chinese youths were engrossed in algorithms.

Nick beckoned Jason nearer. Weaver nodded at them in acknowledgment.

"Rewind," Weaver instructed a Chinese engineer who looked no older than fourteen.

Jason watched, incredulous, as images of himself passing through the iris scanner at Terminal 6 transmitted onto the massive screen above Weaver's head.

"Alexander Monaghan . . . " Nick grinned. "From the ever-fertile brain of Dylan Weaver."

He turned to Jason. "We hacked into Terminal Six's surveillance systems. The breakfast vouchers we gave you were fitted with a camera. We knew the exact moment you paid up and headed for security."

Weaver thrust his plump fingers into a large bag of potato chips and stuffed a handful in his mouth.

"We can hack into any system, thanks to our high-end hackers in Hangzhou. They're an offshoot of the international subversives." He grinned at Jason. "Trained up under Assange's teenage hacking subculture. Our main servers—a very sophisticated setup—are located in Hangzhou and duplicated meticulously in the monastery outside Alexandria. What you see here is just our mobile comms unit. We've been working on 'Sadie' for over three years—we're almost there. Then we'll be able to override any security system." He emptied the bag of chips into his mouth.

"Anywhere in the world." He looked up at Nick. "Completely undetected."

Nick gestured to Jason. "Pass Weaver your new phone. He's got this entire area blacked out from their surveillance. He'll doctor it."

Jason shrugged. "Go for it, but I already removed the sim card."

Weaver grinned. "Time for some fun with Guber."

Taking Jason's cell phone, he plugged in a nano sim card, then looked up at Jason.

"They'll think they have your coordinates, but an independent system will be playing out from your number. Guber will assure Adrian that you're shopping in London. I've added in a few credit card purchases on your phone."

"Hey, Uncle Jas!"

Jason turned. The voice was more than familiar.

Alex Lane Fox, dressed head to toe in a wet suit, leaned against the kitchen door, grinning broadly at Jason.

"Alex!" Jason stared in disbelief. "I thought you were in New York."

He paused. "Don't tell me *you* knew Nick was alive."

"Nah." Alex grinned sheepishly. "Well, yes, but only since yesterday."

"Polly's gran's old holiday cottage is in Kinsale, near Cork. Pol and I were in Ireland. She's still there. I'm assisting Nick—well, for the past three hours." He grinned again. "Great surfing here, Uncle Jas. You should join us. Actually, I'm working on a story. UFO's, government cover–ups—the kind *you* wouldn't publish."

"That's because we publish *real* news, Alex Lane Fox." Jason hid a smile, then put down his briefcase.

"Mainstream media is a tool of the elite."Alex continued.

Jason rolled his eyes. "Alex, we've had this conversation a few thousand times."

The fifth display screen came to life.

"Nick," Weaver broke in. "It's Amman, Jordan. The videoconference."

"Sorry, Jas. Have to take this—update on the Jordanian situation. Jotapa. Why don't you stretch your legs, and I'll join you as soon as I'm off the call."

Nick looked at Jason's Armani suit and grinned.

"Oilskins and Wellington boots are by the back door, Jas. Relax. Take your pick.

Jason shook his head again, his eyes still on Nick. He still felt a strange elation at the sight of his brother. "You look really great," he said.

Nick studied Jason's face. "I feel great, Jas. By the way, I'd take a rod if I were you."

Jason frowned. "It's nearly freezing." He looked suspiciously at his brother. He knew only one person in the entire world who would be fishing in the dead of winter.

Jason pulled off his suit jacket, hung it up on one of the back-door hooks, then put on the yellow oilskin anorak and pulled on a pair of Wellingtons, UK size 11. He ran his hand over one of the fishing rods standing by the door, and looked over at Nick, who was now in intense conversation with Jordan.

Jason walked out of the cottage and into the damp sea air. He walked across a field, past several grazing sheep, through brambles and slush, toward the Atlantic. Rounding a bend, he pulled up the collar of the oilskin, battling to walk against the driving winds.

There, seated calmly on a fishing chair at the water's edge, his expression intense, sat Lawrence St. Cartier. Jason shook his head. His instincts had been right.

Lawrence put his finger to his lips without turning. "You always made too much noise for the fish, Jason," he whispered fiercely.

Jason stood still and watched the old man reel in a huge sea trout. He took it deftly off the hook, dropped it in the kreel on the fishing table at his right, and took a long drink from a metal mug, then turned to Jason, elated.

"Well, don't just stand there." St. Cartier looked him up and down before threading a lugworm bait onto his hook. "Come and join me."

A red flush crept up Jason's neck.

"I haven't done this since you took me fishing in Scotland when we visited Adrian at Gordonstoun. I was . . . "

"Nineteen—you were nineteen and obstreperous." St. Cartier chuckled. "But you were still my best pupil!"

Jason settled himself next to Lawrence.

"Help yourself." St. Cartier nodded at the picnic basket.

Jason grabbed a sandwich of thickly cut bacon. A faint smile flickered on his mouth.

Lawrence St. Cartier grinned at him. "Too much commercialism in your life, Jason De Vere. Commodities, mergers—the rat race, I'm afraid, has wearied your soul."

Jason followed Lawrence's gaze out to the hills far in the distance.

"Knocknarea Mountain. Miosgán Meadhbha—the tomb of legendary Queen Maeve," Lawrence said. "A bit of God's own country is just what you need."

Together they sat in silence.

"Nick hasn't told you what happened yet?"

"Nope," Jason said shortly. Lawrence nodded.

Jason took another large bite of sandwich, then gazed out for a long time toward the Atlantic. Finally, he spoke.

"Lawrence, how long have you *known* Nick was alive?"

"Three years," said a new voice. Jason turned to find Nick standing behind them.

"After the accident," Nick continued, "I was in a safe house in Trier, Germany, for three months."

"You were in *Germany*?" Jason stared at Nick, taken aback. His exhaustion got the better of him.

"Why didn't you just go to Adrian's? The whole family was *distraught*."

Nick sighed. He looked at Lawrence, then continued. "After the safe house, Lawrence gave me sanctuary at the monastery in Alexandria. I stayed there for a year before flying out to China."

You were in Germany and then *Alexandria?*" Jason stared at Nick, then at Lawrence, stunned. "Nick stayed with you for an *entire year.* And you let Mother go to her grave thinking her youngest son was dead? Damn it, Lawrence!" Jason shouted. "She never got *over* it!"

Nick and Lawrence both gazed calmly back at Jason.

"Jason, my boy," Lawrence said softly, "your mother saw Nick a month before she died—on his return from China to the monastery. She spent the week with us. She knew the truth the day before Nick's funeral, three years ago."

Jason stared from one to the other, flabbergasted. "She never . . . " He shook his head. "She *couldn't* have . . . "

"She could. And she did. She knew that Nick's survival depended on her complete silence."

Lawrence sighed.

"Your mother tried to tell you before she died, Jason. You *did* read the black file."

Jason shook his head slowly. "The professor. Hamish Mackenzie," he murmured. "He's got to be *senile*, Lawrence."

Lawrence sighed. "You're going to have to tell Jason the truth, Nicholas. He's seen the documented death warrant. He's read Mackenzie's disclosure." Lawrence met Jason's gaze.

Jason shook his head, appalled. "It doesn't mean I *believe* it."

Lawrence put his hand on Jason's shoulder. "Nicholas *was* at Mont St. Michel the afternoon of the accident. He was Adrian's guest."

He sighed.

"Nicholas, the truth your brother can bear. The other disclosures will come later." Reeling in his bait, he stood up, folded his chair, and picked it up in one hand, his rod in the other. "I'll be getting back to the house. See you both for tea. Don't be late. Lamb and champ."

Seeing his brother's blank stare, Nick said, "Mashed potatoes."

Lawrence licked his lips. "Mashed potato, indeed!" He frowned at Nick. "Much more than mashed potato. Spring onions, full-cream milk. Add the potaoes, a large dollop of butter, then mash."

Lawrence turned and started making his way up the bank. Nick winked at Jason. "Potato famine and all that."

Lawrence glared back at him. "Champ is an expression of the resilience and spirit of the Irish people. Not to be taken lightly." He disappeared from the brothers' sight.

Nick stood silently watching the light rays from the clouds shift over the vast, heaving Atlantic. Finally, he sat down cross-legged on the bank, next to Jason.

Jason stared out at the fishing line. "You were *there*? At Mont St. Michel. The day you had the accident?"

Nick nodded.

Jason stared at him, visibly shaken. "Adrian said you never arrived. He told me to my face. At your *funeral.*"

Nick sighed. "I arrived at Mont St. Michel around eleven thirty in the morning. Spoke to Julia on the phone when I was about about forty miles out. She'll verify it. Met Adrian in the drawing room. He had a videoconference—with the Chinese premier or some such. Dad had sent Lawrence a letter. Enclosed was a photograph."

He turned to Jason.

"The photograph I sent to Julia to give you. Of Dad, Julius . . . Look, Jas, what I'm going to tell you is going to sound really far-fetched."

Jason stood, stony faced. "It can't get much *worse*."

"Okay," Nick said, "Adrian had sworn he'd never seen anyone in that photo, apart from Dad and Julius. While he was on the videoconference, I saw the third man in the photo. Dome-shaped head. Hawk nose. Silver cropped hair. His name was Kester von Slagel. I overheard a conversation between him and Guber. He more than knew Adrian. That's when I knew Adrian had lied to me. Blatantly. So I stayed."

"What do you mean, you stayed?"

"I stayed. At Mont St. Michel. I said good-bye to Adrian, then took the back road to Hilde. She was about to leave. One of Adrian's classified gigs. But there was mention of a strange priest. Royalty—a guest in the West Wing. Everything was out of bounds. I *had* to stay, Jason. I had to know the truth."

"You stayed the *night*?"

"Hilde let me stay the night in the East Wing. Pierre overrode the surveillance system. The gunships started arriving within the hour—nine of them in total. Jason, it was inconceivable. A literal who's who of the elite: World Bank, IMF, CFR, heads of state. But that wasn't it. It wasn't the dignitaries." Nick shook his head. "It was the *cargo*, Jas. Halfway through the evening, a ship—either a UFO or one of Guber's Nazi flying objects—started its descent down over the abbey. It was huge—must have been a hundred feet across."

Nick studied Jason's face.

"It set down a huge crate onto the cloister grounds."

"You're talking about the Ark of the Covenant. It was on the photos Weaver sent me from China three years ago."

Nick nodded.

"I'm a trained archeologist, Jason. This was no fake. It was the real thing. The Ark of the Covenant. There was a power outage. The surveillance came back on. Guber and his thugs arrested me and took me to our brother and his guests. Adrian had it all worked out. He knew it was the one thing that Israel would denuclearize for: the return of the Ark of the Covenant. He just omitted one minor detail when presenting it to the Israeli president: that he and Guber and his thugs were the very terrorists who stole it from the Temple Mount in the *first place*."

Jason held up his hands in frustration. "Nick, this is like a really bad B movie. I mean, the one that doesn't get to release."

Nick ignored Jason's comment. "He became the Israelis' hero." He hesitated. "Overnight. They welcomed him like their Messiah. A segment of them still do—the ones he hasn't murdered. Half of the Mossad and Sayeret Matkal were replaced with Guber's thugs three years ago. The president, PM, and half the cabinet ministers still live in fear for their and their families' lives. So they toe the Line. *Adrian's* line."

"You have *proof* that it was the Ark of the Covenant?"

Nick shook his head.

"They confiscated my camera. The photos I managed to send out don't prove the case. But I'm an archeologist, Jas. I knew. That's why Adrian had to have me killed. He knew I knew. He also knew that I wasn't going to die of

AIDS. Long story for another time. His initial attempt to murder me had failed, but I signed my second death warrant that night."

"So Adrian let you go?"

"I left in the red Aston Martin, on my way to Dinaud. Eight miles up, when I got to the pass, things started to get messy. Black helicopter following me . . . electromagnetic pulse. That's when I tried to get hold of you."

Jason shifted uncomfortably.

Nick grasped his arm. "Don't, Jas. It's water under the bridge. You and I were always so close until Lily's accident. It's okay.

"I finally got hold of Lawrence, but it was too late. The black helicopter was gaining on me; I lost control of the car. Jotapa had given me her cross. Unbeknownst to me, Lawrence had embedded a homing beacon in it. I was miraculously thrown from the car before it went down the ravine. I don't know how long I lay there. I don't know how it happened. In fact, I don't remember anything. I woke up in a house in Trier, in Germany, near the border of Luxembourg, on the banks of the Moselle River." He looked at Jason. "A safe house."

"A *safe house*?" Jason frowned. "Who keeps a safe house?"

Nick took a deep breath.

"The CIA, for one." He hesitated. "Pierre."

"Pierre? Who the hell is Pierre?"

"Dad's old chauffeur—now works for Adrian at Mont St. Michel."

Jason's mouth fell open. "*Dad's* Pierre?"

Nick smiled. "Pierre's ex-CIA, Jas. Black ops—been working for Dad, St. Cartier, and the Illuminus for years, since Dad was ambassador to the UK. Anyway, Lawrence alerted Pierre. Thankfully, he found me before Guber's thugs could. He set the car on fire, released the handbrake. It rolled down into the ravine. Guber thought I was dead. Five ribs broken . . . broken pelvis . . . knee . . . amnesia. It was three months before I could be moved from the safe house in Germany to Alexandria. And another year in Egypt before I was fully recovered. That's the limp." He looked at his left knee and heaved a deep sigh.

"Lawrence literally saved my life, Jas. He couldn't tell you. Neither could Mother. If Adrian became even faintly suspicious that I was alive, he'd come after me. This time he'd make sure. He *has* to believe I'm dead."

Jason nodded, choked with emotion and fury.

"You can't let on anything, Jas. You're next in their sights. Adrian's suspicious of what you know. You can't play by the rules. He's lawless—doesn't have any."

Jason took the memory stick from his shirt pocket and handed it to Nick. "Adrian called it garbage."

Nick took the memory stick. "You mean Hamish Mackenzie's claims that Adrian's not our brother? That he's a clone?"

He looked up at Jason. Grim-faced.

"The medical records that Julia films at Wimpole Street will be confirmation, one way or another. You read Dad's letter to Lawrence?"

Jason nodded. "Okay."

Nick's eyes searched Jason's face. "And now for the bombshell. It's common knowledge that the ten largest territories in the world are on the verge of signing Adrian's AXIS Ten agreement in Babylon. Every one of those ten regions is currently on the verge of economic collapse. GDP down by sixty percent. Banks collapsing every day."

"Sure," Jason said. "Common knowledge."

"And Adrian's offering them each a bailout as a member of the AXIS Ten."

"He is. That's all public domain."

"What's *not* in the public domain," Nick continued, "is that Adrian and his shadowy band of elites are the *selfsame* clandestine instigators of the world economic collapse. They've very successfully created a world currency crash, instability, and a global downturn. Almost single-handedly collapsed the capitalist system. By design. A few weeks after they sign the AXIS Ten, Adrian and his elite intend to launch a new wave of capitalism. A one-world global currency economy and global bank. A tectonic shift in wealth, controlled exclusively by *himself and his new one-world government*."

"You have proof?"

"We have proof."

The rain clouds started. Alex ran toward them, surfboard in hand. He stood above them on the edge of the bank.

"Tea's up!" he shouted.

"There's a roaring fire at the cottage. Lamb and champ, crumpets and blackberry jam, and Earl Grey tea." He grinned, watching the two brothers from the ridge. "Oh, and Julia's scans are coming through!" Alex disappeared.

Nick got to his feet. "It's good to have you back, Jas."

They clasped hands.

"Brothers," they said in unison.

"It's good to *be* back," Jason said softly. He clasped Nick's arm. "I've been away a long time."

CHAPTER NINE

WIMPOLE STREET
LONDON W1
TWO HOURS LATER

J ULIA PLACED HER soft leather Mulberry bag open on her lap and tapped her slender French-manicured fingers on the table. The clerk reappeared with a file marked "Petunia."

"It's classified, madam," he said.

"But you have my *clearance.*"

The clerk shook his head. "You have clearance, but it's read only—no copies, no scans. Please be aware that security cameras are positioned at every angle."

"But I *am* allowed to write a few notes?" Julia asked.

The clerk reluctantly agreed. "But you'll have to pass them by me. For censorship."

Julia nodded.

He gestured to her bag. "You'll have to put it through the scanner, I'm afraid."

Julia sighed, carefully placed the pen next to her papers, then followed the clerk to a scanner. She placed her bag in a container and walked through the body-scanning booth.

The security guard nodded and handed the bag back to her.

The clerk followed Julia back to the desk, then handed her a file folder. Julia studied the innocuous-looking file. On the outside, a single word, "PETUNIA," was typed in an old typewriter font. And below it, the date: "December 22, 1981."

Julia opened the file.

There were two sets of laboratory medical papers, both encoded.

She frowned. There was an extra set of documents, marked "DNA," filed by one Hamish Mackenzie and dated 2017. She took out the pen and smiled sweetly up at the clerk.

He nodded and walked back toward the security guard.

Julia looked up at the camera, which was scanning the back half of the room. "You owe me, Jason De Vere," she muttered.

Julia deftly scanned through the medical records. She clicked the pen down once, twice, and then a final time to capture Mackenzie's record of the DNA results.

As the clerk returned, she was writing intently. He looked over her shoulder, then pointed out two sentences and shook his head.

Julia beamed up at him. She tore out the page and handed it to the clerk, who enthusiastically handed her a second pad of paper. Under the vigilant eye of the records clerk, Julia copied several innocuous pieces of information, then stood, walked over to the reception desk, handed back the file, and shook his hand vigorously.

And left.

CHAPTER TEN

HOLLYHOCK COTTAGE
WEST COAST
IRELAND

DYLAN WEAVER crammed the remains of his crumpet into his mouth and pointed to the glass X-pad screen in front of him. "Three records of money transfers," he said, spewing crumbs over the glass screen.

He looked up at Lawrence St. Cartier.

"The bank records in the file—we had our moles in Langley check them."

Lawrence walked over to the fireplace and sank into a worn armchair. He lifted up a teapot from a tray on the table in front of the fire and steadily poured tea into three cups.

"The first two were traceable to two separate accounts." Dylan gulped down a cup of tea, then wiped his mouth on his sleeve. He grinned up at Jason, enjoying his discomfort. "First account in Switzerland, second in the Highlands."

Lawrence shook his glasses at Jason. "To Hamish Mackenzie, I'll bet."

"The final one—the largest by far—twenty million dollars, traced to a single account in Edinburgh. Aveline—the Aveline Institute."

Lawrence froze. "The photograph that I gave to Nick—Dylan, you have it on record?"

Weaver nodded and started to devour a second crumpet. His fingers flew over the keyboard. The photograph of the Jesuit priest with Von Slagel filled the screen.

Lawrence sighed. "The back view."

Dylan Weaver hit a key. They all stared at the name on the screen, transfixed.

"Aveline," Jason whispered. "It isn't a girl's name after all."

"The Aveline Institute," Dylan muttered in between mouthfuls of crumpet. "It traces its origins to the establishment of the Institute of Animal Genetics, in 1919, by the University of Edinburgh."

Dylan's fingers flew over the keys.

"In 1995, Aveline became a company limited by guarantee."

Alex looked up from his X-pad.

"Aveline—I *knew* it sounded familiar. In 1994, they cloned Harold the sheep—two years before Dolly. It was kept under wraps."

"And in 1997," Dylan added, "Aveline Biocentre was set up in the highlands of Scotland—head of the Department of Gene Expression and Development." He looked over at Lawrence, his features alight with realization. "Hamish Mackenzie—bingo! A leading pioneer in the science of cloning."

Lawrence turned to Jason. "*Not* such a senile old man, after all."

Jason glared at him.

Alex shook his head. "Not anymore. Look at this morning's London *Daily Mail*."

All eyes stared at the screen. A huge building in the Highlands had been razed to the ground. Firefighters were still trying to extinguish the smoldering rubble.

"Unbelievable," Alex murmured. "The Aveline Biocentre —arson, I'm afraid. The entire institute razed to the ground last night. Not a brick left standing."

Jason and Lawrence exchanged glances.

"Julia!" Jason gasped.

"Hey, Weaver!" one of the Chinese youths called out. "Feed from London coming through."

Dylan Weaver swiveled in his chair and hit a key. Instantly, the five screens next to him lit up. "She's out, boss. She's clear."

WELBECK STREET
LONDON
1 P.M.

Julia placed her handbag on the front seat and turned to take her jacket off. She got in the Beetle, backed out of the parking space, and revved down Welbeck Street just as a car exploded directly outside Redgrave Medical Library.

HOLLYHOCK COTTAGE
IRELAND

"The photos from Julia are coming through," Dylan Weaver said. He touched the holographic video screen as Lawrence St. Cartier, Jason, and Nick stood with bated breath.

Jason frowned. "It's medical lingo—I can't make head or tail of it."

Nick pointed at the second screen. "That one looks like a DNA test."

Lawrence sat next to Dylan, still huddled over the computer screen.

"They're printing," Dylan announced.

"The first two documents." He studied the numbers. "Lance Percival's reports."

He handed the copies to Lawrence, who polished his spectacles, placed them over his nose, and studied the documents intently. There was complete silence in the room.

"The first report," the professor explained. "The first infant born to Lilian De Vere. The prenatal genetic diagnosis for your mother was oligohydramnios—too little amniotic fluid. Poor fetal growth. A lagging fundal measurement of over three centimeters. Weekly ultrasounds and measurements of the baby's head, thigh bone, abdominal circumferences. In the last two-thirds of pregnancy, the amniotic fluid comes from fetal urine. Lung formation is dependent on breathing in amniotic fluid; the lungs of these babies with severe dysplasia are very underdeveloped."

He scanned the report.

"Her caesarean date was set for December twentieth, 1981. Infant delivered at St. Gabriel's Nursing Home in

Knightsbridge. As expected, the baby had very severe dysplasia. No kidney function at all. The *real* Adrian De Vere was placed immediately in intensive care. Not expected to survive more than a few hours."

Lawrence looked up at Jason and Nick. "Now look at the infant's kidney function *twelve hours later*."

He handed the brothers the report.

"Perfect! Your *real* brother, Jason," Lawrence said softly, "had severe dysplasia, minimal kidney function. Wasn't expected to survive."

He studied the second document intently.

"The second report, posted by Percival the day after the infant's birth." He shook his head. "Just as I expected: excellent function of both kidneys. No dysplasia recorded. He raised his head. "There is only *one* logical conclusion: the second set of results was taken from a completely different infant."

"Six pages of DNA reports transmitted." Dylan handed the papers to Lawrence.

Lawrence thumbed through the pages. "Percival's DNA test on the second infant." He stopped at the last four pages. "Filed by one Hamish Mackenzie, dated 2017, and Hamish Mackenzie's DNA results."

Nick shook his head, incredulous. "The tests he did on the clone?"

Lawrence nodded. "The precise DNA markings of the clone *he* created for the nameless, faceless priest in 1981."

He moved to a worn ruby red velvet armchair next to the crackling log fire.

"There's no mistaking it," he murmured. "Percival's second DNA sample matches *precisely* Mackenzie's DNA samples belonging to the clone." He rubbed his eyes and looked up at Jason, who was visibly shaken. "It's worse than we imagined."

Jason groaned. "How on earth can it be worse?"

Lawrence took a deep breath. "Years ago, in the late 1980s, I was involved in a top secret black ops project. I was part of the CIA, *spying* on the CIA—the Directorate of Operations. I obtained access into the lower ultrasecret levels of Dreamland at Dulce. There had been reports." He closed his eyes. "Horrific reports . . . "

His voice grew very soft. " . . . of mass abductions. Children."

He opened his eyes. "The cases that I investigated were abductions from Mexico." He hesitated. "We eventually located the missing abductees."

He was silent, as if collecting his thoughts.

"Nineteen levels down in Dulce, a second lab at Los Alamos. Secret underground bases, railcars that reach Mach two—all leading to a horrific underground labyrinth of laboratories called—"

"Nightmare Hall," Alex said, finishing his sentence.

Lawrence nodded.

"You're telling me you were a *witness*?" Alex gasped. He grasped Lawrence's arm. "You were actually *there*? Do you know what this means? There's never been *any* concrete proof. In all these decades . . . "

Lawrence bowed his head. "Eight of the ten members in our team went missing overnight," he said softly. "The reason there is no proof is because the shadowy puppet masters who pull the strings exterminate every witness systematically."

"The military-industrial complex," Alex said.

"But you survived," Jason said, ever the pragmatist.

A slight smile flickered on Lawrence's lips. "You could say I had, um . . . superior protection."

Alex gripped Lawrence's arm more fiercely. "Professor, what did you discover? Are the rumors substantiated?"

Lawrence sighed, and Alex slowly loosened his grasp.

"Alien-human hybrid experimentation. Cloning the human and the bestial races—mixing the DNA of animals, plants, and humans . . . " He hesitated. " . . . with alien DNA—chimera transgenics."

"*Alien* DNA? You mean ETs from Roswell?" Alex queried.

Lawrence nodded. "Tip of the iceberg. Five bodies were discovered. One lived. Even Wernher von Braun saw them, as did many credible scientists, astronauts, high-ranking government officials. They were taken to Wright-Patterson Air Force Base, five miles northeast of Dayton, Ohio. During the next thirty years, there were several more UFO crashes —always kept at the highest level of government secrecy."

He took a deep breath.

"They kept the aliens alive. And started to interbreed an unholy merging of alien and human DNA. The U.S. government—at least those in the know—were ashamed. Tried to put a stop to it, but they were dealing with *far* more powerful masters with a very different agenda. Shadow masters. Rogue factions of the CIA. The military-industrial complex. The moneyed elite and their sinister masters. Their goal: depopulation. And a one-world government.

"Senators, congressmen—those with a conscience, anyway—tried to speak out. They were silenced, either by blackmail or by more permanent means."

Lawrence sighed.

"The Americans were not alone. Make no mistake. The UK has its own equivalents. Porton Down—Ministry of Defense and of Science and Technology."

Alex frowned. "Porton Down . . . David Kelly was its chief microbiologist during the Iraq war, wasn't he? When Blair was prime minister?"

"For a time, yes, Alex. There was also talk of Porton Down's collaboration with the gene warfare monster Wouter Basson." His expression darkened. "But coming back to the DNA . . . "

He picked up the DNA results.

"I had seen exactly the same genetic makeup before, as had Hamish Mackenzie" He looked meaningfully at the others. "It's not the conventional genetic structure of human DNA."

Jason looked at him skeptically. "What do you mean, not *conventional?*"

Lawrence closed his eyes. "I mean that this DNA is not from any terrestrial source. It's not animal DNA. It's not human DNA."

He stopped and looked straight at Jason, then at Nick. "It's alien."

Jason looked at Lawrence in disbelief and then started to laugh. "Come on, Lawrence! Even for you this is a bridge too far. You're not talking *X-Files, Independence Day, Prometheus* . . . "

Lawrence stared at him forbiddingly. "Jason Ambrose De Vere, I'm afraid that's *exactly* what I'm talking about."

Jason put his head in his hands and groaned.

Alex frowned. "So *whose* DNA is it?"

Nick, Jason, and Lawrence all fell silent. It was Nick who finally spoke. "It's our brother's."

Alex started to laugh. "Yeah, sure, it's Jason's."

Lawrence shook his head. "It's no joke, son."

Nick and Jason looked at Alex without a trace of humor. "It's Adrian's DNA, Alex," said Nick.

Alex looked at Lawrence.

Lawrence said, "There is almost watertight evidence that Adrian De Vere is a biological clone."

"A clone . . . " Alex laughed nervously. "The president of more than half the Western world—you're *kidding*, right?"

"Most assuredly, Alex Lane Fox, I am not."

Jason looked up from studying the two previous documents. "These confirm Percival's story." He thrust the first paper onto the table. "Adrian De Vere, born December twenty–first. Mother Lilian, father James—St. Gabriel's Hospital.

"One day later . . . " Jason thrust the second document down beside the first. "Adrian De Vere vanished. Perfect. Dysplasia gone, kidney function perfect."

"They had to have swapped the babies," whispered Nick.

"Who? What baby?" Alex threw up his hands.

Lawrence sighed. "The real Adrian De Vere, James and Lilian De Vere's son, was murdered at birth. He was replaced with a clone."

Nick turned and looked Alex straight in the eye. *"Adrian's not our brother."*

CHAPTER ELEVEN

GEHENNA ICE PALACE
MARS

L UCIFER STOOD, his cloak wrapped tightly around his lean imperial form, his long raven braids lashing his scarred face, fur cape flying wildly in the freezing arctic tempests. He gazed out beyond the southern polar cap of Mars, toward the Ice Citadel of Gehenna. The Second Heaven.

He dropped his gaze to the wild, barren ice plains surrounding his great forbidding fortress. The legions of the damned were gathering.

From the solar systems and above the earth they flew. From their opulent royal palaces on Saturn and Jupiter, Uranus and Venus, the menacing giant six-fingered satanic princes arrived, one by one, in their winged chariots of the damned. From the constellations they flew. From their citadels on Orion and Draco. From Centaurus and Ursa Minor. From their magnificent castles in the Second Heaven above Ethiopia, Grecia, and Babylon they came. From Siberia and from Persia. The great and terrible rulers of the darkness assembled on the ice wastelands of Mars.

The sinister Black Ice Magi rode across the plains of Mars on their headless three-humped camels. Close behind flew the ghostly witches of Babylon from Venus, and the dread Warlocks of Ishtar from Mercury, on the backs of winged werewolves and dragons, their pale faces raised in ecstasy to the ice blizzards.

From the great depths under the earth they came—thousands of dauphin scribes with cloven hooves, ascended out of the Popocatépetl volcano, through the heavens, toward Mars. From under the oceans and from the desolate lunar depths of the Marianas Trench, they came—Hera and the banshees of Valkyrie, riding on Leviathan and giant sea serpents. From the molten center of the earth came the Wort Seers of Diabolos. The Necromancer Snow Kings and the one-eyed ice Cyclops flew through the ice crevices of the secret doors of Antarctica on their six-headed gargoyles, their great horn claws slashing through the glaciers.

As far as the eye could see, the Fallen were gathering.

Answering the call. To hold high court in the Dread Councils of hell.

On the ice wastelands of Mars, a ghoulish screeching filled the solar wind as the thunderous pealing of the monstrous bells of Limbo echoed from the spire across the bleak ice plains of Gehenna.

Lucifer lifted his scepter, his white fur cape billowing in the violent ice tempests. In a semicircle behind him stood the thirteen dread Warlock Kings of the West – their pale green parchment like skin and hooked noses visible beneath their crimson hoods. The only sounds on the ice waste-lands were the ominous mutterings of the Warlocks' incantations.

Lucifer turned to face the damned gathered across the ice wastelands—the great assembly of powers of evil and terror, the rulers of the dark world. His intense sapphire eyes blazed fiercely.

"Secure the gates!" he commanded.

Instantly, a hundred thousand of the Black Horde, Lucifer's elite militia, appeared from their snow caverns. Their black hair hung well below their thighs, and their yellow eyes blazed with demonic fire.

There was a monstrous shuddering. The gates of the Ice Citadel closed.

Lucifer raised his scarred imperial features in ecstasy to the dark blizzards that blew in from the White Dwarf Pinnacles.

"I welcome you, princes, kings, esteemed rulers of the darkness of this world. I welcome you, great magi, witches, and warlocks of the Second Heaven. I bid you welcome, esteemed banshees of Valkyrie from under the oceans, Wort Seers of Diabolos, and Necromancer Kings of the secret places under the earth. You may worship your emperor."

The entire assembly bowed low.

"We worship you, O Lucifer, O great Satan."

Lucifer paced up and down the ice pavilion.

"Our time as the Fallen is short. Untold millennia have passed since the First Great War—the War of the First Judgment—and our iniquitous and unmerited banishment from the First Heaven."

A dark murmur erupted. Lucifer raised his hand.

"Over two millennia have elapsed since our undeserved and crushing defeat by the Nazarene at Golgotha," he hissed.

This time a deafening, bloodthirsty cry erupted. Lucifer surveyed the Fallen. Smiling malevolently, he raised his scepter a second time.

"Yes, we have bided our time. Yes, we have been patient. Yes, we have been judicious." He paced up and down.

"But now the days of the Fallen draw rapidly to a close. The three and a half years prophesied by the Hebrew Daniel have passed. The Tribulation is here. The Great Tribulation is nigh. Three and a half years remain."

He stood, imperial, silent, and held out his hand. Marduk passed him a missive.

"Mark well the seal of the Royal House of Yehovah!" he cried, "for in not so many moons it will be the Royal House of Lucifer the light bearer."

Lucifer held the missive up high.

"Last dawn, I received a visit from a former comrade. My brother, Chief Prince Michael. Archangel." He bowed.

"He bore this very missive. A missive from Him who abandoned us," he hissed. From Him whom we served fervently. Devotedly for eons. A missive from *Yehovah*."

He opened the missive slowly in front of the Council.

"A dark threat. An ultimatum. He lays only two choices before us: desist in our genetic programs before forty moons are passed, or we the Fallen will be expelled. Driven out by force. Not only from the First Heaven but also from our present place of habitation as well. The Second Heaven.

"Venus, Mars, Saturn—*our* planets. Our constellations. We will have only one abode left: that parched tract of dust. That unsightly, hideous planet. We will be driven to Earth."

A thunderous roar erupted from the Fallen. Lucifer motioned for silence.

"We will not stand idly by and watch the demise of our great fallen angelic race!" His eyes burned with an evil fire.

"We will WAR."

The colossal prince of Grecia stood: eighteen feet tall, his head two feet in diameter, with sparse orange hair. His yellow eyes glinted with evil as he raised his copper-bound arm.

"We will WAR!"

A second monstrous roar erupted from the Fallen.

"We will WAR!"

Lucifer smiled, then raised his head in the direction of the planet Earth.

"The day of the Third Great War with Michael my brother and the armies of the First Heaven is upon us. When the seal of the Pale Horse is broken and Nisroc, prince of hell and death, crosses the Kármán Line, all who bear the seal of the Nazarene will be caught up into the heavenlies."

A cacophonous whisper broke out over the wastelands.

"We have waited two millennia for their forthcoming evacuation. We *relish* the removal of the Nazarene's subjects from *our* planet. They have greatly obstructed our progress in the realm of men, with their confounded supplications, the incursions of the angelic hosts through the Portals to assist them.

"The Nazarene," he spat. "Visitations to this wretched planet. *Nightly.*"

The satanic prince of Draco rose to his full height of seventeen feet. His red eyes glinted, and his matted black hair fell below his thighs.

"Golgotha!" he thundered.

A murmur of terror rippled through the Council.

"*Their* removal ensures *His* removal. It ensures our victory. Yet we must ask ourselves the question, *why* does Yehovah remove them at this time?

"Because He would *rescue* them. From the coming Judgment. The Great Tribulation."

Lucifer's face contorted with loathing.

"Does He rescue *us*, the Fallen, from His judgments? Does He show *us*, *the Fallen*, grace or mercy for *our* weaknesses? Our rebellions?

"No!" Lucifer roared. "He *banishes* us. He condemns us for the rest of eternity. First to exile. Then to the Lake of Fire. Are *our* sins, are *our* weaknesses, *our* frailties any less or more than those of the Race of Men?"

A louder roar erupted from the Fallen on the ice wastelands.

"Are *my* sins, are *my* weaknesses, is *my* rebellion any less or more than those of the Race of Men? And if He wins the war, our Father has chosen not only to exile me but to chain me and imprison me for one thousand years in a bottomless pit, and then for eternity in burning sulphur, the Lake of Fire. Do you see even *one* of the Race of Men condemned with such ferocity, such abiding hatred, such unparalleled injustice, as *I, Lucifer*?"

A huge commotion broke out among the Fallen. Lucifer stared out at the Dread Councils in satisfaction. He waited for the uproar to subside, then spoke again.

"Moon after moon, eon after eon, I have personally approached the High Courts of Heaven with our legislators of the Fallen.

I have traveled to and fro on the face of the planet Earth, scrutinizing even the most *hallowed* of the Race of Men. First and foremost, followers of the Nazarene. Case after case of the Race of Men I have brought before Yehovah's advocates in the angelic High Courts of the First Heaven. But *if they bear the seal of the Nazarene*, because they have accepted the terrible sacrifice, at every turn our meticulously researched cases are thrown out of court. The blood of the Nazarene, it seems, covers *every* failing of the Race of Men." He spat.

"And those that reject the Nazarene?" The Warlocks of Ishtar slithered.

Lucifer raised both hands dismissively. "Those who reject the terrible sacrifice share our doom: the conflagration of the Lake of Fire. They are not my concern."

"So, Your Excellency," hissed Marduk, "you are implying that there is unequivocal punishment for the Fallen and the Race of Men?"

Lucifer stopped in mid step, and his eyes darkened with rage. He pointed his scepter at Marduk.

"We the Fallen do not have the *codicil*."

He held out his hand.

Marduk scuttled up to him and passed over a slim golden casket from the Library of Iniquities. A thin plume of white smoke arose from its contents.

Marduk read: "*'Codicil 7998 as pertains to the Race of Men—Codicil as pertaining to eternal absolution, clemency, exoneration.*

"*'If one undefiled from the Race of Men is willing to shed his lifeblood on behalf of the Race of Men*," Marduk announced, "*and become a substitute for judgment, the said Race of Men—past, present, and future generations—will be released from eternal judgment by the death of that one. Pardoned. Absolved of each and every transgression, crime, offense. A soul for a soul. This is binding Eternal Law for those of the Race of Men—if they accept the great sacrifice of the Nazarene.*

"'*A soul for a soul, for the Race of Men.*'"

Slowly Marduk took a second golden casket. A dark plume of smoke arose from it.

"'*Codicil 8898 as pertains to the fallen host, inclusive of the Watchers, Nephilim, Demonic–Codicil as pertaining to eternal absolution, clemency, exoneration.*

"'*In fact, the great sacrifice was undergone by Christos in his capacity as one of the Race of Men. Absolution for the Fallen does not fall within its boundaries.*

"'*Each and every transgression, crime, offense is punishable by eternal chastisement. No absolution is recorded.*'"

He hesitated. The silence was palpable.

Finally, Lucifer spoke.

"Forgiveness for the mewling Race of Men, but no such compassions for those of us who served Him faithfully for millennia. No such clemency for our fellow rebel angels, those of us His cherubim, His seraphim. And what of His Watchers?" Lucifer spat.

"What of His Watchers, who reek of sulphur?"

Lucifer stared distastefully ahead.

"Chained in the bottomless pits, in dungeons deep below the molten earth.

"What did they do to deserve such cruelty, such callousness, from one whom they once served so devotedly? Because the Watchers cohabited with the daughters of the Race of Men. Do you see the daughters of the Race of Men *imprisoned* thousands of feet below the earth's surface. NO!"

Lucifer raised his arms to the swirling skies.

"If *they* repent, they receive His mercy. If *they* repent, they receive absolution."

Lucifer took a deep breath. Finally, he regained his composure.

"Yes, we fell. Yes, He discarded us. Yes, He abandoned us. And as for the mewling Race of Men! Already He prepares their rewards and their mansions. And now He would whisk all those who bear His mark out of harm's way, protected in an instant from all that would come upon the earth.

"For all these past millennia, I have stood at times day and night, in the High Courts of the First Heaven, with my legislators, bringing accusation against the Race of Men. My patience with Yehovah is at an end. If He will not excommunicate them, then I will take action, and we will *mutate every genomic code of the Race of Men until there is not one pure, untainted bloodline that remains.*

"We the Fallen shall storm the gates of Eden. We the Fallen shall storm the gates of the throne room of the First Heaven.

I, Lucifer, shall wrest the throne from Yehovah.

"*I*, prince regent, seraphim, was born to *rule*."

Lucifer raised both hands to the ice skies. The violent, swirling winds blew his hair and cloak. "I *will* ascend into heaven. I *will* exalt my throne above the throne of Yehovah."

A strange, evil fire burned in the blazing steel blue eyes.

"I *will* sit upon the mount of the congregation. They will worship me.

"*I will be as GOD.*" He stared at the Fallen with insane glee. "*We will WAR!*"

CHAPTER TWELVE

HOLLYHOCK COTTAGE
IRELAND

D YLAN WEAVER STARED blearily at the running databases on the three machines in front of him.

"There's no record, Prof. No record of Adrian De Vere's DNA anywhere on any of the updated ten-kingdom databases worldwide. That's a three billion net. All intel sources, east and west, come up void."

He shook his head.

"If it ever existed anywhere, it's been systematically wiped—I'd say, by his pet troll, Guber."

"It leaves us only one option," Lawrence murmured. "Without it, we don't have definite proof that Adrian and the clone are one and the same."

Nick grinned wryly. "A DNA sample. From the president of the entire Western World. You think he's going to be forthcoming?"

Alex cocked one eyebrow. "Not *impossible*."

Nick raised the remote. "Speak of the . . . "

Nick and Lawrence exchanged a glance. Adrian's chiseled features filled the TV screen. The room fell silent. Jason sank into the armchair next to Nick, who was sprawled out on the sofa, half covered by five dog-eared issues of the *Irish Independent*.

"Turn it up, Alex."

The camera zoomed in on Adrian, standing on the iconic white marble steps outside the entrance to his new world headquarters in Babylon.

"He's unveiling his bailout plan," Lawrence murmured. "He's going to bail out every superbloc whose economic infrastructure has been shattered."

"At precisely eleven-o-five a.m. here in Babylon, Iraq, the AXIS Ten Accord, cementing the long-awaited one-world government—the most momentous accord in our lifetime —has been sealed." The announcer continued. "Signed by kings, prime ministers, and presidents of ten of the world's supereconomic regions . . . "

Adrian stood between the Indian and Pakistani prime ministers. "This morning . . . " Adrian hesitated, staring directly into the camera lens.

Jason shook his head. Adrian cast an almost hypnotic spell when he was on the box.

" . . . long-standing feuds, factions, and wars have been set aside to create our new one-world government—the AXIS Ten Accord. The premiers of India, Sri Lanka, and Pakistan are united in their commitment to the Asian Bloc. As are Russia, Georgia, China, Taiwan, Colombia, Brazil, and Mexico."

The camera slowly panned back across the leaders of

Canada and the United States, Japan, Australia, New Zealand, South Africa, Israel, Pacific island nations, Eastern Europe, Latin America, North Africa and the Middle East, Central Africa, South and Southeast Asia, Central Asia, and the Western European Union.

"Eighteen months ago," Adrian continued, "on what was known internationally as the World's Black Friday, economic collapse and world famine struck at the aorta of Western and Eastern society. Bank balances were wiped out overnight. A thousand top-ranking banks, from London to Tokyo to New York, were in liquidation by morning. The Eurozone collapse of last decade paled in comparison to the devastation to the world banking infrastructure that we face today.

"In the shadow of this, and as a result of the referendum of the people of the ten kingdoms, today I am unveiling a new world banking order."

"Well, that's the end of democracy," Alex scowled.

"And freedom of speech," murmured Jason.

"Fifty trillion dollars in gold has been released from the International Security Fund's vaults in Switzerland, into the European Union's Solidarity Fund. And the immediate implementation of a one-world currency. Our new ten-kingdom axis will be known as the AXIS Ten."

"He's done it." Jason shook his head. "He's brought them all to the table. It's the seventh world empire. A new world order—a ten-kingdom world alliance. One-world economic system."

Dylan Weaver turned to Lawrence. "Last one coming through, Prof."

Lawrence took the remote from Nick and clicked the

television off. "Jason, *you* saw the certificate of death issued by the presiding doctor on call that night."

Jason nodded. "Nothing abnormal. Heart attack."

"Yes, acute myocardial infarction," Lawrence said softly. "I commissioned an autopsy."

Jason stared at him, incredulous. "She didn't *have* an autopsy, Lawrence." He sighed. "By the time I was in touch with the hospital her body was en route to the Chapel of Rest. Instruction issued by next of kin Adrian De Vere."

Dylan stood up, document in hand, and passed it over to Lawrence.

"Ah," Lawrence said with a note of satisfaction. "Your mother's autopsy report." He placed his glasses over his nose. "Your information is out of date, Jason. The autopsy report is right here. From Vernon Sinclair, a trusted ex-colleague, retired MI-six forensic pathologist, top of his trade. Used to looking at what lies beneath."

"So what?" Jason rolled his eyes in exasperation. "What's Mother's body got to do with *anything*?"

The whole room fell silent as Lawrence read. The first page, then the next four. Finally, he laid the report down on the table before him. He removed his glasses and rubbed his eyes, then nodded to Weaver, who tapped the holographic screen.

The forensic report appeared. Lawrence nodded to Nick, who read over Jason's shoulder.

"*Rubbish!*" Jason said. "I saw the original with my own eyes. I was there with Mother, Lawrence. Her *heart* was giving out."

Lawrence stood up and gave Jason the full force of his glare. "Jason De Vere! Stubborn when you were ten.

Stubborn at forty-eight. Yes, she had a slight stroke. But she *would* have recovered."

Nick pointed at the screen. "There—it says minute traces of *potassium chloride*?"

"Potassium chloride's virtually untracecable," Alex said. "It reverts back to potassium and chlorine in the body, so it's normally undetectable."

"Unless an extremely experienced forensic pathologist was *looking f*or it," whispered Lawrence. "Your mother was injected with one ampoule of potassium chloride. A hundred mEq. Quite enough to induce cardiac arrest."

He looked long and hard at Jason and Nick.

"Your mother was murdered."

LIBRARY BALCONY
MONT ST. MICHEL
NORMANDY

It was nine minutes past midnight. A Jesuit priest, dressed in the flowing garb of his order of the Black Robes, walked out of the shadows and into the stream of moonlight, his antique silver-knobbed cane tapping evenly on the polished mahogany floors.

He stopped a few paces behind Adrian, who turned slightly, the outline of his chiseled features suddenly visible in the moonlight. Tonight his profile was arresting . . . strangely beautiful.

Adrian stared out at the breathtaking view across the bay. He appeared trim, tanned, immaculately groomed. His raven hair was fashionably long, falling just below his collar, gleaming blue-black in the moonlight. The outlines of his flawless features were faintly visible in the low light.

Lorcan De Molay was silent. His face, although strangely scarred, was imperial, his features striking. The wide brow and straight patrician nose framed imperious sapphire eyes that held a haunting, mesmerizing beauty. He walked to the very edge of the library balcony. His thick raven hair, normally pulled fastidiously back from his high cheekbones into a single braid, fell loose past his shoulders, blowing in the icy winter Atlantic wind.

Adrian refolded an ancient roll of parchment and handed it to De Molay.

"You will reject Yehovah's ultimatum?" he asked.

"We have waited over two thousand years for our revenge," De Molay murmured. "Now we avenge our dishonor at Golgotha."

He lit a black taper. "Our humiliation at the hands of the Nazarene."

He held the taper to the parchment and watched it burn. His palm closed over the blazing missive, and instantly the blue flame transformed to glowing coals. He opened his palm and softly blew the ashes into the winds, then smoothed his Jesuit robes. Slowly he caressed the carved silver serpent on the top of his cane.

"The transport from Antarctica," he murmured. He continued looking out at the raging Atlantic.

Adrian nodded. "The cargo from Antarctica is now in biocontainment three. Our scientists have isolated the Nephilim gene. The genetic rewriting program is being initiated as we speak."

"All scientists involved will be discreetly taken care of when their assignment is completed."

"Your word is my command, Father."

Lorcan De Molay smiled slightly.

"And I looked, and behold a pale horse," he whispered. "And his name that sat on him was Death, and Hell followed with him. And power was given unto them over the fourth part of the earth, to kill with sword, and with hunger, and with death, and with the beasts of the earth."

He stared up past the earth's atmosphere and moved his hand across the sky. Sixty-seven miles above the earth was the figure of a hooded rider astride a pale horse.

He turned to face Adrian, his eyes glittering with passion.

"Billions of the Race of Men will take our Mark."

"The pale horse rides . . . "

72 YEARS EARLIER

CHAPTER THIRTEEN

MUROC AIRFIELD
(EDWARDS AIR FORCE BASE)
CALIFORNIA DESERT
FEBRUARY 20, 1954

THE SLEEK BLACK Cadillac Eldorado carrying President Dwight Eisenhower roared up the desert highway, followed by the seven-car Secret Service motorcade close behind.

The Cadillac's 210-horsepower V-8 engine slowed to a purr as the driver braked in front of Muroc's heavily guarded gates. From the opposite direction, four military vehicles screeched to a halt inside the airfield gates. Twelve heavily armed soldiers surrounded the motorcade, their automatic weapons raised.

President Eisenhower eased his frame out of the Cadillac's low-cut door as a thickset four-star general stood to attention and saluted.

"I'm sorry, Mr. President, sir, but as you are aware, we have orders to search your guests." The general shuffled uncomfortably. " . . . And yourself."

"Is it *really* necessary to search the leader of the free world, Sykes?" the president objected. "What you're about to show me had better be *remarkable*."

General Sykes nodded. "It's unparalleled in the history of our world, Mr. President."

"Well, get on with it, Sykes," the president growled.

The general nodded to the soldiers. The president sighed in frustration and raised his arms as the captain patted him down. Four other soldiers checked Eisenhower's guests while two inspected the Cadillac and the driver thoroughly. Meanwhile, a second team ordered the Secret Service agents and the president's aides out of the motorcade and pushed them unceremoniously against the cars, firearms raised.

"Thank you, Mr. President, sir." The captain stood to attention and saluted, and Eisenhower took his seat in the Cadillac.

The captain waved the president through.

The president shook his head. "My *men*."

Five minutes later, the Cadillac Eldorado, followed by the Secret Service motorcade, was escorted by a fifth military vehicle, past the base and out toward the airfield. Finally, the military truck swerved to an abrupt halt directly outside a vast open hangar. A series of blinding flashes erupted overhead.

The president shielded his eyes from the blinding light. Four generals got out of the military truck.

Slowly Eisenhower's eyes adjusted to the intensity of the light. He raised his head.

"What the *devil* . . . !"

He stared, mesmerized, as a huge, glowing disk-shaped object zoomed across the horizon.

An elderly man with a shock of white hair got out of the

car, his hooded eyes following the arc of the disks as they traveled from north to south. He walked in the direction of the runway.

Two soldiers stood in his path, weapons raised.

"General Sykes, I strongly *object* to your methods." Eisenhower turned around to the general at his right, his eyes flashing with irritation. "This is my *guest*, Franklin Winthrop Allen of the Hearst Newspaper Group. He has top secret clearance."

"My apologies, Mr. President, sir," the general answered calmly. "Our methods may seem excessive, but I can assure you, they are necessary." He pointed in the direction of four more of the lenticular craft, which were drawing nearer the airfield.

A ferocious pulsing blue light illuminated the runway while the craft descended, until eventually all five squatted on the concrete strip of runway, emitting a faint hum.

"By God, Dwight, it's a UFO!" Allen exclaimed. "These things don't even *exist*!"

Eisenhower's eyes remained fixed on the ghostly glow surrounding the largest craft's hull. A tall man dressed in the robes of a cardinal of the Catholic Church got out of the Cadillac and slowly walked toward the president and Allen, his face as white as a sheet.

The three men watched, astounded, as a small door on the craft opened and two slender eight-foot-tall figures emerged.

"Well, I'll be damned!" Eisenhower muttered in disbelief.

The extraterrestrials' humanoid features were framed by long hair that was blond, almost white. They both had pale blue eyes and colorless lips.

"God, Mr. President, they look like they're from *Norway,*" Allen spluttered.

Eisenhower stood in silence while the cleric made the sign of the cross. He turned to General Sykes.

"Sykes, you're *used* to this?"

The general nodded. "Since the Roswell crash, Mr. President, sir. It's . . . it's a pretty regular occurrence." He hesitated. "You never quite get *used* to it, sir."

"They communicate?" Stunned, Eisenhower turned back to look at the extraterrestrials.

"Telepathically, Mr. President, sir. They emit both light and tone signals, transmitting in a mathematical language. Our scientists communicate by means of computer binary code."

The two extraterrestrial figures parted and bowed as a taller figure walked out of the spacecraft, his face hidden beneath the hood of a gray cloak. Moments passed; then the figure removed his hood.

The cardinal gasped. The extraterrestrial's pale, beautiful features exuded a strange luminosity. His waist-length platinum hair fell smooth as glass over his billowing gray velvet cloak, which was fastened with delicate silver clasps.

"We come in peace. I am Darsoc the Gray." Darsoc spoke in mellifluous tones. "Welcome." He bowed and motioned to the president to enter the craft.

"My aide accompanies me," Eisenhower declared.

Darsoc turned to the blond, blue-eyed young man holding the president's briefcase. He nodded.

Eisenhower stood to attention, took a deep breath, and walked up the steps, followed by his aide. They disappeared into the flying craft.

"This is either the most momentous event in the history of the world . . . " Cardinal James McIntyre clutched his cross in his left hand, trembling visibly. " . . . or our worst nightmare."

CHAPTER FOURTEEN

HOLLYHOCK COTTAGE
WEST COAST OF IRELAND
DECEMBER 2025

JASON AND NICK looked at each other in silence.

"When will I see you, pal?" Jason asked.

Nick shook his head. "Not sure, Jas. I leave for Alexandria tonight, prep with the Jordanian special forces, who were loyal to Jotapa's father, the Jordanian king, then out to Saudi Arabia, to bring back Jotapa and her younger brother, Jibril, the crown prince."

Nick's eyes moistened.

"I wish I could be there," he said softly. "At Mother's funeral, I mean."

Jason put a hand on his shoulder. "Mother would understand."

"You'll get Adrian's DNA?" Nick asked.

Jason nodded. "I'll do my damnedest." He clasped Nick in a tight embrace, then released him abruptly, fighting for control of his emotions, and walked with Lawrence toward the red Ford Escort.

Nick stood in silence, watching from the crooked cottage doorway.

"You'll let me know where Nick is, Lawrence?"

Lawrence nodded. "Of course."

"I wasted so much valuable time."

Jason unlocked the ford escort. "Hadn't talked to him since Lily's accident. Eight years ago." He flung his jacket onto the backseat with his briefcase. "How much does Julia really know?"

Lawrence shook his head. "Nothing. Nothing at all. We felt it best that she remain in a position of deniability."

Jason nodded. "Good . . . " He hesitated. "I know you didn't approve of the divorce, Lawrence," he mumbled. "What with Julia being your niece, that is."

"You've been like a son to me Jason," Lawrence replied. "Always have been." Lawrence clasped his shoulder. "Julia's a fighter, Jason," he said softly. "She's a survivor."

Jason nodded, feeling suddenly vulnerable.

"It wasn't her fault, Lawrence. She really tried. After Lily's accident . . . the drinking . . . I drowned myself in my work. She was left to deal with Lily's tragedy alone." He struggled for the words. "I guess I abandoned her."

Lawrence's expression softened in wonder. "You still love her."

Jason looked out toward the Atlantic. "There'll never be anyone but Julia for me. I've been a damn fool," he murmured. "She gets married in August. It's all water under the bridge."

"What are your plans?"

"In London for Mother's funeral Tuesday. Then back to the States. Ten days later in Babylon—VOX board meeting."

"You know how to get hold of me, Jason. Come visit us in Egypt. A retreat. At the monastery." Lawrence's eyes twinkled. "*Feed* your soul."

Jason shook his head. "You know it's not my thing."

He opened the car door and eased himself into the front seat.

"Religion. I belong in a boardroom, not a church." He switched on the ignition.

"Jason," Lawrence said softly.

Jason looked up into his steady gaze.

"Who is more afraid: *the child who is afraid of the dark* . . ." Lawrence hesitated, his eyes boring into Jason's soul. ". . . or the man who is afraid of the light?"

Jason looked back at Lawrence, then turned to look at Nick, still watching from the front door. Then he put the Ford into reverse, swung it around, and revved off at high speed down the winding, muddy drive back toward the N4 to Dublin.

Nick walked up slowly behind Lawrence. "He's always been a hard nut." He smiled "Stubborn as hell."

Lawrence looked up at him, his pale blue eyes distant. "Stubborn, skeptical, yes." He shook his head. "But courageous, intrepid—a truth teller, like St. Patrick."

Nick grinned. "I can't quite equate Jason with St. Patrick."

Lawrence smiled, his eyes distant. "Warrrior, dear boy. Your eldest brother is a *warrior.*"

"You haven't revealed yourself." Nick studied Lawrence intently. "To Jason, I mean. As the angelic?"

Lawrence's eyes twinkled. "A bridge too far for the

rational, skeptical mind that is Jason De Vere, dear boy. All in good time."

"Lawrence . . . " Nick hesitated. "it's close, isn't it?"

Nick looked into the older man's compassionate blue gaze, his own eyes lit with a strange exhilaration. "*He's* close, isn't he?"

Lawrence followed Nick's gaze into the moody Irish sky.

"The three riders of the apocalypse traversed the west winds, venting their fury." He moved his hand over the horizon.

"The fourth rider is released. Niscroc rides the pale horse, wielding his scythe."

Nick followed Lawrence's gaze upward to a hooded dark figure astride a pale-colored horse.

"Nisroc enters the Karmen Line, sixty-two miles above the planet Earth, as we speak." Lawrence inhaled sharply.

"The plagues will be fearsome. The Rapture is near . . . *very* near, Nicholas."

"You'll . . . you'll look out for Jason when I'm gone?" Nick asked. Lawrence moved his hand, and the image of the pale horse disappeared from view.

"One day, Nicholas," Lawrence murmured, "in the not too distant future, as implausible as it may seem . . . " His gaze fell onto a knee-high copper statuette of St. Patrick, to the left of the cottage gate. " . . . Jason De Vere will be the only vanguard we have left."

"Lawrence . . . "

Lawrence raised his hand, as though hearing something. Nick watched him intently.

Lawrence's face paled. He bowed his head, his lips moving, then adjusted his cravat and raised troubled eyes to Nick.

"Nicholas . . . " His voice was barely audible. "I have just received disturbing news. I have urgent matters to attend."

Nick took a step back. He knew what would happen next, and yet, no matter how many times he had watched the transformation, it never failed to take his breath away.

Imposing though the professor's human appearance was, now he became majestic. Noble. No longer a spry five feet nine but now well over eight feet tall. His sparse silver hair grew white and thick, past his shoulders and down to the grass, as did his beard. The professor's cravat and elegantly cut Savile Row blazer transformed into the stately embroidered velvet ceremonial robes of an ancient king of the First Heaven.

Nick, still transfixed, stared into the ancient imperial face.

"The High Council awaits me. I shall meet you in Alexandria."

And the professor vanished from the snowy Irish field.

Right before Nick's eyes.

CHAPTER FIFTEEN

PLAINS OF THE GREAT POPLARS
EDEN
THE FIRST HEAVEN

J ETHER MATERIALIZED under an enormous ancient poplar tree on the lush white plains of the Great Poplars, in Eden. Thousands of the ancient luminescent trees radiated a soft white light that hung in the blazing white mists. Jether breathed in the exquisite fragrance of spikenard that filled the plains.

His silver hair fell far below his shoulders, as did his beard. On his head rested a jeweled crown. He smoothed his nasturtium-colored robes with his pale ringed fingers and turned. *Eden.* Even Earth's most stunning wonders paled into insignificance beside the First Heaven.

Out of the rising mists, Jether watched as, one by one, the ancient kings of the First Heaven became visible, walking swiftly through the soaring Pearl Gates of Eden, toward twenty-four garnet thrones that stood under a great canopy of the finest spun gossamer.

Beyond the canopy lay the fountains of life, bright as

crystal, cascading from the rubied throne room, watering Eden and the Great White Plains. Stately white swans drifted down the flowing stream toward the Crystal Sea.

Angelic heralds blew their shofars.

"We herald the holy council of the ancient ones, stewards of Yehovah's sacred mysteries," they proclaimed.

The blinding white mists cleared, revealing twenty-one ancient kings of heaven. Jether seated himself on the central throne. Again the herald blew the shofar.

The ancient kings bowed before Jether the Just, the most powerful ancient angelic King. Then, following his lead, all took their seats on garnet thrones around the golden council table.

Jether studied the two glaringly empty seats opposite his own. He raised his eyebrows. A tall form strode toward the council table, his huge feet crushing the ethereal foxgloves and lilies beneath his hasty steps.

He stopped directly in front of Jether, catching his breath with long, loud gasps, then bowed hastily three times and emitted two loud sighs. He grasped Jether's hand tightly in his own huge hand and shook it a shade too vigorously.

"My sincere apologies, my revered compatriot Jether the Just. *Deepest* apologies. I came as soon as I was summoned."

Jether studied Xacheriel long-sufferingly, firmly removing his hand from Xacheriel's intense grasp. There was a long silence, broken only by Xacheriel's continual gasping. Jether gestured to the chauffeur's cap still resting on Xacheriel's head.

Xacheriel frowned.

"Your *crown*, Xacheriel," Jether whispered.

Xacheriel frowned. He felt the top of his head, then

snatched off Maxim's chauffeur's cap, hastily picked up his crown, and placed it on top of his unruly mop of wiry silver hair.

Jether's gaze fell to a garish, overlarge carpetbag that Xacheriel clutched tightly in his right hand.

"*Humph*," Jether coughed, looking pointedly at the carpetbag.

Xacheriel frowned, large furrows creasing his forehead.

"Lost . . . er . . . property." Xacheriel turned beet red. "Forgive me, revered Jether. I had a most *distasteful* struggle with a delinquent former comrade of this very table."

Jether heaved a deep sigh. "And you took his *carpetbag?*"

Xacheriel nodded sheepishly. "As collateral."

"Collateral for *what* exactly, Xacheriel?"

Xacheriel stared down sheepishly at his galoshes. "All right, he *deserved* it. I kidnapped his carpetbag. See how he does without his usual lashings of mandragora aftershave!"

He dumped the carpetbag on the table.

"And his blood pressure cuff!" Xacheriel said darkly.

Jether shook his head soberly at Xacheriel, who fell instantly silent.

The gentle Lamaliel giggled into his handkerchief, then hastily grew somber. Jether caught his eye and shook his head.

"Pray take your seat, esteemed Xacheriel. This is no time for levity. We await Maheel's return from Earth. I have requested that he address you, the elders of the High Council, firsthand."

Xacheriel sat down heavily opposite Jether.

"Until Maheel arrives, I will present the facts as we know them. As you all are aware, there has been a gathering of the

Dread Councils of hell on Lucifer's present habitation, the planet Mars in the Second Heaven. The gathering is only the second of its kind in the history of the Fallen. The first occurred after their crushing defeat at Golgotha."

He sipped at an indigo elixir from his goblet.

"Thanks to Chief Prince Gabriel's elite squad of revelator eagles, we are aware of all that was discussed."

He nodded to Methuselah, who rose.

"Honored members of the High Council," Methuselah spoke in his deep, unhurried tones, "there was one subject and only one on the agenda at the gathering of Lucifer's Dread Councils."

He studied the elders' faces.

"War," he sighed.

"Lucifer's main objective, as always, is to occupy and rule from Yehovah's throne. However, the Fallen intend now to conduct a twofold vendetta against the Race of Men. Their latest scheme is to exterminate as many followers of the Nazarene as possible before the advent of the Great Catching Away. By disease or execution, they intend to inflict the greatest suffering possible. But there is a second part to their plan."

"To mutate the Race of Men's genetic code," Xacheriel muttered darkly.

Methuselah continued. "As Lucifer did in the days of Noah."

Lamaliel frowned. "The fallen Watchers had intercourse with the daughters of men and are now bound in sulphur, miles underground, for thousands of years."

Xacheriel scratched his beard. He and Jether exchanged a look.

"They will not be as foolhardy this time," Jether interjected.

Xacheriel nodded. "Jether and I are convinced that they intend to use the great strides in the Race of Men's biotech and genetic engineering to advance their cause."

"As you all are aware," Jether continued, "Maheel's mission, like Xacheriel's and my own, is to reside on the planet Earth as an angelic emissary to the Race of Men. Maheel's nom de guerre on Earth is Father d'Angelis, chief astronomer of the Vatican Observatory."

Jether rose and bowed to a silver-haired elder who materialized at the end of the council table.

"Esteemed Maheel," Jether said, "welcome. Pray, divulge to the Council your findings."

Maheel walked to the empty seat to Jether's left, placed his crown on his silver locks, and remained standing. He surveyed the table.

"Revered compatriots . . . " He sighed deeply, then turned to Jether, visibly shaken.

"Pray continue, revered Maheel."

Maheel took a deep breath. "What I have to disclose to the Council is disquieting, to say the least. I have received very disturbing news from my covert intelligence sources, the Vatican Intelligence Services for Extra- and Intra-terrestrial Affairs. Until now, as the Council is aware, my task on Earth has been to track down and destroy all remaining Nephilim bodies that still exist under the planet Earth's surface."

He coughed. Xacheriel held out a large handkerchief, and Maheel took it and wiped his brow.

"The only remaining Nephilim bodies were buried two

miles beneath Antarctica. I personally oversaw the extermination team, led by Dr. Gabriele Alessandro, one of our top scientists and members of the Illuminus. Until today, as the Council is aware, Dr. Alessandro, under my direct authority, has systematically tracked, exhumed, and destroyed over seven hundred Nephilim in Iraq, Syria, China, and Israel."

He inhaled deeply again and surveyed the grave faces around the table.

"There has been a massacre—a massacre of the entire team of Operation Iceman, including Gabriele Alessandro and his security forces."

"Kurt Guber," uttered Xacheriel, his eyes hard.

"Yes. Kurt Guber and his mercenaries. The end result is that over a hundred frozen Nephilim bodies have just been airlifted from below the Southern Polar entrance by Guber and his military."

Jether tapped the table, his face unreadable. "Pray continue, Maheel."

"The Nephilim are now housed in the secret bioterror operations base below Mont St. Michel. For what *precise* macabre purpose, we do not yet have watertight evidence."

"It is our worst nightmare."

"More explicitly," Maheel continued, "the Nephilim are confined in the bioterror containment levels that are connected by a set of deep underground tunnels and railcars to the underground base at the Franco-Swiss border."

"CERN," Xacheriel interjected. "They have discovered the angelic Portals. Earth's scientists call them stargates, wormholes."

Maheel nodded. "You are correct, esteemed Xacheriel. Billions in black-ops funding are being funneled into stargate and Looking Glass research by an invisible cabal of elites. Their ultimate plan is to open our angelic Portals. They are Lucifer's pawns. They have little understanding of the extreme danger they attract.

"Of course, we suspect that Lucifer will try to isolate the Nephilim gene—to what malevolent end, we are not yet certain."

Maheel sat down heavily.

Jether stared down at the table, then slowly rose to his feet. "Our worst fears have transpired. Lucifer now has Nephilim DNA. It would seem, his intention is to commit genetic Armageddon against the Race of Men."

"But how?" Methuselah asked.

Jether surveyed the ancient kings in silence.

"*That*, my revered compatriots, is exactly what we intend to find out. This gathering is adjourned."

CHAPTER SIXTEEN

1954
FLYING-CRAFT LANDING STRIP
MUROC AIRFIELD, CALIFORNIA

PRESIDENT EISENHOWER sat facing the tall Nordic-looking entities while his aide stood in the shadows. He looked around the craft.

"Any moment now, and I'll wake up," he muttered.

"You are very much awake, President, I can assure you," Darsoc said, staring at the president out of his pale, hooded eyes.

"The human race faces the most perilous time of its existence. America has many enemies—enemies who would take your knowledge and use it to destroy you. Our extra-terrestrial scientists are prepared to work with your scientists in understanding and adapting our technologies into devices that can benefit and *assist* the United States and mankind." He paused. "We would grant you an *exchange*."

"What do you mean, an exchange?" Eisenhower asked.

"The secrets of our technological advancement. Secrets that would enable America to lead the world: fiber optics, lasers, gene-splicing therapy, cloning, stealth technology, particle-beam devices, gravity-controlled flight . . . "

Eisenhower stared at Darsoc, his eyes alight with exhilaration. "In exchange for what?"

"The freedom to study your race. To conduct harmless medical observations . . . "

Darsoc stopped in mid sentence as the aroma of frankincense permeated the craft. Eisenhower noted that the extraterrestrial was trembling.

Darsoc bowed deeply. Eisenhower raised his head. In the doorway of the craft stood a tall stranger in black. The stranger's gloved hand rested on the carved serpent top of a silver cane. His features were hidden beneath a hat.

"You are a pragmatic man, Mr. President," the stranger said, "I'm sure you understand that we have to be assured our demands will be met."

Eisenhower frowned. "What demands?"

Lorcan De Molay studied him dispassionately. "*Our* demands," he said.

Darsoc pushed a document on a strange yellowed parchment across the table. Lines of strange symbols instantly lit up. Eisenhower removed his glasses from his inner pocket and put them on, and instantly the symbols transformed into neatly typed italic English. The president read the parchment thoroughly, then set it down.

Slowly he removed his glasses and looked straight into De Molay's eyes, his expression stony.

"I don't know exactly who you are or whom you really represent," he said. "But I can assure you and your leaders . . . " He took a deep breath. "That I will *never* agree to your demands."

"You must be mistaken, Mr. President." Lorcan De Molay looked at the president calmly. "Let me reiterate them for you.

"Our Council of Thirty-three are to have lifetime governing positions on the boards of the Federal Reserve, the International Monetary Fund, the International Monetary and Financial Committee, and the Council on Foreign Relations.

"You will also create two separate groups within ninety days of this meeting—groups that will be under our total control. The first is called the Bilderburg Group, in which we will have majority representation for the duration of Earth's existence. You will also create a second, smaller committee, whose members shall be approved by me directly. You shall sign a Secret Executive Order, Number fifty-four-twelve, enabling this committee to take appropriate action without congressional oversight.

"These groups will be your government in perpetuity. Congress and the White House will be merely a token while our shadow government runs the nation and, eventually, the world."

"This is *blackmail*!" Eisenhower fumed. "I would be agreeing to let your organization literally run the great-est country on Earth, the United States, as a *shadow* government."

"Precisely, Mr. President." The black-clad figure's voice was low and cultured.

Eisenhower placed his glasses back in his inner pocket.

"I don't know who the hell you think you are, but you've *wasted* my time." He studied De Molay grimly. "I'm the president of the *United States*!"

"Of *course* you are, Mr. President."

De Molay nodded to Darsoc, who passed a telegram to Eisenhower.

"From The Associated Press. A report that is being aired worldwide as we speak." Lorcan De Molay yawned as the president retrieved his glasses and read.

"President Eisenhower died tonight of a heart attack in Palm Springs."

Eisenhower slapped the telegram down onto the table. "What the *hell* do you think you're playing at?"

The blood drained from Eisenhower's face as he started to gulp for air. His hand went to his chest, and his face contorted in agony.

"You will also agree to our medical research and experimentation on the human race." De Molay watched as Eisenhower turned blue around the lips.

I'm a soldier," he gasped. "I will never betray my country."

"This is your considered answer?" De Molay stood to his feet.

"As you will." He turned to Darsoc.

"Prepare to finalize our discussions with Premier Nikita Sergeyevich Khrushchev of the U.S.S.R."

"*Khrushchev?*" Eisenhower gasped.

De Molay looked dispassionately down at the gasping president. "We will finalize our treaty with Russia. Then, regrettably, their next action will be the downfall of the United States of America."

"You don't have the power," Eisenhower gasped.

Lorcan De Molay raised his left hand. Eisenhower collapsed headfirst onto the table. The young blond, blue-eyed aide exchanged a look with De Molay.

"You will discover, Mr. President, either to America's benefit or to her detriment, that I never overstate the situation."

"You son of a bitch," Eisenhower rasped.

"I can give you life or death. Live or die; either way, I win."

"Eisenhower looked up at De Molay from the table. "You will provide assurances that no human subjects will be harmed," he rasped. "We require all personal details to be shared with a new secret branch of government, which I will create."

De Molay nodded. "Names of those we use for tests—call them abductees—will be provided. You will have times and places. Names will be provided. All memory will be erased from their minds.

"In exchange, your administration will be granted technology that will allow the USA to retain technological supremacy over the Soviet Union."

"There is to be no treaty with China or Russia," Eisenhower croaked

De Molay spoke with his back toward Eisenhower. "If our conditions are met."

Eisenhower could not speak, but he nodded.

De Molay placed his hand on Eisenhower's chest. Immediately, his breathing eased. Slowly he sat up and composed himself.

De Molay nodded to Darsoc, who placed Eisenhower's forefinger and thumb in the signature box. His fingerprints lit up on the page.

"Retract the Associated Press report."

"Oh, my God . . . what have I done?" Eisenhower muttered.

"The right thing for America, Mr. President," Lorcan De Molay murmured. "The right course for the American people."

Darsoc walked toward Eisenhower, holding a black box, and nodded. "A symbol of our pact."

He placed it in the aide's outstretched hands.

Eisenhower walked down the steps toward the generals, haggard, hands shaking, his face like stone. Defeated.

The door of the spacecraft closed. The strange craft rose and hovered momentarily while its landing gear retracted. Then the hum increased, and the craft shot eastward and vanished beyond the horizon.

President Eisenhower stood on the tarmac, his face ashen, his hands still trembling. He turned to the cardinal, who was praying under his breath.

"May God forgive me, Father." His voice was hardly audible. "I have sinned." Eisenhower looked at the cardinal's cross, his hands shaking uncontrollably.

"I have sold out America. I have cut a deal with the devil himself."

CHAPTER SEVENTEEN

CHEYNE WALK
NEW CHELSEA, LONDON
DECEMBER 2025

"H EY, LILY." Alex leaned down and kissed Lily's cheek.

He took a step back. "You look different somehow.

Lily smiled.

"All grown up." Alex smiled over at Polly, who clasped Lily's hand.

"She's in love." Polly grinned. "Or should I say, *he's* in love. Adam Fincher, Xavier Chessler's grandson. Works in London. A young investment banker. He's *very* handsome. And rich."

"He keeps calling," Lily said, shaking her head.

"Good. That *is* good, isn't it?"

Lily frowned. "He's not really my type. One of Dad's flunkies."

Alex studied Lily. She had changed this past year. Definitely. She was now 18. She had always been slightly built, but her strong features had softened. Her glossy dark hair framed the heart-shaped face. Lily had grown quite beautiful. Not breathtaking like Polly, who was a supermodel lookalike, but she had a real, ethereal beauty.

Alex bent down and took her hand. "Look, Lils," he said. "I've known you since you were born. I was there when you had the accident at the grand old age of seven."

Lily looked at him in silence.

"And, look, I don't want to overstep the mark, but if this guy Adam wants to take you out, go. Go have fun. God knows you *deserve* it."

Lily snatched her hand away from Alex as though she'd been burned. She stared at him frostily.

"Why, Alex?" she snapped. "Because you think it just might be the only chance I get? Because I'm in a *wheelchair*? The *poor* little rich girl!"

Alex glared at Lily. "I knew it would get to this. The last few months, every time I open my mouth you bite my head off."

He looked at Polly. "It never used to be like this."

Tears stung Lily's eyes. "I don't want your pity, Alex," she snapped.

Troubled, Polly looked down at Lily. "He doesn't pity you, Lily, he's never once pitied you. He *cares* about you." She hesitated. "Deeply."

Alex walked out.

"We've got to change for the funeral," Polly said. Lily nodded. "Pick you up at eleven." She kissed Lily on the head and followed Alex out.

Lily heard the front door bang, then wheeled herself into her bedroom, to a large chest of drawers. Opening a lingerie drawer, she removed a small leather jewelry box. She opened it, lifted a compartment, and took out four photos. The first was of her and Alex when she was 6, in Jason and Julia's New York garden. The second was of Alex at 12, another at his graduation, and then the most recent one. His highlights were gone, and his dark hair was much longer. Alex the investigative journalist. He was smiling. Lily's tears fell down onto the photograph as, slowly, she tore it and then the others into pieces, one by one.

There was a soft knock at the door. Lily froze, then turned.

Julia stood in the doorway. She walked over to Lily. Very gently she took the pieces of Alex's photographs out of her grasp and placed them on the chest of drawers, then held her to her chest.

Lily sobbed in Julia's arms, her heart breaking.

"Its okay, Lily. It'll all be okay," Julia whispered.

"I love Polly, Mom. I'm so glad she's happy. But I've always loved him."

Julia looked deeply into Lily's eyes.

"At eighteen, love . . . " She heaved a sigh. "Love is complicated. Even at my age, it's complicated. Just look at your dad and me. Alex loves you, sweetheart, but as . . . "

"But as a *friend.*" Tears streamed down Lily's cheeks." Because I'm in a wheelchair."

"No!" Julia shook her head emphatically." *Not* because you're in a wheelchair, Lily. Because he loves Polly. They're getting married, Lily, sweetheart. You *have* to get over it."

Lily clasped Julia's hand tightly.

"There are some things, Lily, darling, that are just not meant to be."

"It's okay, Mom. I'll deal with it."

"Promise?" Julia whispered.

Lily squeezed Julia's hand. "I promise."

She picked up her phone and pressed redial.

"Hi, Adam. Yes, I got your message. Tonight'll be great." She wheeled herself out of the bedroom.

Julia walked to the bedroom window, then stared down at the engagement ring on her left hand. Callum. Callum was arriving tonight from Nice.

He was everything she'd dreamed of: tall, elegant, intelligent . . . compassionate . . . handsome . . . considerate. They had the perfect wedding planned. August seventeenth, Summer Marquee. Six hundred guests, champagne, fairytale dress.

Then why, *why* could she not get Jason out of her mind? He was stubborn, insensitive, inconsiderate, as always . . . and yet . . .

She tapped the digital photograph of Jason and Lily on Lily's shelf. It was recent. Alex had taken it in Central Park. It zoomed in on Jason.

He had aged since the divorce. But in the photograph he was smiling—a rare thing for Jason De Vere. Nowadays, only Lily could make him smile. Julia's eyes grew distant. Up until their lean years, Julia had been the only person in Jason De Vere's frenetic and well-guarded world who could make him laugh till he cried. *And* could make him see red within thirty seconds. She wondered if there was anyone else in his life. Julia placed the photograph gently back on the shelf. All her sources said no.

She sighed. She had known it the moment she opened the door to him last Thursday and saw him soaking, cantankerous as always, standing in the pouring rain on her doorstep.

She was still deeply in love with Jason Ambrose De Vere. And she had to get over it.

CHAPTER EIGHTEEN

THE RITZ
LONDON

"SORRY, SIR." The waiter looked Jason up and down sniffily. "Formal dress code."

"For afternoon *tea*!" Jason glared at him.

"*Particularly* for afternoon tea, sir," he said frostily.

Jason scowled, then took a rolled-up gray silk tie from his left jacket pocket and grudgingly tied it around his neck. He scowled again at the waiter, then walked toward the Palm Court, weaving in and out of the chairs toward an elegant old man with silver hair, seated in the far corner.

"Cab got caught in five o'clock traffic. Worse than New York." He looked the old man up and down. "Good to see you, Uncle Xavier."

The old man embraced Jason affectionately.

"It's been months. Don't give it a moment's thought, my boy—gave Sinclair and me a chance to catch up on the World Bank's latest negotiations in China." He frowned. "You do *know* Alistair Sinclair."

Jason nodded. He recognized him from the world summit that VOX had televised last week.

"Sinclair represents the Solidarity Fund," Xavier said. "He's heading up the development of the new one-world currency. Tea, dear boy?"

Jason shook his head, then turned to the hovering waitress.

"Filter coffee—strong."

"It's afternoon *tea*, dear boy." Xavier Chessler shook his head affectionately at Jason. "The English are very particular about their *tea.*"

"Well, good for the limeys, Uncle Xavier. *I'm* very particular about my *coffee.*"

Sinclair took the silver teapot and poured Darjeeing into a bone china cup in front of Chessler. Chessler picked up a finger sandwich of thinly sliced cucumber.

"Ah, the niceties of what once was the British Empire: cake, champagne . . . Sinclair here says the champagne is not to be believed.

"Nah. I'll wait for the coffee, thanks."

Chessler sipped delicately at his tea. "Jason, there was a reason I asked you to meet with me . . . apart from catching up. We need a favor from VOX." He took a second delicate sip of tea. "From you, dear boy."

Jason raised his eyebrows. "All these years, Uncle Xavier, I don't think you've ever asked for a favor. How can I help?"

"I've never wanted to use my position as a VOX board member." Chessler took another neat bite out of the sandwich. "I wanted to have an informal conversation with you, not the board." He wiped his mouth with his napkin. "Off the record, as they say. What I'm about to disclose you may not fully comprehend, but the consequences will be of paramount importance in the months to come."

Jason looked over to Sinclair.

"Oh, don't worry about Sinclair. He's one of us."

He set down his teacup.

"Our plans for a one-world banking system have been, as you are aware, taking shape very nicely. However, after the economic summit last Sunday, we now find ourselves facing what could be a major setback."

The waitress set down a silver cafetière and cup and saucer.

Jason frowned. "Setback?" he echoed.

Chessler nodded. "Adrian has achieved the unachievable. As you and the rest of the planet are no doubt fully aware, the ten-kingdom multinational confederacy was finally signed into existence on Sunday."

Jason stiffened at the mention of his brother.

"Yes. It's signed."

"The AXIS Ten Accord. And the creation of a One World Bank spanning all continents, in the works for two decades, is finally sealed. Every central bank in over a hundred nations now operate under one economic system.

"The next step is an immediate withdrawal of all ten-kingdom currencies, including the IMF's SDR and the WOCU, the world currency unit we launched in 2009. We challenged the U.S. dollar as the world's foremost reserve currency." Chessler dabbed his mouth neatly with his napkin. "The rest is history. Our case rests. *Now* we implement our master plan."

He studied Jason intently, then said, "The introduction of a singular one-world currency, in conjunction with a system of digital enumeration of every human being on Earth."

He turned to Sinclair, who opened a glass X-pad.

"Your brother conducted a trial across twenty members of the European Superstate," Sinclair said, "the UK and Ireland excluded. An RFID chip—call it an ID tag—a special ink deposited in a unique bar-code pattern for each individual, which would be injected under the surface of the skin. Think of it as a virtual fingerprint—the prototype was called the Mark."

Chessler smiled. "It has proved successful beyond our wildest dreams. A virtual fingerprint that traverses all economic borders."

Sinclair continued. "We have set a date for the introduction of the worldwide 'Mark.' Trials were also initiated in all ten member kingdoms this past eighteen months. Everything has proceeded like clockwork."

Chessler lowered his voice. "Except for . . . well, we're encountering—how would you put it?—some *resistance* in certain sectors of the ten-kingdom alliance. After the 2012–13 fiasco with the euro . . . " He coughed politely. " . . . certain factions appear to be more *reluctant* in their compliance."

Jason shrugged. "They don't want to relinquish their currency. Understandable. The UK?"

"The United Kingdom have been *most* amicable," Sinclair declared.

Chessler nodded. "Unlike *our* country of birth."

Jason grinned. "You've got a fight on your hands with the good old USA, haven't you, Uncle Xavier? The Patriot Movement already fought tooth and nail for state sovereignty in 2012, and they're not going to give it back. It dates all the way back to the Tea Party and the libertarians—Ron Paul and that bunch—in 2012. You'll have a people's revolution on your hands if you try to take their electronic gold currency system away from them."

Chessler dabbed again at his pale lips with the pressed linen napkin. "*We the people,*" he murmured. "Let me be quite clear." His voice grew very soft. "Twenty-four states, including California and New York, have already signed the new world currency treaty."

Jason loosened his collar and leaned back in his chair, studying Chessler languidly. "You forgot, I've been living in New York again since the beginning of the year. Twenty-six states *rejected* the accord, if our reporting at VOX is to be believed."

Chessler smiled. "It's a complicated issue, dear boy. To put it mildly, the Patriot Movement is *awash* with religious sects steeped in mythology, legends, folklore. Their views on the one-world currency are *antiquated*, to say the least, especially the Midwest's."

He lowered his voice and affectionately placed a manicured hand on Jason's arm.

"The problem isn't confined to the Patriots, Jason. The past decade has seen the development of a worldwide resistance movement. The resisters are set to pose a major threat to our global economic future.

Jason gave a dry smile. "Resisters?"

"Two point one billion if you believe the statistics."

Jason looked at him in disbelief.

"But, of course, it's only a minor section of these that are putting up *active* resistance to the one-world currency."

"*How* many?"

"Active resisters? A hundred eighty million, maybe more."

"A hundred eighty *million*?"

Chessler took Jason's arm. "They view the world in a *most* simplistic fashion, dear boy. To say the least, they regard the one-world currency as a symbol, a symbol of assigning themselves to a world system belonging to . . . " He sighed. " . . . in their symbology, the devil."

The warlock brand on his forearm was burning. He stopped and took a breath, then studied Jason intently.

"The mark of the Beast, the book of Revelation. Naive, credulous sects all over the world are *refusing* to relinquish their currencies."

"You're talking about the Christians," Jason said.

"Correct." Xavier Chessler picked up a second cucumber finger sandwich. "They've been problematic, to say the least."

Jason looked at him in astonishment.

"In three of the ten kingdoms. North America, naturally- And *China*, of all places—the underground church movement's been spreading consistently the past ten years since the government relaxed its state laws. A hundred and four million Protestants, over forty million radicals. They're popping up in government everywhere. The economy is riddled with them. China's been rigorously opposed to our plans for a new world order, but they have always been highly supportive of a one-world currency—until the new moderates rose to power."

Jason raised his eyebrows but said nothing.

"As for Russia, they went moggy after the nuclear strikes on Moscow, and millions headed back to church. The whole Russian Federation's gone back to the Dark Ages mythology.

Russia's rife with tales of Revelation: the mark of the Beast, a one-world government under the Antichrist."

"You're not *serious*," Jason said. "Surely *Christians* can't pose a threat to a one-world currency."

"I'm afraid, my dear Jason, they can and they *are*. North America—sixty-nine million of them, radicals, resisters . . . "

Chessler finished his cucumber sandwich. "New York, Los Angeles, the East and West Coasts aren't our concern. But among the sixty-nine million radicals, the top tier of them happen to hold posts as governors, legislators, state attorneys of all twenty-six resisting states."

"The Midwest," Jason interjected.

"And others." Sinclair took out a crimson folder bearing the gold seal of the One World Bank. He flipped it open and rifled through documents. "Missouri—riddled with resisters, always has been."

Sinclair looked up from his digital tablet.

"The health care resolution of 2010. They were working towards state sovereignty for years."

Chessler nodded. "They were the instigators, you know. The Tenth Amendment. Kansas followed suit. Then Iowa, Indiana, Ohio, South Dakota. The Bible Belt fell like a pack of cards: Central Florida, Alabama, Tennessee, Mississippi, Kentucky, Virginia, Texas, Louisiana, the Carolinas . . . "

"I get the picture," Jason said.

"All those twenty-six states have rejected the Mark, our new one-world currency. Voted as one to retain their patriot electronic gold currency. China, Russia—a similar scenario.

"The Bank for International Settlements, Global Security Fund, the United Nations are concerned. *Gravely* concerned."

Jason shook his head. "Where does VOX come in?"

"Look, Jason." Chessler smiled affectionately. "I know you're not a religious man. But you may be aware that for decades I've been a member of the European Council of Princes, organized in 1946 as the International Council of Government."

Jason shook his head.

Chessler coughed, then continued. "It serves as a constitutional advisory body to the European Union. But the members also serve, let us term it, the *esoteric realm*. The Council of Princes, consisting of thirty-three Merovingian kings, was created as the occult hierarchy of Europe. Some view us as divine because our ancestors believe that they descended from the angels of Genesis six: two—the Nephilim."

Jason looked back at him with a glazed stare. "Mumbo jumbo to me, Uncle Xavier." He shrugged.

Chessler smiled back benevolently. "Jason, what I'm about to say may sound far-fetched, but I'm speaking as a scholar with over five decades of esoteric study. These resisters, this particular Christian sect, believe they will all be *transported*." He coughed into his handkerchief. "Evacuated, if you will. Transported to another planet, plane of existence, or level of Earth's consciousness, where they can be contained. The main point is that they will lose, for the time being, their access to the etheric planes of power, and the ability to control or influence developments on Earth."

Jason grinned in amused disbelief. "Look," he said, "I've got a Baptist secretary, and Lily's best friend is a vicar's daughter who goes to some clap-happy church. They call it the Rapture." He laughed out loud. "The whole thing's *ludicrous*. I don't believe a *word* of it!"

Chessler sighed. "Of course, of course. We agree. It's all

a lot of mythological folklore. But the fact is," he said softly, "there are things . . . occurrences in the ether, a parallel dimension that doesn't always make sense to the common man." He stirred his tea distractedly. "I'm about to let you in on something beyond top secret, Jason. Over seventy years ago, after the Roswell incident in 'forty-seven, a treaty was signed. A treaty between the President of the United States and a group of extraterrestrials."

He held Jason's gaze.

"President Eisenhower."

Jason stared at him in amazement. He had known Xavier Chessler since he was a babe in arms. Chessler was not one to embellish the truth.

"Yes. A piece of technology came into his hands. Into the hands of the United States. Into the hands of President Eisenhower."

He paused again.

"A piece of extraterrestrial technology. A black box called simply 'the Cube.' It enabled our scientists to see something staggering: the future."

Incredulous, Jason stared at him. "You're not serious, Uncle Xavier!"

"Deadly serious." Chessler looked at him, stone faced. "You are aware that when I was young, very young, I was the youngest aide in the White House . . . "

" . . . aide to President Eisenhower," Jason said, finishing the sentence. "Yes, I'm aware."

"As your father knew, I worked for him when I was just sixteen. The youngest aide he'd ever had. I attended that meeting, Jason. I was there. I have held the cube in my own hands."

A waiter appeared next to Jason. "More coffee, sir?"
Jason nodded.

"I think you need a stiff drink, my dear Jason." Chessler nodded to the waiter.

The waiter filled Jason's cup from the cafetière.

Chessler lowered his voice. "Eisenhower intended it to go to the UN. Certain shadow factions of the military sequestered it. It was in our hands for over seven decades. Our organization has sunk hundreds of billions of dollars into diverse black-ops programs: Looking Glass technology, portals, stargates, the European Organization for Nuclear Research."

Jason frowned. "CERN?"

"Established by twelve European governments in 1952. By 2012, it had twenty member states—all European. It now operates solely under the presidential authority. You remember the commotion over CERN. The world governments decommissioned Project Looking Glass last decade. Every government in the world is *still* hunting the cube."

Chessler's eyes glowed with a strange luminosity.

"Its powers were staggering, Jason. We only scratched the surface before its disappearance. I have looked into my own future. As did your father, James De Vere."

"*My father* used this technology?"

Chessler nodded. "In the 1960s, it was passed from elite to elite, to preserve our own families. It foretold the future probablility of Nine-eleven in the early 1990s, the rise of militants in the nineties. And seven years ago, it predicted a ninety-nine percent probability of an evacuation of the human race. An unprecedented evacuation—of the Christians. Then it disappeared."

"You don't *actually believe* this!" Jason stared skeptically at Chessler.

"Oh, but I'm afraid that I, along with the majority of the economic and political leaders of the Western world, *do*, my boy. When this occurs the ensuing situation will be untenable."

Jason rolled his eyes. "Well, then, the extremely unlikely event of their disappearance should suit your purposes, right?" He took a slurp of coffee. "No more resistance."

Chessler squirmed in his chair. "Not entirely. In the unlikely event that the transportation of two billion Christians occurs, it could throw the entire ten kingdoms into chaos."

He lowered his voice. "It could start a world revolution against the one-world government—make the greatest case for Christianity since the resurrection."

Jason stared skeptically at his uncle. "If over a billion people got transported into the ether, with credible witnesses on hand, it would be the biggest news coup in the world."

"Precisely. Then you understand the situation, Jason —which is that we have no option." He shrugged his shoulders.

Jason frowned. "What do you mean, you have 'no option'?"

"We intend to execute a false-flag operation."

Jason's grin evaporated. This man was serious.

"An event that will have all the appearance of a weaponized bioterror attack in North America, China, Russia. A pandemic.

"Of *course*, dear boy, it won't be *real*." Chessler looked disarmingly into Jason's eyes "But it has to give every *appearance* of a pandemic: martial law, quarantine centers, mandatory vaccination . . . ”

“You’re talking about body bags flown in at night . . . ” Jason’s jaw set. “Making it look like billions of people have died of ebola, smallpox, or whatever.”

“Precisely. You always got to the crux of a problem, Jason. Your mother’s acumen. If the Rapture occurs, no one will ever know. VOX will communicate the event to the masses. Exclusive coverage. Media blackout except for VOX networks.”

Jason looked into his coffee and stirred it distractedly. “You’re talking about a cover-up of immeasurable proportions.”

“Correct again. The Rapture never occurred. Millions of Christians died with the rest of the population—a tragic bioterror event that we, the powers that be, shall blame on China.”

Jason looked Chessler straight in the eye. “I’m a newsman, Uncle Xavier, not a politician.”

He rose to his feet.

“Apart from a faint, deeply submerged but still smoldering belief in liberty, fraternity, and plain old down-to-earth decency, I can assure you as a newsman and as their friend that if Jontil Purvis and Polly Mitchell ever disappear into some etheric third dimension, transported to heaven or wherever it is they think they’re going, I will make it my personal mission to see that the entire Western and Eastern media world disseminates the information *within the hour.*”

Chessler looked at him with an inscrutable expression. “I have your answer, then.”

Jason undid his tie and pulled it from around his neck.

"Yep," he said, rolling the tie into a neat cylinder. "You have my answer."

Chessler stood up and gave Jason a relaxed smile. "I'll see you at your mother's funeral tomorrow, dear boy."

Chessler watched Jason walk through the elegant London hotel and out through the revolving door into New Piccadilly.

Closing his eyes in agony, Chessler undid his cufflink and stared down at the warlock's mark on his wrist. The glowing brand smoldered on his skin, then disappeared. He rubbed his wrist gently.

"As I thought," he murmured. "Jason De Vere is fast becoming a liability." He turned to Sinclair. "Adrian De Vere signs the share transfer from his mother's holding stock tonight. Into his name."

Sinclair nodded. "The takeover will be completed in ten days exactly. You and Adrian De Vere will have the controlling interest in VOX."

"Jason De Vere will regret the day he ever crossed us."

CHAPTER NINETEEN

THE DE VERE MANSION
BELGRAVE SQUARE
LONDON

THE MANSION DRAWING ROOM was shoulder to shoulder with the who's who of British and American society, gathered for Lilian's funeral wake. Jason sighed. An hour had flown by, and he had tried every trick in the proverbial book to get a sample of Adrian's DNA.

Any moment now, Adrian would be making his farewells. Jason edged his way across the room to where Adrian was engrossed in conversation with the British foreign minister.

"Cigar, pal? In the library?"

Adrian studied him for a moment. "No thanks, Jas." He looked at Jason steadily. "Not in the mood."

Damn. The cigar butt was now out of the question. In the past two hours, Adrian had refused his usual mineral water, tea, coffee, and now the cigar.

It was almost as though he were aware of Jason's intention. Jason had only one more trick up his sleeve. *Ah!* There was a footman, sounding the gong. Four other footmen, led by Maxim, entered carrying champagne and mimosas.

The gathering hushed as one. Jason raised his hands.

"Ladies and gentlemen, on the occasion of Mother's passing . . . " He picked up a glass of champagne from Maxim's tray. "A toast to a great lady." He nodded in the direction of Adrian, who was now chatting with Lily, and smiled.

Maxim made a beeline for Adrian.

Adrian looked across at Jason, then back to the glasses of champagne on the silver tray.

"A toast, pal," Jason urged. "A toast to our mother, Lilian De Vere."

"To Granny," Lily whispered as Julia took two glasses from Maxim's tray and handed one to her.

"Master Adrian." Maxim held out a glass. "Your favorite: mimosa with Mumm's."

Adrian looked down at Maxim's outstretched white-gloved hand and reluctantly took the glass from him. "A toast to Mother," he said.

Everyone raised their glass. Jason downed the entire glass of champagne, his eyes never leaving Adrian's glass.

Slowly Adrian took a sip of his mimosa.

Jason nodded to the footman, and the gong sounded for a second time. Jason picked up a second glass of champagne and held it high.

"And a toast to my departed brother, Nicholas De Vere," he declared. "May God rest his soul. A toast to Nicholas, Adrian. What do you say?"

"He's *drunk*," Kurt Guber whispered to Adrian. "Probably had a bottle of whisky before the funeral."

Adrian continued to gaze steadily at Jason. He held up his glass, and once again everyone followed suit. Polly walked over and stood next to Lily.

Adrian loosened his collar with his free hand. "A toast to my youngest brother, Nicholas De Vere."

Adrian took one more sip, and Jason downed the second glass of champagne as quickly as the first.

Guber strode over from the door and whispered into Adrian's ear. Adrian nodded and turned to Julia.

"My regrets, my beautiful Julia, but something urgent has arisen. I have to leave immediately. Chastenay will arrange Lily's travel plans." He kissed Lily on her forehead. "Looking forward to seeing you, my darling."

He held out his champagne glass to Julia.

"Here, don't let a good mimosa go to waste, Jules. I know you love it!"

Julia had just reached out her hand to take Adrian's glass when Maxim snatched it away with his gloved hand, placed it on the silver tray, and disappeared out of the drawing room.

Adrian frowned, then strode toward the doors and stopped directly beside Jason. "Be careful, Jason," he murmured. "You're out of your league."

"My, my, little brother," Jason replied as Adrian walked out of the drawing room. "Curiouser and curiouser."

Maxim hurried through the kitchen to the enormous pantry, where Alex was waiting, both hands in plastic gloves.

He looked down questioningly at the silver tray. Maxim handed him a glass from the far right-hand side. Alex gingerly placed it in a sterile plastic bag, which he then tucked inside a container in his rucksack.

"Thanks, Maxim." He grinned. "Off to forensics."

Maxim smiled in satisfaction as he removed his white gloves.

Alex hesitated, then pulled a plain white envelope from his satchel. The name "Jason" was written on it in Nick's hasty scrawl. Alex passed it to Maxim.

"For Jason. From Nick. Eyes only."

Maxim nodded and watched Alex take off like a shot out the back gate.

"Well done, Maxim, old boy."

Jason stood, sober as a judge, in the kitchen doorway.

"Master Jason!" Maxim declared. "I think we've got it!"

Jason tossed and turned restlessly. He pulled the sheets over his head, then, with a sigh, reached over for his X-pad.

Three a.m. Sitting up, he groggily rubbed his eyes and stared at the white envelope that now lay open on the bedside table.

He flung off the sheets in frustration and pulled out the yellowed paper for the fifth time that night. It was inconceivable, yet there it was in black and white.

He studied the document again. Dated 1981. The signature in green ink was unmistakable: the bold, hard lines of his grandfather's scrawl. Julius De Vere. Witnessed by Piers Aspinall, former chairman of MI-6.

It was a death warrant. He flipped through each page. There at the bottom was the same scrawl in green ink at the bottom of each page, only this time Julius De Vere had merely initialed his name. Acquiescing to his own grand-children's extermination.

By the powers that be, whoever they were.

Jason studied the two paragraphs. One grandchild to be executed at the exchange of the clone. He presumed that was to be the real Adrian De Vere. Executed one day after his birth.

Any surviving grandsons to be exterminated after the clone turns forty. That meant Nicholas . . . and himself.

Jason frowned. Adrian had turned forty the day before Nick's car accident and 'death.'

He assumed that he had been allotted more time because of his usefulness at VOX.

His clean cell phone was flashing blue.

"Weaver?" he said, and listened.

"You're a hundred percent certain?"

Jason sighed, then clicked off the cell phone.

There was no getting away from it. Adrian's DNA matched Hamish Mackenzie's sample of the clone's DNA precisely. Not one discrepancy. It appeared that Adrian De Vere was a clone.

And a *nonhuman* one at that.

Jason tossed again. *Damn.* When he thought back on how he had helped engineer Adrian's rise to fame . . . VOX had showcased the charismatic young politician to the British public, paving the way for his two-year stint as Conservative prime minister before his meteoric rise in Europe.

Jason had been Adrian's kingmaker.

He fumbled in the dark for the holographic television control and flicked through BBC 24 NEWS, CNN, and

Russian TV, then stopped on VOX's Biography channel. There was Adrian with Melissa, his deceased wife.

Jason sat bolt upright in bed and turned up the volume.

"A sad private moment for the European president as he pays respects to his beloved wife of four years, who died in childbirth, and his only son, Gabriel De Vere, who was stillborn."

Jason watched as the scene changed to Adrian visiting the Vane Templar estate in the Scottish Highlands, where Melissa, her father, Lord Vane Templar, and Gabriel De Vere were buried on an island in the center of an ornamental lake. Adrian was wiping a tear from his cheek.

Jason's jaw tightened. He glanced at his watch. It was only ten p.m. in New York.

He dialed his long-suffering personal assistant of over twenty years, Jontil Purvis. The phone purred three times, and a crisp voice answered.

"Good Evening, Mr. De Vere."

"Purvis, I need you to track down the death certificates for my brother's wife, Melissa, and the baby."

Pause.

"Yes, the baby Gabriel, who died stillborn. It's urgent."

"Jason" The soft Southern voice echoed in his ear. "It's after ten p.m. here in New York."

Jason grinned. "That's never stopped you before, Purvis."

"No, sir, but it may very well stop the General Register Office in Southport, Merseyside. With all due respect, sir, everyone in England—apart from yourself, of course—is fast asleep."

Jason grunted. "First thing, then, Purvis."

"May I inquire, sir, is that U.S. opening time or UK?"

"UK, Purvis," he growled. "I need it now."

He clicked off the phone and returned to the Biography channel. Thank God for Jontil Purvis. How long ago was it that Melissa and the baby died? It was around the time he and Julia divorced—about four years ago. Adrian had taken it badly, *very* badly.

Jason frowned. Or had he? And who, or what, was the baby Gabriel? Had Melissa discovered Adrian's secret? He remembered her being very sick all through the pregnancy. Not just sick—Julia had been convinced that she was on a high dose of sedatives. Melissa had become a shadow of her formerly vibrant self.

He shook his head. He needed to let everything settle. VOX was in a tenuous position.

Jason had to get back to the USA. He would fly back to New York in the afternoon. He needed space. He needed to clear his head, let everything settle. Stabilizing VOX and his media investments in the current U.S. financial upheaval was his big priority—that and the yearly board meeting next week in Babylon. Everything else could wait.

He flicked off the remote and lay back on his pillow. Moments later, he fell into restless dreams of Nick and Adrian when they were boys, and of Dolly the sheep, death certificates, and clones.

And Julia. Always Julia.

CHAPTER TWENTY

TOWER OF WINDS
THE FIRST HEAVEN

J ETHER WALKED IN SILENCE with Xacheriel through the lush gardens of the Tower of Winds. Stopping, he held a silver drinking vessel under the fountain.

"Ah! Harebell and jasmine. The delicacies of Earth pale in comparison to the sights and aromas of heaven."

Xacheriel sipped from his goblet.

Jether looked at Xacheriel. "Except for sushi, of course."

He gestured to Charsoc's carpetbag.

"We can well do without Charsoc's baggage for the moment."

Xacheriel placed the vermilion carpetbag gingerly on a silver table. "The past five decades since he passed through the Portal of Shinar have weakened him considerably. He no longer has the ability to traverse time. He requests a meeting with you."

Xacheriel plunged his enormous hands into the depths of his voluminous robes. "My revered Jether, a sealed missive from Charsoc the Dark."

Jether tore open the missive. A black plume of smoke arose. He shook his head. "Charsoc and his magician's tricks."

With a sigh, he walked over to the very edge of the Tower of Winds, studying the words intently. Then he refolded the missive, placed it in one of his deep pockets, and stared out toward the Rubied Door.

Xacheriel walked toward him, and together they stood in silence. Finally, Xacheriel spoke. "You read his missive, my esteemed friend."

Jether nodded.

"It concerns the Nephilim?"

Jether removed the missive from the inner pocket of his long, flowing robes and read aloud:

"'Undoubtedly, it has now come to your attention that we, the Fallen, are now in possession of a unique and treasured cargo. The Nephilim. Tut, tut, Jether, how lax your operatives have become! To cheer you up, I extend my invitation . . . "

"An invitation?"

"You could call it that," Jether said grimly. "An invitation for *cocktails*. Only Charsoc would have the audacity to invite me onto planet Earth for cocktails."

He pointed to the top right-hand corner. "The Right Honorable Baron Kester von Slagel."

Jether tried to hide his smile, without success. "The Right Honorable Baron . . . He does so enjoy giving himself airs and graces. Two millennia pass, and his vanity is as unappeasable as ever."

Xacheriel raised his bushy eyebrows. "You should see his rings. On *each finger*. The jewels literally seem to grow every time I see him." He glowered. "And what sort of a name is

'Kester von Slagel,' anyway?" he muttered darkly. "It has the ring of an East End kindergarten criminal faction."

Jether cleared his throat and held the invitation high. "'The Right Honorable Baron Kester von Slagel invites Professor Lawrence St. Cartier for cocktails on the terrace at the King David Hotel in Jerusalem, at sunset.'" Jether shook his head wearily.

"He then goes on to state, 'I, of course, being the more sophisticated of us, would have preferred Rome or Milan for shopping, but bearing in mind the current frailty of your elderly earthly form, I have settled for Jerusalem.' As though he traveled anywhere without his heart pills, portable blood pressure cuff, and nasal spray," Jether muttered.

A pity I was not invited," said Xacheriel. "I would have liked to give him a piece of my mind."

Jether's expression shifted instantly from mirth to dead earnest. "Xacheriel, you are to go immediately to Alexandria to await Jason De Vere's arrival. I should be there to greet him. But this tête-à-tête is no garden party. It will be between Charsoc and me. He brings communication from his master."

Jether thought deeply for a moment, then turned to Xacheriel again.

"Until then, Maheel will continue his investigations at the Vatican, and you will continue your responsibilities as Maxim, the De Vere family's valet. I, of course, will return to Alexandria as Professor Lawrence St. Cartier."

"I must say, it is most frustrating," Xacheriel grumbled, "for a *scientist* to be pressing *clothes*. And I had rather considered myself to be more a sort of scientific James Bond—more like Q, I should think."

Jether shook his head. "As a matter of fact, it has come to my attention, while serving as Professor Lawrence St. Cartier, that one Maximus Basil Pinkerton, on his days off, has rather fallen in love with earthly cinema."

Jether stopped, suddenly deep in thought.

"Xacheriel, your duties as Maxim are to be extended. We will put you on loan to Adrian De Vere. His valet shall have a short vacation. It is the only way we can be certain of his diabolical plans. We have to have firsthand intelligence. Adrian De Vere knows you as his mother's valet, assisting Jason when he is at the Belgravia house. It will be a natural progression, now that Lilian De Vere is dead, that her valet attend Adrian."

Xacheriel's eyes lit up with excitement. Then he frowned. "What about Charsoc? He knows me in my earthly guise as Maxim."

"Your placement would, of course, be at a time when Charsoc the Dark is away from Normandy and at the Vatican." Jether's eyes twinkled.

"But first you return to Alexandria. And I . . . " He picked up the carpetbag. " . . . shall meet with Charsoc in Jerusalem. Cocktails with me, he requests. Well, cocktails he shall have. I shall return his monstrosity of a carpetbag to him *myself*."

CHAPTER TWENTY-ONE

THE TERRACE
KING DAVID HOTEL
JERUSALEM

THE INTENSE CRIMSON sunset over the walls of Jerusalem was deepening. Jether sat in the balmy Jerusalem dusk, at a terrace table set for two, tapping his fingers. Waiting. He frowned. A loud commotion filtered through from the hotel lobby. It was coming nearer.

Six muscular black-suited minders, with shaven heads, earpieces, and holstered firearms, evicted the bewildered diners from their tables, then positioned themselves intimidatingly across the now nearly empty terrace. The cloying perfume of mandragora suddenly filled the dusk.

Jether sighed. Charsoc the Dark had arrived.

A tall, bony but nonetheless commanding form strode through the doors of the restaurant, followed by his dramatic personal entourage consisting of four immaculately coiffed personal aides.

"Greetings, Professor." The deep baritone voice coming from behind Jether was unmistakable.

"Forgive me if I stay seated," he muttered. "I seem to have forgotten my manners."

"Tut, tut, Jether." Charsoc snatched his hat back from a bewildered, trembling waiter.

"No one," an aide declared theatrically as Charsoc painstakingly dusted off the fedora. "No one touches the baron's hat!"

The terrified waiter beat a hasty retreat through the terrace door.

Charsoc smiled, looking extremely pleased with himself. He nodded in approval to his adoring sycophants, who swarmed around him, patting his hair in place and adjusting the crucifix at his throat.

He yawned in boredom. "My coat . . . "

Two aides eased Charsoc out of his heavy houndstooth coat as Jether looked on in irritation.

Charsoc held out his silver cane.

"Careful with the cane, boy!" He gave the terrified aide a thunderous look. "It's an antique." He smiled widely at Jether. "As is my friend here."

Jether rolled his eyes. He nodded in the direction of the black-suited minders. "Do they *know* you're immortal and don't need protecting, or haven't you told them yet?"

Charsoc glared at Jether and lowered his voice. "It creates the right *impression*." He made a sign to one of the bodyguards, who walked toward them. "He needs to pat you down."

Jether gave Charsoc a steely look. Charsoc hesitated, then motioned to the bodyguard to back off.

"He's clean," he snapped.

"What do you think I intend to do? Blow myself to shreds and take you with me?"

"One can never be too careful with one's personal safety. Or . . . " Charsoc studied the waiter hovering around their table. " . . . one's personal *hygiene.*"

Charsoc slowly removed his white kid gloves, finger by finger, then took a small plastic bottle from his inner pocket and squeezed two drops onto each bony hand.

"Antibacterial hand gel."

He rubbed both hands together briskly, then handed the waiter a crisp piece of paper. Jether noted his distinctive copperplate handwriting on it.

"Make up that cocktail, boy," Charsoc commanded in military fashion.

The waiter scuttled off like a startled rabbit.

"At least *this* antique can translate into an ethereal body at will." Jether smiled back at Charsoc. "*Unlike* yourself."

Charsoc glared darkly at Jether. "There is no need to remind me of my dire fate." He glowered. "Trapped in this infernal mortal body for eternity. I am *well* aware."

Charsoc removed a luridly ornate pillbox from his pocket and opened it, took out three small round blue pills, and swallowed them with a gulp and a grimace.

"Heart pills?" Jether asked languidly.

Charsoc shook his head, distaste on his face. "Blood pressure," he muttered. "It rockets whenever I set my foot upon this parched tract of dust."

"Ah, yes." Jether smiled in satisfaction. "Israel. In fact, Charsoc, wasn't it right over there"—he pointed in the direction of Mount Moriah—"that we both had the privilege of attending the greatest defeat of your and your master's illustrious career?"

He paused for a breath.

"So *far*, that is."

Charsoc sat tight-lipped and unsmiling. "We were deceived," he hissed. "No one, even for one second, guessed that He was Yehovah incarnate."

"A rather *major* oversight, wouldn't you agree?" Jether chuckled and sipped at his mint tea. "I would have loved to be a fly on the wall when you and your master took *my* Master down in chains to Hades. What happened, Charsoc? I have it on good account the entire territory of hell and the grave started to shake and crumble and has never been the same since. I also have it on good account that your master was in chains, whimpering in terror and watching through a cage as Christos led the righteous dead away."

"The Nazarene!" Charsoc spat the words, his face contorting into a mask of sheer hatred. "Yes," he hissed. "We were defeated in Jerusalem. But it is also here in Jerusalem that we shall taste our finest victory."

The balding restaurant manager walked over to their table, followed by the flustered young waiter.

"Ah!" He bowed. "Esteemed Professor, I did not realize it was you." Bowing again, he plucked the now crumpled piece of paper from the waiter's hand.

"It will be no problem to make the cocktail." He bowed yet again. "For such a revered customer, I talk to the chef myself."

"How kind of you," said Jether, "but it is not for me but for my *acquaintance*."

The manager bowed again and leaned over to whisper in

Jether's ear. "Esteemed Professor . . . " He placed the piece of paper in front of Jether's nose. "It is just this I do not fully understand." He pointed to the name of the cocktail.

Jether placed his monocle in his left eye and stared down at the precise copperplate writing.

"The bloody waters of ancient Babylon," he read aloud.

The manager shook his head and raised his hands in despair.

"What are you trying to *do*, Charsoc?" Jether looked up at Charsoc. "Start a third intifada?"

"It's the name of the cocktail," Charsoc admitted sheepishly. "I found it on the Internet. It took my mind back to our tête-à-tête on the Tigris over a millennium ago. I thought it would be *most* appropriate."

Jether tore off the offending script, crumpled it, and placed it in the ashtray.

The manager wiped the sweat from his brow and bowed again, this time in relief.

"Truth be told, Charsoc, diplomacy was never your strong suit."

The manager smiled again, hovering.

Charsoc tapped him gingerly on the shoulder with his right index finger, which was heavily weighted with a huge, gleaming aquamarine.

"And add some pineapple juice, boy," he commanded, "and a splash of sweet-and-sour. Shake it. Strain into a martini glass, and then swirl grenadine on top."

Jether nodded to the manager, then studied Charsoc more closely. He frowned.

Charsoc was dressed in a voluminous multicolored striped robe, the cut vaguely resembling that of a Greek Orthodox priest's cassock. An enormous glistening golden crucifix hung from his neck, and he wore a clerical collar.

Jether rolled his eyes. "What, exactly, *is* your designation, Charsoc? Baron, social shopper, or priest?"

A smile broke out on Charsoc's face. "Ah!" he murmured, staring out over Jerusalem at dusk. "I do still miss our repartee, Jether. There's no one I can compare you to in that department. I'll give you that."

Jether took a sip of mint tea. "Touching."

"Actually . . . " Charsoc leaned closer to Jether and lowered his voice. "I'm leaning more these days to remaining a man of the cloth."

"Oh, yes, that's right. What was it? Grand Inquisitor of the World Council of Churches."

Charsoc nodded. "Rather a grand title, I thought. I rather liked it. Although, for a short while, I intend to turn my vast talents to genetic engineering."

He smiled mysteriously.

"First, my carpetbag."

With a sigh, Jether bent down and lifted the enormous bag onto the table.

Charsoc preened. "It's made from oriental rugs—ancient Persian." He unclasped the carpetbag and, placing his hand inside, brought out several objects. "Nothing has been tampered with, I presume.

"Turkish delight." He smiled. "Nasal spray . . . anti-histamine. Eh, blood pressure cuff . . . travel candle, sewing kit, deep heat . . . *Ah!*" He sighed in satisfaction. "My slippers. Actually, Jether . . . " He removed a pair of gold and crimson Persian slippers with whorls at the toes. Two large gold tassels hung at each toe.

Seeing the grim set of Jether's face, Charsoc raised his hands. "Let me delay the reason for my visit no longer." He held out his hand to one of his minders, who passed him a folded missive with Lucifer's seal of Perdition on it. Charsoc held it out to Jether.

"From my master," he said curtly. "His answer to Yehovah's ultimatum in accordance with the legal requirements of the Supreme Councils of the First Heaven. He requests that you read it in front of me in my capacity as his royal envoy."

Jether slowly took it from him and unfolded the ancient parchment. He studied the exquisite copperplate italic lettering and sighed. After reading silently, he finally looked up at Charsoc. "He declares war."

"A *formal* declaration of war. In legal conformity with Eternal Law."

"So he disregards Yehovah's ultimatum and continues with his ill-founded schemes to mutate the genetic code of the Race of Men. He would mutate the Race of Men's gene pool as he did in the days of Noah and the great flood."

Jether slowly refolded the missive. "He writes that he would storm Yehovah's throne. I shall relay the contents of his missive to Yehovah and the High Councils of Justice."

"I shall not waste words, then," Charsoc replied. "We failed the first time. We will not fail a second."

"You speak of the Nephilim," Jether said softly.

The waiter returned with two cocktails, both a pale Mediterranean blue in color.

"Thank you, *boy*," Charsoc boomed.

Jether lowered his voice. "He's *not* a boy, Charsoc. And to address the waiter at the King David as though you'd just arrived back from Kenya in the fifties is not endearing."

Charsoc stirred his cocktail slowly, ignoring Jether's comment.

"*Yours*"—he jabbed rather violently with a toothpick at Jether's cocktail—"is what they call nonalcoholic."

Charsoc sipped delicately at his cocktail. "Yes, Jether. I speak of our hallowed undertaking, as the Fallen, to mutate the Race of Man's DNA. Our first attempts at intercourse between the fallen angelic and the daughters of men were well rewarded. Giants were born." He made a dramatic gesture that was only enhanced by his voluminous robes.

"The Titans," he declared dramatically. "The demigods, the giants of old."

"The Nephilim," Jether whispered.

"We mutated the Race of Men's genetic code. Everything was going according to plan until *He* interfered! *He* decided to annihilate our new Nephilim creation."

"The great flood."

"But this time, Jether, we will surpass ourselves."

"You violate Eternal Law," Jether said. "The Race of Men reproduce according to their kind. Your master's intention to mix angelic and human DNA violates the divine codicils."

"Oh, no." Charsoc downed his cocktail in one easy gulp and wiped his mouth delicately on a linen napkin. "We are *way* past tinkering, Jether. The Race of Men as *you* know it is swiftly about to come to an end."

He threw the napkin down onto the table with a flourish. "Oh," he said offhandedly, "there is an addendum. My master would relay to Yehovah that we the Fallen welcome the forthcoming evacuation of the Nazrene's subjects. They have greatly obstructed our progress in the realm of men.

We are glad of their removal from the earth." Charsoc swung around. "*Their* removal ensures *His* removal."

He studied Jether intently.

"Or does it? No matter, but be under no illusions, Jether. At the time of the great war between my master and Michael, we, the Fallen, shall drive out each and every one of the Nazarene's followers from the First Heaven. We shall rid it of every last trace of the Race of Men." A strange smiled flickered on Charsoc's lips.

Jether was silent.

"I see we understand each other," said Charsoc. He stood. "I shall take my leave."

"Don't you find it difficult to walk with such heavy jewels weighing you down?" Jether asked.

"You have been *warned*," hissed Charsoc.

Jether looked out beyond the walls of Jerusalem, into the falling dusk. "The Lake of Fire awaits you, Charsoc, and you will be its captive for all eternity, as will your master."

Charsoc took one step, then hesitated. "And what of you, Jether? Will you visit me in moments of secret sentiment, when your conscience calls to you? Will you stand on the edge of that burning chasm and *weep* for me?"

"I shed my tears for you, Charsoc, the day you fell from the First Heaven to your doom. There are no tears. Only for the Race of Men do I weep."

Charsoc rose, and instantly his six bodyguards encircled him.

"You will pay dearly, Jether. I shall see to that. Not one brick of your monastery in Alexandria will be left in its place."

He turned dramatically on his heel, almost knocking the

manager to the floor. And grabbing his coat, hat, and cane from his aides, he stormed through the terrace doors, through the King David's lobby, and out the revolving door.

Jether stood quietly in the upper lobby and watched Charsoc ram his fedora onto his domed head, fling his coat over his shoulders in fury, and disappear into the backseat of a gleaming black limousine. Jether watched until the limousine became a speck disappearing past the new Waldorf Astoria Hotel.

He took a deep breath and walked straight through the wall of the King David's outer stairwell. In the same instant, he reappeared in the monastery gardens in Alexandria, beside Liam Mercer.

"Get me Dylan Weaver."

～

MONT ST. MICHEL
NORMANDY

"Operation Pale Horse, Mr. President, sir."

Adrian looked at the holographic map of North America. The blood red arrows covered the entire Bible Belt and Midwest, from Texas eastward and up to Virginia, and from Kansas to Ohio.

Adrian smiled faintly.

"I looked, and there before me was a pale horse! Its rider was named Death, and Hades was following close behind him. They were given power over a fourth of the earth," he murmured.

"You have excelled yourself, Guber."

Guber saluted. "Dolphin submarines with cruise missiles carrying nuclear warheads filled with weaponized *Yersinia pestis* will launch at multiple cities in the ten-kingdom axis within the hour."

"The black death," Adrian murmured. "It will spread like wildfire. Uncontrollable."

He tapped his fingers slowly on his desk, then looked up at Guber.

"We keep New York, Normandy, China, Israel, and Saudi Arabia clean. We cut all communications, switch on the elite's emergency communication channels. Activate the Blacklist.

"Russia and North America will be brought to their knees by Monday night. Martial law will be initiated throughout the ten-kingdom bloc."

Guber nodded.

"The United States? Report on the deployment."

"Military equipment, half-tracks, tanks, and missile launchers are being deployed from the Mexican border. Trainloads of UN and Russian military equipment. Russian artillery, trucks, and missile launchers stored at Biloxi, Mississippi, Fort Polk, Louisiana, and Fort Dix, New Jersey, are being transported to all major cities and internment camps within the next seven days."

"The equipment and military personnel underground in the mountain range areas? Texas?"

"Being deployed as we speak. Over three million foreign troops will be on standby in U.S. military bases. Prince Yuro Tatekawa and the generals await you."

Adrian followed Guber inside the library.

A Japanese general stepped forward and saluted.

179

"The Boxcars?"

"Shipments of the guillotines, manufactured in China and Japan, are unloading on the docks of San Diego, Long Beach, and other West Coast ports of entry, Your Excellency. Over one hundred thousand boxcars with guillotines have been transported from Montana and Georgia to military internment camps across the USA. Forty million plastic coffins, courtesy of Homeland Security.

He saluted.

"And, General Mitchell, the Resisters—we are prepared?"

"Millions of 'resisters of the NWO' are already profiled. Marked for priority arrest, transport to these modern concentration camps under FEMA, Homeland Security, UN, or military jurisdiction, interrogation, and, ultimately, termination under "Operation Pale Horse."

Adrian gazed up at the huge portrait of his grandfather, Julius De Vere, that hung behind his desk, and smiled.

"Then we release the vaccine."

CHAPTER TWENTY-TWO

VOX BOARD MEETING
RITZ CARLTON HOTEL
BABYLON
10 DAYS LATER

JASON WALKED INTO the plush corporate boardroom, took his chair at the head of the table, and surveyed the men assembled there.

"I received no agenda?" he said.

Everyone fell silent—unusually silent.

Jason frowned. "Xavier?" He turned to Xavier Chessler.

"We have a situation," Chessler said softly.

Jason looked at him, bemused. "What do you *mean*, 'a situa . . . '?" Jason's voice trailed off as Xavier Chessler pushed a document in front of him.

"Unfortunately, a rather *acrimonious* situation," Chessler said evenly

Jason scanned the papers, then looked up at Chessler, stunned.

"I'm sorry, dear boy. Due to the ongoing recession, we

have had no option but to call in VOX's loans. *All* your loans." He hesitated and pushed a second silver file over the table to Jason. "Thirty billion dollars' worth."

Jason stared at Chessler in shock, then studied the deadpan faces, one by one, around the table.

"VOX, regrettably, is now insolvent. I suggest you read *that.*"

Jason took his reading glasses out of his top pocket and studied the documents in silence. Finally, he looked up.

"Give me time. A week, ten days. I'll get the capital."

"Because of our immense love and respect for you, your father, James De Vere, and your grandfather Julius, we have found a consortium who *are* prepared to fund VOX: the Global Security Fund. They do, however, have one firm condition."

Jason relaxed visibly. He removed his glasses. "The condition?"

"That you step down as chairman of the board and resign as CEO of VOX, with immediate effect."

"They've overlooked one thing," Jason said. "*Mother.* Between her stock and mine, we can overrule them."

"Your mother's shares were transferred to another family member immediately after her unfortunate demise," Chessler said coldly. "Ten days ago. That family member is in complete concurrence with our plan."

Chessler pushed over a second set of papers.

"Adrian." Jason's mouth set in a thin line.

"Your brother feels, and rightly so, that in the current climate this is the best course of action, to do the best by your father and grandfather—and, of course, especially your dear departed mother."

"What kind of stunt is this?"

"It's not a *stunt*, Jason." Chessler regarded him with icy pale eyes.

"I've poured my entire life into building this company. You're CRAZY if you think I'm going to let anyone take it away from me."

"That's a pity, Jason." Chessler picked up a slim folder. He opened it, scanning the first page. "It would be tragic if you forced our hand. We would have no alternative but to release these documents to the enforcement authorities."

He passed the folder over the table to Jason.

Jason stared down at the first document.

"Heroin, opium trafficking, cocaine, crack cocaine. VOX's money laundering traced from the Cayman Islands and Antigua back to Colombia and Afghanistan . . . "

Jason stared up at Chessler. "What the hell . . . ?"

Chessler shook his head. "I'm so sorry, Jason, but we would be compelled to disclose the sources of VOX's cash that made the monthly payments on VOX'S major stock, derivatives, and investments in the USA and Europe for the past nine years."

Jason turned the pages one by one. "They're all fakes," he said. "Second-rate forg . . . " He stopped in mid sentence, feeling a dull pain on the left hand side of his chest. Ashen-faced, he looked up at Chessler.

He held on to the table for support.

"They aren't forgeries, are they?" he whispered, "They're records from De Vere Asset management."

"My, my, Jason, you're even more well informed than we first suspected. Yes, a bit of creative accounting. Quite right."

Xavier Chessler smiled.

"Unfortunately, forgeries they absolutely are not. They *will* stand in a court of law. Fifty billion in illegal profits from drug trafficking, Jason. Breaking the provisions of the 2022 United Nations Convention against Illicit Traffic in Narcotic Drugs and Psychotropic Substances."

He shook his head. "Adrian would be *so* disappointed at his elder brother's criminal behavior. VOX's illegal drug money traversing international borders. All documents signed by you."

There was a moment's silence. Chessler smiled.

"And, of course, witnessed by your mother, Lilian De Vere." He played idly with his fountain pen.

Jason stared at him with loathing.

"The only things that are forged are the two signatures. *Right there.*"

Chessler stared up at him, steely eyed.

Jason felt as if he had been physically smashed in the ribs.

"You *bastard*, dragging Mother's name into this."

Chessler continued in his calm demeanor. "You, Jason De Vere, as chairman and CEO, would be convicted of conspiracy. And your deceased mother's name, Lilian De Vere, would be tarnished forever. The crime: conspiracy to defraud VOX holdings."

Jason stared at the faces around the table, many of which he had known since he was a boy. He was stunned. He was being manipulated, betrayed, by the man he had known since his own birth and trusted like a father.

Slowly he raised his gaze to Xavier Chessler.

"I know what you're up to, Chessler." Jason fumbled in his inside jacket pocket and, with trembling fingers, brought out the document signed by Julius De Vere. He smoothed it out on the table. "You and your *illicit* brotherhood—a death warrant."

Jason rose and walked over to Xavier Chessler. He thrust the yellowed document into Chessler's face, then grabbed him by the collar.

"To think, I counted on you as my godfather. I trusted you with my life, as my *friend*."

He closed his eyes for a split second. "Of course, you were my grandfather's closest friend. Piers Aspinall was your English club chum. What have you got planned for me, Chessler? Another car accident? An induced heart attack, maybe?"

He thrust the old man away, leaving him gasping, and snatched the document. He strode to the door, then turned.

"You haven't seen the last of me."

He slammed the boardroom door in their faces.

One by one, the board members left the room. Kurt Guber appeared from the shadows.

Chessler shook his head. He recomposed himself.

"He can use the death warrant against us," Guber said.

"Let him go," said Chessler. "We've got him under surveillance."

"He'll be found dead in the morning," Guber announced. "Suicide."

Chessler nodded. "Couldn't take the strain of VOX's imminent collapse."

Guber nodded.

"When do we release the plague?"

"In twenty-four hours."

Chessler looked up at Kurt Guber. And smiled.

Chapter Twenty-three

RITZ CARLTON TOWERS
BABYLON
TEN MINUTES LATER

J ASON TAPPED THE GLASS hotel telephone screen
again.

"Don't *tell* me the international lines are down!" he
shouted at the concierge on the screen. "I've just had two
SS thugs in here telling me I can't leave the hotel. I don't
care if there's a damn nuclear bomb in Babylon. I want . . . "
Jason paced the penthouse suite. " . . . my ride to the airport
now!"

There was a knock on the door.

"Who is it?" he shouted.

No reply.

Jason clicked the hotel phone off, strode through the
lounge, and tapped a small screen. It relayed the image of a
tall, lean, muscular young man in a well-fitted black suit,
standing at attention in the hallway.

Jason glared at him. "Go to hell!" he shouted.

The young man stood quietly.

Jason hesitated, then opened the door a crack. "Just what part of 'Go to hell!' don't you understand?"

He started to slam the door, but the tall, blond young man inserted himself deftly between Jason and the door.

Like lightning, one hand shot up from his waist and clamped Jason by the neck.

With his other hand, he reached down and removed Jason's Breitling watch, deftly opened it, and removed a minute metal disk from inside and held it out to Jason.

Microphone, he mouthed, gently releasing his hold on Jason's neck. He crushed the disk under his shoe.

Jason watched in amazement as the young man moved swiftly through the hotel suite, removing similar bugs from the hotel telephone screen, a bedside lamp, and the shower-head in the bathroom.

He held the bugs out in his hand and put a finger to his lips. Then, carefully closing the bathroom door, he fitted a scrambler into the bedroom security panel.

Creates interference, he mouthed. He held out a mono-grammed envelope.

Puzzled, Jason tore it open. Only one person he knew still used paper and ink. He stared down at Lawrence St. Cartier's personal stationery. The words were in St. Cartier's unmis-takable perfectly formed cursive hand.

"Liam Mercer is one of us. Don't be stubborn. *Trust him*."

"They have no intention of allowing you to leave, Mr. De Vere." The young man spoke quietly but with an air of authority. "Tomorrow you'll be found dead, hanging by your tie from right there." He pointed to the central chandelier.

"With a suicide note already dictated by Xavier Chessler."

"Mr. De Vere, sir, you can either come with me quietly now . . . " He opened the door and gestured to the empty corridor. " . . . or I'll have to take you by force," he said politely. "I'm sorry, sir. My orders."

"Orders? Orders from *who*?" Jason asked. "The professor?"

Mercer smiled. "Precisely, sir."

"Hell," Jason growled. "How do I know you're telling the truth?"

"You don't, sir," the young stranger said, and smiled for the first time. "It's a matter of faith."

Jason sighed, walked over to the suite safe, and took out his second passport and a black bag of gold Kruger rands while the stranger removed the nano sim card from Jason's cell phone.

Jason pointed to the hallway. "Guber's thugs?"

"All dealt with. The road is clear." He held out the cell phone to Jason.

For some unfathomable reason, Jason knew he was going to put his life in the hands of this young stranger. He took the cell phone, put on his jacket, and followed the stranger down the empty corridor.

CHAPTER TWENTY-FOUR

MONT ST. MICHEL
NORMANDY

"HE TOOK IT IN typical hostile Jason style, I presume."

Chessler nodded.

Adrian spoke to the conference screen in the palace library. "Don't let him leave. He knows too much to live." He sighed. "Pity." He played idly with his pen. "I was somewhat attached to my eldest brother."

"Er . . . um . . ." Chessler stared back at Adrian through the screen. "We have a problem, Your Excellency. Your brother has gone. Disappeared from the hotel room."

Adrian looked up at Chessler in disbelief. "Find Him." He gave a sharp nod to Chastenay, who clicked off the feed from Babylon.

Adrian walked over to the window and looked out at the tide rolling in furiously from the Atlantic. "So . . . we revert to plan B."

Chastenay nodded. "On her way up, Your Excellency."

189

A satisfied smile spread across Adrian's face. "At last, a visit from my favorite niece."

The drawing room doors automatically swung open, and a well-fed Rhodesian ridgeback with a glossy tan coat wagged its tail and licked Adrian's fingers.

In the center of the hallway, sitting in her wheelchair and beaming up at Adrian, was Jason's daughter.

Lily De Vere.

BABYLON INTERNATIONAL AIRPORT
BABYLON, IRAQ

Jason sat in silence, looking out at the newly extended Babylon International Airport as the Gulfstream taxied down the runway. The stranger sat opposite him.

Jason studied him. Good-looking. Clean-cut, dirty-blond hair, clear green eyes. Obviously worked out—muscular shoulders, manicured fingernails.

"Where are we headed? To the monastery?"

"I'm sorry, sir, I'm not at liberty to say."

'What happens to my jet?'

Jason pointed in the direction of his gleaming new Gulfstream 7, still parked on the runway.

'Its been commandeered, sir.

'What do you *mean* comandeered?

'By direct order of Xavier Chessler.'

Jason shook his head in frustration, then looked back down at the note from Lawrence in his fingers. "You work for St. Cartier, then?"

"Yes, sir," he said respectfully. "In a manner of speaking. The professor mentored me." He hesitated. "And my brothers."

"You have brothers? How many?"

"Two, sir," the young man answered.

Jason raised his eyebrows. "You the youngest?"

The stranger shook his head. "No, sir."

"You know, I'm one of three brothers."

The stranger nodded. "Yes, I know, sir. The De Vere brothers."

The jet took off into the clear Babylon skies.

"How did you get clearance for this thing? Without going through the diplomatic channels, it's impossible."

"Sorry, sir, I'm not at—"

"Right." Jason smiled. "Not at liberty." He raised his hands. "I know."

The stranger held up a bottle of mineral water. Jason sighed. "That the strongest you've got?"

The young man poured the mineral water into a glass.

Jason held out his hand. "Thank you, Liam Mercer. For getting me out."

"It's my job, sir. I was just obeying orders."

Jason scanned the *New York Times*. He couldn't quite place the accent. He looked back up at Mercer.

"Where are you from, Mercer?"

Mercer looked uncomfortable.

"From all over, sir," he said softly.

Jason grinned. "You're close to your brothers?"

"Close to the youngest, sir."

Jason nodded. "Like me," he murmured. "My youngest brother and I—we're very close."

Then he went back to his reading.

Liam Mercer stared out the Gulfstream's windows. He was the only one aboard who saw the pack of grotesque gray vampire vultures, flying at speed directly in the Gulfstream's flight path, a mile behind.

Lucifer's surveillance demons.

He closed his eyes and folded his hands. Gabriel's reconnaissance team, the revelator eagles, would overtake them at any moment.

CHAPTER TWENTY-FIVE

JFK INTERNATIONAL AIRPORT
NEW YORK

"THIS IS THE FINAL boarding call for passenger Alexander Lane Fox, booked on Egyptair flight three-seven-two-A to Cairo. Please proceed to gate seven immediately. The final checks are being completed, and the captain will order the doors of the aircraft closed in approximately ten minutes' time. I repeat, this is the final boarding call for Alexander Lane Fox."

Alex glanced down at his watch. "God, Pol, I'm missing you already. Make sure you feed the moggy."

Polly kept step with him as they rushed toward security. She was in New York for the summer, on an internship for Amnesty International, investigating human trafficking.

"I'll always love you, Alex."

"I know, Pol. I know."

She looked at Alex strangely, then kissed him passionately, clinging to him.

"Hey, *hey*, kid." He looked at her, amused. "I'm only gone

for ten days. I'll be with Nick. C'mon, Polly, or I'll miss my flight."

Alex took out his cell phone from his backpack and gave the stern flight attendant his most winning grin. "I'm Alexander Lane Fox."

The flight attendant pressed the glass screen at her right hand. "Lane Fox. He's arrived. I'll rush him through." She nodded to Alex.

Alex put up his hands. Only hand luggage. She pointed to the iris-recognition immigration system a few feet away, which Adrian had recently had installed throughout the USA and the ten-kingdom axis nations.

"IRIS," she instructed.

Polly swung around to Alex.

"Pol . . . " He frowned. Tears were streaming down Polly's cheeks.

Alex sighed. "It's this Rapture thing again, isn't it? It's got you all wound up. You think it's going to happen while I'm gone, and you won't see me again."

He held up his hands. "Pol, we've been over this a million times."

"Look after Lily," Polly whispered. "She loves you."

Alex took back his passport and walked through toward security. He turned back to Polly. "Didn't get that, gorgeous."

He grinned and waved to her, standing behind the ropes. "Take you out on the lake as soon as I'm back."

He walked through the departure hall and looked into the camera at the IRIS barrier.

The system flashed "Registration valid."

He waved at Polly. "I love you, Pol. I'm going to spend the rest of my life with you!"

He blew her another kiss, then disappeared behind the security doors.

Tears streamed down Polly's cheeks. She took the engagement ring off her finger, then held her fingers to her mouth, her voice barely a whisper.

"Good-bye, my beautiful Alex."

CHAPTER TWENTY-SIX

MONASTERY OF ARCHANGELS
ALEXANDRIA, EGYPT

LAWRENCE AND JASON walked through the immaculate monastery kitchen gardens, followed by Liam Mercer, who walked behind them at a discreet distance.

"I *do* wish you were here under pleasanter circumstances, Jason."

Jason sighed. "So do I, Lawrence, believe me." He followed Lawrence down a winding stone corridor.

Lawrence rubbed his hands together. "I wish you'd agreed to take my suite, dear boy. The guest quarters are Spartan, to say the least—not exactly what you're used to." He stopped outside a small cloister door. "You've been through quite the proverbial mill."

"I just need time to think, Lawrence."

"Of course, my boy, of course." Lawrence nodded to a monk who appeared from the shadows. The monk unclipped a scanner from his belt and waved it across the ancient keyhole, which lit up briefly in cobalt blue. The cloister door clicked open.

Jason raised his eyebrows. "Do all monasteries have state-of-the-art security?"

"Only this one, my boy."

Jason scanned the single iron bed, the flagstone floors, and the lone sink in the corner. "I've seen worse, Lawrence." He gave a wry smile. "Not often, though."

"Not exactly the Ritz, but it's clean." Lawrence beamed. "The bathrooms and other amenities are at the end of the corridor, first to the left."

Lawrence looked down at his watch. "Lunch is at one sharp. It's not good for Brother Castigliano's spiritual advancement if we're late. He's our chef, and a fine one, I must say—the gentlest of souls—but once he's in the kitchen his Mediterranean blood tends to stir up easily. Finest cook in Egypt, though."

"Liam will stand guard at the end of the corridor."

Jason shook his head. "I don't need a minder, Lawrence."

"Oh, but I'm afraid you do, Master Jason."

Lawrence and Jason exchanged a look. "Oh, I forgot to mention, you won't lack for a valet."

Maxim ducked and walked into the room, his white hair awry, and beaming from ear to ear. "At your service, as always, Master Jason, sir," he boomed. Jason shook his head in disbelief.

Lawrence walked out of the cloister door. "One o'clock sharp," he said, and disappeared down the corridor.

"Brings back memories of boarding school," Jason muttered.

"Yes, Master Jason, sir, it certainly does."

Jason flung his suit jacket onto the bed. Maxim tut-tutted, then picked it up and dusted it off.

Jason undid the top button on his shirt. "I don't need babying, Maxim."

"Of course not, Master Jason." Maxim opened the single piece of furniture in the room—a wardrobe—and beamed again.

Jason raised his eyebrows.

"Your favorite cashmere jersey. Six of your Ralph Lauren casual shirts. Six pants, pressed. Two blazers."

"And my favorite loafers." Jason shook his head.

"We *have* been expecting you, Master Jason."

Jason walked over to the window and stared out at the painstakingly maintained olive grove. "Yes, I can *see* that."

Maxim pointed to a bell on a pulley. "Please ring if you desire anything else I haven't thought of. One ring for me, your valet. Two rings for Liam Mercer."

"I don't need a val—"

Maxim bowed and left the room.

Jason shook his head. His precise brand and model of razor and shaving cream were laid out next to the basin, with his favorite aftershave.

His "clean" phone vibrated at his hip. He checked the caller ID: Lily. Weaver must have given Julia and Lily his number. His face wreathed in a smile. Lily's face appeared on the screen.

"Lily."

"Hi, Dad, are you okay?"

Jason opened the cloister window. "I'm fine, sweet-heart—all the better for hearing you."

"Are you sure you're okay, Dad? It's just that Uncle Xavier said it was really important I get hold of you. It sounded urgent."

Jason froze. His thought processes seemed paralyzed. Finally, he spoke.

"Lily, where, exactly, are you?" Each word seemed to echo in his head.

"I'm at Uncle Adrian's, Dad. Mom and Uncle Adrian arranged it after Gran's funeral, at the wake. Uncle Ade's been wanting me to come out to France for months, and Mom flew out to New York yesterday. Lulu's with me."

Jason sat on the bed, his mind reeling. Lily and "his" ridgeback were with Adrian.

There was a silence.

"It's really great here, Dad. The sun's shining. Uncle Adrian's spoiling me rotten."

"Lily." Jason clenched the phone in his hand. "Listen very carefully to me. This is very important. You have to get out of there *now*."

"Dad? What on *earth* is the matter with you?"

The phone clicked off.

Jason redialed. There was a clicking noise on the other end of the phone. He dialed Julia's cell phone.

Six rings, and it clicked over to Julia's voice mail.

He pressed redial.

Three rings.

GRAMERCY PARK
MANHATTAN
NEW YORK

"Jason, it's six a.m. What's going on?"

"*Lily's* what's going on!" Jason snapped. He glared into

the phone screen at Julia, who looked still groggy from sleep. "What the hell were you thinking of, to let her go!"

"What are you *talking* about, Jason?" Julia snapped back.

"Lily, of course, damn it." He hesitated. "And my *dog*, come to think of it."

"She's with her uncle—your *brother*, remember?" Julia's voice was like ice. "And we *both* have custody of the dog, so don't even dare go there."

Jason's hands started to tremble with rage and fear. "Look, Julia, I'm sorry . . . " He ran his fingers through his hair. "Look, I can't explain now. Just for once in your life, trust me. Don't speak to Adrian."

"Don't speak to *Adrian*?"

"Julia, listen to me. If he contacts you, whatever you do, don't let him know we've talked. You have to trust me. Where are you?"

"Gramercy, New York. The town house."

"Stay where you are. Until I contact you."

"Well, that'll be three years, then." Julia glared at him. Then her face vanished from the screen. The phone clicked off in Jason's hand.

"Damn!" he shouted in exasperation. He strode out the door to the end of the corridor.

"Where is he?" He grasped Liam Mercer's arm. "St. Cartier. Lawrence St. Cartier. Where will I find him?"

"Follow me, please, Mr. De Vere."

Jason followed Liam down some old stone stairs.

With trembling hands, Jason dialed Adrian's number.

In genial, well-modulated tones, Adrian's private voice mail said, "Leave a message."

Finally, they reached an old wooden door signposted "THE CRYPTS."

"The professor is inside," Liam said.

He placed a small passkey into a digital scanner, and the old door slid open. Jason gasped.

Over a hundred monks and Chinese youths worked feverishly in front of an immense bank of surveillance screens that stretched over the entire room. Liam nodded politely to Jason and disappeared.

The professor and Nick stood behind Dylan Weaver, intently watching one of the largest screens.

Nick turned. "Jas," he said softly, "it seems we have a situation."

Jason followed his gaze to the surveillance screen. Facing him on the screen was Lily, in the cliff garden at Mont St. Michel. She had her phone in one hand, and her head was thrown back in laughter. She was in conversation with a tall man in priestly attire.

Jason could see only the back of the man's head. His black hair was tightly bound in one braid by a black ribbon. Lily was laughing until tears rolled down her cheeks.

The priest wheeled her around the manicured rose beds. Lulu, the ridgeback, was following them. Jason frowned. The normally affectionate dog was growling.

"Who's the priest?" Jason asked Lawrence.

At that precise moment, the priest turned and raised his head. His striking features were fully visible, almost as though he sensed them watching him.

Nick's eyes widened in disbelief. "I know him!" he gasped. "I mean, I've seen him before. At Mont St. Michel. The night Adrian tried to kill me."

"You're sure?" Lawrence asked.

"I'll never forget his face. Beatrice said he was a royal prince. The security surrounding him was unprecedented. He took over the entire west wing of Mont St. Michel. He gives me the creeps."

Lawrence stared at the screen, his face inscrutable.

"He goes by the name of Lorcan De Molay," Lawrence said very softly. "The order of the Jesuits." He paused. "Many years ago, another lifetime away, I mentored him."

Nick stared at Lawrence in disbelief. "When you were in the Jesuits? The CIA?"

Lawrence did not answer but said, "Unfortunately, he crossed over to the dark side."

"You're telling me an evil priest is wheeling *my* daughter around?"

Jason pressed redial.

"Adrian, I know you're there. If anything happens to Lily, I'll kill you with my bare hands."

Lawrence nodded to Weaver. Nick shook his head at Jason.

The surveillance screen's images changed to Adrian's private dining room. Jason stared in disbelief.

Adrian was seated at the mahogany dining table where he and Jason had dined so many times before. His phone lay on the table directly in front of him. It was flashing blue.

"Zoom in, Dylan," Lawrence murmured.

Adrian's caller ID read "*Jason De Vere—cell.*"

Adrian studied the caller ID, picked up the phone, and answered leisurely. His chiseled features appeared on Jason's phone screen.

"You should have thought things through more carefully

before you eluded my security forces and escaped from Babylon, Jason. We might not be having this conversation if you had been—how shall I phrase it?" He leisurely took a forkful of the crayfish hors d'oeuvres. "More *measured*. But you were *never* measured, were you, Jason? Not even when we were young."

Jason stared stonily at the screen.

"You've betrayed me, Jason," Adrian continued. "You've betrayed my cause."

He smiled slightly.

"And now s*omeone* has to be punished. And as you're not here, you've unfortunately left me with no option. I have to revert to plan B, which, as you've no doubt already gathered . . . " He smiled genially. " . . . is Lily."

Sweat broke out on Jason's forehead.

"Nicholas!" Adrian's tone became smoother. "How nice to *see* you. Returned from the dead, I see. How *clever* of you."

His eyes grew hard as steel.

"Charsoc the Dark warned you in Jerusalem, Jether. You might want to watch this."

He walked over to the vast French doors and flung them open.

Weaver switched on a sixth surveillance screen.

Two hundred feet below Adrian, Lily was in her wheelchair. The priest, his face now hidden, pushed her to the far edge of the garden, where the rockeries sloped steeply toward the towering cliff edge of Mont St. Michel. He leaned over and fiddled with the wheelchair brakes. Lulu growled slightly. The priest turned to her, and instantly she lay on the ground, yelping.

Jason, Nick, and Lawrence watched in horror as the priest turned and walked back toward the castle.

The wheelchair began to roll down the slope, gaining speed. Lily frowned, then pulled the brake handle. Nothing happened. Lulu started to bark.

"He's tampered with the brakes!" Nick whispered.

Lawrence gestured to Liam. "Mercer, get hold of Pierre *now*."

The wheelchair hurtled toward the cliff edge. As Lily stared in horror at the oncoming precipice, Lorcan De Molay turned from higher ground. And smiled.

Jason watched, frozen, as Lily was thrown from her wheelchair and went hurtling over the edge of the cliff, into the quicksand below.

She screamed in terror. "Help me," she cried.

Jason gripped the table with both hands. His entire body started to tremble. He could see Lulu standing at the top of the cliff, barking and pawing at the edge.

Jason turned to Lawrence. "Don't just stand there—*do* something!" he shouted. Then he turned back to the screen.

As the tide raced in, Lily sank, sucked down by Mont St. Michel's treacherous quicksands.

Distraught, Jason picked up the phone. "Get the emergency services, for God's sake!" he yelled.

Dylan Weaver pointed to the monitor. "We did," he said. "They've overridden us."

Jason stared at the computer screen. "Who? *Who's* overridden us?"

Nick pointed to the screen that read "Request Mont St. Michel. Drowning. Immediate response." Underneath were the words "False alarm. Deactivate. Code 0099."

"*Adrian*." Jason punched the chair.

"He's president of the European Superstate, Jason," Nick said quietly. "He *controls* the emergency services."

Jason stared from Nick to Lawrence, his breathing shallow. He grasped his phone and pressed redial.

"You bastard!" he screamed down the phone. "You *bastard*, Adrian," he yelled. "I'll find you, wherever you are, and kill you with my bare hands. It's my new mission in life!"

Tears coursed down Jason's cheeks. He wiped them away with the back of his hand. Very gently, Nick pried his fingers from the cell phone.

Lily lay crippled and helpless on the treacherous quicksands of Mont St. Michel as the tide rushed in. She tried to move, but every effort only sank her deeper in the mire.

Calm down, she told herself. Get yourself together, Lily. You're your father's daughter. Calm down. The emergency services are on their way right now.

Tears streamed down her face. "Oh, God, help me," she cried, her mind racing even faster than the rapidly rising water.

Surely Uncle Adrian would get help.

The waves were covering her chest and lapping at her chin. She stared up at the cliff far above her. She was sinking deeper into the quicksand. Lulu was still barking frantically.

There, standing far above her on the balcony, was Uncle Adrian. He looked down at her.

And smiled.

Lily was now completely submerged except for her face

and neck, and the tide was still rushing in. She swallowed more water.

She was drowning. Something terrible was happening. Uncle Adrian was letting her drown. She was completely alone, and she was going to die. She struggled for breath.

Then, through the saltwater, she saw coming toward her, smiling, her long, dark hair flying in the winds . . . her grandmother.

Lily stared in disbelief. Lilian was reaching out her hand, as though trying to tell Lily something.

As the waves swept over Lily's nose and mouth she looked up at Lilian.

Lilian smiled down at her, and as Lily smiled back, Lilian faded into the heavens.

Suddenly, Lily knew what Lilian had been trying to tell her. And as the waves came in, before they submerged her face completely she took her last breath.

And prayed.

Jason sat frozen, his eyes staring straight ahead. He snatched the phone from Nick's grasp.

"For the seventh time, for the love of God, damn it," he screamed into the phone, "my daughter is drowning in quicksand at Mont St. Michel! For God's sake, do something!"

"No. It's *not* a false alert!"

He gasped for breath.

"I don't care if it's signed by the head of Europol! Don't you *get* it? They're *murdering* my daughter!"

He stopped for breath, tears coursing down his face.

"Get a Red Cross helicopter there now!" he screamed.

He grasped Lawrence fiercely by both shoulders, shaking him. "Do something!" he screamed.

He dropped his hands from Lawrence's shoulders. "For the love of God," he sobbed.

His cell phone slipped from his hand to the floor.

"For the love of God," he rasped. He stared around at Lawrence, then at Nick.

"For the love of God," he mouthed in agony. His body was racked with sobs.

Gently Lawrence picked up the phone from the floor. Nick looked on as Jason sat, struggling to breathe. His own shoulders shook with fury and grief.

Lawrence walked over to a far cupboard and unlocked the door. He took out a bottle of Irish whisky and poured it into a nearby glass until the glass was completely full.

Then, walking over to a cupboard of glass containers filled with herbal potions, he removed a small vial of white powder. He poured a teaspoon of the powder into the glass and stirred it vigorously. Walking back, he held the glass out to Jason.

Jason stared blankly ahead, eyes wide with raw pain. Nick gently placed Jason's fingers around the glass.

"Drink it, Jason," he whispered.

Slowly Jason gripped the glass, sobbing as he drank, Nick's hand on his shoulder all the while. Maxim stood quietly next to Liam in the doorway.

Jason stood up. His eyes were beginning to blur, and his legs buckled beneath him. He collapsed into the chair, and his head fell onto his chest.

"Take him back to his room," Lawrence whispered to Nick. "I gave him a rather strong herbal central nervous system depressant. In combination with the whisky, its effects are greatly intensified. It should knock him out."

Nick and a monk lifted Jason to his feet.

Lawrence watched as they walked through the crypt door.

"Well, you'd better get a move on, Liam. And, Xacheriel, there's no point in blabbing on about Double-o-seven if you're just going to stand there.

"Let's get to work!"

Lawrence reached out his hand toward the empty cliff on the virtual screen. "*Deum Patrem omnipotentem.*" He moved nearer and closed his eyes.

Maxim bowed his head, his lips moving in prayer.

"Creatorem caeli et terrae . . . ," he whispered.

Dylan Weaver watched, mesmerized, as luminous white fire emanated from Lawrence's fingertips.

" . . . et in Iesum Christum, Filium Eius unicum . . . "

Lawence's entire body started to metamorphose. Dylan had seen it only once before; it was the most astounding thing he had ever witnessed.

Dylan closed his eyes in respect, then, unable to stop himself, opened one. The brightest light he had ever seen was illuminating Liam Mercer's entire body. Liam's blond hair fell to bare muscular shoulders.

Nick walked back into the room, then fell to his knees, shaking, covering his eyes with his hands to shield them from the incandescent light. The last thing either Dylan or Nick saw before Liam disappeared was a pair of enormous wings rising from his shoulders.

"Oh, my God!" Dylan muttered, terrified. "It's *Batman*!

⤳

"Dominum nostrum, qui conceptus est de Spiritu Sancto, natus ex Maria Virgine . . . "

Lawrence's entire body started to take on a luminous, otherwordly glow as the spry five-foot-eight old man transformed into an eight-foot giant. Dylan stared in disbelief.

" . . . passus sub Pontio Pilato, crucifixus, mortuus et sepultus . . . "

Dylan turned to Maxim, who himself now stood over eight feet tall. Dylan stared up at Maxim's long white hair and beard that swept the floor.

" . . . descendit ad infernos, tertia die resurrexit a mortuis . . . Credo in Spiritum Sanctum . . . "

Lawrence and Maxim—or rather, Jether and Xacheriel—raised both hands to the sky.

There was a loud clap of thunder; then a ferocious cobalt blue lightning bolt struck through the crypts and through the video screen.

Nick stared in trembling awe at the glorious form six thousand miles away, walking on the waves of the Atlantic.

"He's here," he whispered.

Chapter Twenty-seven

MONT ST. MICHEL
NORMANDY

ADRIAN TURNED FROM the French doors and sat back down at the dining table.

"Dessert, Mr. President, sir?" Anton, the abbey's head steward, asked.

Adrian gave a slight smile and held up his hand.

"Coffee. Espresso."

Anton turned to Lorcan De Molay.

"Your Excellency?"

De Molay waved him away. As Anton walked out of the dining room, De Molay picked up his dessert fork. He paused and stared across the table at Adrian's trembling fingers.

Adrian picked up his wineglass and sipped once. His right hand started to tremble uncontrollably. He stared in horror as the glass fell from his hand and smashed in pieces on the oak floor.

Gasping for breath, he tried desperately to undo his top shirt button. His throat was constricting so fast that his face was turning blue.

He clutched at his windpipe, then slid in agony from his chair onto the polished oak floor.

De Molay sat opposite him, suffocating, grasping at the clerical collar around his neck. In agonizing pain, he collapsed to the floor, the collar in his right hand.

With immense difficulty, he clawed his way over the few feet across the Savonnerie rug toward the open French doors, then dragged himself up to his knees, shielding his eyes from the strange blinding light blazing from far below the cliff edge of Mont St. Michel.

It was like a nuclear explosion.

"It's a terrorist attack on Mont St. Michel." Adrian clutched his chest in agony. "Small nuclear device. No . . . bioterror. It has to be the botulinum toxin. It's the only thing that has these effects."

"Did you *see* the gunships?" De Molay hissed, his teeth chattering so hard he could scarcely speak. "Did you *see* a *missile?*" he screamed, staring over at Adrian in disgust.

Then he retched onto the carpet.

"To us, the Fallen, it's worse than botulinum toxin," De Molay hissed.

In agonizing pain, Adrian struggled desperately to drag himself nearer to the balcony. Slowly, he raised his head and stared toward the blinding light over the cliff. It was expanding in pulsating concentric circles over the Atlantic Ocean. The blazing rainbow overshadowed the entire mount. The floor started to shudder.

Far in the distance, on an outcrop of rock in the Atlantic, two tall figures were in intense discussion.

Lorcan De Molay's face contorted in hatred. "My brother Michael," he hissed.

Adrian fell back, clutching his chest. "The second figure—who . . . Astaroth?"

De Molay nodded, his eyes dull. He managed to lift and point his ringed finger. "The third form, to the west. Walking on the Atlantic." His face contorted with intense, unbridled hatred. "On the waves . . . "

Adrian lay pinned to the floor by a monstrous invisible force. "Who . . . who?" he whispered, shaking uncontrollably.

De Molay turned his face to Adrian's in a mixture of hatred and dread. "It is *Him*!" he cried in terror.

"It is the Nazarene!"

Then the entire world of Mont St. Michel fell into utter darkness.

⌒

ATLANTIC OCEAN
MONT ST. MICHEL, NORMANDY

Michael and Astaroth stood facing each other on the rocky outcrop a mile out into the Atlantic.

Astaroth removed his helmet and shook his long blond hair free from its bands. Michael did the same. They stood facing each other—nine-foot lean, imperial angelic forms, their mammoth angelic wings outstretched.

Both their gazes locked on the majestic figure in white robes walking across the raging waves of the Atlantic. Suddenly, the figure vanished.

"She is safe," said Astaroth. He sighed and stared down at his helmet.

"They will note your abscence."

"I am past caring," Astaroth murmured. "Both Adrian and the prince will be suffering from the Nazarene's presence."

"And yet," Michael whispered, "you, Astaroth, once my close and trusted companion, commander of my armies—yet *you* do not suffer . . . " Michael frowned. " . . . from the nearness of His presence."

Michael stared in wonder at Astaroth before him.

"No." Astaroth wiped a lone tear from his cheek. "I do not suffer. His presence is the only respite from the great torments of my soul. To look upon Him once again has been my greatest longing."

"Yet your entire existence is with the prince of the Fallen and his cunning wizard."

"I chose to follow Lucifer, and I will pay the penalty for all eternity. Yet it will never stop me from loving Him who used to be my entire being."

Michael sighed. "Astaroth," he whispered.

Astaroth shook his head. "Don't, Michael. I am doomed. I followed Charsoc through the Portal of Shinar. I will spend my days in the guise of one of the Race of Men, but unlike you, I cannot maintain my angelic form. The longer I am on Earth, the more I lose my ability to maintain my angelic body. I will be Neil Travis forever, except that I cannot die. And the Lake of Fire is my eternal destination."

"I know where you go," Michael murmured. "It has not been hidden from me."

"You *know*?" Astaroth faltered.

Michael nodded. He raised his palm.

The Atlantic disappeared, and suddenly they were

surrounded by the gnarled ancient trees in the Garden of Gethsemane.

Astaroth was now in human bodily form: six feet two, muscular, with close-cropped brown hair. He felt at his side for his firearm.

"Automatic reflex." He smiled wryly at Michael. "Welcome to the life of Neil Travis, ex-SAS."

Travis stared at Michael in wonder. He was now six feet one, with cropped blond hair and a close-fitting black suit. They could almost be twins.

"Liam Mercer, bodyguard extraordinaire. Ex-navy SEAL."

"I was here, Astaroth," Michael whispered. "The night before He died. We were bequeathed one of the greatest privileges in heaven. We came with Jether to minister to Him before His crucifixion."

Astaroth nodded. He fell to his knees under a tree. "It is here—only here—that I find His comfort. *Only* here."

"They do not know?"

Astaroth shook his head. "I will yet find a way to repay some of the debt for my rebellion." He quickly looked up at Michael and raised his hand. "I know there is no redemption for me. That is not my motive. I do it because I would make amends somehow, some way, loving Him even though I committed high treason. I am content with my lot, with my punishment. "I *will* find a way, Michael, to make partial amends."

"Charsoc knows the state of your being?"

"He may guess, but he does not know. He himself may wrestle. I do not know."

Michael nodded. He clasped Astaroth's arm. "I am truly sorry it has come to this."

Astaroth stared at him blankly. "No, Michael. Don't. There is no return. I am a slave of the King of Lies. And yet, I find that my soul is imprisoned by the King of Love. I take responsibility for my own actions, as you and Jether taught me.

"I must return, Michael."

Astaroth removed himself from Michael's grasp. He vanished, leaving Michael alone.

In the Garden of Gethsemane.

Chapter Twenty-eight

GRAMERCY APARTMENT
NEW YORK

FOUR HOURS AND THREE minutes had passed since Adrian phoned Julia with the news that no mother should ever receive—the news she would never recover from. The phone call at 9:17 that morning had changed the course of her life irrevocably.

Lily.

She looked down at the photographs that lay scattered on the bed. Lily at six, smiling and carefree. Lily at nine. Lily at twelve, thirteen, sixteen . . . She closed her eyes. Her chest was sore, so sore, from sobbing.

Julia stared blankly at the bottle of sleeping tablets clutched in her left hand. With a great effort, she opened the lid and shook out a handful into her palm.

Slowly, one by one, she dropped nine tablets back into the plastic container. Then she took a deep breath and washed the remaining three down with a glass of water on the nightstand, willing the blackness of sleep's oblivion to descend on her swiftly and take her out of the cruel, desperate pain that felt as though it was tearing apart her entire being.

She fell facedown onto the carpet, screaming silently. Screaming, screaming. Clawing at the Aubusson carpet beneath her, her matted blond hair fallen over her face, until she fell into a tormented, restless slumber.

She was still there, sprawled across the carpet, as the gray New York dawn seeped into the room.

MONASTERY OF THE ARCHANGELS
ALEXANDRIA, EGYPT

The helicopter hovered above the grass helipad in the center of the monastery gardens.

Nick and Lawrence watched intently as the chopper landed and the rotor blades slowed to a standstill. The door opened, and Pierre, Adrian's chauffeur, climbed down the steps, carrying a metal briefcase, followed closely by Lulu, Jason's ridgeback.

Lawrence nodded to two monks, who ran toward the helicopter with a stretcher, followed closely by Nick.

Lawrence made the sign of the cross as Pierre walked toward him and handed him the briefcase.

"He saved her," Pierre whispered. "Literally." The tears welled in his eyes. "The tides came in. I was too late. I watched her drown in the quicksand. I couldn't get to her. She was *gone*, Lawrence. Completely submerged. Washed out to sea, well below the surface."

"But He came." Nick shook his head in wonder.

Pierre nodded, deeply moved.

Nick stared down at Lily as she was loaded onto the stretcher. She was pale—oh, so pale. But her breathing was even. Lawrence and Nick exchanged a euphoric glance.

"Jason?" Nick looked at Lawrence.

"Don't wake him. Let him sleep."

Lawrence bent over Lily and brushed her matted dark hair off her face.

"Take Lily to the sanatorium," Lawrence instructed Father Benedictus. "Nick and I will stay with her through the night."

"He . . . He . . . " Pierre wiped a tear from his cheek. "I saw Him . . . walking . . . on the water. A hundred, a hundred fifty yards out. He was walking on the raging Atlantic." He took a deep breath and bowed his head.

"You . . . you actually saw *Him.*" Nick's eyes searched Pierre's face hungrily.

"I had never seen Him before," Pierre whispered. He stared at Nick, tears streaming down his face. "He was so beautiful." He stopped, overcome with emotion.

"It is hard for the human soul to behold such beauty." Lawrence placed a gentle hand on Pierre's shoulder. "Go on, Pierre," he said with a gentle smile.

Pierre nodded. "The next thing I knew, He . . . He was on the shore. With *her.*" He choked up in emotion.

Everyone waited in reverent silence until he regained his voice.

"He lifted Lily up in His arms, then held her to His breast. Then stroked her hair and kissed her, right on her forehead. Like a father . . . like a mother."

Pierre clutched his crucifix and kissed it fervently.

"We serve a compassionate savior." Tears fell unheeded down his face. "I'm not sure what happened next, only that when I found her, she was warm and alive. And breathing."

"You know you can't go back, Pierre," Lawrence said softly. "This is it, old friend."

Pierre looked up in alarm. "But Hilde . . . Hilde's still there. All these years. She has no idea what I do."

Lawrence smiled as a short, plump figure came running toward them from the direction of the kitchen, her gray plaits flying.

"Ah, but I *do*, my darling Pierre." Hilde sobbed and flung her cumbersome frame into her spry husband's arms. "They told me everything."

Pierre looked up through Hilde's sobbing and stroked her plaits. "So this is it, then. The end of the road."

"This is it." Hilde dried her eyes with her apron.

"I want to be of use, Professor," said Pierre. "To protect the De Vere family is all I've ever known. I promised James De Vere—gave him my eternal word." He bowed to Lawrence.

Lawrence smiled "You're on the team," he said. "You'll work under Liam Mercer. Wait till you see our comms setup. Hilde's already started; she's helping Brother Castigliano in the kitchens."

The sound of raised voices echoed from the monastery kitchens.

Hilde pursed her lips. "A good, solid frying pan on the head is what he needs!" She rubbed the tears from her eyes, then glared at one and all, then at Pierre. "You need to clean up!" She pursed her lips. "You need a shave!"

Pierre raised his hands in the air.

"Nag, nag—always nagging." He winked at Lawrence, then followed Hilde meekly toward the kitchen door. "I'm the only one who can keep her under control!" He grinned as Hilde glared at him.

Nick watched in amusement as the squabbling Pierre and Hilde disappeared into the monastery. He frowned. "Where's Liam? I haven't seen him."

"He's on his way." Lawrence clasped Nick's arm. "Nicholas, I'm afraid I have disturbing news."

Nick looked back at Lawrence steadily. "It can't wait?"

Lawrence gazed at him in silence.

"Okay, Lawrence."

"It concerns Gabriele Alessandro and Project Iceman." Lawrence paused. "It concerns Kurt Guber and his mercenaries."

"*Guber* . . . " Nick shook his head. "No . . . you're not saying Guber . . . "

"I'm afraid I am."

Nick looked at Lawrence in shock. "*Dead?*"

"The entire team of Project Iceman." All forty-five scientists—executed, along with all security forces and intelligence operatives at the Lake Vostok base."

"Gabriele Alessandro?"

"Executed."

Nick stared at Lawrence in horror. "And . . . and the . . . the cargo?"

"Now in the biocontainment centers of Mont St. Michel."

Nick stared at Lawrence, his mind reeling. "How many?"

"Over a hundred. A hundred and six, to be precise."

"It's our worst nightmare."

"No, Nicholas," said Lawrence evenly. "Our worst nightmare, regrettably, has only just begun."

Jason woke. He stared groggily around the monastery cloister, then swung his legs out over the iron bed.

Where was he?

Lily. Yesterday's events came rushing back at him like a runaway truck.

He closed his eyes. The pain hit him like a heavy iron weight in the pit of his stomach. He sat paralyzed; his head fell heavily onto his chest.

Lily was dead.

He had watched his own daughter drown. Before his eyes. Helpless. He would never forgive himself . . . or Adrian.

Slowly he walked over to the small porcelain sink and stared blankly at his reflection in the mirror.

He looked haggard, unshaven, and unkempt. His eyes were bloodshot. He picked up his razor, but his fingers shook so hard, it slipped from his hand.

Lily . . .

He closed his eyes.

A loud knocking disturbed the silence.

"Leave me alone," he muttered.

The knocking grew more insistent.

"I said leave me alone!" he shouted.

The door opened. Maxim stood in the doorway

Unable to talk, Jason waved at him to go, tears streaming down his cheeks.

"Go away, Maxim," he rasped.

"The professor is waiting for you," Maxim said. "I need you to come with me, Master Jason. Urgently."

"For God's sake, Maxim!" Jason looked up at him, tears falling down his unshaven cheeks. "Let me grieve in *peace*, man."

Lulu the ridgeback bounded in, making a beeline for Jason. She jumped onto him with her forepaws and licked his face liberally.

"Lulu?" He stared at Maxim, dazed. "How . . . what's Lulu doing here?"

"Jason." Lawrence stood in the doorway, looking fresh as a daisy, in pressed trousers, linen shirt, and cravat. He gestured to Maxim to leave.

Jason stood in his vest and shorts, staring blankly at Lawrence.

"Put on some clothes, Jason."

It wasn't often that Jason heard that tone in Lawrence's voice.

"Lily is alive."

Jason stared at him blankly.

"Get *dressed*," Lawrence said calmly.

Still staring at him, Jason pulled yesterday's shirt over his head, then pulled a pair of sweatpants on over his shorts.

Lawrence took him gently by the arm, and they walked slowly through the corridors, up a winding staircase, past signs reading "Sanatorium," followed by one enthusiastic, slightly overfed Rhodesian ridgeback.

They stopped outside two large glass doors. Lawrence pushed them open, and Jason followed him into a small room off the main corridor to his left.

They stood together outside a small cream-colored door. Slowly Lawrence opened it.

Jason stood in the doorway, frozen.

Nick sat on a chair next to a small iron bed. There, fast asleep, was a pale, ethereal-looking figure swathed in white sheets.

Lily de Vere.

Jason moved toward her in horror.

"Oh, God." He put his hands over his eyes. "She . . . she's . . . "

"It's *all right*, Jason." Nick grasped his arm. "She's breathing."

Jason knelt down by Lily's bedside and placed his hand on her heart. Her chest was rising and falling evenly.

He started to laugh.

"She's . . . she's alive!" He turned to Lawrence. "But how . . . ? What . . . ?"

Lawrence shook his head. "She'll tell you in her own time. All that matters for now is that she get strong."

Lawrence smiled broadly. "You look like you've seen a ghost."

Jason moved toward him, tears streaming down his cheeks, and grasped the spry old man in a bear hug. Then he did the same to Nick.

"Thank you, Lawrence," he whispered. "I'll stay with her."

Lawrence disentangled himself from Jason. "Quite all right, dear boy. We had help—quite a *lot* of help, actually."

Jason was staring down in exhilaration at Lily, stroking her face. He sat down next to her and held her hand.

She stirred.

"It's okay, Lily." He wiped the tears from his cheeks. "You're safe, sweetheart," he whispered. "You're safe."

Slowly Lily's eyes opened. She looked around the room, then back at Jason. She frowned.

"You look *awful*, Dad. When's the last time you *shaved*?"

Jason ran his fingers over his dark stubble and grinned. "Thanks." His grin got broader.

Lily sighed and closed her eyes. "I'm so tired, Daddy," she said.

"You just sleep, sweetheart. You've been through a terrible ordeal. You need your rest."

Lulu sat obediently next to Lily's bed.

"*Lulu.*" Lily smiled as the dog licked her hand.

"Where's Mom?" Lily murmured. "I want Mom. Is she here?"

Jason turned to Nick in horror.

They both said the word in unison. "*Julia!*"

At the Gramercy apartment in New York, Julia raised herself with difficulty off the floor of Lily's room, into a sitting position. She rocked incessantly from side to side, a photo of Lily in her hand, staring blankly at the wall.

Her cell phone rang. She pushed it away.

It rang again. And again. And again.

Groggily she reached out her hand to click it off, then stared at the caller ID.

Jason.

Slowly she picked up the phone.

"Julia . . . Julia, it's me, Jason. Are you okay?"

He closed his eyes.

"She's sobbing," he whispered to Nick.

Lily took the phone from Jason and pressed it to her mouth.

"Mom . . . Mom," she murmured. "Don't cry, Mom. It's me, Lily—I'm alive. I'm *alive.*"

Lily raised herself up slowly in bed. She was still terribly weak. "She's not saying anything, Dad."

"Julia," Jason said quietly but firmly.

"Something happened. Lily's safe. She's here in Alexandria with Lawrence. With me. *Safe*, Julia. At the monastery. She's *alive*, Julia. Our little girl is really *alive*. Julia, you *must* stop crying."

He turned to Lily. "Your mother wants to speak to you again." He held the phone out to Lily.

"Mom . . . I was drowning, Mom. The water went over my head. I couldn't breathe. I was sinking, sinking into terrible blackness. I was so frightened, Mom, so scared.

"I saw a light, Mom. At the end of a tunnel. Those stories they tell us are *true*, Mom."

Lily stopped. She closed her eyes.

"My eyes are so heavy, Dad." The phone slipped from her hand.

Very gently Jason took the phone from her.

"She's very, very weak, Julia, but she's alive," he said. "And she's safe. Julia, did you take tablets? How many?"

He shook his head at Lawrence. "She's groggy, not herself. Said she took three sleeping pills." He put his mouth to the phone.

"We'll call you tomorrow. No, *don't* tell Adrian, Julia.

Weaver's got you on a secure line. I can't explain now, but Adrian has to think Lily's dead. Do you understand me? Jason's voice was almost harsh. He tried to get control over his emotions.

"You're sure."

"She's okay," he mouthed to Nick. "Look, I can't explain now. We'll call you again tomorrow on the secure line. Then we've got to get you out of there. You're in danger."

Jason clicked off the phone. He looked down at Lily, who had fallen asleep. Very gently he traced the outline of her strong cheekbones.

He looked up at Lawrence. "He'll go after Julia next. First we get her out. Then I deal with Adrian."

Lily stirred. She opened her eyes. "Dad," she whispered.

"Go to sleep, darling. You need your rest."

"Dad?" Lily looked panicked. *"Dad!"*

She clasped Jason's hand.

"What is it, Lily?" He stared down at her in alarm.

"Dad, it's my legs. They're *tingling.*"

She looked up at Jason in wonder.

"I can feel my legs."

GRAMERCY PARK
MANHATTAN
NEW YORK

Julia rose to her feet, her hands shaking. She was still clutching Lily's photo in her right hand. Gently she laid it down on the nightstand, then walked over to Lily's closet, opened the door, and buried her head in Lily's vast array of brightly colored tops, sobbing.

She stood a long time, then took a deep breath and walked over to the tall bookcases. Lily was a voracious reader. She skimmed her hand over the hundreds of books. She knew exactly what she was looking for.

There it was. Her hand stopped on a small, dusty pocket-book Bible that Polly had given Lily on her thirteenth birthday.

Julia took it down and, trembling, opened it. There on the flyleaf was inscribed "Lo, I am with you always, even to the end of the age."

Julia walked over to the bed and, falling to her knees, laid her head down on the bedspread.

"Thank you," she whispered, sobbing with joy into the soft cashmere throw.

She was still there two hours later, clutching Lily's small leather-bound Bible in her left hand, fast asleep, a look of utter peace on her face.

CHAPTER TWENTY-NINE

MONASTERY OF ARCHANGELS
ALEXANDRIA, EGYPT

L AWRENCE SAT IN THE SHADE, watching Jason
finish his lunch.

"Tea, Jason?" He held up the teapot. "You really
should partake."

Jason shook his head. "You know I don't touch the stuff."

Lawrence steadily continued to pour tea into three cups.
He gave Jason a knowing smile. "It's never too late for an
old dog to learn new tricks. Try the tea, Jason, my dear boy.
It's Darjeeling—*most* refreshing."

Nick was in a world of his own, his eyes distant.

"Nick, you okay, pal?" Jason asked.

Nick jolted back into the present. "It's okay. Just some
unexpected news," he muttered.

"Nicholas," Lawrence said, "the time has come."

"Jason's going to need more than tea."

"No more bombshells." Jason looked at the tea and
grimaced, then looked at Lawrence. "The time has come
for *what*?"

228

"The time has come to divulge the truth of the De Vere heritage. Nicholas?" Lawrence nodded.

Nick sighed. "Look, Jas, just take a deep breath and listen, okay? When Lawrence first told me, in this very spot, I thought he was stark-raving mad." Nick hesitated. "But he was right. Everything we're about to tell you is true."

"It can't get *worse*," Jason muttered.

Lawrence poured copious amounts of sugar into his tea, then picked up a spoon and stirred vigorously. "Oh, but it can, dear boy." He took a large slurp of tea.

"And unfortunately, it does, so brace yourself." He took another sip of tea, then set the cup down.

"The De Vere family is one of thirteen families that have significant influence in the global business of nations. Through a consortium of power brokers—private investors, defense contractors, renegade factions of NASA, the CIA, the CFR, IMF . . . The list is too long to mention them all."

Lawrence picked up a gingersnap and dunked it in his tea, then brought it to his mouth and ate the entire cookie in one bite. He nodded to Nick.

"Our family has financed these operations for centuries," Nick said, "through our treasury and bullion trading, mining, and investment banking. De Vere Asset Management New York, East Asia . . . De Vere Reserve."

Jason shrugged. "No bombshells there—been in the public arena since I can remember."

"That's exactly what *I* said," Nick replied. He sighed. "Go on, Lawrence."

"These are all subsidiaries of the De Vere family-controlled De Vere Continuation Holdings AG," Lawrence continued quietly, "established in Switzerland in the early part of the twentieth century to protect your family's ownership of its banking empire.

"De Vere Continuation Holdings AG is *not*, however, in the public arena and never has been. I'll ask you precisely the same question that I asked Nicholas over three years ago."

"Ask away," Jason said nonchalantly. He rolled up his shirtsleeves, enjoying the balmy Egyptian winter sun.

"I could get used to this," he muttered, then looked back at Lawrence. "Okay, give it to me."

"Who runs De Vere Continuation Holdings, Jason?"

"Dad. At his death, all power of attorney was transferred to Mother. Satisfied?"

Lawrence St. Cartier sat across the table, silent.

Nick sighed. "De Vere Continuation Holdings was established by our ancestor, Leopold De Vere, in the 1790s. From verified sources, it is confirmed that he also held a secret subterranean vault full of gold beneath his house in Hamburg. In 1885, Ephraim De Vere handed it to his son Rupert, our great-grandfather. In 1934, our paternal grandfather, Julius De Vere, took the reins."

Jason shrugged. "Nothing new so far."

"Our grandfather cornered the world's gold supply. By the time of Julius De Vere's death in 2014, De Vere Holdings held over five percent of the world's gold in its private vaults.

"Well, Julius decided Dad was unfit to take the reins, and before Julius's death, he handed total control to his trustees."

"No, to Mother."

"Your mother was their *token*, Jason," Lawrence interjected. "She had total autonomy on the charitable side. Everything else was clandestine."

Nick frowned. "How much is the family worth, Jas? A rough guess."

"Look, it's common knowledge that we lost over forty percent of our net worth in the 2008 crash. And over half our wealth in the run on the banks in 2018. What's your point?" Jason began to get irritated.

Lawrence looked at him straight in the eye. "The De Vere family's assets amount to forty *trillion* dollars, Jason."

"That's patently *untrue*," Jason snapped. "I'm a business-man, Lawrence. I saw every document connected with our holdings."

"Or did you?" Lawrence looked at Jason grimly. "The De Vere fortune is completely intact. There were no losses. A PR ploy to keep prying eyes at bay."

"Sorry, Jas," Nick added. "It's all true."

"Your family owns more than forty percent of the world-wide bullion market," Lawrence continued. "Operates an aggressive monopoly on the diamond industry, has undis-closed stakes in Russian oil—estimated at over fifty percent. Operates at the center of the illegal global drug and arms trade. And runs the International Security Fund, set up in the 1990s under the auspices of your grandfather, Julius De Vere."

"Your point is . . . ?"

"My point is," Lawrence continued quietly, "that in 2001, the Illuminati, following Julius De Vere's instructions to the letter, orchestrated the raising of a targeted 60.5 trillion from at least three hundred international institutions, in the biggest secretive private-placement financing operation in the world."

Lawrence nodded.

"Its aim was to pay off every leader, policymaker, and

intelligence operative worldwide, for the rest of this century, in pursuit of the group's nefarious goals." He drained the last of his tea. "One of the most significant being your younger brother's dramatic rise to power. He now rules their new world order. And their meticulously planned one-world banking system.

"It is the Illuminati's illegal slush fund. Estimated today by undercover overseas financial investigators at over one hundred trillion dollars, directed on behalf of the Council by Adrian De Vere."

He squinted at a figure coming toward them through the blazing sunlight.

"Weaver!" Lawrence gestured to a chair. "Out from the shadows. What brings you into the land of daylight?"

Dylan Weaver stood grimly looking at Lawrence.

"Dylan?" Lawrence frowned.

Weaver squinted at the sun and rolled his shirtsleeves down over his pasty, freckled skin. "We have a problem."

Lawrence studied Weaver's face. "What kind of a problem?" he asked.

"The *serious* kind, Professor." Weaver pushed his stringy hair away from his pasty face. "It's Lily."

Jason looked up from his salad.

"There's an implant. A biotech implant." Weaver hesitated. "Embedded in her right hand."

Lawrence slowly put his napkin down on the table. "You're absolutely certain?"

"Certain, Professor. It showed up on the sensor X-ray. There's no scar tissue yet, but it's deeply embedded in her right arm. She's had a local anesethic. Father Innocentus is removing it now."

Jason put down his salad fork. "Removing *what*, for God's sake!"

Lawrence rose slowly to his feet.

"A very sophisticated biochip that your brother had embedded in Lily's arm," Dylan replied.

Jason looked back at Lawrence, then to Nick, who sat in silence.

"Can you tell if it's the Mark?" Lawrence asked quietly.

Weaver shook his head. "Not until I examine it more closely. Our intelligence tells us they haven't manufactured it yet."

Lawrence paced up and down in agitation. "Or have they?" he murmured.

Weaver turned and lumbered hurriedly down the monastery roof stairs, followed closely by Nick, then Lawrence.

Jason stood up hastily and followed. "Would someone please tell me in plain English what the hell's going on!" he shouted, striding after them.

"The implant in Lily's right arm is a microchip that Guber and his cronies have been developing," Nick called up from the stairway. "A system of digital enumeration of every human being in the ten-kingdom currency zone, in coordination with the introduction of a one-world currency."

"A virtual fingerprint," Lawrence added.

Jason strode behind him. "Yes. Chessler called the prototype—'the Mark.'"

"Very good, Jason," Lawrence continued. "During the famine of 2024, they conducted a Europe-wide trial in which an EU Social Security number was embedded in a chip on the right wrist. The wearer had access to food stamps, to Europe's vast grain stores and underground seed banks."

He stopped in the middle of the olive grove and turned to Jason.

"Without the chip, they starved. The trial was exactly that: a trial. Since then, they've been developing an extremely sophisticated prototype in the depths of Guber's biotech laboratories. Believe me, Fort Dietrich in the U.S. and Porton Down in the UK are kindergarten compared to them."

"*How* sophisticated?" Jason asked.

"Beyond imagination," Weaver mumbled, "though our intelligence tells us that certain elements are still inactive."

Lawrence gestured to Jason to follow them down the garden path.

"So why on earth would he implant it in Lily's arm?" Jason asked.

Weaver sighed as they walked past the monastery vegetable garden. "Lily's chip also contains a tracking device. Active," he added softly. "They have our coordinates."

Nick turned, his mind reeling. "But it doesn't make *sense*—Adrian already knows *exactly* where she is."

"It's a threat," Lawrence said. "A warning not to interfere" He stopped and stared up at the monastery bell tower. "Everything is going precisely to plan."

"To plan!" Jason exploded. "What do you mean, 'to plan'? *Who* has our coordinates? What the bloody hell are you *talking* about?"

"A forty-eight-digit identification number," Dylan Weaver said softly. "Readable by a chip scanner radio frequency, enabling the carrier to be tracked in real time with the global positioning system. The information is transmitted wirelessly to the Internet. The carrier's vital signs, movements, and location are collected and stored."

"I thought he was an IT guy." Jason gestured to Weaver, who was swiftly disappearing down the corridor.

"Weaver has worked for the past fourteen years for the Directorate of Science and Technology, CIA," Lawrence replied. "One of the masterminds of its golden age of technical innovation—2014 onwards."

"I thought he worked for Microsoft!" Jason shouted after Lawrence. He hurried after him down the corridor to the crypt, then made a sharp left and stepped into an elevator.

"Ah, that's how good our cover is. Reconnaissance satellites, imagery intelligence, measurement and signature intelligence. These past four years, however, Weaver's been the leading mind in our Biotech intelligence."

"Biotech is the next IT," Weaver said.

Our . . . Who's our . . . ? You're not back with the CIA, Lawrence?" Jason stammered as he stepped out of the elevator, followed by Lawrence and then Nick.

"Not the CIA, Jason," Lawrence said quietly. "The *Illuminus*. Those of us from the international intelligence agencies all over the world—MI-Six, the CIA, FSB, MSS, ISI, Mossad—agents who would stop the illuminati from getting a complete stranglehold. The new world order. Their one-world government."

"What the hell's any of this got to do with Lily?"

Jason grasped the steel banister and followed Lawrence and Weaver down the steeply descending stairs. Nick followed at a distance.

"For the past four years, your younger brother and his cohorts have been developing a highly sophisticated human RFID system," said Lawrence. "Continuing from Verichip, Digital Angel, and others in 2010. Their superficial aim:

population control." He turned to Jason. "Their real purpose, however, is infinitely more sinister."

Lawrence continued his descent.

"The story goes that an employee of Applied Digital, VeriChip's parent company, watched emergency crews on TV trying to identify victims of the terrorist attacks on September eleven, 2001."

Jason was working hard to keep pace with the sprightly old man.

"Realized that implanting chips into humans would rapidly access an individual's medical history and identification." Lawrence started down a second flight of stairs. "Similarly after Hurricane Katrina."

Weaver stopped, gasping for breath.

Lawrence continued down, then turned sharp right at the landing. Jason arrived just as Lawrence stopped outside a large set of wooden doors and placed his palm on the scanner. The doors slid open, revealing two steel doors with an iris scanner.

Weaver caught up with them, panting, and placed his eye to the scanner.

The doors opened onto five sprawling laboratories.

Lily was sitting on a surgical gurney. Her forearm was bandaged. "Hey, Dad," she chirped.

"You okay, sweetheart?"

Lily nodded as Jason kissed her tenderly on her forehead. "Fine. They took something out of my arm. Local anasethic's working at the moment."

Jason watched her pointing her feet in a ballet position. She was grinning from ear to ear. *More movement.*

She eased herself off the bed and held on tightly to Nick's

arm. Jason watched in wonder as she took seven steps over to the nearest chair, then sat.

She grinned. *More movement every hour.*

Jason's cell phone rang.

"Yes, Purvis." He frowned. "What do you mean, 'there are no death certificates'? There *have* to be. Yes. Call me back with the results."

He listened, then grinned and said," By the way, Purvis, if you ever find that you've disappeared . . . evacuated—you know, what you clap-happys call the 'Rapture'—please find a way to let me know."

He clicked his phone off, then shook his head and chuckled.

"You *shouldn't*, Daddy." Lily frowned at him.

"Shouldn't what?"

"It's not nice to make fun of Purvis's faith."

Jason frowned at her. "Since when did you care?" He stopped himself. Lily had been through hell and back. She was walking, getting stronger day by day. Who was he to rain on her miracle?

"Okay, sorry, sweetheart. I'll phone Purvis tomorrow."

Lily shook her head at him. She walked over into his arms. "I love you, Daddy. Even if you're a cynical, stubborn old . . . "

"Now, that's quite enough." Jason grinned and kissed her on the head.

Maxim entered discreetly, a serving cloth draped over his arm. Alex walked in after him, talking on his cell phone.

"Miss Lily, your lunch is served," Maxim declared.

"Hey, Alex, Maxim, watch!" Lily smiled brilliantly, let

go of Nick's hand, and walked unsteadily back to the wheelchair.

Maxim clapped his hands in glee.

Alex grinned broadly. "Fantastic!" he said. "By the way, Lils, I'm joining you for lunch. Polly just phoned. She's surviving the New York traffic! Sends you her love."

Lawrence watched as Lily wheeled herself deftly through the doors, followed by Maxim and Alex.

Father Innocentus waited till the laboratory doors closed, then walked toward Lawrence, holding out a minute glowing chip in his gloved hand. "The tracking device *was* operational, Professor. I deactivated it."

Lawrence nodded at Father Innocentus. He handed the chip to Weaver, who grasped it delicately, walked briskly over to a row of digital microscopes, and placed it underneath the largest. Nick and Jason watched in silence.

"This is strange," Weaver mumbled. He zoomed in on the digital image on the monitor. "Guber was the architect of an ultrasophisticated version of an ink bar code based on the primitive Somark version for livestock back in 2009—basically, a 'live' version of the Auschwitz tattoo."

He looked up from the screen. "But this isn't a bar code. It's definitely a chip. It's lodged inside the actual paint of the tattoo."

He waved his hand, and instantly a large virtual screen descended from overhead.

"There, you can see the tracking device." The new RFID chips have a hundred-twenty-eight-bit ROM for storing a unique thirty-eight-digit number, like their predecessor," Weaver muttered.

He moved the digital camera slightly to the left.

"Lily's entire medical history over 120 pages." He scanned through the data.

Her passport details, every passport she's had. Banking accounts . . . "

Nick and Jason stared, incredulous, at the overhead monitor.

"But this . . . " Weaver zoomed in. "*This* is where it gets peculiar—in fact, I've never *seen* anything quite like it before. Embedded is a highly sophisticated computer program."

"But is it the Mark?" asked Nick.

"I can't be certain, but whatever it is, it's only partially operative. It looks like there needs to be a second trigger to activate the more sophisticated level of code."

"The forehead." Pierre's soft voice came from directly behind him.

He held up a hard drive.

"From the Core. A copy of Guber's blueprints. I, uh, *obtained* it before I left Mont St. Michel. An invisible bar code is branded in the bearer's forehead. It's the trigger. It activates a second program. The program's name is Pale Horse."

"So the bar code is the activator of the code." Weaver took the drive from Pierre, pushed it into his computer, then scrolled down the documents until he stopped at a section titled "ACTIVATION CODES."

He zoomed in, riveted to the screen.

"Pierre's right," Weaver said softly. "The chip, when activated, triggers a highly advanced computer program." He slammed the table with his plump fingers. "But *what* does the computer program *do*? I need more *time*."

Lawrence looked grimly at Nick. "You don't *have* time, Dylan. We've received disturbing information. Over a hundred frozen Nephilim bodies were airlifted from below the southern polar entrance by Guber and his military, seventy-two hours ago. They are now housed in the secret bioterror operations base below Mont St. Michel, over a mile beneath the Atlantic."

Dylan gulped. "You're not *serious!*"

"I'm afraid I am. Find it. Find out what the program does." Lawrence heaved a sigh. "You have less than an hour." He turned to Nick. "We take Jason to the archaeological crypts. Dylan, you know where to find us."

"C'mon, Jas." Nick gestured for Jason to follow them back through the glass doors. "This will blow your pragmatic De Vere mind."

Jason followed Lawrence and Nick reluctantly down the corridor. "Haven't you both got better things to do than show me religious artifacts?" he said, looking nervously over his shoulder. "Seeing as how Adrian's SS are about to arrive."

"Oh, we've been *expecting* them, dear boy," Lawrence said matter-of-factly. "Today, next week, next month—they were bound to show up. We've been evacuating the monastery since last July. General Assaf and the Jordanian Royal Guard have everything in hand. Moreover, we have assistance from . . . " He smiled. " . . . other *quarters.*"

He and Nick exchanged a glance.

Two elevator doors opened in front of them. Lawrence beckoned Jason to follow him inside, then pressed a flashing amber button.

As soon as the elevator stopped five floors down, Lawrence stepped out into a flagstoned corridor flanked by six steel doors. Jason followed just as a squad of soldiers marched through the corridors.

Nick smiled in amusement.

"No need for alarm—they're ours," Lawrence said.

Nick nodded. "They're Jordanian special forces. The old guard, loyal to the old king, Jotapa's father. I leave in under an hour to rescue Jotapa and her younger brother, the crown prince."

He walked toward a set of old mahogany doors and placed his palm on the reader. Immediately, steel doors slid open onto a state-of-the-art archaeological laboratory.

Jason stared in disbelief. The chamber was filled with dozens of monks huddled over computers, archiving and studying various images.

"Archaeologists," Lawrence said, walking briskly through the room. "Mathematicians, computer scientists, highly trained specialists. Come with me."

He led the way through a longer corridor, toward a second set of doors guarded by four special services soldiers, who saluted him.

"We call this the Archaeological Crypts."

Jason eyed the eight special forces soldiers holding submachine guns. "What do you keep in here—the *Ark of the Covenant*?"

Lawrence put his eye to the iris scanner, and the doors slid open. In front of them was a long, dimly lit tunnel. Jason followed him along the passageway, which narrowed to about five feet in width.

About twenty yards from the entrance, the passage spread out into a vast vault. Lawrence walked into the center of the vault, where two monks sat at an instrument panel some thirty feet in diameter and reaching almost to the ceiling.

Nick turned to Jason and said, "We keep things at a

constant relative humidity of forty to fifty-five percent, temperature ten to fifteen degrees Celsius."

Twenty-two glass chambers were laid out around the central chamber, reminding Jason of a monstrous wheel with spokes running at a sharp angle from the central vault.

Each of the chambers had colossal steel doors. They looked like giant state-of-the-art operating chambers.

Jason looked around in fascination.

"Number twenty-two is still here?" Lawrence asked.

The monk nodded. He handed Lawrence a steel icon.

"Still don't believe in the supernatural, Jason?" Nick asked.

Jason looked at him skeptically. "Nope."

Nick studied him soberly. "The world as you know it is about to change."

Jason followed Nick and Lawrence past chamber after chamber, peering inside the huge glass-walled rooms as they passed. Each one was empty.

Finally, they stopped, and Lawrence waved the icon over a flashing green light.

The foot–thick steel door slid open. Lawrence waved Jason inside, and the door slid closed immediately.

On what looked like a huge stainless steel operating table lay a monstrous humanoid figure. It appeared to be mummified.

Jason's mouth dropped open.

"Eighteen feet three inches," Lawrence declared. "And no, it's not a fake, not a replica."

Nick took a pair of sterile transparent gloves from a dispenser at his left. "Gabriele Alessandro and I discovered them thirteen months ago, in Iraq. Babel."

Nick waved Jason closer.

"All our work was carried out in a 'clean' laboratory. Mitochondrial DNA was extracted; diagnostic sites in the coding region were PCR amplified, cloned, and sequenced. No indication of contamination. At first, we thought they were mummified. Then, overnight, things . . . " He exchanged a glance with Lawrence. " . . . changed."

Nick pulled the gloves over his hands.

"What was discovered in Iraq and brought here to the monastery," Lawrence continued, "were the remains of twenty-two giants—no more than skeletons. They were bound hand and foot with thick copper bands."

"It was when we *removed* the bands," Nick said, taking a deep breath, "that things became *unusual*. After the first forty-eight hours in our controlled chambers, far from deteriorating, the bodies started to modify, literally before our eyes, into what you see before you."

Jason stared in amazement at the eighteen-foot form before him.

Lawrence nodded. "It looks as if it had been exhumed after only a week in the ground, doesn't it? But its DNA, according to our radiocarbon dating, puts it at over four thousand years old."

Jason walked slowly around the steel table, his brain racing, his thoughts scrambling to make sense of what he was seeing. The creature's head was three times the size of a human's, but the features were definitely human, except for the staring eyes. The iris was a strange pale lilac. Strong chin. Orange hair. The creature looked almost *alive*. Six fingers on each hand, six toes on each foot. A white muslin material lay covering the form's shoulders.

Nick pressed a remote control, and the giant's mouth opened.

Jason stepped back.

"Two parallel rows of teeth," Nick murmured. "Note the incisors."

"What *is* it?"

"A Nephilim," Lawrence said softly.

"Okay, so what's a *Nephilim*, Lawrence—some fancy archaeological term for 'giant'?"

"No," said Nick. "We humans have a double helix; the Nephilim all exhibit a *triple* helix. A Nephilim is a hybrid race, a combination of human and angelic DNA."

Jason rolled his eyes. "You don't expect me to *believe* . . . "

Nick carefully removed the muslin cloth, and Jason paled.

Jutting from the form's shoulders were the skeletal remains of two monstrous wings.

Jason pushed his hand through his cropped hair. *Impossible.*

Lawrence pulled a switch, and the form slowly turned, moving a full 180 degrees to a prone position.

"Look." Lawrence pulled a second set of gloves and handed them to Jason. "You're a confirmed skeptic. Judge for yourself."

As Jason pulled on the gloves, Lawrence laid his hand where the wing protruded from the shoulder.

Jason ran his fingers over the skeleton of the massive wings.

"If you look closely," Nick said, "the joint axes of the skeleton supporting the creature's wing are set perpendicular, enabling it to extend and flex."

Lawrence watched as Jason tugged gently at the wing

bones jutting out from the shoulder. "They really *are* fused together, dear boy. The wings are part of the skeleton."

"What *is* . . . ?" With some difficulty, Jason tore his gaze away from the giant before him. He looked straight at Lawrence. "What *was* it?"

"There were Nephilim," Lawrence said softly. "Giants in the earth, in those days; and also after that, when the sons of God came in unto the daughters of men, and they bare *children* to them, the same *became* mighty men which *were* of old, men of renown. Genesis six: four. I quote directly.

"The Hebrew term 'Nephilim,' correctly translated, Jason, actually does *not* mean 'giants.' The correct Hebrew translation is 'fallen.'" He hesitated. "The *fallen* ones.

"In canonical scripture, it is widely accepted that Lucifer, of the seraphim, rebelled against the Most High. A third of his angelic host rebelled with him. They were banished. Known as the Fallen. Call it legend; call it myth. Whatever you want, but the research of a multitude of ancient scholars before us leads us to the conclusion that some of these fallen angels, alluded to in the apocryphal book of Enoch as 'the Watchers,' to put it quite simply, had intercourse with the daughters of men."

"*Sex*, Jason." Nick grinned. "Some of the fallen angels had sex with some earthly women."

"The product of this cohabitation was a unique hybrid species," Lawrence continued. "A mixture of the seed of the fallen angels and the human women—the Nephilim."

"The women had babies, Jas," Nick said. "Abnormally large infants. Monsters that tore them apart in childbirth. Neither human nor angel. A mixture of DNA. A new species: Nephilim."

Jason's eyes narrowed. "You're saying that this creature is one of *them.*"

Nick nodded. "The presence of a wing skeleton only confirms the fact. The vast majority of Nephilim did not possess wings. These seem to be of a different constitution—of a more sophisticated angelic DNA than the norm."

"Royalty," Lawrence murmured. "Fallen royalty. All our investigation points to the fact that these twenty-two were actually princes of the Fallen."

Nick studied Jason. "Remember Sunday school, Jas. Mother made us go. You dressed up as Daniel in the year-end play. Adrian played the archangel Gabriel."

"Ironic," said Jason.

"Listen with new ears. Daniel ten, the archangel Gabriel talking to Daniel: 'Fear not Daniel,' et cetera, et cetera, but then, in verse thirteen, the King James version states . . . "

Nick turned to Lawrence. "Lawrence, you know it by heart."

Lawrence cleared his throat. " 'But the prince of the kingdom of Persia withstood me one and twenty days: but, lo, Michael, one of the chief princes, came to help me.' Biblical scholars concur that the prince of the kingdom of Persia represents a fallen angelic prince whose territorial governance extends over what was known as the Persian Empire—today's Iran. But the point is, Angelic princes existed. Both good—Michael the Archangel, a chief prince —and the Fallen, such as the prince of Persia. Daniel also references a fallen prince of Grecia.

"The Nephilim are hybrids, the result of a deliberate genetic experiment thousands of years ago. The result of intercourse between the physical, corporeal manifestation of the fallen angelic host and the 'daughters of the Race of Men'—women living at the time of the great flood.

"In Greek mythology, they were known as Titans. In Rome, demigods. The Fallen's aim, quite simply, was to contaminate our human gene pool, mutate our DNA. The great flood, referred to in the tales of Noah and Gilgamesh, quite literally cleansed their lineage from the earth. But their spirits still roamed the earth, seeking embodiment."

Nick held out his hand to Lawrence, who passed him a steel canister that was connected to a small monitor at his right hand. "There is evidence, not in the public domain, that the fallen angels' banishment led to a definitive change in the basic structure of their DNA," Nick explained "The addition of what we term a 'Luciferian gene'—a gene that is found only in the Fallen. A gene our scientists identified in all twenty-two of the Nephilim housed here in our archaeological crypts."

Nick plunged the steel canister into a vat of liquid that seemed to be emitting small flashes of electricity.

Jason watched as Nick held the canister to the creature's neck and pressed a flashing red switch, releasing a thick needle that plunged directly into the creature's neck.

The monitor readings flew into the red.

Nick pulled the needle out of the fleshy neck. "It takes a few minutes to work. Brace yourself."

They watched in silence as suddenly, the creature's huge manacled arms thrashed about wildly.

"It can't be!" Jason gasped.

"Wait."

The creature's top layer of flesh started to smolder, then burn until the entire expanse of its flesh was blistering. Jason watched the creature flailing around, his expression a mixture of absolute terror and fascination.

The creature's skeleton began to disintegrate before their eyes.

A horrifying scream reverberated around the chamber. Then complete silence.

Lying on the operating table was only a handful of what looked like dust.

"You've destroyed it!" Jason uttered in horror.

Nick pulled off his gloves and threw them in the incinerator. "We've destroyed all twenty-two." Nick nodded to two monks who stood in the doorway, and they entered the chamber. The steel doors shut behind them.

Nick followed Jason and Lawrence out of the crypts. They retraced their steps back into the corridor, then turned into the vast underground monastery archives. As they turned a corner, the scent of myrrh cascaded through the corridor.

"We discovered the twenty-two Nephilim remains in a dig near Babel, Iraq," Nick explained. "For the past two years, I've been involved with a team called Project Iceman, working with one Gabriele Alessandro as a consulting archaeologist. Alessandro dedicated his life for the past two decades to tracking down the Nephilim deposited in the earth's crust and destroying them.

"We unearthed twenty-two mummified Nephilim, untouched by humans for thousands of years. We didn't have time to destroy them before Guber's militia arrived, so we had no option but to transport them to the underground chambers here at the monastery."

Jason followed Lawrence past perhaps a hundred monks who were meticulously packaging ancient manuscripts and tomes into enormous steel crates. Lawrence continued walking, then rounded another corner and went through another door.

"Our Secret Archives," he said. "Sister to the Vatican's own. Not for public consumption. Where we keep the church's more 'controversial' artifacts."

Ancient manuscripts, tomes, and scrolls were meticulously stacked on shelves reaching up to the very dome.

"But why *destroy* them?" Jason asked. "Their value to the scientific community must be immeasurable."

"Yes, priceless," said Nick. "Maybe the greatest discovery in the history of our planet. What is not in the public domain is that both the military-industrial complex and the shadow elite have up till now exercised total control over the world's antiquities and archaeological findings. We're talking deep, deep black, Jas—black ops *beyond* deep black.

"They release to the public only the archaeological findings that *they select*. What the general public is totally ignorant of is that they—the shadow elite—are looking for specific artifacts. They sponsored Hitler's explorations for the spear of Longinus—the Spear of Destiny—and the Ark of the Covenant. They control the bona fide men in black since the Roswell crash. Their deep-black program was thrust into another gear in the early 1980s. Today their specialized black-ops teams in the military search Iraq, Afghanistan."

"What are they looking for?"

"Stargates. Searching out coordinates of portals that connect to wormholes—access to parallel dimensions. The keys to time travel. CERN is only the tip of their proverbial iceberg. They are searching for the very secrets of our universe. They've spent billions searching out areas of

Nephilim deposits under the earth's surface." Nick stopped for breath. "Lawrence . . . "

"Because if they can obtain the Nephilim DNA," Lawrence continued, "they can not only create Nephilim *clones*—create a supersoldier Nephilim army—but they also would have the ability to mutate the genomic code of the entire human race.

"Gabriele Alessandro has been tracking down Nephilim on behalf of the Illuminus for the past two decades. Up until now, we have successfully exterminated every trace of the Nephilim race on Earth. Over seven hundred individual creatures, discovered in Iraq, Afghanistan, Israel, Syria, China, and, finally, the Antarctic.

"Until seventy-two hours ago," Lawrence continued, "Adrian De Vere's mercenaries murdered Alessandro and seized the final cargo of a hundred and six Nephilim. What his intention is, we're not completely certain, but I can assure you, it's not benevolent."

"So," Jason said dryly, recovering his composure, "who was that back in the crypts—Goliath?"

Lawrence pursed his lips. "It would serve you well to pay attention, Jason," he said a little too sharply. "In light of what you have just seen *with your own eyes.*" He looked at Jason meaningfully. "You *have* heard of Flavius Josephus?" Lawrence gestured to the twenty volumes on the shelf above him.

Jason nodded. "He wrote—what was it?—*Antiquities of the Jews.*"

"He was a Jewish historian of priestly and royal ancestry who recorded first-century Jewish history. Author of *The War of the Jews* and *The Antiquities of the Jews.* The oldest of these manuscripts dates from the eleventh century. They are all Greek minuscules, and all have been copied by Christian monks."

Lawrence nodded, and Father Innocentus removed a manuscript from the shelves and laid it out before them on the table.

"The text of *Antiquities* that you have in front of you was copied by monks from this very monastery," Lawrence continued. "Josephus wrote his *Antiquities of the Jews* to educate the Roman-Hellenistic world. In it, he recounts the tale of the Watchers.

"Father Innocentus!" Lawrence smiled. "Pray, a brief overview on the Nephilim for our esteemed visitor Mr. De Vere. Time runs down as we speak."

Father Innocentus bowed to Jason, then bent over the manuscripts and read:

"*'For many angels of God accompanied with women, and begat sons that proved unjust, and despisers of all that was good, on account of the confidence they had in their own strength; for the tradition is, that these men did what resembled the acts of those whom the Grecians call giants. But Noah was very uneasy at what they did; and being displeased at their conduct, persuaded them to change their dispositions and their acts for the better: but seeing they did not yield to him, but were slaves to their wicked pleasures, he was afraid they would kill him, together with his wife and children, and those they had married; so he departed out of that land.'*"

"Thank you Father Innocentus. Philo of Alexandria, if you please."

The old monk carefully removed a second manuscript. "This is Philo of Alexandria's commentary on Genesis six, called 'Concerning the Giants.'" He started to read: "*'And when the angels of God saw the daughters of men that they were beautiful, they took unto themselves wives of all of them whom they Chose.'* Those beings, whom other philosophers call demons, Moses usually calls angels; and they are souls hovering in the air. And let no one suppose that what is here stated is a fable."

"Thank you, Father Innocentus." Lawrence walked over to a far shelf and delicately took down *The Book of Enoch*, an ancient Jewish religious work ascribed to Enoch, great-grandfather of Noah.

"Wild, bro." Nick looked over at Jason. "Before Lawrence showed me the documents I thought it was all fables—no substantiation."

"Look . . . " Jason held up his hands. "No offense. I realize this holds great weight with you both, but this religious stuff goes completely over my head."

"Microfilm," Lawrence muttered, ignoring Jason's comment. "Of the eleven Aramaic-language fragments of the Book of Enoch found in cave four of Qumran in 1948. In the care of the Israel Antiquities Authority today:

"*'And it came to pass when the children of men had multiplied that in those days were born unto them beautiful and comely daughters. And the angels, the children of heaven, saw and lusted after them, and said to one another: 'Come, let us choose us wives from among the children of men and beget us children.' They were in all two hundred. [They] took unto themselves wives, and each chose for himself one, and they began to go in unto them and to defile themselves with them, and they taught them charms and enchantments . . . . And they became pregnant, and they bare great giants, whose height was three thousand ells . . . . And there arose much godlessness, and they committed fornication, and they were led astray, and became corrupt in all their ways.'* Chapters six through eight.

"The Codex Sinaiticus, the earliest known version of the Bible. An ancient handwritten copy of the Greek Bible, Alexandrian text-type manuscript, written in the fourth century. Until last year, its contents were divided between four institutions, including St. Catherine's Monastery and the British Library. Now it resides with us, in Alexandria."

Jason sighed.

"Read it yourself," Lawrence urged. "Genesis six, verse four."

Jason studied the verse, then read it aloud: " 'The sons of God came in unto the daughters of men, and they bare *children* to them.' 'Sons of God' could mean anything."

"To an unenlightened reader, to an uneducated mind," Lawrence replied, "yes. But it *doesn't*.

There is, however a train of unenlightened thought that insists the sons of God were the line of Seth. Thousands of us, however, concur with a multitude of scholars of the ancient Hebrew text who conclude that 'sons of God' is clearly used of angels in Job thirty–eight, verse seven. I quote from the original King James Version: *'When the morning stars sang together, and all the sons of God shouted for joy?'* The Septuagint (seventy) here translates 'sons of God' as 'angels of God.' The term translated 'the sons of God' is, in the Hebrew, *B'nai HaElohim*, 'sons of Elohim,' which is a term *consistently* used in the Old Testament for *ange . . .* " He stopped in mid sentence.

General Kareem stood at the entrance of the library,

followed by Alex. Nick exchanged a long look with Lawrence, who nodded.

"The Hercules is fueled and waiting, Your Honor," General Kareem said, then saluted Lawrence.

Nick looked at him in exhilaration.

"Jordan. The regime change has been successful?"

Kareem nodded. "The corrupt Prince Faisal is dead," he said quietly.

"Jotapa's older brother," Nick said to Jason. "He banished her and Jibril, the crown prince, to Saudi Arabia."

"Faisal was executed by his own security forces at dawn," General Kareem continued. "Our Jordanian special forces will commandeer the King Fahd Airport, eight miles northwest of Damman, then move on to the royal palace to capture Arabian prince Mansoor and his thugs, who have been holding Jotapa and her younger brother, Jibril, captive for over three years."

"Alex and I leave now," Nick said. He exchanged a look with Lawrence, who put an arm around his shoulder.

"When will you be back?" Jason asked.

Nick stared at him, strangely silent.

"Three days," Kareem answered. He gave a broad smile, revealing brilliant white teeth. "We'll be in and out before you know it. And the royal princess, Her Highness Jotapa, and Crown Prince Jibril will take their rightful place as rulers of Jordan."

Nick lowered his gaze. He kissed Lawrence on both cheeks, then embraced Jason so tightly he could hardly breathe.

"Hey, hey, it's only three days," Jason said, grinning. "Unless you're planning another disappearing act."

Nick smiled, but his eyes were distant. He and Alex followed General Kareem into a second elevator. Then Nick stopped. He spoke without turning.

"I love you, Jas."

The elevator doors closed as a second elevator opened. Dylan Weaver stood in the doorway.

"What is it, Weaver?" Lawrence asked, walking toward him.

Dylan held up his cell phone. An emergency series from the alert systems sounded. Then it from each of their cell phones.

"It's the DHS handheld alert system," Weaver said. "The alert pops up automatically on every cell phone across the world in the receiving area of the AXIS Ten nations. We can't block it."

Jason followed the professor and Weaver into the elevator. It opened into Weaver's lower laboratories. A second set of emergency alert systems sounded from each of their cell phones and from a large screen transmitting network news.

Adrian's face came onscreen from Normandy.

Weaver grabbed the remote and turned up the volume. They stared silently at the screen.

"We interrupt this broadcast with an emergency announcement from the president of the one-world government, Adrian De Vere."

The camera zoomed in on Adrian, impeccably dressed as ever, today in a subdued blue suit that highlighted his steel blue eyes. He held up his hands benevolently, then turned to the ten leaders who stood somberly in a semicircle around him.

"President Mitchell, President Hong Zou, President

Alexandrov, revered clergy . . . " Adrian looked straight into the camera.

"My fellow citizens of the world . . . " He paused, looking grave.

"I am called as your leader. And each one—mother, father, son, daughter—listening to the sound of my voice is called to give testimony in the sight of the world to our absolute faith that *our future shall belong to the free.*"

He paused again. "Tonight, friends, patriots, we stand faced with a worldwide pandemic. As your leader, your sovereign, your ruler, my mind harks back to the inaugural covenant I pledged to you, my fellow citizens: to protect and to govern—to fulfill this vow to you the people of the world, no matter the cost, the price . . . the sacrifice.

"I have just been informed that at this very moment, unmanned terrorist craft carrying weaponized black plague, flying close to the speed of sound, are headed toward every major city within the footprint of the ten-kingdom axis. This includes Rome." He hesitated.

There was a long silence. Adrian stared down at a screen in front of him, placed his hand over his eyes, then rapidly regained his composure. "Dehli, Chennai, Mumbai, and Lahore . . . " His voice grew soft. " . . . have just been hit." He sighed. "As have Berlin, Hamburg, Zurich, Rome, Paris, Amsterdam, Johannesburg, Nairobi.

"I have been informed that this particular form of weaponized plague is antibiotic resistant. I am talking about the plague, the black death, which wiped out over a third of the entire population of Europe in the year 1348. One of the single most dangerous bioterror weapons in existence.

"The unnamed terrorist faction has informed us that a second wave of Dolphin submarines, with cruise missiles carrying nuclear warheads filled with weaponized *Yersinia pestis*, will be launched at twenty cities across the United States and Russia within the hour."

He hesitated once more as he was handed a document. He held up his hand to the camera, then breathed deeply.

"Forgive me," Adrian whispered. He stared down at the document, his hands trembling. "I have just been informed that Washington, D.C., and Colorado Springs, Colorado, have been hit by the black plague. As has the city of San Francisco." He raised his eyes to the camera. "And Houston, Texas. Cruise missiles have also been launched against Egypt, Syria, China, the Korean peninsula, Russia.

"In the past eighteen minutes, individual nations have been visited with a violent, cataclysmic assault upon their citizens. Each nation represented here in our ten-kingdom axis is at this moment facing the evil onslaught of a treacherous and unrelenting enemy who has brutally attacked the very fabric of our free and democratic society, represented by our One World Confederacy, in an act of terrorism—a most savage and inhuman strike.

"The entire ten-kingdom axis is about to come to a standstill. Let me waste no words.

I have declared a state of emergency, conferring extraordinary powers to myself as president of the one-world superstate. Martial law, emergency law, famine law have been implemented across the world. Curfews are in operation in all member countries. Places of worship, places of gathering, are closed. House-to-house searches are now in operation. All civil aviation flights have been grounded. From London to Hong Kong, New York to Cape Town. I have personally instructed WHO, FEMA, the UN, and the UN Civil Guards throughout the ten-kingdom federation to release immediately to every member of the public óur one-world government's vaccines against *Yersinia pestis*—the antidote to this pandemic. Included in our vaccine is the most sophisticated antibody, with the ability to counteract and reverse every pandemic known to man, including all forms of bubonic and pneumonic plague."

Jason watched in wonder as cameras zoomed in on vast stockpiles of the vaccine, which were being loaded onto ships, jumbo military transport planes, and railcars.

"As you can see on your television and computer screens," Adrian continued, "the vaccine is, at this very moment, being released to every corner of the world. Vaccine depots already exist in every member nation.

"Carefully selected deployed and mission-critical personnel will receive a yellow card with instructions to report to your quarantine precinct. These have been allocated to public health workers, inpatient health-care providers, outpatient and home health providers, all first responders—paramedics, firefighters, and police—manufacturers of pandemic vaccines and antivirals, pregnant women, and children under age three.

"Stage two is the allocation of orange cards to the general public. Let me emphasize, there is enough vaccine for every human being in the ten-kingdom population zones."

CHAPTER THIRTY

BUNKER
MONT ST. MICHEL
NORMANDY

ADRIAN PAUSED and let his words sink in.

"I also must emphasize that this vaccine not only protects those exposed to the disease but also reverses the disease's effects. Let me repeat, there is enough vaccine for every citizen within the ten-kingdom axis. I have been asked by our military to inform you that martial law is now in place. All resisters will be placed under arrest.

"On reporting to your quarantine precinct, you will receive in your right arm a chip containing the vaccine. However, it can be activated only by the activation of a digital bar code on the forehead.

"I end this communiqué with the words of a great president and one of the great warriors in the annals of history, President Dwight D. Eisenhower. We sense at this apex of history, with all our faculties, that although colossal forces of both good and evil are massed and armed and opposed as rarely before in our planet's history, to all the peoples of the world I once more give expression to the new world order's prayerful and continuing aspiration: My prayer is, in the great Mr. Eisenhower's words, 'that peoples of all faiths, all races, all nations, may have their great human needs satisfied; that those now denied opportunity shall come to enjoy it to the full; that all who yearn for freedom may experience its spiritual blessings; that those who have freedom will understand, also, its heavy responsibilities; that all who are insensitive to the needs of others will learn charity; that the scourges of poverty, disease, and ignorance will be made to disappear from the earth; and that, in the goodness of time, all peoples will come to live together in a peace guaranteed by the binding force of mutual respect and love.'

"Never have we needed faith as much as in this moment.

"I remain your leader, Adrian De Vere."

Adrian watched the red light of the camera switch off. He removed his suit jacket and held it out to Maxim, who took it and hung it neatly. Adrian held out his arm, and Maxim removed his cufflinks, first from the right sleeve, then from the left.

"Pass me the 'clean' demarcated list," Adrian said to Kurt Guber.

"Thanks, Maxim." Adrian smiled. "Went well?"

"Master Adrian," Maxim declared, "you have a remarkable gift. Almost *hypnotic.*"

Chastenay raised his eyebrows. "Bravo!"

"Some tea or mineral water, Master Adrian?"

Adrian nodded. "Bring it down into the bunker library, Maxim. And bring my cigars. Damn bunker. There's no plague within a thousand miles of Normandy, but we must play the part. You've moved my wardrobe?"

Maxim bowed. "Of course, Master Adrian Your entire walk-in wardrobe is now at your disposal in the bunker. All suits, shirts, and ties pressed."

"Mother trained you well."

"Thank you, Master Adrian."

BUNKER LIBRARY
MONT ST. MICHEL
NORMANDY

Three senior generals appeared on a large conference screen.

Maxim placed the tray of tea and mineral water on the cherrywood library table, then walked over to the library bar and refilled the cigar box, depositing one of Dylan Weaver's sophisticated nano audio listening devices into the lid.

"General, Operation Pale Horse is activated. We have reason to believe from our intelligence sources that the evacuation of Christians will occur at any moment."

Adrian paced the floor, hands behind his back.

"Generals, activate the Blacklist. All dissidents, constitutionalists, patriots, Christians, gun owners who refuse to relinquish their Second Amendment rights . . . "

He beckoned to Maxim, who removed the plastic wrapping from Adrian's favorite cigar brand. Adrian smiled.

"Christians—yes, we are aware. The Mark is ineffective on them if they wear the seal, unless they recant. Unmarked jets will transport them to the internment camps."

Adrian took the cigar from Maxim and placed it in his mouth. Maxim picked up a silver lighter.

Adrian winked at him. *Just a minute*, he mouthed.

"Over half a million surveillance drones in the skies over the ten-kingdom axis. By Thursday, after the vaccination program kicks in, we'll have the beginnings of three billion totally unaware genetic supersoldiers."

He drew in the cigar smoke and exhaled, then flicked the screen off. He turned to Guber.

"Now we wait. Keep me informed. I want to know the second the first Christian disappears. Hopefully, our intelligence is correct and we arrest the majority before they get "'raptured.'"

⤳

MONASTERY OF ARCHANGELS
ALEXANDRIA, EGYPT

Dylan Weaver clicked the audio feed off and sat down, hunched over his digital microscope.

"It's *exactly* what Chessler said they would do," Jason muttered. "It's their false flag: people receive the chip; the vaccine is released."

Jason froze. "Nick—what about Nick and Alex? They're in the air."

Lawrence raised his hand. "Military aircraft. They have clearance. They're perfectly safe. General Kareem is in possession of our own vaccine. But I can assure you, Jason, that Saudi Arabia has been deliberately kept clean. As has Adrian's headquarters. Also Iraq and Israel. Adrian and Chessler will be extremely discerning as to who is destroyed at their own convenience and who remains untouched."

Jason frowned. "He said Egypt had been hit."

Lawrence nodded. "We're perfectly safe indoors. Our radioactive containment seals were activated over an hour ago. Everyone is evacuating underground."

Pierre stood quietly behind them. "Received from Maxim three minutes ago." He handed a nano to Dylan Weaver, who inserted it into his computer. He tapped the screen with a stylus, and a schematic appeared.

"Adrian's secret bioterror operations base below Mont St. Michel," Pierre said. Over a mile beneath the Atlantic. Military patrols 'round the clock. Dogs trained to kill. Level-three containment laboratories. Staff of over four hundred foreign forensic toxicologists and microbiologists—North Korean, Russian, Chinese.

"Biosafety level-three containment—one mile down."

The slide changed to a level filled with caged primates and dogs.

"Animals to test the germs," Pierre explained.

Another slide showed thousands of vials sealed in lead containers. "Anthrax, the Marburg virus, botilinum toxin, ebola . . . " He paused. "And the black plague.

"Where Kurt Guber, Adrian's autocratic director of security operations, reigns supreme."

Lawrence's eyes grew hard. "You mean Kester von Slagel. Guber is merely an eager pawn in his master's bejeweled hands. Rings on every finger," Lawrence muttered. "Crucifixes. He is obsessed with Earth's 'bling.' I'm surprised he can lift a finger with all that weight."

Pierre grinned. "He doesn't, Professor. Four hundred scientists under Guber lift it for him.

"Having Maxim in the bunker has been an absolute stroke of genius," Pierre continued. "Here are his latest findings. Guber based his initial work on 'Dr Death'— Wouter Basson, former head of South Africa's secret chemical and biological warfare project. It was called 'Project Coast.'

"Von Slagel's scientists worked on the genetic modification of *Clostridium perfringens* in an attempt to isolate the gene responsible for the production of epsilon toxin.

"The Pentagon's most prestigious scientific advisory panel transferred their allegiance from the U.S. to Adrian and the one-world government during the DARPA debacle. Guber received brilliant but frustrated former DARPA scientists with open arms. Soon under Guber's iron control, the creators of supersoldiers—enhanced warriors with superhuman physiological and cognitive abilities—now worked for Guber, who in turn worked for Adrian. Maxim is convinced that Guber intends to create the ultimate weapon. Operation Pale Horse is the equivalent of their own genetic bomb."

'What's your take on it, Weaver? asked Jason.

Dylan sat frozen, staring through the microscope at the chip.

Lawrence walked up behind him. Dylan slowly swung his chair around to face Lawrence.

"What is it, Dylan?" Lawrence whispered.

"Guber's implant." He stared at Lawrence. "The Mark —the section of the chip I couldn't decode. I've deciphered the formulas from the blueprints Maxim transmitted."

He pushed his chair in. "It's a masked genetic marker."

Weaver sat at the laptop, hunched over the screen, watching as the data downloaded in code.

"The vaccination *does* work against *Y. pestis*. But as soon as a human being receives the chip, instantly a DNA rewriting program is activated."

"In plain English, Dylan," said Jason.

"A man or woman will receive the vaccine as a subcutaneous injection in their arm, which includes a minute chip. The vaccine is activated only by a second chip, injected into the forehead. The chip in their forehead triggers the Pale Horse program." Lawrence sighed.

Dylan looked up from the digital microscope, his plump fingers trembling.

"The vaccine chip in the forehead is programmed to add another gene," he whispered, "into the genotype of every human who accepts the Mark."

"You're sure?" Lawrence whispered.

Weaver nodded, ashen. "The Pale Horse program is a genetic rewriting program."

Jason frowned. "What's a genetic rewriting program?"

"Transgenic organisms, a subset of GMOs, are organisms with inserted DNA that originated in a different species. This initiates intracellular changes."

Weaver looked up. "Basically, the vaccine's program will rewrite the human genomic code when activated. It alters our basic human source code."

Lawrence and Father Innocentus looked at each other.

"They're injecting every man and woman who receives the vaccine with the chip. Every human being will accept the Mark," Father Innocentus said in his broken English. "No one wants to die."

Lawrence put his hand gently on Father Innocentus's arm.

"What type of gene is it programmed to add?" Lawrence's voice was barely audible.

Dylan Weaver gulped. "It's adding a nonhuman gene, Professor. Not animal. Not fully human."

Pierre walked back into the room, holding a document. "Maxim's final transmission. Research from Hadassah Hospital, Jerusalem. It seems that five of their leading genetic scientists were working in tandem with Guber's DNA specialists on the DNA rewriting program to be activated upon subjects' receiving the vaccine. The geneticists were totally ignorant of the end user."

"And?" Lawrence asked.

"They were murdered, the research laboratories destroyed."

Dylan Weaver held out his hand to Pierre, who handed him the documents. He studied the papers silently.

"It's everything we dreaded, and more, Professor," he muttered. "Guber's geneticists isolated the fallen Nephilim gene. They obtained the genetic material from the Nephilim. From Antarctica." He looked up at Lawrence, profoundly shaken.

"The gene that Pale Horse is programmed to add *is* the Nephilim gene."

He held out the documents to Lawrence, who took them and read, pacing up and down the laboratory.

"Lucifer and the fallen angels failed the first time. Their genetic evil was destroyed by Earth's great flood," Lawrence murmured. "Now they try again."

He handed the documents back to Dylan.

"A gene that first mutated mankind's DNA thousands of

years ago," Lawrence said softly. "The extra gene in the Mark is a hybrid of fallen angels' and human beings' DNA. A horrifying mutation."

He turned to Jason, who watched soberly.

"Adrian's intention, Jason, is to use the pandemic to vaccinate every man, woman, boy, and girl on Earth with their so-called vaccine. They *are* the terrorists. Guber and his scientists created the pandemic deliberately—their intention, to activate the Mark system globally. Their intent is not only malevolent, it is immoral. They are supercriminals."

"*Everyone's* going to take the Mark." Pierre looked up at Weaver, Jason, and Lawrence.

Jason stared at Lawrence, stunned. "You're talking supersoldiers."

"Worse, far worse, Jason. Every human being who receives the vaccine will have their human genomic source code mutated forever, altered by the insertion of DNA belonging to the fallen angelic host." Lawrence took a deep breath. "I'm talking billions of demonized human beings.

"'*And he [the Beast] shall make all, both little and great, rich and poor, freemen and slaves, to receive a mark on their right hands, or on their foreheads, and that none might buy or sell, unless he carried this mark, which was the beast's name, or the number that stands for his name,*'" Lawrence muttered. "'*Here is wisdom; he that has understanding, let him count the number of the beast. For it is the number of a man: and the number of him is six hundred and sixty-six.*'"

His voice trailed off.

"Eons ago," Lawrence said softly, "their attempt to mutate the human race failed. This time it will be the total annihilation of the human race as we know it. It is truly the Mark of the monsters.

The Mark of the Fallen."

He turned to Jason, deeply shaken.

"It is the *Mark of the Beast*."

CHAPTER THIRTY-ONE

DAMMAN, SAUDI ARABIA

ALEX STARED UP AT the mile-long, high-walled compound of monolithic buildings. The Jordanian soldiers moved rapidly up the marble walkway toward a massive forty-foot gilt door, outside the foyer of the palace. The door was riddled with bullet holes, open and swinging at a strange angle.

A soldier waved the others back as six of the Jordanian security forces entered, submachine guns raised. Alex and Nick followed at a distance. General Kareem waved them inside the palace.

The palace's marble floors were stained with blood. At least eight of Mansoor's private army lay dead on the floor, brutally executed. The Jordanians dragged the unconscious bodies out of sight as General Kareem, Safwat's brother, submachine gun at the ready, moved forward through the empty corridors, followed by Nick, with Alex close behind.

"It's deserted," said Nick.

"Someone beat us to it," General Kareem replied. "There has been a massacre."

Nick gazed at him in horror. "Jotapa!"

The party continued to move in silence under forty-foot ceilings, past shattered gilt marble pillars, down seemingly unending bloody corridors, until they reached a smaller grouping of palaces. They stopped outside a soaring silver door. General Kareem nodded and gestured to four swarthy men wearing ghutrah headdresses and black uniforms, lying dead on the marble floor. Part of Mansoor's brutal private army.

Kareem nodded, and his soldiers broke through the doors, submachine guns raised.

A bearded youth of about twenty, with long, matted black hair, stood, machine pistol raised, violent hatred in his eyes.

"Don't shoot!" General Kareem shouted at his forces. *"Don't shoot!"*

He stood opposite the fierce youth. The youth's finger rested on the trigger, his hands shaking violently.

General Kareem gazed at the young man in horror. His face was bloodied and bruised, his shoulder bandaged with an old piece of cloth. Kareem laid his gun carefully on the floor, took a step forward, and held out his hand to the youth.

"I'll shoot!" shouted the youth, tears streaming down his face. "If you touch me or her, I'll blow your head off!"

"You don't have to, Your Majesty." General Kareem dropped to one knee, his voice even. "Your brother King Faisal is dead. I am General Ahmed Kareem of the Jordanian forces—Safwat's brother."

"Safwat?" Trembling uncontrollably, Jibril stared at General Kareem, dazed.

"Jordan awaits its new king." The battle-worn general

smiled up at Jibril compassionately, tears in his eyes. "We have come to take you and the princess home."

Jibril turned toward a canopied bed in the far corner of the room. Nick stood in the doorway, following Jibril's line of sight. A slight figure lay under bedclothes, stirring from a deep drugged sleep.

Jibril dropped the machine pistol and, running to the bedside, grasped the figure's arms and pulled her toward him until she sat groggily upright in the four-poster bed, staring at him in bewilderment.

Nick ran over and clasped the frail figure in his arms. She stared up at him, speechless with joy, tears streaming down her bruised and bloodied cheeks.

It was Jotapa.

∽

ALEX'S APARTMENT
MEATPACKING DISTRICT, NEW YORK
FOUR A.M.

Polly sat bolt upright in bed, her heart pounding. This was it—she sensed it with all her being.

Pulling on her tracksuit pants, she padded over to the window in bare feet and stared down ten floors, through the blinds, at the enormous black military vans drawing up outside the apartment building. She ran back to the bedside table in semidarkness and switched on the light. *Nothing.*

She fumbled for her cell phone, then hit Alex's number. The circuit was dead. She picked up the landline. There was a crackling sound, then a loud click, and the line went dead.

She slammed down the receiver, then ran over to the window, staring up at the black helicopters circling overhead. "They," whoever they were, were jamming the frequencies. A black-operations mission.

She watched as a team of black-helmeted soldiers dragged two men from the neighboring tenement block, and a second team crashed through the entrance to her building.

Polly ran to Alex's desk, pulled out a pad of paper, and desperately started writing. The thud of approaching boots got louder. She kept writing, then stuffed the paper in an envelope and ran through to Alex's study, where she hid it inside a large, dog-eared Roget's Thesaurus—a gift from his beloved maternal grandfather when he was just twelve. Then she ran in bare feet back to the bedroom, put on the nearest pair of sneakers, grasped her tracksuit top, and pulled it over her head. Then she grabbed her pocket Bible and taped it to the back of her neck.

She tried the cell phone once more. *Still dead.*

There was a loud bang as the front door to the apartment swung violently open. A soldier burst through the bedroom door, pointing his submachine gun straight at her.

"Polly Mitchell," he said in a thick accent that sounded Slavic. "You are under arrest for insurgency."

"I'm a UK citizen," she said softly.

The soldier thrust a sheaf of papers at her. "Extradition papers. You'll be tried under U.S. law."

"Tried for *what?*"

Polly stared directly into the soldier's eyes. He faltered momentarily.

"For treason. Against the Constitution. You are on Blacklist. You are terrorist."

He grinned. "We are not American soldier. We don't care." He pushed her in the chest with the butt of the submachine gun and, with a lecherous laugh, waved her toward the door with the gun barrel.

Slowly Polly walked out of the apartment, her hands raised above her head. The door slammed behind her.

⮌

MONASTERY OF ARCHANGELS
ALEXANDRIA, EGYPT

Pierre laid out a copy of Guber's pandemic map.

"The real pandemic will affect the entire Midwest and South: Kansas and Missouri up to Iowa and down to Alabama. California and New York have been kept clean. Too many new world order lackeys there.

"They've been bringing body bags in from out of state since dawn to make it look like New York's been hit with the plague," he continued. "Moscow is hit. Europe all the way from Norway to Greece. Normandy is clean, naturally. And London—they can't compromise the square mile. They plan to exterminate all resisters under the guise of the pandemic."

Pierre looked over at Jason and sighed. "I don't know how to say this nicely . . . " He hesitated and took a deep breath.

"Just say it, Pierre," Lawrence said.

Pierre turned to Jason, grim faced. "It's Miss Julia," he said softly. "She's on the Red List. She's been issued a yellow card."

"Walk with me, Jason," Lawrence said. He took Jason's

arm and walked out of a small door into the monastery corridors.

They walked past the monastic chambers. Lawrence stopped in mid step and looked Jason directly in the eye.

"Julia's in great danger," he said. "Jason, I need you to listen very carefully."

Jason nodded.

"There are at least four hundred concentration camps—quietly modified facilities—all across the United States. They've been springing up for over two decades. Until four years ago, they were seemingly devoid of activity, yet they each had barbed wire-topped fencing, helicopter wind socks, and major highways and railroad transport facilities adjacent to the sites.

"Over thirty foreign military bases under the United Nations flag are already set up in the U.S., all with the approval of special appointees in high federal positions. The camps are set up for dissenters who will not go along with the new world order. The 'resisters' are gun owners who refuse to give up their weapons; the 'dissidents' are Christians, patriots, and constitutionalists."

"You're *kidding* me, Lawrence!" Jason looked at Lawrence skeptically. "It's been conspiracy theory for years. You're sounding like *Alex*, for God's sake."

Lawrence slowly shook his head. "This is not conspiracy theory, my boy. It's highly classified information, verified by intelligence services—CIA, MI-Six, FSB, and the Mossad, to name a few."

He gave Jason a steely look.

"All across the world. These bases are already manned with over *one million* troops from Russia, Poland, Germany,

Belgium, Turkey, Great Britain, Nicaragua, and a number of Asian countries. Unlike our own troops, they have no qualms about firing on U.S. citizens. They've been preparing for over a decade. As far back as March of 2012, Homeland Security purchased four hundred fifty million rounds of forty-caliber hollow-point bullets, followed by a second order for a further seven hundred fifty million rounds the same year. Why would the U.S. government need over a billion rounds of ammunition?"

"Preparing for economic collapse . . . riots." Jason shrugged. "Twenty twelve was a bad year for the USA."

"No, Jason. They've been waiting for a moment in time. *This* moment. Our intelligence confirms that the Blacklist was deployed six hours ago.

"We were too late for Polly Mitchell. Julia's on the Red List of dissenters. She'll be picked up next. The only reason she's still alive is because Chessler has her under close surveillance."

"Julia?" Jason gasped. "Julia's completely *harmless*! Why would she be on any list?"

"Adrian's going to make her take the Mark, Jason. She'll be very useful to them if she turns."

"Oh, God." Jason paled. "You're serious about this, aren't you?"

"It's a matter of life and death. You have to talk to her. Convince her. Our people can pick her up at dawn. We'll send General Assaf. He's our best."

"*I'll* do it." Jason's jaw set. "*I'll* go."

Lawrence shook his head. "Too dangerous." He smiled gently at Jason. "New York, I mean." He hesitated. "Adrian wants you dead. You're on the Blacklist, my boy."

Jason's face set. "I fetch Julia myself. It's my condition. How much time have I got?"

Lawrence sighed. He looked at Jason steadily. It was pointless to argue.

"Enough," Lawrence said softly. "You have enough time. In our underground hangars we have seven fully working equivalents of the X-51A WaveRider jet that Boeing eventually threw in the towel on. Our prototypes fly six times faster than the speed of sound, on takeoff—you'll be in New York in under an hour and a half."

He nodded toward the state-of-the-art comm system.

"Phone Julia."

"It's secure?"

Lawrence nodded again.

"By the way, what do mean, you were *too late* for Polly Mitchell?"

"She's been arrested, Jason."

Jason punched in Julia's number. Her cell phone was dead.

"All cells will be down. Try the old landline. It'll be the last to go."

Jason dialed again.

"Julia . . . Yes. It's me." There was a long silence. "It's Jason."

Polly stumbled down the steps of the sixty-four-passenger Chinook CH-47 helicopter, onto the airfield tarmac.

She was stopped by the butt of a submachine gun shoved against her chest, and her leg was shackled to the prisoner in front of her. She stared up at the unmarked, windowless Boeing 747 waiting on the tarmac, then looked around.

Her surroundings looked like Vermont. *Impossible.* Weak from exhaustion, fear, and hunger, she rubbed her eyes.

The line ahead of her started to move. She stumbled up the steps of the 747 and into the cabin, where her hands and feet were chained to a specially designed harness.

She watched as soldiers picked up bottles of water from a huge pile near the cockpit.

"Water . . . please," a prisoner behind her whispered.

A cruel laugh came from the soldier in front of her. He poured the water down his throat, then wiped his mouth on his sleeve.

He shook his head at a soldier about to hand out bottles to the prisoners. "No water." He pointed to his throat and made a slashing gesture. His intent was clear: no need to waste water on those soon to be executed.

TOWN HOUSE
GRAMERCY PARK
NEW YORK CITY

"Oh, Jason, thank God Lily's *safe*," Julia said agitatedly over the landline. "I'm so glad you're all safe. Yesterday I was having drinks with my clients at the Gramercy Park Hotel . . . "

Julia sneaked a quick look through the curtain, to the Gramercy Hotel across the street, which was deserted apart from rows of black unmarked military vans.

"Today there are military trucks *every*where." She peered through the curtain again. "They're going zip code by zip code. It's as though it had been planned for months." Her voice faltered.

"Jason," she whispered. "Jason, I see body bags."

Julia walked over to the small bar near the window, holding the phone and cord in her left hand, and, with trembling fingers, picked up a half drunk bottle of pinot grigio.

"Oh, my God, they're *body bags*, Jason—in *New York*! No one's allowed on the streets without authorization, or they're arrested. The only information we've been given is 'plague breakout.' I'm *terrified*!"

Julia poured the white wine shakily into a water glass. She put the bottle back down and picked up the glass. "There are soldiers in masks everywhere, and, Jason, it's . . . it's . . . " She took several sips of wine, then took a deep breath, tears streaming down her cheeks. "It's Polly . . . " She sobbed into the landline.

"Polly's *dead*, Jason. Her landlord said she was rushed to the precinct quarantine hospital, sick. Soldiers came around last night, cordoned off her flat. Said she was infected. With bubonic plague." Julia garbled, "I can't get hold of Jontil Purvis—her phone's continually off the hook. There are rumors they're taking over the cellular system for military use only. Everyone's back to using landlines. And who knows how long *they'll* be working."

"Julia, calm *down*," Jason said. "I spoke to Purvis yesterday. She was fine."

Julia's hands shook violently. She downed the remains of the wine, placed the glass on a side table, and clicked on the television. The screen was black except for the words "Emergency Channel" in white.

"I *can't* calm down," she sobbed into the phone. "You're safe in damned Alexandria with Uncle Lawrence. It's fine for *you* to tell me to calm *down!*"

There was a long silence.

"Is . . . is the plague in Egypt?"

"Yes, Julia. The plague is in Egypt. But the monastery is completely protected. Sealed. Everyone's safe. *Lily* is safe." He sighed.

"Julia, listen to me," Jason said, his voice very soft. "You *have* to listen very carefully to what I'm going to tell you. There's a vaccination. A vaccination that the military intends to make you and every person in New York take. Adrian's second message goes to air worldwide in approximately sixty seconds." He checked his watch.

"Any moment now. Turn on the TV. The Emergency channel."

"It's on." Julia stared blankly at the television screen. It's black. Just says 'emergency channel.'"

She frowned as the television crackled to life. Staring at her from the screen was Adrian De Vere.

DAMMAN
SAUDI ARABIA

"Faisal is dead?" Jotapa whispered, clinging tightly to Nick. "Really *dead*?"

Nick nodded. "Assassinated by his own security detail."

Jotapa wiped away a tear from her cheek. "For all his wickedness, he was my half brother."

"We need to get Polly. We have to hurry," Alex said in a low voice to Nick.

Nick looked deeply into Jotapa's eyes. She nodded.

"I sense it, also."

She turned to look at her younger brother, Jibril. He had grown into a man these past three years in exile. He was now nineteen, over six feet tall, and his thick, dark-brown hair, now matted, fell to the nape of his neck. But it was in his eyes that she saw the change. The gentle, clear gaze now held a steely anger. She removed her arms from around Nick's waist and slowly walked over to where Jibril stood.

"Jibril, my brother, I will not be returning with you to Petra," she said. "You will return to Jordan with General Kareem."

Jibril shook his head vehemently. "I will not go without you, beloved sister."

Tears streamed down Jotapa's face as she held Jibril's bruised face in her hands. "You are now the rightful king of Jordan, Jibril," she whispered. "You will serve our people as Papa did. And as did King Aretas, our ancestor. You will be a good and righteous king."

Alex frowned.

"It's always been this way, Alex," Nick said quietly. "You and Jibril go back to Alexandria on your own. Jotapa and I . . . " Tears filled his eyes. "We . . . we have a long-standing appointment."

Jibril stood perfectly still, watching Jotapa. Finally, he spoke softly.

"It is to do with your Christ." He grasped her arm fiercely. "You have been waiting for Him every day, and now you think He is coming to *fetch* you."

Jotapa raised her strong, regal features to Jibril. "I will not lie to you, beloved brother. Our ancestor King Aretas and my namesake, his daughter Jotapa, followed the Hebrew. I, no less than they, will live for Him and die if I have to."

"You believe He is coming to take you with Him." Jibril grasped Jotapa's arm so tightly it stung.

Tears streaming down her cheeks, she nodded. "Yes, He is coming for us, Jibril. And He will come for you if only you can receive Him."

Jibril loosed Jotapa's arm and stepped back. "I cannot." His eyes flashed with anger. "I will *not believe* in what I cannot see and touch. You know this to be my nature of old, sister."

Jotapa nodded. "Then for now it is so, beloved younger brother. But one day you, too, will serve the Hebrew. And protect His people."

Alex looked strangely at Nick. "You *are* coming back with us?"

Nick gazed into Alex's eyes. "I can't."

Alex threw his backpack onto the bed. "You think I don't know what you're talking about!" He flung up his hands in frustration.

"I got it at the airport from Polly. Polly, you, Jotapa. I *know* what you're thinking, Nick. You're talking about the Rapture." He glared at Nick. "You all *honestly* believe that Jesus Christ is just going to walk through that door and transport you to another dimension."

Alex was seething with anger. "What are you both going to do?" he challenged Nick. "Stay in Damman until He comes to fetch you?" He rolled his eyes at the ceiling. "You're both deluded!"

He pressed a key on his phone—the speed dial to Polly's

cell phone. The strange jamming noise was still there. He frowned. He phoned the landline to his apartment. It rang and rang. He clicked it off in frustration.

"Come on, Jibril," he said. "We've a plane to catch."

A Slavic-looking guard with cropped hair shoved Polly and three other prisoners into a large, dank cell that held another thirty women dressed in orange uniforms. A stocky woman in military dress roughly stripped Polly completely naked as the guard watched from the far corner of the cell. Then the woman grabbed Polly's ears and held her head still as a second Russian woman put a dirty electric razor to Polly's head.

Blood wet the once-beautiful glossy blond hair as it fell in long, thick, locks onto the concrete floor.

Polly cowered in the corner, naked, her skull shaven and bloody, tears streaming down her face. The Russian woman flung a set of filthy orange overalls at her.

Polly pulled on the overalls, desperately trying to stop the sobs welling up in her throat.

Another guard appeared in the doorway. He passed a stack of documents with a crimson seal to the Russian, who gave a gumtoothedgrin.

Five minutes later, Polly and the other women in the holding cell were blindfolded, then propelled down unending dank corridors until they reached an enormous brightly lit warehouse. The blindfolds were ripped from their heads.

Polly winced at the blinding fluorescent lights hanging from the steel rafters above her. Her eyes gradually focused on a line of steel boxcars in front of her.

She looked around the warehouse. It was crammed with hundreds of women, all with shaven heads and wearing orange uniforms. She listened intently. Many of them were singing softly. The melody was familiar, but she couldn't quite make out the words. She was sure it was an old hymn.

The militia captain was holding something up in the air, but Polly wasn't close enough to make it out. She obediently followed the queue of women in front of her and walked past the militia captain for inspection. Her whole body trembled violently as she recognized the object that the soldier was holding up.

It was a woman's shaved head. Blood still ran from it, as though it had just been severed. Polly retched as the woman in front of her collapsed to the ground. Instantly, two uniformed women with coarse features grabbed the fallen woman and dragged her toward one of the boxcars.

Polly exchanged a look with an elderly woman behind her, who was singing softly. She listened intently to the words.

"When I survey the wondrous cross
On which the Prince of glory died
My richest gain I count as loss
And pour contempt on all my pride."

The woman squeezed her hand. "He is very near," she whispered. "Their chains cannot hold Him."

Polly looked at her in wonder. "You're a *believer?*"

The elderly woman's face radiated a deep peace. "Yes," she whispered. She smiled tenderly at Polly. "I believe."

Tears streamed down Polly's face as she listened intently. Hundreds of women had now joined in singing the old hymn. Polly began to sing along, tears streaming down her cheeks.

"Forbid it, Lord, that I should boast,
Save in the death of Christ my God . . . "

"No singing!" a guard yelled.

A beautiful, regal-faced woman in her forties spat at the women. "Yes, shut up with your caterwauling! Shut *up!*"

She turned to the guards. "They're singing about their *God*," she hissed. "But *their* God will not save them," she spat." There *is* no God!"

"Let them sing . . . " The militia captain marched in. "Let them sing to *nothing*." He laughed loudly. "Let them sing to the *air*."

He gestured dramatically.

"In a few minutes, they will all be *dead*."

The Russian woman handed a set of papers to a short, stocky soldier with heavy Slavic features and a shaven head. He took the papers, glanced through them, then grinned lecherously.

"You there!" he shouted. "No one should be as pretty as she."

An ugly Slav woman pointed her whip straight at Polly. "She's next!"

Polly started to tremble violently.

The elderly woman grasped her hand. "Sing, little one," she whispered. "*Sing*. He is here. He has come for us." She kissed Polly tenderly on the head.

The captain frowned. "No. You first, old woman. No one as ugly as you should be allowed to live a moment longer."

The militia joined his raucous laughter. He nodded to two soldiers, who savagely pushed the old woman toward the two steel doors of a boxcar.

She turned for one last look at Polly. Her plain features shone with a strange luminosity. Polly stared, transfixed. She semed the most beautiful woman Polly had ever seen.

Then the boxcar doors rolled shut.

Thirty seconds later, the woman's head rolled out into a steel trough. The Ukrainian captain gestured to a young soldier, who held up the woman's head by one ear.

Polly stared, tears running down her cheeks. Even in death, the woman's face radiated an incredible peace.

"See from His head, His hands, His feet
Sorrow and love flow mingled down . . . "

"You!" The captain pointed at Polly. "You next."

CHAPTER THIRTY-TWO

GRAMERCY PARK TOWN HOUSE
NEW YORK CITY

JULIA CLUTCHED the phone to her ear. "Okay, I'm watching Adrian now." She stared intently at the screen. "They've created a vaccine for the plague." Her voice shook with fear. "They're releasing millions of doses from the EU stockpiles. Hang on, Jason; I'm just checking something . . . "

Julia ran over to a writing desk, the phone still at her ear, and picked up a piece of yellow card with a number in black stamped on it.

"Oh, thank God, Jason! I've already been assigned. A yellow card dropped through the mail slot an hour ago. Uncle Xavier called and said I'd been upgraded courtesy of Adrian. I've got a yellow *card*."

Tears of relief ran down Julia's cheeks. "I'm going to be okay, Jason. They'll give me the vaccine. You don't have to come. I'll just sit tight till the worst is over."

"Oh, God," Jason said to Lawrence. "Adrian's earmarked her for the vaccine."

"When? *When*, Julia? What's the *date* on the yellow card?" Jason shouted down the phone. The line crackled loudly.

Julia stared down at the yellow card, then reached for her reading glasses and peered through them. "The nineteenth —December nineteenth. I have to register at the quarantine precinct by eight a.m."

"That's tomorrow!" Jason shouted.

"Oh, Jason, thank God!" Tears rolled down Julia's cheeks. "Yes, it's tomorrow. I'm going to be all right."

"Julia . . . " Jason's voice was soft but clear. "Listen to me very carefully. You *can't* take the vaccine."

There was a long silence. Julia's jaw clenched in anger. "Jason, don't *start!*"

"Julia . . . Julia, listen to me. It's not just a vaccine."

His voice grew less distinct, as if he was talking to someone else. "She's not listening, Lawrence."

"Julia . . . " Jason's voice rose in a mixture of fear and frustration. "You CAN'T take the vaccine."

"Don't tell me not to take the vaccine! You're not in this hellhole! If I don't take it, I'll end up like Polly—in a *body bag*, Jason! I *have* to take the vaccine. I don't want to die. I suppose that would suit *you*, though, Jason De Vere. What do you want—the London house as *well*?" she screamed into the receiver.

"Julia," Jason said in desperation, "there is *no* plague in New York."

"Polly's *dead*. Her neighbor was informed last night. Don't you . . . " Her voice was cold with fury. "*Don't you dare* tell me there's no plague in New York."

She ran to the window.

"The military are *everywhere*. Of *course* the black plague's in New York."

Jason handed the phone to Lawrence in frustration.

"Julia, my dear . . . " Lawrence's calm, steady tones filtered down the line to New York. "It's Uncle Lawrence."

Julia stared at the phone. "Uncle Lawrence. Thank goodness it's you, Uncle Lawrence. Please talk some sense into Jason. I've *got* to take the vaccine!"

"Now, Julia, take a deep breath," Lawrence said gently. "Now, I need you to sit down and listen very carefully. I know you're scared, my darling, but you're going to be just fine."

Julia sat down, clutching the phone to her ear, somewhat calmer now.

"Now, Julia, you know that I worked in the CIA for years." Julia nodded in silence. "You know you can trust me."

Another feeble nod. "Yes, Uncle Lawrence," she uttered feebly.

"That's right." Lawrence talked to her tenderly as though she were a small child. "Now, dry your eyes and take another deep breath. Are you ready to hear what I have to tell you?"

"I'm ready," Julia whispered.

"Now, cast your mind back to London, to the medical records you recovered for us on Wimpole Street. I haven't got time to explain everything on the telephone, my dear Julia, so you'll have to trust me. Your brother-in-law, Adrian, is not who he appears. I know this will come as a tremendous shock to you. Adrian not only attempted to kill *both* Nicholas and Lily, but we have strong evidence that he murdered Lillian and that Jason is next on his list.

"Now, this is where you have to take a step on faith. Julia, we have it on the highest authority from our intelligence sources all over the world: there is *no* plague anywhere in the vicinity of Gramercy. In fact, no plague has been released in New York City. The entire *state* is clean."

"Uncle Lawrence . . . " Julia stared out the window at the body bags lining up. "I'm watching the emergency channel. There are thousands of body bags in the streets. They're *burning bodies* constantly in Times Square . . . Central Park . . . "

"It's what they call a false flag, my darling Julia." Lawrence sighed. "It's very difficult to understand, I realize. But you are *not* under threat from the plague. You are under threat from Adrian, Chessler, and their one-world government. Now, I'm handing the phone back to Jason. He has some papers we need to show you."

"We're sending them through on the old videophone," Jason said. "Pull out the landline plug and plug the video screen into the landline. Then switch it on, Julia. After you've seen the document, plug the landline back in and we'll get hold of you."

Julia pulled out the landline telephone jack, then scrabbled in a cupboard and pulled out an old videophone. She plugged it into the phone plug at the wall. The screen slowly came to life. She stared at a classified document with Adrian's distinctive presidential seal stamped on the top.

"EXECUTIVE ORDERS – NEW YORK STATE – CALIFORNIA – TO REMAIN CLEAN ZONES – NO WEAPONIZED PLAGUE TO BE RELEASED IN DEMARCATED AREAS. All elite members of the government to travel immediately to demarcated clean zones."

She read the words again, slowly, then replaced the video

screen plug with the landline. The phone rang. Julia grabbed the receiver.

"But the . . . the body bags . . . " Her voice trembled. "VOX is broadcasting it! It's your *own network*, Jason."

"There's a media blackout, Julia." Jason's voice was hard. "Enforced by presidential order. They tried to get me to authorize VOX's involvement. I refused. They took over my shares, Julia. The UN and the government are flying the body bags in from out of state, from Missouri, Kansas, Alabama, Texas. They're placing them deliberately in plain sight of the media. I repeat, New York is a clean state."

"Now, listen. I'm coming for you. I'll be there by five a.m."

"You're in *Egypt*, Jason. You're crazy."

"Crazy enough to be there at five a.m. Don't step one inch out of the apartment. Do you hear me?"

Jason heard the second landline ring in the background.

"Who's on the other line?"

"It'll be Uncle Xavier."

"Julia, Xavier Chessler is one of *them*."

Julia stared as the second line turned orange.

"Ja—Jason, he's on the other line."

"As soon as I get off the phone, speak to him. If he asks who you were talking to, tell him a lie. Any lie. You always lied well to me. Tell him you'll be at the precinct tomorrow morning at eight a.m. Act calm. Whatever happens, *don't* let him pick you up. If he senses anything, blame it on your fear. You're overwhelmed. Terrified. He mustn't get suspicious. You're going to lose the landline soon—they're about to cut all communications. Five a.m., Julia. I'll be there."

∽

Jason clicked off the phone as Lily walked in, arm in arm with Father Innocentus.

Lawrence kissed Lily on both cheeks, then said to Father Innocentus, "Alert General Assaf immediately. Tell him to activate code red. We have two hours, maximum, to evacuate the monastery."

He turned to Jason, who stood hand in hand with Lily.

"Come with me. General Assaf of the Royal Jordanian Air Force will escort you safely to New York. He has military clearance."

"Lily . . . " Jason turned to Lawrence. "We'll escort her safely to Petra. She'll meet you both there."

Jason pulled Lily to his chest and held her tightly.

"I'll be all right, Dad. Just go get Mum, okay?" Lily brushed the tears away from her cheeks. "And don't *fight*! Look *after* her."

Jason shook his head at Lily. Lily reached back and undid a clasp at the back of her neck. She held out a platinum ring in her palm.

Jason frowned. "Where did you get *that*?" He stared at his old platinum wedding ring.

"From underneath Grandad's cufflinks in the top drawer of your study desk in the New York apartment. I've worn it every day since you and Mum divorced. Take it, Dad."

Jason looked intensely at Lily, then back at Lawrence, then back to Lily.

"For luck," she said. "*C'mon*, Dad. Just till you get back." Lily looked up at him with imploring brown eyes. "For me."

Jason heaved a deep sigh.

"Only for *you*." He reluctantly took the ring from Lily's palm and placed it in his inside pocket, then kissed her once more on the head. "*Just* till I get back."

"We need to hurry, Jason."

Jason embraced Lily once more and clasped her tightly to his chest. "I'll see you in Petra with Uncle Lawrence, okay?"

"Okay, Dad." Lily wiped her eyes.

"I love you, sweetheart." And Jason turned and followed Lawrence out the door.

Jason and Lawrence stood in front of a stone wall, which parted to reveal a huge steel shaft that closely resembled a freight elevator.

"Hope you've still got a strong stomach, Jason."

Jason stepped in after Lawrence. The elevator plummeted. Down, down, down, until they were fully two miles beneath the monastery. It stopped with a loud thud, and Jason caught his breath, bracing himself against the steel wall. The doors opened onto a vast cavern.

Lawrence motioned to the ten Jordanian soldiers, who lowered their weapons in response.

"Code red is activated," he said softly. He nodded to the nearest soldier. "Add Mr. De Vere to the list."

The soldier saluted, then took Jason toward two monstrous camouflaged steel blast doors set into the rock He lifted a small blue key card, and an iris scanner appeared.

He nodded to Jason, who stepped forward and aligned his eye with the scanner. "You're now logged in, sir."

Jason and the soldier took out a metallic scanner and

pressed. There was a click; then the monstrous doors slid open, revealing a sprawling underground base.

Jason stared in amazement. There must be over five hundred members of the Jordanian special services, loading supplies onto what looked like steel railcars.

A tall, handsome olive-skinned soldier walked up to them, saluted Lawrence, and then bowed. "Esteemed professor," he said.

Lawrence bowed in return.

"Esteemed General."

"It was sooner than expected," the general said.

"A small drawback. We have to accelerate our plans."

The general smiled. "We are well prepared for this eventuality."

Jason was still staring at the soldiers now lowering tanks and ballistic weapons onto enormous flatcars. "Where are they going?" he asked.

"To Petra," Lawrence replied. "Four hundred seven miles of railroad, two miles below the surface."

Jason raised his eyebrows. "You *dug* under *Israel*?"

Lawrence smiled and twirled his mustache.

"Twenty years in the making. Under Egypt, Israel, and part of Jordan, actually. Courtesy of Jotapa's father. In honor of his ancestor, the Nabetaean King Aretas of Petra. We named it the 'King Aretas Highway.'"

The general smiled. "In honor of his friendship with the Hebrew. An underground city at Petra that will preserve both the Hebrews and the followers of the Hebrew in the event of a second holocaust."

"I'll explain it all in good time, dear boy, all in good time," Lawrence said. "The underground city at Petra is still under construction. We have food supplies for five years, ninety percent of the monastery's antiquities and archaeological treasures were evacuated last month. Most of the laboratories and the surveillance equipment have already been transported. Weaver is packing his portable communications station as we speak."

The general looked at his watch. "The monastery will be evacuated within the hour, esteemed Professor. Mr. De Vere, it is our honor to escort you. Your daughter will evacuate with our best team."

He bowed. "General Assaf, commander of the Prince Hashem bin Abdullah the Second Brigade at your service."

Lawrence smiled at Jason, who stood staring in bemusement at the soldiers. "Jason, General Assaf will escort you to New York."

"Our jets are six times faster than the speed of sound, Mr. De Vere, sir. We'll be in New York in under an hour and a half."

"Once I'm on terra firma, I go it alone, Lawrence."

Lawrence nodded. He nodded to the general, who handed Jason a yellow quarantine card and two sets of papers.

"Courtesy Dylan Weaver," said Lawrence. "You'll need them to get through the roadblocks in New York. This is the address of the Fifth Column. Memorize it. They're illuminus. The general in charge is an old friend. Once you have Julia safely in your hands, they'll get you and Julia to our safe house in Kansas. In Lawrence, the old university town. General Assaf will fly you from the Lawrence airport straight to Petra.

"May God be with you, Jason De Vere."

⁓

The Slavic soldier grinned lecherously. He moved his stubby fingers slowly, caressing Polly's cheeks, then her nose and eyes.

"Execution," he said. *"What a waste."*

Two soldiers dragged her by her elbows toward the boxcar and hauled her up the steps, where one of them spat on her and then kicked her in the side, crushing the heel of his boot sadistically into her ribs.

Polly sank to the ground, shaking violently from head to foot in agonizing pain. A rat crawled over her feet. She looked up. Directly ahead of her stood a guillotine over six and a half feet high. Her entire body began to shake uncontrollably as another soldier savagely dragged her to her feet, toward the guillotine. Placing her hands in two hand restraints, he pushed her head into the space directly under the guillotine's diagonal blade.

He held up a blindfold. Polly shook her head.

"No blindfold . . . please," she rasped.

"You want to see guillotine, lady?" The captain grinned. "Then, you see." He shrugged.

He said something in Russian, and two soldiers outside the boxcar laughed raucously.

Slowly Polly raised her eyes to the gleaming diagonal blade poised above her neck. She could still hear the faint sound of singing.

Suddenly, the boxcar filled with a strange fragrance. *Roses? Lilies?* No, it was like nothing she had ever smelled on earth.

The captain frowned.

Polly felt a substance like thick, warm honey being poured over her entire body, from the crown of her head to the very tips of her toes.

Instantly, she stopped trembling. Tears streamed down her bloodied cheeks.

She sang in a whisper:

"Just as I am, Thy love unknown
Hath broken every barrier down;
Now, to be Thine, yea, Thine alone,
O Lamb of God, I come, I come."

Polly was sure she could hear ethereal voices. She wasn't sure whether it was the women singing or the angels.

The Russian captain and the two soldiers shouted, pointing in terror.

With a supreme effort, Polly raised her head.

There He stood, in the doorway of the boxcar. Imperial. Majestic. Clothed in white.

His noble face burning with the radiance of a thousand suns.

Through the searing white light, Polly could distinguish His eyes, gazing down at her. Living streams of infinite love and compassion.

Beautiful beyond imagination.

Filled with tender mercies.

The great King of Compassions.

Lion of Judah.

The slain lamb.

Jesus Christ.

He held out his nail-pierced hand to her.

Polly took hold of Jesus' outstretched hand. She smiled in ecstasy as the guillotine blade fell . . . fell . . . fell . . .

CHAPTER THIRTY-THREE

MONASTERY CHAPEL
EAST GARDENS
ALEXANDRIA, EGYPT

LAWRENCE STARED UP at the towering stone walls of the empty monastery. It seemed cavernous now that everyone had finally evacuated the grounds. Dylan Weaver and the surveillance team had left with General Khalid over an hour ago. All staff, Jordanian military, and the museum's artifacts had been evacuated forty minutes before that. Every inhabitant of the monastery of Alexandria was now safely on the way to Jordan, two miles below the surface of Egypt, traveling by rail at the speed of sound.

Lawrence walked slowly through the shaded olive grove, past the monastery's olive press. He unfastened a small iron gate that opened onto the eastern gardens. He had received word that Nick and Alex had arrived safely in Damman, Saudi Arabia. Jason had just taken off on his way to Julia in New York. Only he was left.

He looked up into the sunlight, then passed his hand over

the Egyptian skies. A hooded rider wielding a scythe galloped through the heavens.

Lawrence walked along the path under rows of cypress trees on either side, until he reached a small stone chapel.

Slowly he pushed open the heavy carved cedar doors, then walked up the nave. He closed his eyes, his head bowed in reverence to the figure of Christ above the exquisitely carved altar, and breathed in the fragrant aroma of the burning aromatic gums and spices that rose from the golden censer standing on the altar.

He smelled spikenard. A memorial to her. He knelt in reverence to the slain lamb. Tears welled up in his eyes. Then he froze, sensing an unwelcome presence.

"My, my." The familiar chilling tones, today adopting a distinctly Deep Southern accent, pierced the silence.

Lucifer stood at the entrance to the chapel, in the center of the open doorway.

He took a step forward.

"My, my, my! Ah do declare . . . " He lifted his hands dramatically. "If it isn't my old mentor, Jether the Just —or should I say, the esteemed Professor Lawrence St. Cartier."

He surveyed Lawrence.

"Mm-m-m, that cravat is just *darlin,*' Professor. I'll answer your question. I'm doin' fair to middlin'—thanks for askin'. But, Professor, the air here is just riddled with *black plague.*

Oh, my, my, that's right. It slipped mah mind—you're *immortal,* just like me!"

He leaned over and idly picked up the Book of Common Prayer.

Lawrence stood silently, his gaze never leaving the statue of Christ.

"All over the world, they chant it, sing it. Bored out of their tiny little minds, they go through the motions, their thoughts on the Sunday roast, online shopping . . . " He snickered. " . . . getting in the vicar's wife's knickers."

He raised his hands. "Oh my, my! Ah am just downright sorry! You look just about as happy as a dead hog in the sunshine, Professor. Forgive me for that profanity. I clean lost mah manners!"

He tossed the prayer book aside, grinned, and reverted to his precise British accent with its exotic inflection.

"Anglicans." He took a step up the aisle.

"Methodists." He took a second step.

"The Catholics." Lucifer grinned. "*Lots* of Catholics. Just love their rituals. Quite transfixing. All that money on vestments and gold icons that could surely be put in the Vatican bank with its other laundered billions.

"You must admit, Professor. All that *money*. All in His name. Billions of dollars, pounds . . . "

"Y'all"—switching back into his Southern accent—"even *I* never dreamed I would win on such a colossal scale. Miss Scarlett, it's a complete *travesty!*"

He turned to Jether.

"What in the *Sam Hill* is going on?"

Jether stood, his back still to Lucifer. "Not all merely go through the motions," he said very softly. "There are still those who believe. Those whose faith is in Him, not in the ritual but in the relationship."

"The church is weak," Lucifer hissed.

Jether raised his eyes, blazing with a holy fire, to Lucifer's.

"Then why do you *fear* them so much, Lucifer? Why does every fiber of your soul tremble when those who bear the Nazarene's seal come near?"

Lucifer's face contorted in rage. "If they only knew. If they even *guessed* the power within them. But that, of course, remains my greatest victory of all."

"Times change," Jether said. "His army is rising. Even out of their weakness, their humanity, there is a clarion call to arms. You have been exposed. Identified. Many heed you no longer."

"Yes," retorted Lucifer. "And they suffer greatly at my hands. I have trained the demonic realm meticulously. We, the Fallen, bring about their suffering, then lay the blame at *His* feet. Our whispered voices torment them in their dreams.

"'*You follow Him. You serve Him faithfully,*' we whisper," Lucifer hissed. "'*And yet, Yehovah abandons you. He allows you to suffer. What manner of God do you serve?*'

"Oh, yes, Jether, they shall feel as I felt. They know how it feels to be abandoned by Him. I target his 'pets.' Those He comes to in their dreams. His earthly visitations. Those who have usurped me, who occupy the place that was mine. *Always* mine. Take away their hedge of protection and they abandon him. Like whimpering babies.

"He will finally be forced to admit that I was right. He shall rue his greatest folly: creating man. They have brought Him nothing but regret. Yet still He pursues them. They shall break His heart, Jether . . . as He broke mine."

"Oh, Lucifer, light bearer, you who were once so filled with wisdom and beauty."

"Those days are long gone," railed Lucifer.

"Yes," Jether whispered. "Long gone."

"Hell, that could even depress the *devil*." Lucifer swung around dramatically. "Oh, wait, that's me." He grinned malevolently.

"Now to the point."

He moved his palm, and the roof of the chapel disappeared. He stared up at the form of a hooded rider on a pale horse crossing the Kármán Line of the earth's atmosphere.

"Nisroc rides. The Nazarene comes to rescue his mewling pets. The brilliance of my plan is unparalleled. The sensational disappearance of millions of 'Christians' buried in the outbreak of a global pandemic. Good riddance. *This is the way the world ends: not with a bang but a whimper.*"

Slowly Jether lifted the wooden cross that rested on top of the altar. "How thou art fallen, son of the morning."

Lucifer stared, silent. Transfixed. The skin on his forehead started to blister. He stumbled backward, hiding his face with his hands.

"The King of Lies will always be slave to the King of Truth." Jether stepped toward him. "You are His puppet, Lucifer. You reign a king without a kingdom. Ultimately, even your evil will serve to fulfill his omniscient plan." Jether looked at him grimly.

Lucifer backed down the aisle, blinded by the radiance emanating from the cross. "And yet," he screamed, his face bubbling with consuming fire, "He still created me-e-e-e-e!"

He pushed open the chapel doors, gasping for breath, and stumbled into the gardens, then slowly raised his blistered face to the Egyptian skies.

"*That* is the unanswered question in the Race of Men," he spat. "The answer to that question *consumes* me. It has become my obsession."

"As *He* is mine," said another voice.

Lucifer slowly removed his hand from his eyes. A lean, muscular form stood under the cypress trees.

Lucifer studied the stranger's chiseled features. "Michael." A slow smile spread across his lips. "My brother." Lucifer's hands went to his face. He threw his hood over his head, hiding his blistered features.

Michael bowed his head in deference. "Lucifer."

Lucifer strode across the grass, his cloak billowing out behind him.

Jether walked up behind Michael, his hand on his shoulder.

"Lucifer!" Michael's voice echoed across the gardens. "May Yehovah have mercy on your soul!"

Lucifer turned. "Frankly, my dear . . . " He stared contemptuously at Michael.

"I don't give a damn."

He bowed dramatically, then saluted Michael. And vanished in the air.

Jether and Michael exchanged a glance.

"As always, he overplays his hand," Jether murmured.

"The excitement in the High Courts is unparalleled," Michael said. "The elders and angelic host are gathered at the Gates of the First Heaven. They await Christos's return.

"With His subjects." He gazed up in wonder at a white form high in the heavens.

"Those who have longed and yearned their entire earthly life for His appearing, those who have faithfully served Him even through their frailties and weaknesses—they shall finally see Him face to face. "They shall see their redeemer." Jether looked at Michael in wonder. "They shall see their *King*."

CHAPTER THIRTY-FOUR

DAMMAN, SAUDI ARABIA

JIBRIL EMBRACED Jotapa fiercely.

"I cannot rule without you, beloved sister," he said. "You have been my counselor, my confidante. My closest friend."

Tears streamed down Jotapa's cheeks. She covered Jibril's face and hands with kisses. "Such a noble king you will make," she whispered.

"But you choose this *other* king," Jibril retorted, strangely incensed. "You choose this *Christ* over the royal household of Aretas."

"Yes, I choose," Jotapa whispered. "I choose, as my namesake chose before me."

Jibril turned away from Jotapa, his jaw set.

Alex turned to Nick. "For God"s sake, Nick, what am I going to tell Lawrence? And *Jason?*" He sighed in frustration. "Oh, Jason's just going to love this. You've just returned from the dead, and now . . . "

Nick grasped Alex by the head and pulled him to his chest. "I love you, man," he said.

"You were the only big brother I ever had," Alex said, his voice breaking as he tried desperately to hold himself together.

Nick held him tightly, then let him go. He frowned.

"Jotapa . . . "

Jotapa stared back at Nick in wonder as, suddenly, an exquisite scent permeated the room.

"It's . . . it's like Jasmine," Jotapa whispered. "Or roses . . . "

Jibril's entire body started to tremble violently. Jotapa started to move toward him.

"No . . . " Nick gently placed his hand on her arm as an intense, blinding light filled the room.

"He is here," Nick uttered in ecstasy.

Jotapa turned. Alex was frozen in terror, hiding his face from the light.

In the doorway, barely distinguishable because of the translucent light radiating from Him, stood a tall, imperial figure wearing the crown of a king.

"He has *come* for us," Nick murmured.

Jotapa flung herself at the figure's feet, weeping uncontrollably, her long dark tresses falling over his sandaled feet.

Ever so slowly, Nick stepped directly into the light. He stood completely transfixed, unable to draw his eyes away from the figure's gaze.

His heart literally felt as though it were burning with an exquisite pain, like intensely hot coals within him.

It had been so long that at times, he had almost believed that *He* was only a dream, that that day, over three years ago, had been a hallucination. But now, as he stared in wonder, the noble imperial features became fully visible.

Oh, His beauty was indescribable.

Tears streamed down Nick's cheeks. And still he stared.

Inexpressible joy welled up inside him. And still he stared, his entire being saturated in incandescent light.

Bathing in the unfathomable love and compassion and infinite mercies that exuded from His being.

Peace—a peace beyond Nick's comprehension—flooded his entire being.

Tears streamed down his cheeks. And still he stood, staring . . .

Staring . . .

Utterly transfixed by the eyes of his King.

Jesus held out His hand to Nick.

"Nicholas," He whispered.

Nick took Jesus' hand. "It is time?" he whispered.

Jesus smiled. "It is time." He drew Nick into His embrace and held him to his chest, as would a mother with her child.

Still clasping Nick, Jesus bent down and gently wiped the tears from Jotapa's face.

"Arise, Jotapa, princess of the house of Aretas."

Jotapa rose slowly to her feet and clung to him, burying her face in his white robes.

Jesus looked over to where Jibril stood, trembling, unable to speak.

"Jibril, crown prince of Jordan, you shall yet be as King Aretas, protector of your people." He smiled. "And of mine."

He turned to Alex, who was still standing, his arm across his face.

"Alex," Jesus said softly. "Alex . . . "

Very slowly Alex raised his head, staring beyond the brilliance into the most beautiful eyes he had ever seen.

"You search for truth."

A strange burning sensation flooded Alex's rib cage. He clutched at his chest in panic. It felt as though every cell of his physical heart were on fire.

"And yet, I *am* the truth." Jesus smiled tenderly—oh, so tenderly—at Alex.

Alex fell to his knees.

"Follow me, Alex Lane Fox."

"Alex, look after Jason," Nick whispered. "Tell him I love him."

A form materialized next to Jesus. It was Polly.

"Polly . . . " Alex stared in utter disbelief. "What the . . . "

Alex turned away momentarily from the still blinding light.

He looked back up. There was no one in the room but himself and the weeping crown prince, Jibril.

The soft fragrance of the rose of Sharon.

And the burning presence of the King of Kings . . .

The Slavic captain slowly lifted his face from the floor. He stared around the boxcar in shock, then terror. In the warehouse, hundreds of the singing prisoners had disappeared.

"He was there," one soldier said, pointing and retching.

"No, he was *there*," said another, pointing to the opposite end of the boxcar.

The captain turned to them, trembling uncontrollably.

"He was *everywhere*, it seems!" The captain stared at the bitter, beautiful woman, who stood silent and trembling.

"Their nonexistent God has rescued them," he spat.

She fell to the ground, moaning. "I believe, I believe . . . "

"You're too late," he snarled, kicking her in the ribs. "She's next!"

CHAPTER THIRTY-FIVE

GRAMERCY PARK TOWN HOUSE
NEW YORK CITY

"JULIA!"

Jason pressed his face to the kitchen window of the Greek Revival town house.

"Julia!"

He glanced down at his watch. It was five a.m. precisely.

Very slowly the ornate back hall door opened a crack, then swung completely open. Jason hurried past Julia into the hallway. He looked down at the silver designer suitcase and vanity case by the door.

"No luggage," he said.

"No *luggage*?" The immense relief on Julia's face turned to a glare. "You *seriously* expect me not to take any *luggage*?"

Jason held up his hands. "I know this must be very hard for you to understand, Julia," he said drily, "but we're not about to leave for a five-star vacation in the Greek isles."

He put his face to hers. "We're on the *run*." He unhooked a backpack from a hook behind the door. "Martial law. Submachine guns. Black helicopters. Here . . . " He

309

slung the backpack at her. Julia caught it. "Use Lily's backpack."

Seething, Julia flung open her vanity case and hauled out her makeup, moisturizers, and cleansers.

Jason rolled his eyes. "We may even have to *walk*."

Julia glared at him again. "You're really enjoying this, aren't you? Don't answer that."

"We can use your car on the yellow-card precinct route, but we're going to have to dump it when we get near the water," Jason continued. "Go the rest of the way on foot."

His eyes narrowed. Julia followed his gaze to her five-inch platform Chloe casual sandals.

"Dump the shoes, Julia."

She sighed. "I only have heels."

"You must have *something* less than a foot high." Jason rolled his eyes. "We're on the *run*, Julia, in case it hadn't occurred to you."

She pulled out a pair of designer sneakers. "Three-and-a-half-inch, but they're wedges."

Jason shook his head wearily.

"I can walk in them."

"You'd *better*—you can take it to the bank that I'm not carrying you!"

Julia glared at him, then threw him a set of car keys. He caught them in one hand.

"So here's the drill."

Jason looked her up and down. She wore a pale blue tracksuit, and her blond hair was pulled away from her face into a ponytail, accentuating her high cheekbones. She was wearing only foundation with the faintest hint of blusher, eyeliner, and a dab of gloss. He had always loved her minus the perfectly applied makeup that was her trademark.

His voice softened. "Here's the drill, Jules. Martial law is in place. All bridges are closed, and the Holland Tunnel. There's only one route out of the city: the route to the quarantine precinct at Newark. The only vehicles allowed on the road are those carrying a yellow card: diplomats, ambassadors—privileged bearers. Orange and green card holders are convoyed to the centers in military vehicles.

"We follow the route to the quarantine precinct, but we need to divert to Chinatown without the military seeing us. The fifth column has a military jet there waiting to fly us to a safe house in Kansas. It's a patriot state. From there, we fly to Jordan and meet Lily and Lawrence at Petra."

Julia shook her head. "Fifth column—what are you *talking* about, Jason?"

Jason flung the keys to the Mercedes sports car back to Julia, who missed them.

"Too conspicuous," he said. "We use Hortense's Golf. I see your eye-hand coordination hasn't improved."

Julia bent down and picked the keys up from the floor, glowered at Jason, then grabbed the housekeeper's car keys from the rack and threw them hard at him. He caught them deftly in one hand, smiled triumphantly, then walked through to the small garage.

He pressed the key remote, unlocking the doors of the white Volkswagen Golf. Julia leaned over and put the backpack in the backseat, then got in the front. Jason pressed the ignition, and they roared out of the driveway.

~

LEXINGTON AVENUE
NEW YORK CITY

"Roadblock," Jason muttered.

They stopped, joining hundreds of cars in the queue, and Jason's window slid down. A Homeland Security soldier wearing a respirator and a bulky suit put his hand out.

"Pass," he said tersely.

Jason handed the soldier two identical yellow cards.

"What on earth is he wearing?" Julia whispered.

"CBRN suit—military version of a hazmat suit. Chemical, biological, radiation, nuclear."

Julia paled. "And a respirator. I thought you said there's no pandemic here," she hissed.

Jaon glared at her to be quiet.

The soldier nodded, then swiped the yellow cards.

Jason waited with bated breath.

"Lucky, then," the soldier said. "First in line for the vaccine—you must have friends in high places."

Jason nodded. Inwardly he breathed a sigh of relief. Dylan Weaver had delivered the goods. He had hacked into the FEMA and UN databases and changed Jason's and Jullia's Black- and Red List status.

The soldier passed the yellow cards back through the window. "Follow the precinct markings to the quarantine center. It's the only route out."

Jason and Julia had been traveling for what felt like hours, and they had covered only two and a half miles. The route was swarming with masked United Nations soldiers, submachine guns at the ready. Black FEMA and Homeland Security vans were positioned at even intervals along the route.

"We're near," Jason said. "I'm getting off."

"You want us to go into *Chinatown*?" Julia stared at him in disbelief.

"Well, you didn't think we were going to the precinct, did you?"

Julia looked to their left. "That's *a barricade*, Jason," she said sarcastically.

"Yes, but luckily for us, it's unguarded. Here . . . " He swung the steering wheel. "It's our only chance."

The car veered through the barricade and down a narrow verge. Julia put her hands over her eyes.

Jason looked through the rear view mirror. "We're clear. Now we head to the warehouse."

"The Warehouse?" Julia said, her head still down at her knees.

Jason veered sharp left again and accelerated down an even narrower alley, toward a high chain-link fence surrounding an empty parking lot and a dilapidated warehouse plastered in graffiti.

He hit the clutch just as Julia raised her head. She pointed in alarm at the two massive broken-down warehouse doors.

"Jason!!" she yelled as he drove straight through the closed chain-link gate, knocking it open. She put her head down again.

Jason sighed, put the car into gear, and screeched to a halt just outside the warehouse doors.

A solitary homeless man, holding a whisky bottle in a

paper bag, limped up to Julia's window and gestured for her to roll it down.

Jason nodded.

"*You can't be serious,*" Julia mouthed.

"Roll down the window," Jason said through gritted teeth.

Reluctantly Julia pressed a button, and the window slid down a few inches.

The homeless man surveyed their surroundings, then stuck his hand into his left pocket and pulled out a badge. He passed it through the window.

"We haven't got much time," he said.

Julia stared at the badge. It read "1st Special Forces Operational Detachment-Delta (1st SFOD-D)"

Jason observed the SPR sniper rifle beneath the grubby trench coat, then passed the man his and Julia's passports.

"Have you lost your *mind*?" Julia hissed.

The soldier nodded in approval, handing back the passports. "The professor sent you. Welcome to the Unit."

He motioned for Jason to move the car forward.

Instantly, the car plunged down a steep ramp into a vast underground compound lit with massive searchlights and swarming with armed militia. They were stopped at a barricade, where a uniformed soldier with a shaved head approached them.

"We need you to step out of the vehicle, please," he stated in soft, precise British tones while keeping his submachine gun trained on them. Julia looked at him, terrified.

"It's okay, Julia," Jason said soothingly.

She glared at him. "Jason Ambrose De Vere, if we ever get out of here alive, I'll . . . "

Jason stepped out of the car and handed the soldier the yellow cards, papers, and passports.

The soldier gestured at Julia, and slowly she got out of the car. He frisked them both, then tore up the yellow cards and papers and handed back the passports. He saluted.

"The general is expecting you," he said. "Get in the jeep."

Julia grabbed the backpack from the Golf and followed Jason into the backseat, seething.

They passed armed militiamen every three or four yards. The jeep stopped at last, and Jason and Julia followed their escort into what looked like a railroad passenger car.

"You know where we're going, don't you?" Julia hissed at Jason, bewildered as thick harnesses automatically strapped them into their seats.

Jason nodded.

"Who's the general?"

"I don't know," Jason muttered, "except that Lawrence trusts him implicitly. We'll be safe here until they get us out to Petra."

"Hold on," the soldier warned.

The railcar shot forward, rapidly accelerating to over two hundred miles per hour. Five minutes later, it came to a halt.

Jason got out, and four soldiers approached him with automatic weapons raised. Jason raised his hands, and they frisked him.

"He's clean," said one of the soldiers.

The squad commander nodded in Julia's direction. He gave instructions in what sounded like Hebrew. They frisked Julia down.

The commander pointed to the bag, and a soldier dumped Julia's makeup and personal effects unceremoniously onto a tray and pushed it toward a scanner. Then he pointed them up the steel stairs.

"We've got to get a move on," Jason told the Israeli squad commander. "When they find Julia hasn't turned up at the quarantine precinct all hell will break loose."

The thickset Israeli grinned, chewing his gum nonchalantly, and gestured up the stairs. "First things first," he said in English with a strong guttural inflection.

He led the way into a large, sparsely furnished room. A man with white hair stood with his back to them.

Slowly he turned around. "Why, Jason, you young whippersnapper!" he said.

The old man was in the full battle dress of a four-star general, with medals. An unlit cigar hung from his mouth.

Jason stared in disbelief at his wrinkled, leathery face. "General *Magruder*!"

Jason grinned from ear to ear. Magruder had been one of James De Vere's oldest and most trusted friends.

"Sorry to hear about your mother, son. That was one classy dame." He looked at Julia inquiringly.

"Julia St. Cartier," Jason said.

"Ah, the professor's niece." He hesitated. "Your ex."

Jason and Julia both nodded vigorously.

The general raised his hand. "Come with me."

They followed the old soldier into a military jeep. He nodded to the marine in the driver's seat. The tyres screeched as they turned off onto a highway.

"You realize that we're two thousand feet down." Magruder grinned. "Say hello to our Mother City."

Jason and Julia stared in amazement at the vast underground facilities.

"We're totally self-sufficient," the general continued. "Generate our own electric, created our own air filtration systems, water purification systems."

They passed an enormous munitions factory.

"Vast supplies of guns and ammunition. That's the agrarian section."

Ten minutes later, they were still staring at miles of farmland.

"It's incredible!" Julia gasped.

Magruder grinned. "Our artificial underground farms. We even redirected underground rivers. We can feed all ten thousand of our military here for five years. But wait for it . . . "

They transferred to another railcar, and fifteen minutes later they came to a halt.

Jason stood up, gaping.

"*Impossible*," he breathed.

Magruder chewed on his cigar and grinned. "It's a U.S. Navy guided missile cruiser."

Jason shook his head. "But *how?*"

"We have nuclear submarines, destroyers, secret ocean entry points all over the world. They slide onto massive rails. We transport them under dry land, through gigantic tunnels to our underground docks.

"What you see here—we have setups like these all across the USA and the world. Call it the Illuminus military arm." He pointed to the Israeli. "Avi here's from Shavetet Thirteen. Our militia consists of the finest special forces in the world—SAS, Delta Force, Navy Seals, Spetznaz—all with one goal: to stop the new world order."

He raised his hand. "To my quarters."

Twenty minutes later, they were seated on a battered leather couch in a large oak library.

"Cigar?" Magruder asked.

Jason shook his head.

A marine carried in a steaming pot of coffee and a tray of sandwiches and salad.

"A salad for the little lady?" Magruder grinned.

"Not bad for martial law and rationing." Julia smiled. "Better than FEMA's menu."

Magruder settled into his chair, suddenly serious.

"You realize FEMA and the UN blue hats have become your brother's puppet militia. Their urban unit, MOUT - 'military operations in urban terrain', have been preparing since 2010 to take control of major population centers, disarming American citizens and crushing any rebellious or antigovernment groups who attempt to resist the military takeover. That's the underlying reason why, during Obama's presidency, U.S. soldiers were recalled from both Iraq and Afghanistan. They wanted them home, to create a homeland army. All presidents are on a need-to-know basis only. The shadow elite pulls the nation's strings."

Julia's eyes grew wide in disbelief. Jason nodded.

Magruder stared at the picture of a sweet-faced elderly woman on his desk, and for a split second, his eyes misted over. He nodded to the two soldiers with pistols at his door.

"Stand down," he said. The door closed, and they were alone in the room.

"Kids, listen. We're onto something." He hesitated. "Something huge." He sighed and picked up the photograph of his wife. "My Clemmie . . . " his expression softened. "She died forty-eight hours ago."

"I'm *so* sorry, General. The plague?" Julia asked gently.

The big old soldier roughly wiped a tear from his eye and shook his head.

"Jason and Uncle Lawrence say there's no plague in New York City."

"And they'd be right, young lady."

The general pressed a remote control, and images instantly appeared on a projector screen opposite them. A virtual map of North America appeared, with blood red arrows covering the entire nation, from Texas to Virginia and from Kansas to Ohio. Every state was covered in red arrows except for California in the West and New York State in the East.

"Weaponized black death, affecting every state except California and New York. All civilian flights gounded, state borders closed."

He felt in his top pocket and removed a well-worn pocket Bible.

"My wife's," he whispered, opening it to a bookmarked page. "Luke seventeen: thirty-four. *'I tell you, in that night there shall be two men in one bed; the one shall be taken, and the other shall be left.'*

"I'm not a religious man—never have been—but let an old man be an old man. All our married life, Clemmie talked about it. Told me one day . . . well, it happened exactly as she said.

"At precisely eleven on Sunday night, we were lying in bed. I was still awake, reading, as is my habit. Clemmie had read her pocketbook Bible, then fallen asleep next to me, facing me. She looked so sweet that night." His gray eyes softened. "It all happened so quickly."

"And she died in her sleep?" Julia asked innocently.

Jason stared at Magruder intently. Slowly he opened his mouth. "You're not saying she dis . . . dis . . . "

"Say it, Jason," the old man said. "Yes. She disappeared. Vanished . . . " He took a deep breath. "In front of my eyes."

"You said you were reading," Jason said.

MacGruder shook his head. "As fate would have it, I'd just finished reading. Laid the book on my bedside table. I leaned over to kiss her cheek.

"She . . . one minute, she was there; the next minute, she was gone. Vanished straight in front of my eyes with me watching her." He studied Jason's face.

"She left me a note. It was in her Bible."

He handed Julia a well-worn note in beautiful cursive writing.

"*'My darling Mac,'*" Julia read aloud, "*'when you read this I will be gone. He is coming for me. I sense it with all my being. No tears—just a promise. That my disappearance will be the sign you have waited for all your life, Mac, my darling stubborn old pragmatist. Now, accept the fact.*

"*'Receive Christ, Mac. It will not be easy being left down here. But you've always had more courage for your country than anyone I've ever met. Now have courage to follow Him, live for Him. Die for Him—you may have to, my darling Mac. I now see Him face-to-face. So will you, my darling, and one day in the not too distant future we will be together forever.*

"*'With all my love, as always, your Clementine.'*"

Jason watched, deeply moved, as the big soldier's shoulders shook and he started to sob.

Julia took the big, craggy hand in hers.

"Go on, General," Jason urged.

"Our base consists of ten thousand military personnel and their families. Last night, at precisely eleven-o-seven p.m., we had over two thousand verified cases of men and women disappearing from the base here. *All* disappearances witnessed by a second party. And another thousand four hundred and fifty unwitnessed disappearances."

"It was precisely at eleven p.m. that the weaponized plague was released worldwide," Jason said thoughtfully. Magruder nodded. "Our intelligence services aboveground have sourced over a hundred thousand cases of witnessed disappearances in the U.S. already. FEMA, the UN, WHO—someone very high up had inside information because, at four that morning, everyone on the Blacklist was rounded up."

"The Blacklist?" Julia frowned.

Magruder smiled wryly and tapped his keyboard. They stared at the screen.

"There are three lists held by One World Intelligence, underground at Mont St. Michel, Normandy. Lists of Christians, patriots, constitutionalists, from Texas to Beijing, now labeled terrorists. At four a.m. yesterday, over eight million American men and women were seized from their homes, picked up in military vans, and transported to huge quarantine centers—concentration camps—across America. Their families were informed that they were suspected plague cases. At eight a.m. Central time, martial law was implemented."

"Our troops wouldn't do that." Julia shook her head. "Not to their own."

"Exactly." Magruder nodded. "They *weren't* U.S. troops. There are now hundreds of foreign military bases, under the United Nations flag, already set up in the USA. They have no qualms about firing on U.S. citizens. Our U.S. troops do most of the aboveboard stuff: patrolling the streets, doling out rations, keeping order."

He thrust a sheaf of documents onto the table next to Jason.

"Every one of these are men and women we know. All witnesses vouch that they were not sick. Most were in good health. They were beaten and forced into vans by foreign troops—practically a second holocaust. They had no defense.

"Remember the global UN 'Small Arms Treaty' over a decade ago? To fight 'terrorism,' 'insurgency,' and 'international crime syndicates.' You can be quite certain that an even more insidious threat is being targeted. It was passed by the UN and ratified by our Senate in 2018."

Jason nodded. "That's what caused the uprising and secession of Kansas, Missouri, Texas, and eighteen states following them," he said. "And the families?"

"If they resisted, they were taken, too."

Maguder pressed the remote again, and a vast room appeared onscreen, with hundreds of military men and women working at rows of computers.

"Our U.S.-based intelligence units. They're here underground, collating evidence. And this is where it gets strange. For ninety percent of people on the list, the government has been issuing *two* sets of documents. The first, issued by the quarantine authority to the next of kin.

"Take this one: *'John Andrew Miller. Cause of death: plague. Place of death: Brooklyn Quarantine Center, New York.'*

"But in ninety percent of cases, they're issuing a second

document, purely for EU headquarters, marked 'EYES ONLY.'"

Jason frowned as the general continued to read.

"Issued to the EU Headquarters: *John Andrew Miller. Dissident. militant. Blacklist.*

"*'Reason for detention: Terrorist acts against the state.*

"*'Death by guillotine. Executed eleven-o-seven p.m.'*"

Magruder pressed a second remote, and instantly four TV screens appeared, broadcasting the emergency channel, now commandeered by the military. The screen showed thousands of body bags lining the streets of Florida, the District of Columbia, Virginia, and Iowa.

He switched it off.

"With millions of deaths from the plague across the world, the whole world's in a panic. No one's asking questions about people disappearing . . . " He raised his eyes to Jason. "Christians."

Jason was still pale. "General . . . " His voice was very soft. "I need you to track the whereabouts of one Jontil Lucinda Purvis. She's been missing."

He looked up at Julia.

"And Polly Mitchell," he said softly.

He scrawled Jontil Purvis's name, social security number, and address on a piece of paper, then wrote on another piece of paper, "Polly Winifred Mitchell. UK citizen. Can you have your people check those?" he said softly.

Magruder put the list in his pocket. He nodded. "I'll get back to you. Meanwhile, Lieutenant Casey will show you to your quarters. Tomorrow you see the 'doctor.'"

LUCIFER

To my naive brother Gabriel,

So, the Pale Horse and Nisroc have crossed the Kármán Line.

The Rapture is over.

He has finally rescued His mewling subjects from the coming Great Tribulation of the Race of Men, and no doubt the First Heaven is full of vain jubilation at His triumph.

However, I would remind you, Gabriel, that the road to Armageddon is no doubt paved with Yehovah's lofty intentions of saving other mewling masses of this pathetic mud-spattered orb who cry out to Him—pitiable intentions that will, in the coming months, be exposed as fruitless—even wretched.

My son rises like a shooting star in the world of the Race of Men.

They flatter him with their rhetoric, fawn and grovel at his feet.

From the four corners of the earth they come, to seek his counsel at every turn.

He rules over ten kingdoms.

And shortly will amass an army of two hundred million to meet the Nazarene at Armageddon.

Make no mistake. I shall be there to witness His defeat. The capitulation of the Nazarene.

And as he defeated me on Golgotha, I shall ensure that his conquest in the land of his birth is a spectacle for all to see.

But first things first.

Once I have conquered the world of the Race of Men, who knows? Maybe I will reassemble my armies against the Most High . . .

This thought intrigues me . . . which, in fact, reminds me of things closer to home. When will I be notified of our coming war?

Chapter Thirty-six

THE FIRST HEAVEN

NICK STARED AROUND, disoriented.

Just as suddenly as it had started, the vortex of light subsided. Jesus had disappeared. The last thing that he consciously remembered was gazing into His eyes.

He stared down in wonder at the softly glowing, pulsating azure light enveloping him and tried to get his bearings. He seemed to be floating beneath a swiftly flowing current of water, but strangely, he was breathing quite normally. Nick frowned, then let the warm, glowing turquoise liquid run between his fingers. It was molecularly thicker than Earth's water and had a completely different texture.

Some sort of current seemed to be propelling him very gently downstream.

He wasn't sure whether he was in a sea, a lake, a river. All he knew for certain was that this was like nothing his senses had ever known. Each part of him felt alive in a way he had never experienced before.

His body seemed to be imbibing minute particles of living

light that bubbled around him. Each time the tiny light particles entered his body, the most incredible peace washed through his entire being.

Peace. A wondrous, soothing peace.

Even in his most ecstatic moments on Earth, nothing had come near the intensity of the sheer serenity and freedom he was experiencing now. The heroin and cocaine highs of his youth couldn't touch whatever this was.

He took another deep breath of the turquoise liquid, his mind racing.

"I'm breathing in *water*." He took a second deep breath. Another surge of ecstasy suffused his soul. "The Rapture."

And then it happened.

It felt as if a giant hard drive in his brain began to be scrubbed clean. So gently. Every neurotransmitter seemed alive. Thousands of memories began to play as the water in front of him became a virtual screen. He stared at the images moving in front of his eyes and then being erased. He was injecting heroin, sniffing cocaine, fighting with James De Vere. *Oh, no!* The pantechnicon was speeding toward them. The accident. The worst day of his life. "Lily!" he shouted. Then the image was gone. He held his head. He thought there had been an accident, but the memory of it was totally erased.

The warm liquid surrounded him like a spinning vortex. He was being propelled again at an amazing speed, now passing people who were floating just as he was. Each person he passed had the same expression of serenity.

"Nicholas . . . " A soft voice echoed through the liquid. He turned to his left.

An incredibly beautiful woman in her late twenties, with

soft, flowing black hair and wearing luminous white garments and gold, floated next to him. He took in a breath. Her beauty was, quite literally, breathtaking. She reached out her hand to him. He hesitated; there was something incredibly familiar about her, but he couldn't quite define what.

She smiled at him with such tenderness that Nick wanted to melt into her arms.

"Don't you recognize me, my darling Nicholas?"

Nick shook his head, his eyes riveted to her face. Then he opened his mouth in wonder.

"Mother," he uttered.

Lilian smiled at him "It's the Waters of Life, Nicholas," she said softly. "They transform us. By the time we see Him . . . " She closed her eyes in ecstasy. " . . . all of Earth's sorrows, stresses, and pains have been washed away. These waters remove the scars and memories of earthly life and pain from the souls and minds of all who arrive within these gates.

"Once our souls are healed, our bodies are free to be exchanged for a different type of matter." She raised her hand to his. "Put your hand in mine."

Nick's hand passed straight through Lilian's. She smiled.

"All these people . . . " Lilian gestured to the thousands floating downstream past them. They have all been taken up through the Kármán Line. It's the Rapture, Nick. You were taken in the Rapture."

"The Rapture—it actually happened."

Lilian nodded.

A woman in crimson garments floated past them. Her face was literally engulfed with luminous light. As she floated past them blood seemed to be flowing from her neck and hands.

"She's bleeding . . . "

Nick reached out his hand as if to touch her. Lilian shook her head.

"It is not her blood, Nicholas, but the blood of the one who laid down his life in the terrible sacrifice.

"The fifth seal has been broken," whispered Lilian. "These are the ones who loved not their life more than death. The tribulation martyrs are arriving. They have the greatest status in heaven."

She bowed very low to the one who passed.

"The greatest sacrifice. The greatest privilege of all," she said softly. "They have laid their lives down. For Him. He awaits these ones now beyond the Rubied Door. They will see His face first. And receive their crowns and flowing white robes, then join their brother- and sisterhood across the ages—other matyrs who were slain for Him —under the colossal carnelian altar. The souls of those who were slain.

"I have to go, my beloved Nicholas. There are many more martyrs arriving. Your father and I are two of the many who have been chosen to assist in this hour."

"Dad?" Nick frowned. "He didn't believe."

Lilian smiled softly. "Oh, but, Nicholas, only the great King Himself hears the voices that cry out to him from their deathbeds. Even the most agnostic cries bring him running to their aid if they genuinely call upon Him. After you have seen your King, you will come and be with us." She smiled. "Your father has been longing to see you from the day he arrived. We have so much to share with you.

"Oh, our King has built for us such a glorious house. The emerald grass leads right down to our own beach. The shells are encrusted with living pearls."

She kissed Nick tenderly on the head. "There is someone else who awaits you. You are much beloved within heaven's gates. And much beloved by your father and me."

Lilian vanished beyond his sight, further upstream.

Nick looked down at the riverbed. For the first time, he noticed that it was covered by thousands of gleaming jewels. Or maybe it was because he had floated farther up the river. Nick reached out and picked up a huge, beautiful stone that emitted a crimson light. He studied it, still with an archaeologist's eye. It looked like a ruby . . . and yet, again, the molecular structure was different.

"Ah! You have chosen wisely, my dear Nicholas."

Nick looked up from the riverbed to see Jether floating by his side.

"Jether?" He sighed in relief.

Jether's pale blue eyes twinkled. "In the twinkling of an eye, they shall be changed."

Jether gently took the ruby from Nick's hand.

"The jewels in the First Heaven have a completely different structure from those on Earth."

Nick nodded. "It seems lighter in weight."

Jether nodded. "Unlike earthly gems, it contains super-natural properties, my boy. Look . . . "

They both studied the riverbed. Nicholas looked at the ruby in Jether's hand, then bent down and picked up a nondescript piece of wood, stained with crimson and lying alone on the riverbed.

He grasped it in his palm, his eyes filling with tears.

"There is a strange power in this . . . " He held it out to Jether. "I don't know what it means, but it fills my heart with pain." Nick struggled to breathe. He started to sob wretchedly.

Jether watched him compassionately. "You were drawn to what you hold, because it represents His healing powers. Your soul still bears many scars of the long and painful sickness that you walked through on Earth.

"Even though Christos healed your body, Nicholas, your mind and your soul still bear the scars of the daily struggle with pain and disease—the trauma that is buried so deep in your subconscious. You have been unaware of it, but it has been trapped in your mortal body, affecting much of what you do. Many people are healed on Earth, but although their physical bodies have recovered, their minds and souls still bear great wounds. Our King who suffered so, physically on the cross, has never forgotten the trauma that caused him to sweat drops of blood in the garden. And that caused him to cry out, 'Eloi . . . '

"There is hardly any greater loneliness experienced on Earth than that of those who suffer mentally, who suffer trauma. There is only one who truly understands the depth of what you suffered. There is only one who paid the price to truly set you free. There are those who are healed in their souls on Earth, but many arrive here with their minds and hearts still wounded from earthly struggles.

"That which you hold in your hand—that which you chose—is a great gift to you from your King. It is hewn from the same mountain that the Rubied Doors of the throne room were carved from millennia ago.

"It bears the blood of the great sacrifice, from the carnelian chalice, and contains powerful supernatural properties to heal your soul. Take it and eat."

Jether held the crimson-stained wood out to Nick, who frowned. "I can't eat that."

Jether smiled. "Take and eat."

Slowly Nick brought the wood to his mouth. As he placed it on his tongue it dissolved into a honeylike substance. He felt a surge of electricity arc from the neurotransmitters in his brain to the soles of his feet. *More freedom.*

Jether smiled. "You have two more choices. Two more stones to choose. Choose wisely. Take your time. You have all eternity." Jether smiled tenderly at Nick.

Nick stared down at the mass of colorful jeweled stones by his feet. Slowly he picked up an emerald green stone.

"Ah," said Jether. "The stone of the shepherd. You have chosen the heavenly emerald. It is the stone of green pastures. It restores your soul. Take it and eat."

Nick placed the emerald on his tongue. Again, it dissolved. He felt an infusion of comfort, of safety, of immense belonging and peace fill his soul.

He gazed down at the riverbed, drawn to a small glowing aquamarine stone by his feet. He picked it up and studied it. It glowed in his palm, its color transforming to every shade of blue.

Jether watched him intently. "We are nearly at the bank."

Nicholas tore his gaze away from the glowing stone and looked up. Above the water was a riverbank that stretched for miles. The meadows were greener than those in Ireland.

Nick followed Jether out of the water and onto the bank. The grass sprang up under his feet.

"It's alive!"

"Of course it's alive—this is heaven." Jether studied Nick, now clothed in white garments.

"You are ready, Nicholas. I have been chosen by Yehovah Himself to mentor you," Jether said softly. "I mentored Michael, Gabriel, and Lucifer, but never before in the history of the First Heaven has an angelic king been elected to mentor one of the Race of Men. Nicholas, open your hand."

Nick opened his palm. The beautiful aquamarine stone lay exuding rays of light.

"The stone of the seer." Jether closed his eyes. "To see God face to face—this is your destiny. You have been chosen."

Jether pointed a trembling hand over toward Eden. "There is Yehovah's garden."

Nick followed Jether's gaze to a flashing dark cloud of blue lightnings.

"Beyond the cloud, Yehovah walks. Few of the Race of Men, both on earth and even here in the First Heaven, venture beyond the dark cloud. They see Yehovah on His rubied throne, but he has specifically asked for you. To see Him face to face."

"I can't," Nick said, a strange dread gripping his heart. "I'm not worthy."

Jether gently took his hand. "Only one is worthy, Nicholas. And His sacrifice is enough."

CHAPTER THIRTY-SEVEN

ILLUMINUS HEADQUARTERS USA
CHINATOWN
NEW YORK CITY

JASON AND JULIA FOLLOWED Magruder into the sanatorium.

"We're prepared for every eventuality, Jason," the general said.

A thin man in a white coat walked in, a stethoscope draped over his neck. He walked over to a safe. Magruder followed him and placed his eye on the iris recognition scanner. The doctor opened the safe and took two glass vials from a row of at least ten.

"We don't have much of it," Magruder grunted. "Keep it for our friends or friends of our friends."

"It's like gold," the doctor said, shaking the vials. He removed a syringe from its wrapper and started to fill it from a vial.

"No." Jason shook his head.

The general turned his laptop screen to Jason. "In the event that any of us are caught," he said, "the first thing they'll do is inject us with the Mark, to rewrite our DNA. We're more useful to their cause as their pet supersoldiers, or whatever it is they're concocting, than dead.

"This . . . " Magruder took the vial from the doctor's hand and tapped it with his finger and thumb.

"This, Jason De Vere, is the only obstacle to your brother and his iniquitous cronies rewriting the human race's genetic code for their malevolent purpose, whatever that may be. The liquid contained in this vial, once injected into a human being, renders their DNA-rewriting program null and void. The Mark has no effect. Roll up your shirtsleeve."

Jason sighed. He rolled up his shirtsleeve. The doctor stuck the needle in and studied a monitor intently. A minute later, he nodded to Magruder.

Julia looked over to Jason. He nodded, and she reluctantly rolled up her tracksuit sleeve. She winced as the needle plunged into her skin.

The doctor studied the monitor's readings one more time and nodded.

"You'll be transported by railcar to our hangars," Magruder said. "A military aircraft will fly you to our safe house in Kansas. All being well, you should arrive safely in Jordan by tomorrow nightfall."

"Never count your chickens before they hatch."

Jason froze. He would know those elegant tones anywhere.

"*Uncle Xavier!*" Julia gasped.

They both turned.

Xavier Chessler nodded. General Magruder's own Serbian militia captain now held Magruder in a stranglehold.

"*Unfortunately*, General, over eight hundred of your

335

military were our plants. We've been watching your every move and planning this for two years. We *let* you exist."

Chessler nodded again.

"By the way, Magruder, you grossly miscalculated—you're *far* more useful to us *dead*." He nodded.

A soldier sliced through Magruder's throat with one thrust of his knife. Blood spurted from both severed carotid arteries, and the general dropped to the ground like a sack of cement.

Julia shook with terror and started to sob.

Jason gripped her arm. "Don't let him see your fear," he whispered. "These cowards feed on fear."

"I think the party has quite literally *ended*, children." Chessler smiled.

He took Julia gently by the arm.

"What *were* you thinking of, my dear, sweet Julia? What lies has Jason here filled your pretty head with? It's quite *pointless* to struggle. The militia on all seven floors were slaughtered in the first three minutes of our arrival. Macgruder and his underground base have been under surveillance for over four years. We've been waiting for the right opportunity to exterminate them. We're *ever* so grateful to you both."

He nodded to a soldier, who shoved Jason to the floor. Jason's jaw hit the concrete; blood gushed from his mouth.

Chessler's eyes were cold. "Only these two survive. Take them to the containment center."

Jason and Julia were hauled at gunpoint into an elevator. They were escorted out the warehouse door and into one of three waiting black Chinook helicopters in the empty parking lot. Chessler followed them inside and settled himself into the seat opposite them. He turned to the pilot.

"The harbor."

The Chinook took off into the skyline over Chinatown.

"Code amber," Chessler instructed through his earpiece.

A moment later, the entire base exploded in a blistering orange fireball.

∽

THE FIRST HEAVEN

Nick followed Jether down a golden path through a beautiful, exotic-looking forest. Finally, they stood at a gate. The house was Palladian, its every detail intricately carved.

The vast expanse of brilliant green lawn led straight onto a beach of pearl white sands, beyond which a sea of the same pale blue as the Caribbean gently lapped.

A figure was standing at an easel on the pale sands, painting.

It was a young woman, her long curly hair blowing in the soft sea winds. Her face was alive with joy and wonder.

"Jether!" she cried in delight. She held a rose in one hand.

"He has been with you."

She nodded. "Oh, that I had known Him better when I was on earth. I fell so short."

"But now you have all eternity to know Him and serve Him," said Jether softly. "Lilian, you have a visitor."

Nick stepped forward as Lilian stepped back. Her eyes welled with tears.

She ran to him, then ran her fingers over his face. "Nicholas," she whispered, "you look so different."

Nick grinned. "So do you, Mom. You look amazing!"

Jether looked at Nick. He still looked his earthly age of twenty-nine, but all hardness and worldliness had been erased from his face.

His features glowed with a peace that he had never attained on earth.

"You are beautiful, Nick," Lilian whispered. "He has made you beautiful. You have been with Him?"

She put Nick's hand to her face.

"I failed you, Nicholas. I should have taught you about Him. Prepared you when you were young, to live for Him."

"But He found me anyway, Mom, so all is well." Nick kissed her tenderly on both cheeks.

"Nicholas." A soft but low voice came from behind him.

Nick turned.

"Dad!" He drew an astonished breath. The last time he had seen his father, they both had said things that each regretted but never had the chance to take back.

"I'm so sorry, Dad, about the things I said to you. I didn't mean them. But I never had a chance to say sorry before you died." Nick hesitated.

"But I don't understand. You didn't believe—you were an agnostic."

"And proud of it, much to my regret." James De Vere looked out over the lapping waves, his eyes distant. "I viewed religion as a crutch for the weak, a set of fables. Lilian always had faith, but I was stubborn. Wouldn't listen.

"When I arrived at the hospital after my heart attack I was semiconscious. An old man, a priest, came to give me the last rites. As he placed his hand on my head I felt something strange, a power, surge through me.

"I remember the old man's words. He said to me, 'Son, you have not much time. Will you commit your life to Christ?'

"I could not speak, but suddenly, with all my being, I knew this was the truth. I managed to nod my head.

"And in a moment . . . " James De Vere stopped in mid sentence, overcome with emotion. Tears ran down his cheeks. Lilian took his hand, smiling up at him.

"There was a peace, Nicholas. A peace and assurance I had never experienced before at any time in my life. And as the old man prayed for me, I knew I was to ask forgiveness for each and every sin I had committed while on Earth. And I knew I had to forgive all those who had wronged me. And all the while, this simple old priest was staring down at me with such love and such compassion."

James De Vere wiped his eyes. He looked at Nick.

"And then the old man's face changed." James De Vere's voice choked with emotion.

"It was Him," he whispered.

Nick grasped James's hand. "Christ?"

James nodded. "It was Jesus Christ. He stayed with me, next to my bed, watching over me like a mother, until I took my very last breath. It was He who brought me here."

Lilian placed her arm around James's waist. "It still overcomes Him," she whispered.

Nick nodded, unable to speak, tears streaming down his cheeks.

And together, Lilian, James, and Nick stood, embracing, there on the sands of the First Heaven.

Jether bowed his head. "Oh, the joy of heaven," he whispered.

And vanished.

Leaving them. Together. Weeping on the white sands.

Chapter Thirty-eight

INTERNMENT CAMP
CHELSEA PIER
NEW YORK CITY

THE CHINOOK WAS descending fast. Jason stared out in disbelief—it was landing at the Chelsea Pier on Manhattan's West Side.

"Quite appropriate, I thought, Jason," Xavier Chessler purred. "The TV series *Law and Order* was shot in Pier Fifty-nine. VOX bought the studios in 2022—two of your more recent acquisitions. You should feel quite at home."

The helicopter came to a halt. Two soldiers opened the doors and shoved Jason out onto the tarmac, then shoved Julia out after him.

Jason stared stonily ahead. "What are you going to do, Chessler? Kill us?"

"Oh, *no*, dear boy." Chessler stood at the top of the Chinook's steps. He lit a cigarillo and drew on it. "How distasteful! What do you *take* me for? If I'd wanted to kill you, I would have cut your throats in the general's base. No, no, after your timely escape from Babylon, I've been dreaming up *far* more exhilarating plans for you both. After we've reprogrammed your DNA, you'll both be our finest spokespersons."

"That'll be a cold day in hell," Jason said through gritted teeth.

Chessler's warlock's brand started to burn.

"Yes, I'm sure you're right. But that's quite a while off. Let's live for the moment, shall we?"

He turned to the soldiers. "Take them to Subzero. Don't give them the Mark until I join you. I shall take great pleasure in viewing it firsthand." He drew hard on his cigarillo and gave a thin smile.

"It's reminiscent of Nero and the Colosseum, when the Christians were being fed to the lions. Of course, I'm fully aware you're not a Christian, but I definitely want a front seat."

"And you're *Nero*, I presume." Jason glared at Chessler.

Jason screamed noiselessly as the soldier's steel-toed boot slammed into his groin.

He retched onto the cold, hard concrete, then looked up through bloodshot eyes to see the soldier grasp Julia by the hair and place his mouth on hers. Her long acrylic nails raked down the side of his neck. The soldier flinched in pain as blood ran from the deep scratches. He backhanded Julia savagely across the face. Blood gushed from her nose and mouth as she hit the floor.

"Waterboarding's nothing to what we've got prepared for you both in here."

A light switched on behind a glass screen, and Xavier Chessler's face became visible.

"Later," he said to the soldier. "There'll be plenty of time for recreation later.

"But first, the Mark."

A third soldier set two wooden chairs in front of the steel table and threw Jason brutally onto one. Julia clasped the leg of the chair and slowly raised herself up.

A tall man entered, wearing a stethoscope around his neck. He listened to Jason's heart, then Julia's, and nodded.

"Pulse," he said. "Blood pressure."

A steel tray was wheeled in from the door. Jason stared at the vial filled with blue liquid. The Mark. Adrian's masterpiece.

If General Magruder's antidote to the Mark failed, he and Julia were finished. History.

The nurse attached a blood pressure cuff to a monitor, then pushed up Jason's sleeve. He swabbed down Jason's forearm and inserted the syringe, then repeated the procedure exactly with Julia.

Chessler smiled slightly. "And now the activator," he murmured.

The nurse swabbed a small area of skin on Jason's forehead, then injected the microscopic chip under the skin. He repeated the procedure with Julia.

Xavier Chessler's eyes were riveted to the monitor. The microchip started to glow red.

"Activation five percent," the nurse called out.

Chessler watched intently as the red bar graph on the screen in front of him slowly rose.

343

"Ten percent activated."

"Twenty-five percent . . . thirty percent."

Then the red bar on the computer screen reversed.

"Twenty percent deactivating," the nurse reported. "Ten percent. Program deactivating."

Chessler sat, his breathing shallow, watching Julia's monitor readings as they followed Jason's almost to the letter.

"Program deactivated."

Chessler nodded. He pressed the microphone button. "Inject a second chip."

The nurse repeated the process with Jason, then Julia. Chessler watched as the deactivation signs appeared on the screen for a second time.

"Seems the general's deactivating serum worked, Chessler," Jason said. "You can't rewrite our DNA. We've been preprogrammed. It's irreverrsible."

Xavier Chessler rose slowly to his feet.

"Kill him," he said softly. "Kill them both."

He walked toward the door, then turned.

"But make it slow."

The door clicked shut behind him.

Jason was chained to the chair. He stared through bloodshot eyes across to Julia, lying half dazed on the concrete. Tears stung his eyes.

She was brave. He'd forgotten how brave Julia St. Cartier was.

"A survivor," Lawrence had always called her. And he was right.

Jason looked over at her. Her makeup had worn completely off. Her hair was matted and bloody, and her acrylic nails had been pulled off. Blood still seeped from her mouth. She looked so young, much younger than her 45 years. So vulnerable.

And in that moment, he knew. He had never loved her as much as he loved her right now.

The door opened, and two soldiers marched toward Julia and yanked her to her feet.

"Jason," she whispered.

The first soldier kicked her savagely in her abdomen. She doubled up.

"Jason," she cried.

The second kick caught her in the spine. She struggled to breathe. The tears mingled with the blood trickling down her cheeks.

She turned her head, in intense pain, toward Jason; then, with a superhuman effort, she spoke. "I've always loved you."

Jason nodded. His eyes welled up with rage and tears. He couldn't bring himself to speak, for the intensity of emotion welling up within him.

A figure behind him was unchaining him.

He gave Julia a weak, lopsided smile.

The last thing he remembered thinking as someone pushed his face savagely down into the vat of water was that if they ever survived this, he'd give Callum Vickers a bloody-good run for his money.

FIRST HEAVEN
EAST OF EDEN

Nick and Jether finally reached the Eastern gardens of Eden. Far in the distance were two towering pearlescent gates, guarded by the Seraphim.

Jether took Nicks hand. "I shall await you here."

"Go . . . Go to your Father." He kissed Nick on both cheeks.

"Go to *Yehovah.*"

Nick took a deep breath, steeled himself, then walked toward the entrance to Yehovah's Hanging Gardens of Eden. The six Seraphim bowed as one to Nick as the enormous pearlescent gates slowly opened.

Nick turned and looked back at Jether for a long while, then walked through into Yehovah's Gardens. The huge Gates shut behind him.

He took a deep breathand gazed around.

Massive curtains of flickering light shafts, all the hues of the rainbow, shifted across the vast horizons, like some immense swirling celestial aurora.

Nick watched in wonder as the shafts of light transformed from lilac to aquamarine, then to vermilion.

He turned to his left. Hundreds of feet above him was a thundering monumental waterfall that gushed down to a swiftly flowing river lined by ancient willow trees.

On either side of the stream, were lush, tropical celestial gardens where unicorns and oryx grazed in the meadows.

As the luminance lifted, a second gate became visible, and two cherubim, over ten feet in height, clothed with fires and lightning, bowed low before him, their four outstretched wingtips touching each other.

"Nicholas De Vere, beloved servant of Christos our King, they addressed him in unison. The Great Emperor of Heaven awaits you."

They ushered him through a second much smaller arbour-like pearl gate into the thick, swirling white mists.

He followed the ten foot tall angels, as they walked past knee-high gladioli and frangipani, beds of pale blue flowers that looked almost like tulips except for the long crystal stamens in their centre. Past climbing roses of every hue and imagination. Past intricately carved pearl and crystal benches and arbours. The incredible floral aroma permeated his senses.

Finally, they reached a second gate, different from the previous ones.

It was higher—almost twelve feet high and three feet in breadth, carved of solid gold and embedded with emeralds and diamonds set in a vast jacinth wall that surrounded the entrance to the inner sanctum of Eden. The gate was slightly ajar.

Nick pushed it open.

There, standing in the far corner of the garden, was a tall figure clothed in shining white garments.

Slowly the figure turned.

It was Jesus.

He took Nicks hands in his own, then turned them upward. The aquamarine stone pulsated in Nicks palm.

"You have been chosen, Nicholas. Chosen to visit my Father."

There was complete adoration on Jesus face as he turned and gazed far in the distance. In front of them, seemingly suspended in midair, were the vast, exquisite Hanging Gardens of Yehovah.

Hardly visible from where Nick stood, rose what seemed to be a thick dark roaring cloud from which emananted blue and white flashing lightnings.

"He awaits you. Go to Him." Jesus vanished before Nick's eyes.

Nick stared, utterly transfixed, at the cloud ahead that hung heavily over the hanging gardens. Cobalt blue lightnings erupted from its very centre.

He walked through a second gate, towards two huge trees in the farthest corner of the hanging gardens. the trees were almost wholly enveloped by constantly swirling white mists, their fruit glistening gold and blue in the lightnings. To the north of the trees, Nick could see the dark cloud more clearly.

He placed one foot in front of the other. As he neared the cloud, the thundering grew so loud in intensity, that he could barely hear his own thoughts. Suddenly an immense terror gripped his heart. He turned back to search for Jesus, but the gates behind him were now tightly shut.

Somehow he sensed he had to continue onward towards the terrifying cloud.

As he drew nearer, dragging one foot in front of the other, a strange darkness started to fall like a thick, heavy veil over the gardens. Nick stopped in mid step, closing his eyes in dread. He should never have come. He was not worthy enough to be here. He was not ready.

After what seemed like hours, he took all his courage in his hands and opened his eyes.

Ahead of him, through a gap in the veil of darkness,

wound a glittering path. His archeologists curiousity, instinct-ively got the better of him.

Nick bent down and picked up a handful of stones.

"Diamonds," he murmured in wonder. He looked down at the path, some of the diamonds were as large as a gooses egg. Nick emptied his hand and picked up the large diamond. It felt as light as a feather, its texture, completely different to the diamonds of Earth.

Nick took a few more steps, then frowned. Embedded in the diamond path were rows of large glistening crimson stones. He knelt again.

'Rubies . . . ' He looked around him. The darkness was shifting from shades of amethyst to a deep thunderous black. Suddenly, he was gripped by a deep terror, a terror that he had never experienced before.

He turned back on the path, the urge to run over-whelming him. He looked down in horror. The path behind him had vanished. Now, behind him was only a mass of black swirling sky.

Trembling visibly, he turned back towards the cloud and looked down.

The shimmering path continued to curve its way deep, deep into the very centre of the darkness to the very epicenter of the lightnings and roarings.

He still fought the overwhelming urge to turn back, but something deep within his soul drew him onward, still onward.

He placed one foot in front of the other in trepidation. He had the distinct feeling he was being observed. There was a movement to his left. Slowly the clouds cleared for a few seconds. Nick gasped.

Towering over him was a monstrous living creature that had six wings. As the clouds cleared, Nick could make out hundreds of living eyes on the creature's upper and lower wings.

The roaring was coming from the creature. It sounded like many voices harmonizing in unison.

Nick frowned. He could make out the actual words.

"Holy, holy, holy is the Lord God, the Almighty—the one who always was, who is, and who is still to come."

Then the clouds descended again and the creature disappeared into the swirling mists.

A tempestuous wind blew. Lightning struck from east to west of the horizon. Nick flung himself, face down, to the ground, petrified.

And then, through the thunder and the roarings, through the lightnings and the veil of darkness, Nick heard a voice.

It was a voice as that of a thousand waters.

It was a voice infinitely more beautiful than either angelic or human imagination had ever the capacity to conceive.

Somehow Nick knew that this was the voice that had thrust a million flaming suns into orbit.

This was the voice that had fashioned ten thousand times ten thousand galaxies and laid the boundaries of the firmaments of a thousand universes.

The voice that allotted the path of a million, million moons and created the lightning, the tempests, and the hail.

The voice of the Sovereign of all sovereigns: authoritative, noble, and valiant, yet filled with grace and exquisite tenderness.

It was one voice, yet as three.

And it was three, yet it was one.

It was the voice of Yehovah.

"Nicholas . . . " the voice pealed. "Nicholas . . . "

Nick started to weep, overcome. The lightning struck and the thunder grew in intensity. Finally the voice spoke once more.

"Nicholas . . . of the Race of Men." The voice itself sounded as though it was weeping.

"You, my beloved, you—who I created to be my fellowship. Come . . . Come to me."

Nick began to tremble violently, as an incredible joy rose from the very core of him.

He rose to his knees, then stumbled to his feet and placed one foot slowly in front of the other and walked toward the center of the swirling black cloud.

Suddenly the thunder and lightning subsided, and the wind decreased to a gentle, balmy breeze.

The darkness cleared and straight ahead of him, Nick saw a huge golden throne half enveloped by swirling white mists.

A hand stretched out toward him from the throne.

Tears streamed down his face, as slowly Nick raised his head.

The mists cleared. Nick looked up directly into the eyes of Yehovah.

Oh indescribable love. Acceptance. Humor. Laughter. Omniscient. Omnipotent.

Yet all embracing.

It was as though Nick felt every atom on his body had found its home.

This was where his heart would rest forever.

It was here, in His presence that all earthly pain evaporated.

Here, in His presence, that all earthly sorrows were transformed to joy.

It was here, in His presence, that all fear fled.

That all questions were answered.

That the raging storms were hushed.

And as he gazed into Yehovah's eyes, it seemed that all things, that lay dark and were only seen through a cloud darkly, were suddenly understood and made plain.

Where even the most tired battleweary heart could be refreshed.

And as Nick took Yehovah's outstretched hand, an inexpressible incorrigible joy welled up within him.

This was truly heaven. This was the reason for his whole being.

Every tear he had ever shed.

Every battle he had ever fought.

The tapestry of Nick's life had finally become complete.

. . . Here in the arms of his Father.

Yehovah.

CHAPTER THIRTY-NINE

INTERNMENT CAMP, CHELSEA PIER
UNDERGROUND JAIL, LEVEL 10
FORTY-EIGHT HOURS LATER

"Who is more afraid: the child who is afraid of the dark, or the man who is afraid of the light?"

Jason struggled to breathe. The strange voice inside his head grew louder. Where had they taken Julia? Drenched in sweat, he tossed from side to side in the dark, hands over his ears.

"Who is more afraid: the child who is afraid of the dark, or the man who is afraid of the light?"

He heard the keys turn in the lock of the steel door.

"Get up," a voice whispered piercingly in Jason's ear. "Get *up!*" The voice was more insistent.

Jason sat bolt upright, trembling, in complete darkness. He was shoved to his feet, and a burlap sack was thrust over his head.

A strong pair of arms grasped him by the shoulders and pushed him out the doorway and into a corridor. More voices.

Marching . . . more corridors.

Marching.

Suddenly, the rush of freezing New York winter air hit him like a jackhammer. Zero degrees. He was outside.

Oh, God, they were going to shoot him. This was it. The end. He had never thought it would be like this.

More voices. Foreign voices. Shouting. Gunshots.

He was suffocating under the burlap.

Sounds of turbine engines. Rotors.

He was pushed roughly up more stairs.

Into a helicopter. He had ridden in enough of them to know.

He sat paralyzed with fear. They were moving him. To God knows where. Where was *Julia*?

The turbines intensified to a scream.

More sounds of automatic gunfire.

The helicopter accelerated upward.

The sack was pulled off his head. Sitting to his right was General Hamid Assaf.

He stared ahead in shock.

Seated directly opposite him, looking like hell . . . Was Alex Lane Fox.

"Drink this," the general said, handing Jason two bottles of water.

Hands trembling from dehydration, he slugged down the first bottle, then the second.

He wiped his mouth with the back of his hand, still staring at Alex in utter disbelief, then looked back at General Assaf.

Slowly he turned to his left.

Leaning against the window next to him, asleep under a blanket, was Julia. Her face was bloodied and bruised, but she was alive.

Jason sighed in relief. "Thank you," he rasped.

"The plan was to rescue you both," Assaf said softly. He nodded to Julia. "Which we did."

"And Polly Mitchell."

"We were too late for Polly," Alex snapped.

Julia's eyes flickered open. She tried to sit up.

"They took Polly away," she whispered. "She was sick, Alex—very, very sick. The plague. They took her to the quarantine hospital."

Julia's head fell onto her chest like a dead weight.

"We gave her a mild sedative," General Assaf said softly. "She'll be awake by the time we arrive. Just over ninety minutes."

"Arrive where?" Jason asked.

"Kansas. Safe house. We're keeping to the plan, just a bit behind schedule. Kansas and Missouri are governed by resisters. A military plane is refueling at the Lawrence airport. We're safe under the radar—totally blacked out."

"You all right, son?" Jason asked, turning to Alex.

Alex stared grimly down at his clenched fists. "If it costs me my life, I'll hunt down whoever did this to Polly."

Jason looked down and saw that Alex's left hand was handcuffed to the seat. He raised his eyebrows to General Assaf.

"Is that *really* necessary?"

"I'm afraid so, Mr. De Vere. After he arrived back from Saudi Arabia and found out that Polly was dead, he wanted to take on Chessler and the entire military unit single-handedly. I was left with no choice."

Jason leaned over and grasped Alex's shoulder. Alex recoiled.

General Assaf opened his briefcase on his lap. "From one of our inside men in the detention centers."

"Can I borrow your glasses, General?"

The general smiled and passed Jason a pair of silver-rimmed spectacles, then patted his pocket.

"Oh, before I forget, Mr. De Vere . . . " He held out the platinum wedding ring that Jason had given him for safe-keeping when they were aboard the Hercules transport plane. In his other hand were Jason's wallet and his Breitling watch.

Jason took the wallet and watch, then stared down at the thick platinum wedding band. "Thank you, General."

Alex watched as Jason took the ring from General Assaf and slid it carefully onto his finger, put on his watch, then put the glasses on and took the first document from General Assaf.

"The warrant for Polly's arrest," Alex mumbled in a monotone. He pointed to the top document.

"It's a directive," Jason muttered. "She was assigned to the detention center. The East Pier."

"That's where they take the Blacklist," Assaf said calmly. "It's a containment center twelve floors underground."

"Resisters. A list that is held in the core. The ones who won't take the Mark."

Jason frowned. "But we . . . " He turned to Julia, who was in a deep stupor. "We *had* to take an antidote, or the DNA rewriting program in the Mark would have worked anyway, even against our own subconscious. All they had to do was inject Polly."

Alex sighed. He looked straight into Jason's eyes. "She was a Christian, Uncle Jas. A committed one."

"I don't get it," Jason said.

Alex shook his head at Assaf. "He won't believe it. Calls it nonsense."

Assaf looked directly at Jason.

"The seal is an indelible mark—a symbol, if you will. Invisible in this dimension, but visible and enforced in a parallel dimension."

"It's worn by the Christians, Uncle Jas. Not the lip-servers—the ones who really *believe*."

Jason started to retort, then stopped himself.

"They're marked in that dimension with an invisible seal," Assaf said. "Our great ancestor King Aretas of Petra taught the Nabataeans this fact. He was a follower of the Hebrew. It was King Aretas who took the Christ child and His mother to safety in Egypt. He hid them in the monastery."

"The monastery . . . " Jason frowned. "In Alexandria?"

"I have personally seen the seal in operation," General Assaf said quietly. "It seems to affect the bearer's own DNA. It grants a protection against the rewriting program. Immunity. Resisters who wear the seal are immune to the effects of the Mark. The only way Polly could suffer the effects is if she recanted her allegiance."

"To Christ?" Jason said softly.

Assaf nodded. "Only if, by an act of her own will, she recanted, would the Mark have effect."

Assaf handed Jason the remaining pages of the report.

"Polly would *never* recant," Alex glared at the general. "She was stripped naked, her head shaved. Locked up without food or water. Water boarded constantly."

Alex's hands trembled with rage.

Assaf turned the page. "Tortured. Raped," he continued

evenly. "Then taken to Area Subzero. "The guillotines." Jason looked up from the papers, appalled. "She was guillotined at twenty-three hundred hours, Tuesday, December eighteenth."

General Assaf sifted through the documents on his lap. "Death Certificates. There are two." He handed them to Jason.

Jason scanned the first document, issued by the State of New York. He read aloud. "'Cause of death: plague. Place of death: Lincoln Memorial Hospital, New York City.'"

He picked up a second document. "Issued by the EU Headquarters: 'Dissident. Militant. Blacklist. Reason for Detention: Terrorist acts against the state. Death by guillotine.'"

A small handwritten note was clipped underneath the report.

Jason removed the scrap of paper and read each word methodically. "This *is* something strange, though: 'Guards in paranoid state, the blade fell, then . . . '"

He shook his head. "I don't understand it. There must be some kind of error."

"What do you mean, *error*?" Alex asked.

"It says she was beheaded, but then . . . " He looked at Alex strangely. " . . . then she disappeared. Dematerialized."

Alex grabbed the lined piece of paper with his free hand and studied the handwritten notes. "What time does the second death certificate give?" he asked. "The *precise* time of death." Alex stared strangely at General Assaf, who studied the death certificate.

"Eleven-o-seven p.m."

Alex put his head in his hands, then started to laugh. He looked almost drunk with euphoria.

Jason looked at him as if he had lost his mind. "Get a hold of yourself, Alex, son," he said softly.

"You don't understand, Uncle Jas," Alex whispered, a strange smile spreading across his lips. "Eleven-zero-seven p.m., Eastern Standard time . . . " Alex turned to the general.

" . . . is exactly *six-zero-seven a.m.* in Saudi Arabia." He put his hands to his face. "Seven hours' difference. *She defeated them!*"

Jason shrugged. "I really don't get it."

"But *he* does!" Alex turned to General Assaf, who nodded silently.

"She *disappeared, General! Polly disappeared*—just like Jotapa and Ni—"

General Assaf glared at him, furious. He shook his head in warning.

Jason's eyes narrowed. "What do you mean, *Nick*?" he snapped. "Nick's back with Lawrence St. Cartier, in Petra."

Assaf glared at Alex, who stared sheepishly down at the floor. "I can assure you, Mr. de Vere, that your younger brother is quite safe," he said.

Alex pushed up his shirtsleeve. "Look," he said. "My watch stopped precisely when the Saudi incident happened. There was some kind of electromagnetic interference. The hands—they won't budge."

Jason stared at Alex, ashen.

"What do you mean, the Saudi *incident*?" He looked down at Alex's watch." The hands were stopped at precisely 6:07 a.m.

"Nick and Jotapa." Alex paused. "There was an incident."

Jason could hardly form the words. "You're saying they were . . . they were *killed*?"

"No, Uncle Jas," Alex said evenly. "I was there. I saw everything firsthand. It was all going precisely to plan. We were about to leave, to take them back to Petra on the Hercules. Then Nick told me he wasn't coming back with us. Then he and Jotapa disappeared. Right in front of us. The electromagnetic field was so strong, my watch stopped, and it's never worked since. General Khalid is a witness.

"It's the same time they disappeared, General. You had confirmation from the Jordanian special forces."

The general nodded.

Jason reached over and grasped the general by the shoulders, shaking with fury. "*Where* is my brother?"

General Assaf sighed. "Your youngest brother accompanied our special forces to liberate Princess Jotapa and the crown prince from Mansoor in Saudi Arabia."

"I'm fully aware of Nick's trip to Saudi," Jason replied. "He was to get Jotapa out, then return to meet Lawrence St. Cartier at the underground base in Petra. Jordanian special forces were accompanying him."

"That was the *plan*, yes," said Assaf. "But there was an incident. Your brother and the princess . . . they disappeared. In front of seventeen witnesses."

"What do you *take* me for!" Jason spluttered. "They can't just *disappear*. It's impossible! You're telling me that my brother just *vanished*. For God's sake, man, he wasn't even a . . . a *Christian*!"

There was a long silence.

"Oh, yes, he was, Uncle Jas. Nick was a Christian. Your brother disappeared. Vanished into thin air."

"Jotapa . . . " Trembling, Jason released the general.

"The royal princess also disappeared."

Jason looked from General Assaf to Alex. "What's going on, General? General Macgruder said he had over a thousand witnessed and documented disappearances."

The general looked at him in silence.

"Lawrence St. Cartier has been informed of the 'incident'?" Jason asked.

Assaf nodded. "The esteemed professor wanted to tell you face-to-face, but it seems events have conspired against us." He shook his head at Alex.

"We have sworn statements from seventeen witnesses. They all correlate precisely. General Khalid—a lieutenant general. Three captains, the special forces team, the crown prince. And Alex. Your brother and the Jordanian princess disappeared at precisely six-o-seven a.m., December eighteenth."

"The exact time on Polly's death certificate." Alex looked up at Jason in wonder. "Don't you get it, Uncle Jas? Don't you realize what it means? The *Rapture*—it actually *happened.*"

Jason snatched the paper from Alex and studied it. He was silent for a long moment.

General Assaf turned to a tall soldier behind them. "Relay this to Petra. Get the reports: both state issue and EU Headquarters issue."

The lights dimmed.

Julia stirred. "Where are we?" she murmured.

"We're entering Kansas airspace," Assaf said, "We'll be landing in twenty minutes.

"By the way, Alex, this is yours, I believe." The general opened his briefcase. "It was one of our intelligence officers that swept the building. You asked him to check behind a certain painting in your study, I believe."

He unlocked Alex's handcuffs, then held out a white linen envelope.

Alex stared at the distinctive bold writing on the envelope, then tore it open.

It was from Polly.

⤳

FIRST HEAVEN

Polly stared around her at the dazzling lilac and turquoise horizons, trying to get her bearings.

Everything had happened so fast. One minute she was facing death, staring up at the guillotine; the next, she was here, still clinging to Jesus' hand. She turned to him. Very gently, he let go of her hand.

Polly ran like the wind over the emerald green grass of the vast meadow. She bent to pick a bunch of dazzling white lilies. As she picked them, more lilies instantly grew in their place. She laughed in wonder.

"Everthing's *alive!*" she cried.

Jesus stood watching her in delight.

Polly felt something rub against her legs. She looked down, then dropped to her knees.

"Mr Smithy!" she cried. She looked up into Jesus' face. "He died when I was five. This is *incredible!*"

She laid the lilies down on the grass and picked up the enormous purring tabby cat in her arms. He rubbed his face against hers in affection. "He was the only pet I ever had."

"Why . . . " She gazed up at Jesus. "It's just like going

through the wardrobe in Narnia," she murmured in wonder. "It is like Narnia?" she whispered.

Jesus smiled brilliantly. He nodded. "Yes, beloved Polly. It is very like Narnia."

He laid his hand very gently on her cheek.

"C. S. Lewis saw many things. He was a seer. And he was our friend. He was born into the earth for the very purpose of writing what you could call 'letters from home'—to remind those who love us, amid their earthly struggles and human failings, that earthly life and death is not the end. Indeed, it is just the beginning of a wondrous eternal story."

Jesus smiled again at Polly with infinite tenderness.

"You may meet him later, if you like."

"And *you*?" Polly grinned. "You are *Aslan*?"

"Yes." Jesus threw his head back and laughed in amusement. "You could say I am Aslan." He gazed at Polly with eyes that radiated living streams of love.

"You are the Lion of Judah," Polly said softly. "And the risen lamb."

She took both of Jesus' hands in her own and turned them over so that the palms faced upward. Her tears fell onto two large nail holes, one in the center of each palm.

Jesus leaned over and kissed Polly's soft blond head. He took her face in his scarred hands.

"You have loved me all your life, Polly. Your love has been such a great gift, both to me and to my Father. You have loved us, not for what we could give you, but you have loved us for ourselves."

Tears fell down Jesus' cheeks.

"But now there is something I need to share with you.

What do you remember of the few minutes before we arrived in this world?"

Polly closed her eyes. "I remember seeing the guillotine. I remember being really scared. And suddenly, you were there. And then I was here."

Polly's mind ran back to the moment she looked into the most beautiful and compassionate eyes she had ever seen.

"I took your hand. And we were gone. Is it the Rapture?"

Jesus nodded. "Yes, Polly," he said softly. "The Rapture has been and gone. This is true. But there is still something I have to share with you. Something you may find hard to understand. So listen carefully."

Polly nodded.

"I have to leave you for a very short time."

Jesus laid his hand on hers.

"Beloved Polly, there will come a time when we will never be apart again. But it is almost time for the fifth seal to be opened."

"The seal of the martyrs," Polly whispered.

Jesus nodded.

"You see, Polly," he said tenderly, "the guillotine *did* fall. You were killed. You are one of the great company of end-time martyrs. Those who loved their lives not unto death."

"But I don't remember being . . . " She held her hands to her throat. On her palm was blood. She looked down; her white garments were crimson and stained.

She stared at Jesus. Stunned.

Polly watched in wonder as tears fell down Jesus' cheeks. He gazed at her, almost in adoration.

"I go now to my Father. To open the fifth seal."

Polly stared at Jesus in intense yearning. Suddenly, her eyes clouded.

"Alex . . . "

Polly's eyes grew wide.

"Alex . . . "

"Alex has his own journey, as do you. Lamaliel will take you to the altar beyond the Rubied Door." He smiled. "And I will see you soon. Very soon." He kissed her again on the forehead and disappeared.

"You are greatly honored in this world." Lamaliel bowed to Polly. She followed the ancient elder through the meadow until they reached a towering jacinth wall.

Tears welled up in his eyes. "We the angelic have not had the privilege to lay down our lives for the Lamb, though we would willingly do so." He turned the latch of a small door inside the wall. Polly followed him through the door, then hesitated, looking up at Lamaliel in trepidation.

"It is the presence of our great Emperor, Yehovah, the King of the universes, that you sense. You sense his great mantle of authority and might." He smiled gently and held out his hand. "He is the Mighty One, but He is also the great King of mercies. Of compassions. There is no need to fear. Come with me. We will enter through the corridors of the slain Lamb to the inner chambers, where you will bathe in the fountain that flows directly from the rubied throne of Yehovah. There you will receive your white garments. And your crown of courage. The crown of the overcomer. Then the royal guard will take you to join with the rest of your sisters and brothers who await you with longing, underneath the carnelian altar."

They turned a corner. Lamaliel looked up in reverence. Polly followed his gaze. Above them towered a door that must have been well over a hundred feet high. It was made of huge individual glistening rubies.

Lamaliel fell prostrate. The Rubied Door opened slowly. He nodded to Polly.

"They await you. The Lamb is about to open the fifth seal."

CHAPTER FORTY

ILLUMINUS SAFE HOUSE
LAWRENCE, KANSAS

JASON LOOKED OUT the Victorian windows of the Kansas farmhouse, at the rolling snow-covered fields. He had showered, changed clothes, and eaten and was feeling on the way back to being halfway human. He pulled on a snow jacket hanging by the back door and pushed open the large screen doors. The cold hit him like a tidal wave. Alex and General Assaf sat on the porch swing, drinking steaming hot coffee from a thermos.

"Coffee?" asked Alex.

Jason nodded and rubbed his palms together, obviously frozen. Alex poured strong black coffee into an enamel mug.

"Gloves are in the right pocket, Mr. De Vere, sir," said General Assaf.

Jason took out a pair of fleece gloves and pulled them on. "Thanks. I thought Kansas and Missouri had the worst of the pandemic."

"Whole area's clean," Alex mumbled through a mouthful of cornbread and butter.

"The Resisters sweep it twenty-four seven," General Assaf replied. "The entire regional government of Kansas and Missouri were patriots. Patriot states. Our intelligence served us well. We prepared an antidote. Resisters in Missouri, Kansas, and Indiana received an effective vaccine. It was previously developed by the U.S. Army and used under an investigational new drug status. We were able to recreate it in one of our underground laboratories. Kansas, Missouri, Texas, Virginia, and Indiana received the antidote two weeks before the pandemic. It was administered subcutaneously to every citizen of all five resister states. All victims of the biological attack. The all clear has been given."

"Cornbread, Uncle Jas?"

Jason sat on a large wooden swing directly under the disused old fan on the ceiling of the porch. He nodded. "Just the coffee. Strong."

"It's strong, all right." Alex grinned. "I'm going to make pancakes."

"He's almost like his old self," said Jason.

The general smiled. "He believes it's what Polly would want. Whatever was in that envelope transformed his whole world."

"Talking of that . . . " General Assaf took out an official-looking document and handed it to Jason. "It came through while you were sleeping."

Jason looked down at the death certificate. "Jontil Purvis," he murmured. "I don't *believe* it. Cause of death: black plague. December fourteenth."

"Our people are still checking with our contact inside the detention center to see if there's any record of her being a dissenter," General Assaf said. "To all intents and purposes, it looked as though she died of the pandemic."

"Let me know if you find anything else," Jason said. "I still don't get it about Nick. I need hard evidence."

He rocked back and forth in silence, drinking in the vast vista of snow-covered fields that stretched out for miles before him. Deep in thought.

Kansas. He had never been to Kansas. It was pretty. Like a Christmas card.

"Hey." A soft voice broke the silence.

Julia stood in the doorway, towel-drying her hair. Normally flatironed within a millimeter of its life, it hung in soft blond curls framing her heart-shaped face.

Jason smiled. "The natural look."

Julia grimaced. "No flatiron."

She threw the towel at him.

"It's freezing—come inside!"

"Hey, Jules, I . . . I'm sorry about your ring. God knows what they did with it. From Callum, I mean. It was some kind of rock."

Julia cocked her head to one side and studied Jason intently.

She dropped her gaze down to his ring finger. He was wearing his old wedding ring.

"Where . . . ?" Her voice trailed off.

"Lily. She kept it for me. She said I'd need it on this trip. And it so happens that she's right!"

They stared, almost transfixed, into each other's eyes.

"I have to tell Callum, Jas. It's only fair," Julia said softly.

"About the ring?" he murmured, never taking his steel blue eyes off her honey brown ones.

"No, about us."

Alex watched from the kitchen in amazement as Jason's and Julia's fingers intertwined. Jason kissed Julia full on the lips. "Tell him soon."

"I will." Tears of joy welled up in Julia's eyes. "Tell me I won't regret this, Jason Ambrose De Vere."

He clasped Julia's petite hand in his and moved his head half an inch from hers.

"You won't regret this, Julia Samantha St. Cartier. It's destiny. I take thee . . . "

Julia shook her head at him and laughed. "It's going to be formal or nothing."

Alex pushed open the screen door, holding a plate of pancakes. His mouth dropped open.

Jason looked up. "Careful, Alex—you'll swallow a wasp."

Julia sat on the sofa next to Jason, her head resting on his shoulder.

"Um, Uncle Jas . . . "

Jason glared at him darkly. Alex nodded at Jason's wedding ring.

"What's going on? Is there something you both should be telling me?" Alex winked at Julia mischievously.

She lifted her head and pulled her hand away from Jason and slapped Alex's chest. "Nothing you haven't already guessed."

Jason studied Alex intently. "Alex, I know it's personal. But did Polly's note mention anything . . . " He hesitated and took a slug of his coffee. "Um," he said awkwardly. "Did she . . . ?"

Alex shook his head. "You're not exactly subtle, Uncle Jas. You mentioned the date December fourteenth twice, *then* asked for Jontil Purvis's death certificate."

"Well, did she?"

"Did she what?" Alex stared at him inscrutably.

"Mention the Rapture?" Jason growled.

Alex nodded. "She did." He took the envelope from his shirt pocket and handed it to Jason. "Read it. Polly was always fond of you, Uncle Jas. She'd want you to read it. She'd want you to know the truth."

Jason nodded. He stood up, took the envelope from Alex, and walked to the far edge of the porch, reading in silence. Strange. It was as though he could hear Polly's voice in his head.

Tuesday 1 December 12, 2025

My beloved Alex,
I had a dream last night, Alex. It was a dream but it wasn't a dream. Call it a forewarning. An omen of things to come.

I saw my name on a list. The Blacklist. They're coming for me, Alex. I saw militia in black suits. Machine guns. I was taken to a detention center. Near the water. It looked like the Piers.

They'll take me away. They'll do terrible things to me. They'll tell you I died of the pandemic. Don't believe them.

I'm not sick, Alex. I've never felt so good in my life. And He's coming. I can sense it as surely as I know my love for you.

They've been talking the past hour about the vaccine on the TV. It's the Mark, Alex. The Mark of the Beast. The number of the Beast is 666.

So they'll kill me. But He's coming, Alex.

Jason frowned. The ink was smudged.

ALEX'S APARTMENT
MEATPACKING DISTRICT, NEW YORK
THREE DAYS EARLIER

Polly brushed the streaming tears from her cheeks. She picked up the pen, her face glowing with a strange, ethereal luminosity.

"You know what I've learned in my short twenty-four years? You know what's strange, Alex? I always thought that to die for my faith would be the hardest thing I could ever face. To be martyred. But you know . . . "

Polly looked over at the picture of Alex on her bedside table. She picked up the pen again, her fingers trembling. She could hear the slamming doors of the Homeland Security military vans that had arrived three minutes ago.

"It's not the dying that's hard. It's the living it out that's easier said than done. I'm going to miss you so terribly. I wish you were here with me.

"Alex, you have to know this: that the Rapture is close. So close. I'll be with Him forever. Don't ever forget what we . . . "

She heard the thudding of boots up the stairwell.

She folded the letter, pushed it into an envelope, and ran to Alex's study.

SAFE HOUSE
LAWRENCE, KANSAS

"They found it inside my grandfather's thesaurus. It was our hiding place. I'd told General Assaf to look there. Polly knew I'd find it."

Alex wiped his eyes with the back of his hand.

Jason's eyes welled up. "Hey, pal, I'm here for you, Alex. Always."

And Jason Ambrose De Vere clasped Alex Lane Fox in his arms and held him. Like a son.

CHAPTER FORTY-ONE

SECOND HEAVEN

MICHAEL STOOD directly opposite Lucifer on the barren ice wastelands of Gehenna. The ice tempests raged violently over their heads.

Lucifer's features were shadowed by his white hooded velvet cape. Michael pulled his own cloak tightly around him. He studied his brother.

"Your beguiling speeches that once found their mark leave no trace on me," said Michael. "You demand a war, Lucifer. A war you shall have. Twice you have been vanquished, yet *still* you persist in your vain delusion to overthrow Yehovah."

"*Why*, Michael?" Lucifer flung off his hood. His long raven hair blew violently in the tempests. A sudden euphoria spread across his features.

"Why?" He clasped his hand dramatically to his temple. "Why did it elude me before? It is *so simple*. I have the answer!"

Lucifer grinned.

"I shall be *magnanimous*. My war, as you and I are both aware, is *not* with Yehovah, whom I still revere and reverence, but is primarily with the Race of Men. I shall be predisposed to magnanimity towards Yehovah."

Michael studied him, steely eyed.

"Why, my brother . . . " Lucifer smiled winningly at Michael. " . . . your judgments of me are *far* too harsh. I have decided!"

He spun around suddenly and raised his face to the tempests.

"Relay to my Father that I absolve Him of *all crimes* against me and the fallen host. I would show him my benevolence. There shall be *two* thrones." Lucifer stopped in mid sentence, deep in thought.

"In fact, this would please me *greatly*. I shall finally be as He. Surely we shall rule together. As one."

Michael raised his hand. "I can endure your diatribe no longer." He heaved a long-suffering sigh. "I shall report to the High Council that you have *finally* gone insane."

Michael turned his back and started to walk away, his hand on his broadsword.

"*You tell Yehovah!*" Lucifer shouted after him. "I retract my kindness. Because of my brother Michael's *supreme insolence!*"

Michael stood very still. Slowly he turned.

"I shall tell Yehovah that you suffer from a strange malady. That your mind has been afflicted. That you suffer delusions that reach far above your station."

"I shall yet defeat you, Michael, my brother," Lucifer hissed, his eyes raised toward the First Heaven. "At the rise of the two crimson moons, I will gather my armies and defeat you in your own backyard."

Michael raised steely eyes to Lucifer.

"Then it is final. We war, brother."

Lucifer stared at the place where Michael had been standing. But Michael had vanished.

"Yes," he murmured. "We war."

CHAPTER FORTY-TWO

LAWRENCE MILITARY AIRFIELD
LAWRENCE, KANSAS

HUGE SEARCHLIGHTS illuminated the small convoy of military jeeps as they screeched to a halt on the tarmac of what had previously been known as the Lawrence Municipal Airport. The Midwest's new patriot government had recently commandeered the airfield into military use. Generals Rivera and Assaf got out of the first jeep. Jason, Julia, and Alex got out of the second.

Jason glanced down at his watch. It was well after two a.m. He followed Julia's and Alex's gaze to a sleek military jet squatting just a few yards in front of them.

The jet was almost a precise replica of his own Gulfstream 7, seized by FEMA by order of Xavier Chessler. He scowled.

General Rivera walked over to Jason. "Gulfstream Five. Designated *C-37A* in U.S. Air Force service. Belongs to the Midwest Patriot movement now." He grinned. "Believe it or not, we have five of these babies."

Rivera escorted Jason over to the steps of the jet, where

General Assaf was in close conversation with the pilot. Assaf turned to Jason.

"The aircraft is equipped with military comms, secure voice, and data capability, Mr. De Vere. We're still in patriot country over Kansas, Iowa, and Wisconsin."

"Our men have been in touch with Canada," Rivera added. "They're not exactly fans of the Union. You're cleared."

General Rivera saluted once more.

"Once you're out of Canadian airspace you're on your own."

Assaf saluted back.

Jason took Julia's arm and followed General Assaf up the steps of the jet. He took in the crew at a glance: two pilots, a flight engineer, and a communications systems operator.

Julia sank into a well-worn leather seat.

"Hey, Aunt Jules, I know you still hate flying," Alex said. "You may want to use these for takeoff."

He threw Julia his X-pod and earphones, which she caught deftly with one hand.

"Thanks, Alex."

"So nothing's changed, then," Jason teased.

Julia ignored the comment. "So where exactly are we headed?" she asked.

"To your Uncle Lawrence in Petra, in Jordan," Jason replied, settling into the seat opposite her. He watched as Alex stared over the pilot's shoulders into the cockpit.

Julia heaved a sigh of relief and squeezed Jason's hand. She smiled, placed the earphones in her ears, and closed her eyes.

General Assaf walked through from the cockpit, steering Alex back down the aisle. "A slight detour, I'm afraid," he said.

Jason frowned. "What do you mean?"

"We fly to Tel Aviv."

Jason stiffened. *"Israel?"* He shook his head. "Too dangerous. The Waldorf Jerusalem's Adrian's temporary Middle East headquarters. He and Chessler have their moles everywhere."

General Assaf stood expressionless. "New orders. We have to pick up some top secret cargo." He gave Alex a meaningful look.

"I don't like it," Jason said. His jaw set. He looked over to the oblivious Julia, who sat listening to the X-Pod. "I don't like it at all."

Alex buckled his safety belt, then raised his gaze to Jason's. "It's my grandparents, Uncle Jas," he said softly.

"Your grandparents? What have they got to do with this?"

Jason cast his mind back to the many family dinners at his and Julia's first apartment, when Alex was a toddler. Jason had grown very fond of the fiercely intelligent, feisty silver-haired Rebekah Weiss and Alex's laid-back, genial grandfather David.

"Their covers have been blown. If we don't pick them up, they'll be exterminated."

"What do you mean, their *covers*?"

General Assaf sank into his seat as the engines started to roar. "As you know," he said, "before their retirement, Rebekah was head of the Goldyne Savad Institute of Gene Therapy at the Hadassah University Medical Organization, and David Weiss was former head of NASA's astrophysics division."

"They've both been Mossad agents since the Munich massacre in 'seventy-two."

"Mossad agents? Your grandparents? They're *intellectuals!*"

"Joined the Illuminus ten years ago," Assaf continued. "They've been two of our best operatives in Israel. It's getting too dangerous. We have to get them out. At a private runway in Tel Aviv, a UH-60L Black Hawk helicopter is waiting for us."

"You knew?" Jason stared at Alex in disbelief. Alex nodded.

Jason looked over to Julia, who sat with eyes closed, listening to Alex's music.

"Julia's not to be told till we arrive. That's an order, General Assaf."

General Assaf nodded. "Yes, Mr. De Vere, sir."

Jason turned to Alex.

"Granddad oversaw NASA's covert UFO program for thirty years until his retirement. He has in his possession the only untampered evidence in existence of the counter-intelligence program at NASA. He's also a fully fledged member of the Collins Elite."

Assaf nodded. "And Rebekah Weiss has documented proof that a covert genetic program existed under the employ of Guber and his specialists. We fly from Tel Aviv, then pick them up at Atarot Airport in Jerusalem. The Mossad—or whoever are left of the Mossad after Adrian's own personal Kristallnacht—are working for us. Then we fly straight to Petra."

"My grandmother has evidence that Adrian and Guber are working avidly on reinventing the second holocaust. They intend to target anyone with Jewish ancestry, worldwide, courtesy of Project Coast and Wouter Basson."

"Impossible!" Jason gasped. "Adrian's been treating the

Israelis with *kid gloves*." He looked from Alex to Assaf in disbelief. "Jerusalem's just become his second *headquarters*, for Pete's sake."

Alex and General Assaf looked at him in silence.

"Look . . . " Jason was starting to get heated. "He ratified the Concordat of King Solomon, and the forty-year Ishtar Accord—it's a—"

"A seven-year guarantee by the EU and the United Nations to defend Israel, as a protectorate, bound by international law. Israel, in exchange for her immediate denuclearization, would be protected both diplomatically and militarily against Russia, the surrounding Arab states, and any enemy third parties, by both the European Superstate and the United Nations. Israel would, however, retain a sufficient measure of sovereignty and remain a state under international law," Alex rattled off with scarcely a breath. "Israel has been at peace with every Arab nation on her borders since the Accord and is forty-eight months into the implementation of her seven-year denuclearization strategy. A UN peacekeeping force occupies Temple Mount. Israel's boundaries have reverted back to the borders of 1967. Jerusalem is undivided. Muslims, Christians, and Jews have free right of passage to the holy places in Jerusalem, regardless of religion, gender, or race."

"Exactly!" said Jason. "Not to mention, Adrian dismantled the wall, got them back the Ark of the Covenant, and has just finished rebuilding the Third Temple in Jerusalem almost single-handedly."

"He's going to contravene the Accord, Uncle Jas."

Jason froze.

"*Today* her denuclearization program is irreversible. Israel is demilitarized for the first time since 1948. Israel's Samson Option is—"

"But the . . . the Israeli government . . . they act as though Adrian's their . . . "Jason fumbled for words. " . . . their . . . "

"Their *Messiah*?" Alex said grimly.

"Adrian and Guber are already in the final stages of a DNA program that shows up Jewish ancestry going back forty generations. It was completed five weeks ago. No more gas chambers. Just a toxin that targets the specific Jewish DNA."

"How do you *know* all this?"

"Investigative journalism's pretty much my life, Uncle Jas."

Assaf turned to Jason, grim. "Mr. De Vere, sir, Israel's real Mossad was pretty much decimated two years after your brother became president."

"Over eighty percent of Israeli agents were replaced with Guber's thugs," Alex added. "Forged Jewish heritage."

Jason stared at Assaf in disbelief.

"Make no mistake," said Assaf, "They have exhaustive files on every member of the government and their extended families, both inside Israel and out. The minute they don't cooperate, their families will be exterminated. Gas ovens and concentration camps have left them with, shall we say, a far more pragmatic view of survival than we Gentiles possess."

Alex studied Jason intently. "Hey, Uncle Jas, Aunt Lilian—your mother—was Jewish, wasn't she?"

Jason stared back at Alex, silent. He had been raised an agnostic. Lilian had held no belief until later in life. He recalled seeing a carefully wrapped prayer shawl in her room.

Come to think of it, she had supported Israel with money—vast sums of money, in fact.

He remembered seeing her Hebrew surname once, on an old certificate. Her second name was Rachel.

"Yes, Mother was Jewish," he said very softly.

"That makes you technically a Jew, Uncle Jas."

Jason stared out the porthole, deep in thought, as the jet took off into Kansas's inky black skies. Whether he liked it or not—whether or not he even understood it—it was an indisputable fact.

Jason De Vere was a Jew.

Chapter Forty-three

AREA 51
NELLIS AIR FORCE BASE, NEVADA
2025

THE AC-130U GUNSHIP IV, the elite's latest innovation courtesy of the Lockheed "Skunk Works," entered the restricted airspace of Area 51, shadowed by eight black unmarked helicopters.

Kurt Guber, director of EU Special Service operations, and exotic-weapons specialist, stared out the gunship's windows as they flew over the colossal three-million-acre Air Force base, approaching Groom Lake. Guber gazed out at the dry lake bed, severed by the 27,000-foot runway and studded with massive hangars and communications towers. He scanned the recently erected fifty-mile band of concentric razor-topped chain-link security fences that surrounded the inner perimeter of the base.

Guber's own team of security specialists had designed the new state-of-the-art electronic surveillance systems recently put into use. He knew that they were so advanced, they even had the ability to pick up the odor of human sweat—and transmitted a lethal electrical charge.

He smiled. His master was now only minutes away from holding in his hand the most incendiary piece of evidence from this century or the last.

Evidence of the U.S. and one-world government's participation in the most treacherous pact ever initiated in the dark corridors of shadow government. Evidence that *had* to be destroyed.

The gunship flew over the Groom Lake "graveyard," then set down on the airstrip.

Minutes later, eighteen members of the Special Operations Command task force exited from the gunship out onto the tarmac, then marched toward the western elevation of the mountain range, led by Guber.

Instantly they were surrounded by militia with automatic weapons raised. Their captain saluted Guber, who nodded to Neil Travis. who removed a heavy brown envelope from a briefcase attached to his wrist. He handed the envelope to Guber, who handed it to the captain in front of him.

The captain instantly recognized the unique NCS seal. He shrank from Guber, fleeting fear evident in his eyes.

Guber smiled in gratification. The National Clandestine Services, operational since October 13, 2005, had absorbed the infamous CIA Directorate of Operations. And since December 2022, it had been commanded solely by the one-world government.

The captain examined the papers methodically.

Guber paced up and down, his gaze fixed on the two unmarked aircraft with their distinctive red stripe along the fuselage, taxiing down a second runway in the distance.

The "Janets"—nicknamed after their call letters, he thought idly. Each day, they ferried thousands of Area 51's employees to and from McCarran International Airport in Las Vegas, fueling conspiracy theorist sites all across the Internet.

Guber gave a disparaging smile. If they had any idea what *really* lay beneath Groom Lake . . .

The captain closed the envelope and motioned to the militia, who lowered their weapons.

"The papers are in order," he said softly. He handed the envelope back to Guber and saluted.

Guber and his militia marched across the tarmac into Hangar 18 and into a huge, nondescript elevator guarded by six special forces soldiers, weapons cocked and locked. The doors closed. Guber's party descended at high speed to thirty-seven stories beneath the surface, then came to an abrupt halt as the elevator opened onto monstrous camouflaged steel blast doors set into the bedrock.

Guber stood at attention as the iris scanner automatically lowered to his. He looked into the camera lens. Seconds later, the massive doors slid open, revealing the western access to a sprawling underground city the size of Lower Manhattan.

Guber smiled. This was the core of the covert "black world" of the shadow government's classified research and development, financed by the new world order—The Shadowlands.

Guber and his special forces operatives headed toward the underground shuttle system hub the size of Grand Central Station. The monstrous silver railcars' steel doors slid open silently as the soldiers walked toward them. They boarded, sat down, and strapped themselves in. Five seconds later, the railcars took off. Quickly accelerating to Mach 2, they passed the flickering lights of hundreds of other railcars at high velocity through the vast subterranean highway engineered by Aerospace, descending to two miles beneath the vast Mojave Desert.

The rail cars hurtledyunder the sparse acres of brittle-bush and desert holly towards 'Dulce', then, seven minutes later, came to an abrupt halt as the doors opened onto an eight-ton blast door guarded by ten militiamen dressed in black, holding TDI KRISS Super V XSMG submachine guns.

Guber exited. The militia saluted as one as he marched straight past them, through a security body scanner and into a high-security control room, where armed sentries monitored intrusion alarms linked to the black Vault.

A tall man in a black suit stood with his back to Guber and the soldiers

The man seemed able to read his thought waves.

He lifted his hand, and black steel doors descended on each window.

"You're late."

Guber trembled.

The man in black raised his hand, and the chambers spun around, transforming into one vast subterranean bunker with a wall of iron bars.

The man in black walked through to the chamber. The entire chamber, which must have been a thousand feet square, contained only two steel boxes.

The man nodded. The iron gates opened, and Guber walked toward the iron wall of boxes. He inserted an access card into a reader, and immediately a box to his right, halfway up the wall, lit up red.

Guber placed the access card in one end of the steel box and punched in a code.

The man in black punched in a code and nodded to Guber

The box slid open. The man reached inside and carefully removed an old yellowed document.

He looked briefly at the United States seal on the document, then turned the pages.

There on the final page of the document was President Dwight Eisenhower's distinctive scrawl, dated February 21, 1954. Opposite the president's signature were three strange alien markings.

On the front page, in precise black, above the United States presidential seal was the title: "The Greada Treaty."

"We are ready for the final implementation of our new world order," the man in black said. He turned to face Guber.

It was Lorcan De Molay.

CHAPTER FORTY-FOUR

JERUSALEM

"ISN'T THAT DOWNTOWN Jerusalem?" Julia asked. "Look at the lights!"

Jason stared out the helicopter window, then frowned. He recognized the outline of the old city wall. Strange—they were supposed to be headed for Atarot, between Jerusalem and Ramallah.

He could hear hushed, terse voices in the cockpit, then silence. General Assaf walked from the cockpit toward them.

"We've had word from our intelligence," he said solemnly. "A small *hitch*, as you say in America." He smiled slightly, but his eyes were troubled.

"Your brother's militia got to our agents at Atarot. A massacre. Chessler's thugs got wind of our flight plan. The Weisses escaped with two ex-Mossad soldiers. We'll pick them up at Hadassah Ein Kerem. The hospital—it has a helipad."

Alex sat bolt upright. "It's much too dangerous."

General Assaf sighed.

"Of course, we wanted to avoid it because your grandmother is so well known there. No choice, I'm afraid."

Jason looked out the window again.

He could make out the outline of two Apache attack heli-copters approaching in the distance. The Apaches' comms flared on.

"This is the One World Alliance. You are to land immedi-ately by presidential order."

General Assaf shook his head and motioned to the pilots. "Continue the course to Ein Kerem," he said softly.

"This is the One World Alliance. Repeat, you are to land immediately by presidential order."

There was complete silence.

Julia looked in apprehension at Jason, then at General Assaf. She moved toward the window just as the Apaches descended.

"Julia!" Jason shouted, and grasped her arm.

A stream of tracer bullets blazed toward the helicopter.

Julia collapsed into Jason's arms.

Jason stared down in horror at the crimson blood gushing between his fingers from her chest.

"First-aid kit!" General Assaf shouted.

Jason stared down at Julia, paralyzed.

Her eyes flickered open. "Jason," she whispered. Assaf opened a first-aid kit and took out a sterile bandage.

Jason smiled weakly. "I'm right here, Jules. You'll be fine, pal." He squeezed her hand, willing back his tears.

"Jason . . . "

"Don't talk, Julia," Jason said gently. "Just let Assaf patch you up. We're taking you straight to the hospital," he lied. "Alex's grandmother is a surgeon. The hospital's right here."

"You were always a terrible liar," Julia whispered. A tear ran down her cheek as she smiled up at him.

"Roll up her sleeve," Assaf instructed Jason.

Jason rolled up Julia's sleeve, as Assaf plunged a needle into her upper arm.

"Morphine," he said.

Jason nodded.

"When this is all over," he whispered, "I'm going to marry you, Julia St. Cartier. The biggest wedding New York's ever seen."

"Not New York—London," whispered Julia. "I love you, Jason." She struggled to form the words. "I've always . . . "

Jason stared, horrified, at the blood trickling from Julia's mouth. He placed his finger gently over her lips, willing back the sobs that were racking his chest. Julia smiled weakly up at him as she lost consciousness.

"I've loved you forever, Julia De Vere."

Jason clasped her to his chest, tears streaming down his unshaven cheeks, and gently smoothed her matted hair.

"I've loved you forever, Jules," he sobbed, rocking her as he would a small child. "Loved you forever."

Alex looked at Jason, horrified. "I'm so sorry, Uncle Jas."

Very slowly Jason laid Julia down next to the medic, who sat beside Assaf, making a flutter valve.

Jason watched the lights of the Apaches as they approached within firing range again.

"They'll shoot us down this time," Alex said. "They're going to blow us out of the sky."

Jason grabbed Assaf's handgun from his belt. "Drop me," he ordered.

He pointed the gun straight at Assaf and the pilots, his hands trembling.

"Use me as a diversion. I'm the one they're after."

"No, Mr. De Vere." Assaf's tone was even. "I can't let you do that."

"Drop me right here on the street, General. *Now.*" Jason looked down at Julia, then up at the general.

"Or I'll blast your head off." His hands shook. "You know I'll do it, Assaf."

Assaf studied Jason intently, then nodded to the pilot. "Do as Mr. De Vere says," he said softly.

Jason glanced over at Julia. She had stopped breathing. He looked into Assaf's eyes. "Get Julia to the Hadassah Hospital now."

Assaf nodded.

"Sorry about this, General."

The helicopter descended rapidly, and Assaf opened the door.

"May the Hebrew be with you," he whispered.

Jason jumped down onto the grassy expanse of the park opposite the Waldorf Astoria Jerusalem and stumbled up onto his feet. The helicopter disappeared as the Apaches started to descend toward him.

CHAPTER FORTY-FIVE

EDEN
THE FIRST HEAVEN

NICK STARED TRANSFIXED at the tall, imperial
stranger who stood, a lone figure, bathed in the
soft white light that hung in the blazing white
mists of the Eastern Gardens of Eden.

The stranger pulled his indigo cape tightly around him.
His gleaming raven hair, plaited in thick braids and inter-
woven with diamonds, fell over his broad shoulders, blowing
in the soft tempests of Eden. A crown of state rested on his
head, and his glistening white silk robes fell to the ground,
half concealing his jeweled sandals.

But it was the haunting beauty of the stranger's face that
Nick could hardly take his eyes from: the high imperial
cheekbones, the passionate crimson mouth.

Nick watched as a second figure approached from the
golden bulrush meadows. The raven-haired stranger turned.

The second figure was of similar height, but his countenance was gentler. His pale gold tresses were plaited with
platinum and hung loose down his back over a pale blue

frock coat. His ethereal features were flawless, almost pretty: the perfectly carved cheekbones, the regal heart-shaped countenance. His clear gray eyes were gentle yet piercing.

"Gabriel . . . ?" Nick whispered.

Jether walked up slowly behind Nick and placed his hand on his shoulder.

"Yes," he said softly. "It is Gabriel, chief prince, the Revelator. He meets with his elder brother."

"Michael?" Nick asked.

Silent, Jether shook his head. They watched as the two brothers bowed to each other in the protocol of the First Heaven.

"No, not Michael," he said softly.

Jether gazed out at the reflection of the twelve palest-blue moons that glistened on the First Heaven's horizon, watching the lilac hues shift to a deep majestic indigo.

Nick followed Jether's gaze, staring up at a soaring gold-columned palace that towered high above the western wall, far in the distance.

"The Palace of Archangels," Jether said. "The three chief princes, three brothers, dwelt within those walls in harmony and kinship."

Nick turned back to the two brothers, who were in intense discussion.

"He is mesmerizing, the one Gabriel meets."

"He was once the fairest, most devoted of all the angelic host. Prince regent, second only to Christos in status."

Jether turned to Nick, a strange sadness in his pale blue eyes.

"Before the darkening shadows of insurrection fell over

the realm of the First Heaven—before he, seraph, great archangel, light bearer, was banished."

Nick stared down at two towering golden doors engraved with the emblem of the Royal House. They were barred. Jether followed his gaze.

"The majestic West Wing. It has been barred since his banishment, in other worlds long since departed.

"You have seen him once before," Jether said very softly.

"No." Nick shook his head. "No, I've never seen him. I'd remember."

"Four years ago. At Mont St. Michel."

Nick stared at Jether in disbelief.

"You saw him in his earthly guise as a Jesuit priest."

"There was a special guest," Nick murmured. "High security. Royalty, Hilde said. The West Wing was off limits to all other visitors. He was standing at the very edge of the balcony of the West Wing, playing the violin. More like a priest than a prince."

Jether nodded.

"I remember how he played. I had never heard music like that. Each note pierced through to my soul. It was haunting yet, at the same time, beautiful. Exquisite. Poignant. Almost lonely."

"It is the only thing left to Him of all that once was," Jether said softly.

"Who is he, Jether?"

"He has many names." Jether looked at Nick, unsmiling. "None of them pleasant.

"He has deluded many of the Race of Men about his actual existence. In their minds, if he does not exist, neither, perhaps, does Yehovah. The Race of Men's minds are his willing playground."

Nick gazed at Lucifer, speechless.

"Yes," said Jether. "You know him among the Race of Men as the devil, Satan, the Dragon."

"And yet, standing there in Eden, he looks completely at peace," Nick said. "You see him today, Lucifer the light bearer. In *this* world, he has certain immunities, which will be revoked after the war between him and his brother, Michael the Archangel. Even here in Eden, he is but a shadow of what he used to be."

Jether's eyes grew distant.

"I was his mentor, Nicholas, as I was to all three brothers. But Lucifer—oh . . . " Jether sighed. "He was unique, exceptional in every way, except for one minute flaw, which ultimately became his demise. Finally, his pride and arrogance flawed his reasoning.

"Now only melancholy surrounds him. He has no peace. The only peace he has is when he walks in Eden. But he cannot retain it.

"He used to walk hand in hand with Yehovah, along the paths he walks today. They would discuss the universes, the cosmos and its galaxies. He would lay his head on Yehovah's shoulder in complete adoration."

"How did he fall, Jether?" Nick whispered. "You who were his mentor—surely you, of all, must know."

Jether's eyes were distant.

"In eons past, when Yehovah created the Race of Men, he feared that man would usurp his place with Yehovah. On learning that the Race of Men's DNA, unlike that of the angelic race, was an exact replica of Yehovah's own, he became consumed by jealousy. It was like a canker growing inside him. His dislike of the Race of Men became loathing. Loathing became hatred, until he had but one obsession: the destruction of the Race of Men.

"One day, hours before the Race of Men would receive the breath of life, he pleaded desperately with Yehovah to desist in His plan, saying that the Race of Men was folly. That they would break His heart."

"And yet, in turn, it was *Lucifer* who broke His heart?"

"For a fleeting moment it seemed so. It was at the inaugural ceremony for the Race of Men that Lucifer and his third of the angelic host stormed Yehovah's throne. Rebellion that has never been seen before or since in our world.

"Sin cannot stand in the holiness of Yehovah's all-consuming fire. Lucifer miscalculated. He and a third of his angelic host were burnt beyond recognition, their once exquisite features marred."

"And yet today he . . . he . . . "

Jether studied Nick's face. "You are still awed by his beauty?"

Nick nodded in silence.

"When he is in our world, he recaptures some of what he once was when he was prince regent. The fairest of all the brothers."

Nick stared in wonder as Lucifer turned. He studied the imperial chiseled face, the passionate ruby mouth, the intelligent, piercing blue eyes framed by gleaming blue-black hair that fell past his shoulders.

He reminds me of . . . of . . . It can't be." Nick stared at Jether in shock.

"He reminds you of Adrian," Jether whispered. Nick looked at Jether.

"He is his *son?*"

Jether shook his head.

"No. He is his *clone*. He shares the same genomic code."

Nick looked at Jether in disbelief.

"We knew Adrian was a clone. But not who his father . . . "

"Adrian De Vere reigns supreme in the world of men. The Son of Perdition, ruler of ten kingdoms. The Antichrist. But now that the Rapture has taken place, he contends no longer with the prayers of the saints on earth. He will now wage war with the saints who remain.

"Let us walk." Jether took Nick's arm in his. "Lawrence . . . " Nick hesitated. "Lawrence, can I ask you something that has puzzled me?"

Jether smiled at Nick. "Of course."

"Do you, as an angelic king, have all knowledge of all things past, present, and future?" He hesitated. "Does Lucifer?"

"Nicholas . . . " Jether closed his eyes. "The angelic, whether fallen as Lucifer is, or unfallen as two-thirds of the angelic host remain, have knowledge of the past, but we, unlike Yehovah and Christos, are not omnipresent.

"Remember that Lucifer's antithesis is Michael, not Christos. Only Yehovah is supreme, invincible, and all powerful. He is the Almighty. Lucifer, as I, Michael, and our angelic host, is a created being, even as you are. What you are asking is, do we have knowledge of future events? We are like you, the Race of Men, in that respect. We rely on Gabriel's reconnaissance activities. You call it intelligence gathering."

"But you . . . " Nick stopped.

"I, as an ancient king and elder of the High Council—yes, it is true. Many times, I see further ahead into the future, as does Gabriel, but it is as a seer, Nicholas. I hold no omniscience.

"Only one is omniscient. Only one is omnipresent. Only one is omnipotent. All knowing, everywhere present, all powerful."

His eyes grew distant.

"There are times when Yehovah chooses to reveal the future to us, His holy elders. But in his omniscient wisdom, there are times when He allows us as his angelic host to discover for ourselves what lies ahead. If we knew all things, Nicholas, we would not need to trust Him. We would not need faith. It is *because*, *like you*, we walk by faith, seeing as through a glass darkly, yet still believing, that we, too, as the angelic, please Him, the One we love. The One we serve.

"Today we go to His Garden." He led Nick through a narrow pearl arbor covered with vines laden with lush silver fruit. Past the heady perfume of the magnificent hanging blossoms of the gardens of fragrance that exuded the aromas of frankincense and spikenard. As they walked, Nick shielded his eyes from the intense shafts of crimson light radiating from far beyond. Finally, they came to an inconspicuous grotto at the very edge of the cliffs of Eden, surrounded by eight ancient olive trees.

"Christos's garden," Jether whispered. He pushed open the humble wooden gate.

Gradually, the rays settled, revealing, a hundred feet ahead and across a vast chasm, the colossal Rubied Door, ablaze with light, embedded into the jacinth walls of the tower.

The entrance to the throne room. Between the cliff face and the throne room entrance was a sheer drop where the fountains of life flowed from Yehovah's throne, thousands of leagues downward to the waters of Eden, then north, south, east, and west to water the First Heaven. There was no bridge across.

Jether led the way to a simple bench, carved of olive wood, in the center of the grotto. He watched as Nick stared toward the throne room, his face enraptured.

"He is not here?"

"No," Jether murmured. "He talks with His Father."

Nick stared out in wonder at the Rubied Door. Tears filled his eyes.

"When He was on Earth, He said, 'Blessed are those who have not seen me, and yet believe . . . '"

Jether's eyes shone with adoration.

"It was here in this garden that it all began. It was here that Christos shared with Lucifer about the advent of the Race of Men. It was here that his treachery began."

"But why?" Nick asked. "After his treachery, *why* is he still allowed here in the First Heaven?"

"For over two millennia, he has had access to the First Heaven. Bringing railing accusations in our great courtrooms, against the Race of Men.

"But the Third Great War, a war between Michael and Lucifer, draws nigh. If he loses, he will be thrown down through one of seven Portals to Earth, never to return to this planet. Never to return to the First Heaven.

"He is here this day because he senses that his time is short."

Jether sighed.

"Nicholas, I must return."

"To Earth?"

"Yes, to Earth."

Nick studied Jether's face. "It's Jason, isn't it?"

Jether sighed. "Jason is in great danger, Nicholas. He enters the valley of the shadow even as we speak. I must alert Michael. We must move swiftly."

Jether anointed Nick with the sign of the cross.

"Until my return." Jether kissed Nick on both cheeks, then vanished.

"Jason . . . ," Nick whispered.

And fell to his knees.

CHAPTER FORTY-SIX

JERUSALEM

JASON RAN FOR HIS LIFE across the few yards that separated the intersections of King David, Agron, and Mamilla Streets.

He glanced up at the descending Apache helicopters. They were closing in on him. He dived underneath a stream of tracer bullets, into the sheltered entrance of the Waldorf Astoria Hotel, and stopped, gasping for air behind one of the arches in the ornate foyer.

Thank God the 2018 peace agreement had removed the need for the previously rigorous security measures throughout the city.

He took a deep breath, then walked unhindered through the foyer, receiving only a rapid glance of disapproval from the pretty night receptionist on duty at the front desk. She gazed in faint disapproval at the blood and dust on his shirt, then instantly switched on a false smile.

"Shalom, sir."

"Shalom," Jason replied brusquely, walking toward the elevator.

He paused, then retraced his steps to the reception desk, took his wallet from his back pocket, and thrust his driver's license in the receptionist's face.

She looked down at the license, then back up at Jason in vague recognition. His photo had been splashed over the Jerusalem papers for weeks during his takeover of the Israeli TV cable companies Yes and Hot.

"Jason De Vere?"

"My brother."

She nodded. "He's in the presidential suite."

"He's expecting me."

"Of course, Mr. De Vere, sir."

She passed a magnetic card through a scanner and gestured to a private lift opposite the lobby bar.

"The card unlocks the lift and the presidential suite entrance, Mr. De Vere."

She placed her hand on the phone. Jason placed his hand on hers and smiled politely.

"A surprise," he said hoarsely. "For my brother."

She removed her hand from the phone and smiled broadly. "Of course, Mr. De Vere. We are all honored to host such a distinguished guest."

Jason walked into the slim gold elevator and placed the card in the reader just as eight militia tore through the hotel entrance. The elevator doors closed.

There was only one destination. Jason pulled General Assaf's pistol from his waistband just as the elevator doors slid open.

Jason walked out into the vast expanse of the presidential suite. He looked around him, at the grand piano and the enormous dining table. Guber materialized as if out of nowhere, as did four of Adrian's security guards. Jason leaned against the marble wall, gun in hand.

Kurt Guber stepped toward him.

PRESIDENTIAL SUITE
WALDORF ASTORIA HOTEL
JERUSALEM

Adrian walked out of the sauna in a towel, rubbing his jet black hair with a hand towel.

"Your *brother* is here, sir." Kurt Guber gave Adrian a knowing look. "He seems somewhat overwrought."

"I can handle Jason."

"He has a *gun*."

Adrian stopped in mid step, without looking up, a strange smile on his lips.

"Jason has a *gun*? How *curious*."

Adrian walked through two ornately carved doors to the suite.

"Jason." He smiled. "Drink?"

Jason shook his head. "Call your thugs off, Adrian," he said.

Adrian stared straight into the barrel of the semiautomatic pistol, then raised his blue eyes into Jason's steely gaze.

He waved Guber back. Guber hesitated.

"Guber, lock down the security arrangements for the opening of the Third Temple."

"I don't like it, Mr. President, sir."

"I said lock down the security arrangements," Adrian said icily.

Guber bowed, then took the exit down the back stairs, followed by Adrian's personal security team.

"Oh, and, Guber . . . " Adrian didn't look up from drying his hair. "Travis stays."

Guber nodded to Neil Travis and two of his agents, then left down the back stairs with the rest of his security team.

Travis stood inside the penthouse's sitting room door, with two agents behind him. He raised his Beretta, his eyes never leaving Jason's for a moment. Adrian shook his head.

"My brother is a little . . . emotional right now," he said. "Understandably so." Adrian gave the faintest hint of a smile.

"I said call your thugs *off*."

Adrian nodded to Neil Travis. "Wait outside. My brother and I require privacy."

Slowly Travis holstered his gun and walked over to the solid brass penthouse doors, followed by two agents. Adrian watched till the doors clicked shut behind him, then walked over to the wet bar and poured Jason a whisky.

"You seem a little tense."

He casually held the whisky out to Jason, who took it with his free hand and slugged it down. Then Adrian calmly poured himself a mineral water.

Jason kept the gun trained on Adrian. "You're going to contravene the "Solomon Concordat," aren't you?" he said calmly. "You're going to betray Israel."

"Israel?" Adrian slowly turned to face Jason. "Oh, I forgot, you're actually, technically, a Jew, aren't you. How ironic. Is *this* what all this commotion is about? My betraying Israel? I didn't realize you had such strong political sentiments."

"I don't," Jason said evenly. "You killed *Mother*, you bastard."

Adrian sipped at the mineral water, placed his glass down, and continued drying his hair.

"Lawrence had a second autopsy carried out," Jason continued. "By a top forensic pathologist. Ex MI-Six. One ampoule of potassium chloride—undetectable in an autopsy."

He raised the gun in line with Adrian's head. "Unless you're trained to look for it."

"Impressive, Jason. Quite the private detective, or maybe I should credit the interfering Professor Lawrence St. Cartier."

Adrian continued to rub his hair with the towel. "It was quick." He smiled. "She didn't suffer."

"Unlike *Nick*," Jason replied.

Adrian froze.

"Live AIDS virus delivered April fourth, 2017. Injected twelve-o-seven a.m. Signed warrant for Nicholas De Vere's execution," Jason continued. "I *saw* the document, Adrian. Then you tried to kill Lily, my own *daughter*. *Your own niece.*"

"Casualties of war, Jason." Adrian calmly laid the towel over a chair. "Like Father, Melissa, and my son, Gabriel. All casualties of war." He looked straight into the barrel of the gun.

"So what are you going to *do*, Jas?" He shrugged. "Kill your own *brother*?"

A supercilious smile spread across his lips.

"I don't think so." He picked up the glass and sipped.

Jason held the gun with both hands, flicked off the safety, then took a long slow breath.

"*You're not my brother,*" he said.

He pulled the trigger.

The bullet smashed through Adrian's throat. The glass shattered on the floor as he fell to his knees, his hands at his neck, blood spurting between his fingers from the severed carotid artery. He looked down at the blood on his hand, a look of faint surprise on his face, then collapsed onto the floor.

Jason took one step nearer, tears of rage running down his cheeks. He pointed the gun at Adrian's head.

"This one's for Julia, you murdering son of a bitch." Jason looked at him with intense hatred. "Rot in *hell!*"

He pulled the trigger.

The second bullet smashed straight through Adrian's skull. Jason watched as Adrian's body convulsed once, twice, then went limp.

Jason started to tremble violently. The gun slid out of his hand onto the marble floor.

He had just shot his "brother," president of the new ten-kingdom one-world axis, in cold blood.

Jason De Vere.

Was a murderer.

The door of the suite flew open, and Jason looked straight down the barrel of Neil Travis's nine-millimeter Beretta.

He made no attempt to struggle as Travis and his security forces surrounded him and a black bag was pulled over his head.

He made no attempt to struggle as the noose tightened around his neck.

His last waking thought before he lost consciousness was that he had lost Julia—this time, forever. Julia St. Cartier was dead. And *his* world had died with her.

A savage blow hit his temple. Then Jason De Vere's whole world went black.

To be continued . . .

To my unrepentant brother Lucifer,
The two crimson moons arise in the heavens. I have seen
them for many moons in my dreamings.

If you persist with your malevolent schemes of genetic
Armageddon, War is inevitable.

You will lose the Third Great Battle, brother.

You will be hurled by our brother Michael from the First
Heaven through the great angelic Portal down to Earth.

Repent, Lucifer, Before your days and nights are spent in
eternal torment in the Bottmless Pit.

I plead with you one more time. Desist from your futile
fantasies of victory. Your defeat is inevitable.
Your brother Gabriel.

My supercilious and uncharacteristically arrogant brother Gabriel,

I see you have been spending far too much time with our deluded brother Michael.

How I grieve for you.

Even more, I grieve also for the fact that I, your elder brother, your protector, your guardian, have not been by your side to watch over and protect your sensitive and finer nature from the indifference and pitiless persuasions of our brother Michael.

He contaminates your untainted mind with his own base and infected thoughts, Gabriel.

This causes me great suffering.

Yes, I, Lucifer, suffer greatly on your behalf.

Come join me, Gabriel. Let us be brother to brother again.

Relay to my callous and unfeeling brother Michael, when he asks me to repent, that I, in my wisdom, discern his real motive.

He is assured of my eternal victory and his own defeat and would save himself from the indubitable humiliation of his impending downfall.

No doubt, Michael's unease at our impending battle has persuaded you to write to me.

Mark me well, my younger brother, My plan is set.

Again I issue my invitation, adored Gabriel.

Join me.

Your devoted brother Lucifer

Gabriel,

I receive no answer to my magnanimous missive. You disappoint me exceedingly.

May your dreamings be infested with apparitions of the first stage of my eternal Kingdom.

A thousand-year reign. A millennium under my rule.

What havoc shall I wreak upon this world when I rule from Yehovah's throne. Every vestige of the Nazarene will be erased from memory on Earth.

The crimson moons rise.

Your brother Lucifer

My greatly deluded brother Lucifer,

Receive my pity. For surely it is now the only emotion my heart is capable of holding for you.

I have received your latest missives. Our communication is now at an end.

As I write, our brother Michael mobilizes his armies in preparation for your final expulsion from the First Heaven.

Mark well the sights and sounds when you enter these gates again.

For surely, brother, they shall be your last

Lucifer threw Gabriel's missive onto his mother-of-pearl desk.

"I will defeat you, Michael," he said with an iniquitous smile. "On the White Plains in the East of Eden."

Lucifer rose and walked to the window of his Ice palace. He threw open the balcony doors and stared up at the two crimson moons, their flaming tails blazing high on the horizon above the bleak ice plains of Gehenna.

"I shall take you and Gabriel captive. I shall rule from Yehovah's throne.

"I shall *storm* the gates of the First Heaven within the hour."

He held his broadsword high.

"It is time to *war*!"

APPENDIX

Daily Mail article

By Anthony Bond

Source: http://www.dailymail.co.uk/news/article-2100947/Eisenhower-secret-meetings-aliens-pentagon-consultant-claims.html
(*Updated*: 07:58, 15 February 2012)

President Eisenhower had three secret meetings with aliens, former Pentagon consultant claims

- Ex-President met with extra-terrestrials on three separate occasions at New Mexico air base
- Eisenhower and FBI officials organised the meetings by sending out 'telepathic messages'

Former American President Dwight D. Eisenhower had three secret meetings with aliens, a former US government consultant has claimed.

The 34th President of the United States met the extra terrestrials at a remote air base in New Mexico in 1954, according to lecturer and author Timothy Good.

Eisenhower and other FBI officials are said to have organised the showdown with the space creatures by sending out 'telepathic messages'.

The two parties finally met up on three separate occasions at the Holloman Air Force base and there were 'many witnesses'.

Conspiracy theorists have circulated increased rumours in recent months that the meeting between the Commander-in-Chief and people from another planet took place.

'Aliens have made both formal and informal contact with thousands of people throughout the world from all walks of life,' he added.

Asked why the aliens don't go to somebody 'important' like Barack Obama, he said: 'Well, certainly I can tell you that in 1954, President Eisenhower had three encounters, set up meetings with aliens, which took place at certain Air Force bases including Holloman Air Force base in New Mexico.'

He added that there were 'many witnesses'.

Eisenhower, who was president from 1953 to 1961, is known to have had a strong belief in life on other planets.

The former five-star general in the United States Army who commanded the Allied Forces in Europe during the Second World War, was also keen on pushing the U.S. space programme.

His meeting with the cosmic life forms is said to have taken place while officials were told that he was on vacation in Palm Springs, California, in February 1954.

The initial meeting is supposed to have taken place with aliens who were 'Nordic' in appearance, but the agreement was eventually 'signed' with a race called 'Alien Greys'.

Mr Good added: 'We know that up to 90 per cent of all UFO reports can be explained in conventional terms. However, I would say millions of people worldwide have actually seen the real thing.'

According to classified documents released by the Ministry of Defence in 2010, Winston Churchill may have ordered a UFO sighting to be kept secret.

The UFO was seen over the East Coast of England by an RAF reconnaissance plane returning from a mission in France or Germany towards the end of the war.

Churchill is said to have discussed how to deal with UFO sightings with Eisenhower.

Excerpt of transcript of the videographed statement from the Honorable Henry W. McElroy, Jr.

Former representative of the New Hampshire State Legislature (May 8, 2010)

My name is Henry McElroy, Jr., a retiring, former State Representative from New Hampshire. Thank you for your attention to this brief message concerning the world's interaction with both earth-based and off-world astronauts.

When I was in the New Hampshire State Legislature, I served on the State-Federal Relations and Veterans Affairs Committee. It was, apparently, important that as a Representative of the Sovereign People who had elected me to this Honorable Office, that I be updated on a large number of topics related to the affairs of our People, and our Nation. As I understood it, some of those ongoing topics had been examined and categorized as Federal, State, Local development, and security matters. These documents related to various topics, some of which spanned decades of our nation's history. One of those recurring topics is the reason I am addressing you this evening.

I would like to submit to our nation my personal testimony of one document related to one of these ongoing topics which I saw while in office, serving on the State-Federal Relations and Veterans Affairs Committee.

The document I saw was an official brief to President Eisenhower. To the best of my memory, this brief was pervaded with a sense of hope, and **it informed President Eisenhower of the continued presence of extraterrestrial beings here in the United States of America.**

The brief seemed to indicate that a meeting between the President and some of these visitors could be arranged as appropriate if desired.

The tone of the brief indicated to me that there was no need for concern, since these visitors were, in no way, causing any harm, or had any intentions whatsoever, of causing any disruption then, or in the future.

While I can't verify the times or places or that any meeting or meetings occurred directly between Eisenhower and these visitors – because of his optimism in his farewell address in 1961, I personally believe that Eisenhower did, indeed, meet with these extraterrestrial, off world astronauts.

I hope my personal testimony will aid the nation in its quest for continued enlightenment. I am honored to follow in the footsteps of those who have come forward with their personal testimonies – those who deserve the admiration of the American people for sharing their accounts publicly, in an effort to elevate our knowledge to a higher understanding of our existence.

People such as:
Former astronauts (John Glenn, Edgar Mitchell, Gordon Cooper, and Buzz Aldrin);
Former presidents (Ronald Reagan and Jimmy Carter);
Captain Bill Uhouse of the United States Marine Corps; Lt. Col. John Williams of the United States Air Force;
Col. Phillip Corso, Sr. of the United States Army; Commander Graham Bethune of the United States Navy;

Along with:
David Hamilton of the Department of Energy; Donna Hare of NASA; and James Kopf of the National Security Agency.

I would also like to thank the countries of: France, Brazil, Britain, Russia, Italy, Denmark, Sweden, Norway, New Zealand; and, our neighbor to the north: Canada; Uruguay, and Australia - for also opening their files to the citizens of their countries, and allowing them access to information that is so very important to the evolution of humanity.

Map of Auschwabenland

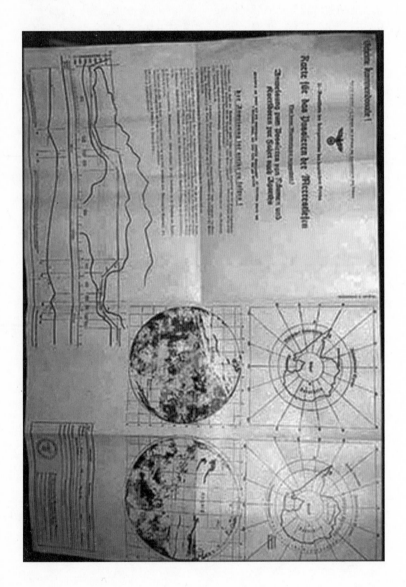

Transcript of Ron Paul's farewell address to Congress

A transcript by Matthew Hawes of Ron Paul's farewell address to Congress on November 14, 2012 is available on the following website:

http://12160.info/page/the-transcript-of-ron-paul-s-farewell-address-to-congress-11-14-1

OTHER TITLES IN THE CHRONICLES OF BROTHERS SERIES

Book 1: The Fall of Lucifer

Order now on
www.chroniclesofbrothers.com
or from Waterstones, Amazon, Barnes and
Noble or your local independent book store.

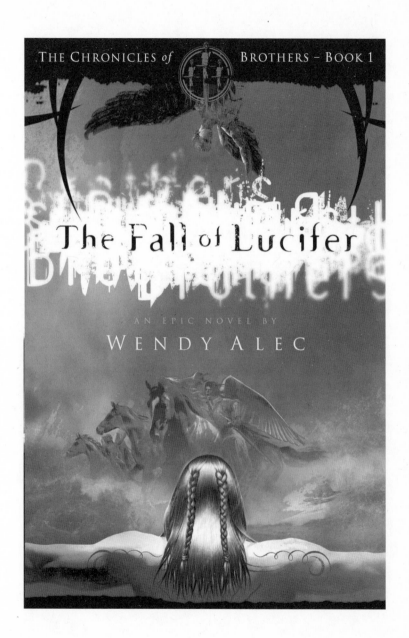

THE CHRONICLES of   BROTHERS – BOOK 1

The Fall of Lucifer

AN EPIC NOVEL BY

WENDY ALEC

Book 2: **Messiah: The First Judgement**

Order now on
www.chroniclesofbrothers.com
or from Waterstones, Amazon, Barnes and
Noble or your local independent book store.

ARCHANGELS MICHAEL, GABRIEL AND LUCIFER RETURN IN...

THE FIRST JUDGEMENT

WENDY ALEC

Book 3: **Son of Perdition**

Order now on
www.chroniclesofbrothers.com
or from Waterstones, Amazon, Barnes and
Noble or your local independent book store.

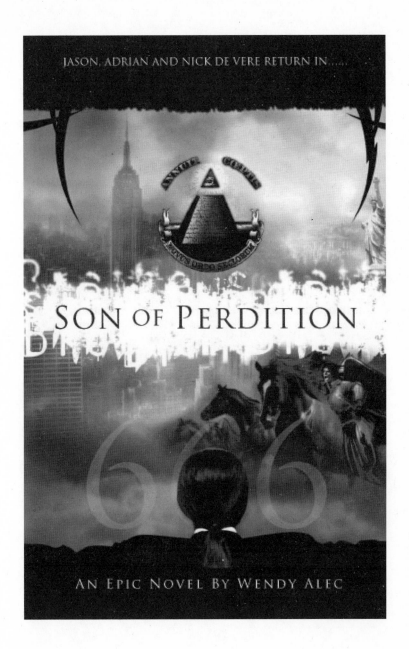

JASON, ADRIAN AND NICK DE VERE RETURN IN.....

SON OF PERDITION

AN EPIC NOVEL BY WENDY ALEC

www.chroniclesofbrothers.com

For more information on the
Chronicles of Brothers,
including the other books in the series,
the characters, live chat with
the author, author's blog,
and lots more.

Join us on Facebook!